The Woman in Grey

THE WOMAN IN GREY

Carola Salisbury

$\overline{C}$

CENTURY
LONDON MELBOURNE AUCKLAND JOHANNESBURG

First published in Great Britain in 1987 by
Century Hutchinson Ltd
Brookmount House, 62–65 Chandos Place,
London WC2N 4NW

Century Hutchinson Australia Pty Ltd
PO Box 496
16–22 Church Street, Hawthorn, Victoria 3122, Australia

Century Hutchinson New Zealand Ltd
PO Box 40–086, Glenfield,
Auckland 10, New Zealand

Century Hutchinson South Africa (Pty) Ltd
PO Box 337, Bergvlei,
2012 South Africa

ISBN 0 7126 1446 X

Set by Input Typesetting Ltd, London
Printed and bound in Great Britain by
Anchor Brendon Ltd, Tiptree, Essex

For Joan Young

PART ONE

The Evil Eye

One

More than a year passed before I summoned up the courage even to think of going out into the streets of Venice again.

I told Assunta, and she was horrified. She crossed herself with gnarled, work-calloused hands.

'No, Isolda – no!'

'Assunta, I must. I can't spend the rest of my life hiding away.'

'Then at least go out at night – for the first time, try it at night, I beg you.'

'I'm going out now. Having made up my mind, I mustn't back down. If I do, I shall never find the courage again.'

'They will crucify you!'

I was unshakeable. She offered – even begged – to go with me, though I knew the very notion filled her with dread. Even she, my faithful old nurse who was midwife at my birth, who would have plunged her hands in fire for my sake, shrank from being a witness to what I might encounter in the dark streets and alleyways, the broad piazzas and the crowded quays of our native city. If only for that reason, I would have refused her. As it was, the ordeal was something which, for my sins, I had to face alone.

Accordingly, at seven o'clock on that spring evening – the loveliest time of the day and the year in Venice, when the low-cast sun catches every dome and pinnacle, and touches every wave in its golden light – I put on my good grey cloak and a bonnet to match, and took stock of myself in the long pier-glass in my dressing room.

There stood – myself. Isolda Mazzini-Forsca. In my early

3

twenties. A spinster of the See of San Marco. Not greatly changed during the last twelvemonth – not on the outside, at any rate.

Tall – and the tallness comes from my English ancestry on my father's side. Pale of complexion in the currently fashionable manner. Dark hair and deep blue eyes – legacies of my mixed Irish and Italian descent on my mother's side.

And the eyes – *haunted*.

I did not leave the palazzo by the great wrought-iron gates that let out on to the marble steps leading down to the edge of the Grand Canal, where in happier days my father kept no less than three private gondolas bearing the Mazzini-Forsca escutcheon, nor by a scarcely less splendid, marble-canopied door leading to the piazza at the rear of the mansion, but by the back gate in the kitchen yard which gave access to an alleyway that was lapped by the scummy green waters of a narrow canal.

No one was about. No sound but the gentle plash of the water and a dog that barked in the distance. Gathering my cloak more closely about me, I crossed a humpbacked bridge and directed my footsteps towards St Mark's Square, which would be my testing ground, I told myself. If I could pass by Florian's café, if – and the very notion made me catch my breath – if I could summon up the courage to enter and order a cup of coffee or an aperitif – then everything would fall into place. I would have conquered my fears. And, master of myself, nothing and no one could ever harm me again.

Alas for forlorn hopes. . . .

I rounded a corner, out of shadow and into sudden sunlight. There was a child, a little girl in a ragged apron, playing with a doll outside an open doorway. As I approached, she picked up the doll and held it out to me, mouthing something happy and treating me to a delicious smile, so that I paused to touch her tousled head and admire her doll. There was a cry of alarm, and a woman rushed out of the door, snatched at the child and dragged her away from me, treating me to a glance of such malevolence that it was as tangible as a blow in the face.

I knew that woman, though we had never exchanged a

4

word in our lives. I had known her by sight since she was a girl, could remember the day of her wedding, when she had been led into that selfsame door on the arm of her proud groom with his flowery buttonhole and his plastered-down hair, and she all in white. I could remember seeing her with the new baby, proudly pushing her bassinet, the beaming father at her side. We had never done more than exchange a glance in all that time.

And now – this.

I went on my way, diminished. If the encounter had been only slightly more protracted, if the woman had said something to me, something that matched the look of loathing, I think I might have turned back home there and then. As it was, she left me with just sufficient fortitude to carry on. But, oh, by so narrow a margin.

The road between the tall buildings began to widen, and I passed through a couple of small squares, over two or three bridges. There were a few people about now. It was nearly the time of the evening promenade. No one gave me so much as a passing look, and my defences were strengthened in consequence. Here was I, who had been a self-condemned prisoner of the Palazzo Mazzini-Forsca for over a year – and for no good reason. In all of Venice – so far – I had been recognized and reviled by one person only. My step lightened. The great bell of San Marco sonorously boomed the hour of seven. I could almost imagine the scent of Florian's delicious coffee that awaited me in the great square.

And then – my world fell apart again.

Two elderly women – black-garbed from head to foot like all of their age and class, simple peasant women – were coming towards me. Why they should have recognized me I have no way of telling. Perhaps they had noticed me at Mass many times, and whispered and nudged each other: 'See – there's the Mazzini-Forsca woman.'

No whispering and nudging this time. Together, they saw me as one, and each reacted after her own inclinations.

One of them crossed herself and averted her eyes. The other raised a clenched fist with thumb and little finger extended like horns – the sign to avert the Evil Eye, the defence against encroaching evil. And I was the evil object against which the woman had raised her defence!

I fled, turning on my heel and ducking down an alleyway that led through a rabbit warren of tall tenements that seemed to offer me a place in which to hide. Before I had gone more than a little way down the alley the high walls had risen all about me, shutting out everything but an irregular shape of cerulean sky, and bathing me in chill shadows. I was hemmed in by flaking walls and windows like blind eyes, shuttered. There was no sign of anyone, but when my steps brought me round a corner, I heard the laughter of children from somewhere ahead. It was not the laughter of gay innocence; there was mockery and menace there.

The quality of the laughter heightened my unease, so that I nearly turned back, even at the risk of encountering again the two women in black, but another bend brought the children into sight.

There were about six or eight of them – urchin boys in faded and ragged shirts and breeches, barefoot. They were playing with – tormenting – a small kitten. Laughing and chanting, they were tossing the writhing scrap of white fur from one to another like a handball. Sooner or later, it had to fall and be injured – this was clearly a concomitant of the game; the throwing and catching were loose and haphazard, and a fumbling catch brought fresh shrieks of mockery.

'Stop it!'

The echo of my shout, reflected back from the enclosing walls, seemed unnaturally loud, and some obscure prompting made me repeat the words in a harsh whisper.

'You horrid creatures. How can you be so cruel?' I added for good measure.

The one who was holding the kitten – he was older and taller than most of the others, and there were the beginnings of a moustache on his upper lip, though he could scarcely have been more than eleven – stared at me in something like alarm as I approached him, hands extended.

'Give that poor little thing to me!' I demanded.

It might have ended there. Receiving no support from his silent and overawed companions, the boy was within an ace

6

of obeying – when his sullen eyes lit up with a flash of recognition. My heart missed a beat.

He pointed at me, called out to his friends, his mean little mouth twisted in a grin of malevolence. 'Hey! look who it is! Don't you recognize her? She's the woman who . . .'

Another took up the cry. 'Yes – it's her!'

I waited to hear no more. Pausing only to snatch up the kitten which had taken the opportunity of wriggling free of its captor's grasp, I continued on my way as fast as I could run, and my tormentor cried out to his companions to follow me. Heart pounding, I ducked and twisted through the alleyways, in and out of sunlight and shadow, under low arches, over humpbacked bridges, and the yelling urchins came after me.

Presently, I came to a shop on a corner of a building so old and dilapidated that it was propped up by long baulks of wood. There was an indecipherable sign hanging drunkenly on a gallows above the door, and through the grimy windows the eye of faith could dimly discern the outlines of statuary and tumbled bric-a-brac. Seeking sanctuary from my pursuers, I pushed open the shop door and burst in, breathless. A bell tinkled thinly above my head. The door closed behind me, and through its dusty panes of glass I saw the urchins pause, look at each other irresolutely, but make no attempt to follow me in.

'Who's there? What are you seeking?' A wavering voice came from the dark recesses at the rear of the shop, and an old woman shuffled into view. Treading with infinite care, she made her way towards me past mountains of crockery, brassware, statuary, knick-knacks, bits and pieces of heaven knows what, all jumbled precariously on rickety-looking tables and piled upon the dusty floor.

'What are you looking for?' she repeated. 'It's all for sale. Speak up.'

She was incredibly old and dressed in black, with a shawl draped over her head. The eyes that stared out at me were opaque in whiteness like the eyes of a dead fish. She was blind.

'I – I hadn't anything particular in mind,' I faltered, with a backward glance to the door. The urchins were still outside. Waiting.

'How much do you want to spend?' she demanded.

'I don't know,' I replied. 'I was looking for – um – a present. Yes, a present.'

'Is it for a birthday, a saint's day? A wedding?'

'A wedding,' I lied. From what I could see, my pursuers showed no signs of going away.

'For the bride, is it?'

'Yes.'

Reaching out, her hand wavered searchingly for a moment, then closed about my wrist. 'Come with me,' she said, 'I've the very thing for you in the back of the shop. This way. . . .'

I allowed myself to be led, she continuing to hold me in a quite implacable grasp. There was a narrow corridor at the rear of the main showroom, its narrowness further circumscribed by a row of statuary ranged along each wall. There were gesticulating figures in the classical style, winged angels, putti, armoured knights, heraldic animals and all manner of grotesques. Everything was thick with ancient dust. We came at length to a small room that was cluttered like all the rest, and lit only by such evening sunlight as was able to filter through a round cupola set in the middle of the ceiling.

Still holding me tightly by the wrist, my guide reached out with the other hand and drew aside a coverlet, from which a great cloud of dust arose, catching innumerable pinpoints of the thin daylight descending from above.

'There! What do you think of that?' she demanded.

I drew a sharp and involuntary breath.

'Don't you like it?' she snapped.

It was some kind of chest, perhaps a dower chest, made of a dark tropical wood, with a hinged lid. What I found so distasteful, what had made me gasp and shrink away, was the lifelike representation of a snake coiled up on the lid. Whether it was all of a piece with the lid, or stuck on afterwards, there was no way of telling, but the thing was most cunningly carved to present the image of the reptile as if in the act of being surprised. Its head and neck were raised and the evil mouth was agape to show cruel fangs made of

8

ivory. The eyes were of some variety of semi-precious stone and looked like drowned seed pearls. To me it was utterly revolting, for I have a deep-seated horror of snakes.

'Just the thing for a bride to keep her linen in,' said the old woman. 'Made of sandalwood. You can smell it. See?' She sniffed. 'And it's cheap.' She named a figure that I could well meet from the money I carried with me in my reticule.

As I hesitated she let go of my arm. Her whole demeanour took on an air of hostility. I had a vision of being dismissed from her shop as someone who had simply come in to waste her time, and I thought of the young tormentors who were waiting outside for me – and was afraid.

'I – I'll have it,' I blurted out.

Her face softened. 'You won't regret it,' she said. 'The bride will bless you.'

'But I can't take it now,' I added.

'Take it when you like,' she countered. 'Only, pay me now.'

I delved into my reticule for the money, meanwhile puzzling my mind as to how I could further protract my stay in my sinister sanctuary till such a time as the urchins, tired of waiting for their victim to emerge, might go away. After I had counted the coins into her palm (no easy matter with the small white kitten still held in my other hand), I chanced to notice that there was a door at one end of the room. The fact that it had bolts and a lock suggested another avenue of escape.

'Does that door lead out to the street at the back?' I asked.

She confirmed that this was the case, and I contrived some tale about wanting to return home by another way so as not to meet someone I preferred to avoid. The old woman accepted it without interest and proceeded to unlock and unbolt the door. I thanked her and made mention of sending a servant round to collect the chest – while being determined to do nothing of the kind.

Just as I was about to step out into the empty street at the rear of the building the old woman once again took hold of my wrist and put her gnarled face close to mine. It seemed to me that the blind eyes saw, and probed into my very mind.

'I am the seventh child of a seventh child,' she said, 'and nothing is hidden from me.' She paused for a few moments after this astonishing declaration, and then went on: 'I saw the fear in you when you entered. You carry it with you like the lanterns that we children in the old days used to carry under our cloaks, a light that no one else knew about, secret only to ourselves. But a seventh child of a seventh child – she can see that light. And I saw it in you.' The grip on my wrist intensified. 'I see much pain ahead of you, my child,' she went on. 'It is possible that there will be no end to it. I cannot tell you, because that much is hidden even from me.'

Staring at her in mounting alarm, I struggled to be free, but she would not let me go.

'This much I see,' she said, 'your only hope is to endure. That way only lies your salvation. If you give in, you are lost for ever and the grass will grow over your grave untended.'

'Please!' I pleaded. 'Let me go, whoever you are.'

She would not release me. 'One thing more,' she said. 'He who will come to you from over the sea, listen to his words. Your only hope of salvation may lie in him. But even he may not be able to hold at bay the dark shadows that I see closing about you.'

She freed me. I backed away from her, out of the door. One last look into those all-seeing, blind eyes and I turned to run.

Her words came after me: 'Your only hope is to endure!'

I do not remember my return flight to the palazzo, only the act of slamming the yard gate behind me and driving home the bolt, then resting my cheek against the cool wood-work, breathless, eyes closed in agony of mind. I was summoned back to the there and then by a small paw – soft, its tiny claws withdrawn into the velvety pads – gently probing at my cheek.

I stroked its neck, and the old woman's strange words came back to me – 'He who will come to you from over the sea . . . your only hope of salvation may lie in him. . . . '

In my father's day, and earlier still when my dear mother was alive, the palazzo blazed with light every night. My mother kept a salon twice weekly, one of them political, to which came most of the great figures in Venice and Italy generally. From a safe place of refuge behind my mother's chair, I, a young girl, saw and heard world-famous politicians and statesmen holding forth. One evening, never to be forgotten, King Victor Emmanuel himself graced our salon, and I gave our Sovereign a deep curtsy, as I had been taught.

The alternative salon was artistic, at which I have listened to the great writers and artists of Europe discussing their works, and enjoyed some of the finest singers and instrumentalists of our time.

But now — all gone. . . .

The night of my disastrous foray into the streets, as on so many other nights, I wandered through the high-ceilinged rooms of the great mansion, in and out of the dust-sheeted furniture, under the massive crystal chandeliers that had once spread their light over jewelled corsages and proud tiaras — now darkened for ever, leaving only my solitary candle throwing my huge shadow on the silent walls.

My secret, which was no secret because all Venice knew of it, but spoke of it only in whispers, was not freely discussed between Assunta and me. Nor was I able to think of it save in abstractions. From time to time — and that particular night was such a time — I took out certain strands from the tangled web of my secret and examined them for a short while before letting them fall back into obscurity again. Never could I bring myself to trace the whole course of events right through, in chronological order. I could abide only the disembodied fragments, the single strands of memory. The whole of it was too much for my sanity to encompass.

That night, alone in my mother's salon that had once resounded to some of the greatest singers and instrumentalists of the age, and echoed the visions of Cavour, I let my mind take the painful journey back to a certain late afternoon in February when the living nightmare really began.

The funeral procession left from the Fondamente Nuove, that long, straight quay which faces the cemetery isle of San Michele, with the tips of sad cypresses standing sentinel above its enclosing walls. Six gondolas in all. First, the floating hearse, black overall and sable-plumed, the black-draped coffin lying within the crystal catafalque with a single sheaf of red roses resting upon the lid. Next followed the five covered gondolas bearing the mourners, myself included.

The cortège set out from the quay and was immediately assaulted by the wind-whipped waves that tried to the full the strength and skill of the gondoliers. I remember shrinking against Assunta, and she holding my hand more tightly, as I looked out over the grey water and the flung spume, towards the isle of the dead silhouetted against the darkening sky. It took powerful men and long oars over half an hour to battle against wind and current to cross the short distance, but presently the cortège came to its resting place and we were filing after the coffin, through the cloister, watched by silent Franciscan monks, and into the high-naved church that smelled of beeswax and incense.

Somehow I ordered my mind and kept my resolve not to break down. Even when the bronze coffin was slowly lowered into the family crypt, and the chaplain to the Cardinal Archbishop of Venice intoned the liturgy for the dead, scattering earth from a silver scallop shell down upon the sheaf of red roses, I fought back the worst of the anguish but let the tears flow unchecked behind my enveloping veil.

And then it was over. The last of the Latin, the final plume of burnt incense drifted over the dark maw of the vault, the monks shuffled away on sandalled feet, the mourners looked at each other, waiting for one of our number to take charge and lead the way out.

I remained to the last, and became separated from Assunta during the move towards the door. The Cardinal Archbishop's chaplain stood at the door in his funereal vestments of black embroidered with silver skulls and crossed bones. He was a young man, and marked for high office, so they said, perhaps even the papacy. His eyes scarcely touched upon mine for more than a passing moment as he addressed me in a whisper.

'You have suffered greatly, my child. I will pray for you.'

'Thank you, Father.'

'Such tragedy coming on the heels of supreme joy – it is a terrible burden for shoulders as young as yours. But you have many loving friends to support you in your time of grief.'

'I hope so, Father.'

'And I will pray for you,' he repeated, and looked away.

I thanked him again.

Outside the cloisters, the rain had started. It came down in a steady stream, a rain determined to stay. The overcast had turned late afternoon into early night, and the wind was chill. I shivered in the light coat that I wore, and looked about me for Assunta. She must have thought I had gone on ahead and would be waiting for me at the foot of the steps by the gondola. I quickened my pace.

Emerging from under the arch in the cemetery wall, leaving behind me the forest of Carrara marble figures set among the dark cypresses, I saw that the cortège was already departing. Three of the mourners' gondolas remained – and there was another craft: a very workmanlike-looking barge with a crew of uniformed oarsmen and a cloaked man in a tall hat standing at the tiller.

Three men stood at the top of the steps, and I knew from their attitude that they were waiting for me. Two of them were uniformed, the third was a hard-eyed personage dressed like a minor civil servant, in a seedy frock coat that was green with age and shining wet from the rain. He doffed his hat upon my approach and sketched the travesty of a bow.

'Signorina Mazzini-Forsca.' It was not a question. 'Police. You will wish, please, to accompany us.'

He gestured down towards the waiting barge.

Two

After that first essay into the streets, I kept not only to the palazzo, but also ventured out of my own suite of rooms and into the state apartments and the main part of the mansion only after dark, when Assunta was asleep and I could wander undisturbed, raising ghosts of the past with my flickering candlelight.

Memories are one thing, present fears another. And I had a present fear which, though I tried my best to force it back into a dark recess of my mind, kept returning like a grim reproof. It was Assunta who, a few days after my disastrous attempt to return to normal life, herself raised the question.

'Have you given any thought about what's to be done regarding Julietta?'

'Please, not now, Assunta,' I replied. She had come upon me in my sitting room that overlooked the Grand Canal. I had been daydreaming with the kitten asleep on my lap. 'Some other time.'

She shook her head and sighed heavily – a reaction that, as I remembered from my childhood, she had always employed when I was being particularly irritating. 'Isolda, you can't sweep it away under the carpet any longer,' she said. 'Julietta will be home soon and asking questions. You've managed to keep her far away from Venice ever since – ever since it happened – but the time's fast approaching when you'll have to make a clean breast of everything.'

I felt the chill edges of panic assaulting my nerve ends. 'I'll find some way of telling her,' I said. 'But not now. I have to give it more thought. Don't hurry me.'

14

She looked down at me, arms akimbo, her button-black eyes stripping away my subterfuges and evasions, layer by layer, and revealing me to myself as I was, naked and vulnerable.

'You know there is no way you'll be able to keep it from her,' she declared. 'You've known it all along, and yet you still fool yourself.'

'Why should she know?' I retorted. 'Why can't she go on thinking a lie, since she's contented with the lie? Why break her heart in the relentless pursuit of truth for its own sake?'

She shook her head again – this stolid peasant woman who had been, and still was, the one rock in my life upon which I could lean and know she would never let me fall.

'That's not good enough, Isolda,' she said gently, 'and you know it's not good enough. It was one thing to send the child to the convent school in Ireland till the worst of the trouble had blown over, but the pigeon is coming home to roost this summer, and no power on earth is going to prevent someone from telling her everything. Why, the very children in the streets will shout it after her.'

I got to my feet, still holding the kitten, and went over to the tall window that let out on to the balcony overhanging the canal. Out in mid-stream a solitary gondola was being sculled towards the Rialto bridge. There was a young couple, boy and girl, seated in the stern. They were holding hands and looked very much in love.

'I'll take her to the villa,' I said at length. 'We'll all go there, Assunta, the three of us.'

'That will only be putting off the evil day,' was her response. 'And even on the Brenta, there are folks who'll talk.'

'But not so many,' I reasoned. 'There are no busy streets, no cafés, no places where people congregate and gossip. On the Brenta, she will only have her solitary walks, the company of we two, the quiet of the garden. See to it, will you Assunta? Send word to Signore Nevi to go in and prepare the villa for us.'

Assunta pursed her lips and nodded grudging agreement. But, as usual, she had the last word. 'You'll not keep it from the child for ever,' she declared. 'Better forfeit her love by

15

telling her straight out, yet perhaps keep her whole, rather than she be torn apart by a few cruel words from a stranger.'

To this I could only reply that I would pray for the strength to do what must be done – knowing full well that, from where I stood, I could never in all my life see myself confessing all to the beloved young sister who idolized me.

So I kept to my suite, taking my meals in the sitting room with the kitten, whom I had named Michou. There, I spun out the long days with my books, my sewing, and watching the world go past my window. Also, I had plenty of food for memory. I speak of memory of the sweeter sort. I had kept copious diaries since childhood, together with souvenirs such as theatre programmes, invitation cards, *carnets de bal*, letters – all carefully guarded in velvet-bound albums. They told of my life as a pampered daughter of the Venetian nobility, elder of two sisters, whose upbringing had been an endless summertime of picnics and masked balls, carnivals and fêtes; a life spent in a magnificent Venetian palazzo, with an army of servants at one's beck and call, and a villa on the Brenta nearby; a roundelay broken only by a year at a finishing school in Lausanne, from which I ran away on two occasions. Two dark shadows, only, lay across the memories of those early years: the deaths of my beloved parents. My mother was taken from us when I was eleven years of age, but we had come to accept the inevitable after many years of her illness and her long, hopeless stays in Swiss sanitoria. Father's death, which was sudden and unexpected, came as a far worse shock, and left me bereft of all support save that provided by my faithful Assunta. In one stroke it left me parent, guide, confidante and mentor to my sister Julietta, who was six years younger than me. She, wayward, high-spirited and mercurial, was like an unbroken colt who responded only to one pair of hands – and those hands were mine. How I blessed the understanding there was between us, and the confidence that she reposed in me, so that I was able, if only in some degree, to help shape and guide that bright and beautiful spirit and watch her grow in knowledge of the world about her.

16

How bright had been the promise then – and how dark and threatening the storm clouds now.

Among my souvenirs I treasured most of all the invitation cards – those mute pasteboard signposts of my childhood and youth. Here was the relic of the very first birthday party to which I went in my first long dress, and was sick from eating too much ice cream. And here, a memory of a state ball at the ducal palace, when I and my fellow debutantes were presented to their Excellencies and I danced with a most handsome midshipman who afterwards wrote to me every day for three months and never again.

Balls, soirées, receptions, banquets, parties on the canal, excursions to bathe on the Lido, picnics on the Brenta, firework fêtes on the Giudecca during the Feast of the Redemption when we stayed up all night, boat parties at the historic Regatta – they were all there, marking the passing years.

And the later invitations, the ones dated the previous year and the one preceding it, bore another name after mine. . . .

'. . . *request the pleasure of the company of the Signorina Isolda Mazzini-Forsca and the noble Count Bruno Ferrara. . . .* '

The earliest memory of Bruno. . . .

It was the Easter Mass in San Marco, and I with my mother and father in our private pew above the nave, with the carved wooden sides so high that father was able to doze off, unseen, during any particularly long and boring sermon, and I was only just tall enough to see over the top and down into the standing congregation below. Shortly after the Elevation of the Host, I became aware that a pair of dark eyes were thoughtfully regarding me from an adjacent pew which I knew to belong to the Giolitti family, with whom, for political reasons, the Mazzini-Forscas were not on speaking terms.

The intense scrutiny lasted considerably longer than mere curiosity allowed, and I was at last compelled to look away with my cheeks flaming with embarrassment. I would add that I was ten years old at the time and totally ignorant about boys, since I had never exchanged more than half a dozen words with one of those rather alarming creatures in my life. Much later, during the singing of the recessional hymn, I sneaked another glance towards the next-door pew, where Senator Giolitti, his pompous wife and their seven children were singing lustily. He of the thoughtful dark eyes was merely looking down at his hymn card, silent. It seemed to me that I had never gazed upon so beautiful a face, which, in its olive-skinned, smooth perfection, in the lustrous profusion of sable curls that framed the noble brow, put me in mind of a young Christian martyr in one of the dark paintings that hung in our *piano nobile*.

As I continued to regard him covertly, he glanced up and caught me at it. Once more I hastily looked away. Nor did I attempt to search him out again.

I determined to discover the identity of the strange boy, and did so sooner than I had hoped. Those were the days, of course, when we had a veritable army of servants at the palazzo, and I used to spend a lot of time in the housekeeper's parlour where the senior servants – the butler, head cook, my father's valet and suchlike – spent their brief leisure times drinking coffee and gossiping about people and happenings in the city. One day soon after Easter they touched upon the Giolitti family, and Aldo the butler said that the senator had taken under his wing the young ward of a distant relation who had died during an outbreak of typhus which had racked the city of Pisa during the previous summer. The boy, said Aldo, was the Count Bruno Ferrara and heir to a considerable fortune and widespread estates in Europe. Also – according to Aldo's brother, who was an under-footman at the Palazzo Giolitti – young Bruno was very much of a handful, the scourge of all the servants and a trial to his new foster parents. He was to be sent away to a school in England, said Aldo. The English knew how to tame boys, he said.

This was undoubtedly the young Christian martyr of my imaginings, though the description of his character scarcely matched up with my impression of him. And now he was going away to school in England, and I might never see him again, even from afar. I hasten to add that the very notion

18

of meeting him at close quarters was almost too frightening to contemplate.

But the unimaginable came to pass, and in this manner. . . .

It was during the Feast of the Redemption, four long months after my first, slight encounter with the boy Bruno, and I had resigned myself to the thought of never seeing him again. This traditional feast of ours, which takes place on the night of Saturday to Sunday in the third week of July every year, is held on the Guidecca Canal which separates Giudecca island from the main mass of the city. From the early evening onwards every boat in Venice gathers in the canal, all decorated with lanterns and coloured branches, while the rest of the population crowds the shores to watch the spectacular display of fireworks lasting right through the night. At the first light of dawn in the east, the entire armada makes across the lagoon to the Lido to await the sunrise over the Adriatic. Nor is that the end of the celebrations, for later in the morning there is a great religious procession across a temporary bridge of boats reaching over the wide span of water separating San Marco from the Church of the Redemption on the Guidecca, which was built in the sixteenth century in thanksgiving for the end of a terrible plague, and in memory of which the annual fête will be held for as long as Venice remains above the waters of the lagoon. The whole proceeding is a most marvellous experience and one which remains with an impressionable child, like myself, her whole life through.

It happened during the height of the festivities, when the last of the fireworks were exploding in cascades of descending colours above San Giorgio island and every eye present was straying towards the eastern horizon for the first intimation of dawn. I was in a gondola with my family – my little sister Julietta included, she being fast asleep in Assunta's arms, for not even the tiniest babies are put to bed on the feast night of the Redemption. The canal was packed tightly with craft of all kinds, bow to stern, side by side and touching. During a particularly dazzling display of rocketry, when a cascade of stars illuminated the entire scene in searing, breath-robbing whiteness, I became aware of someone regarding me from the gondola alongside ours. Before the sky was plunged again into temporary darkness I discerned, with a sudden leap of the heart, that Bruno Ferrara was close to me – so near that I could have reached out and touched him.

I can only guess by what means Bruno contrived it so that the Giolittis' gondola stayed close to ours during the journey across to the Lido, perhaps he himself took a hand at the oar – he certainly became a most adept amateur gondolier in later years – but it is certain that when the Mazzini-Forscas alighted on the quay of the Lido, the Giolittis were next ashore. And both families made great play of ignoring each other completely.

Later, also, on the Adriatic beach, barefoot in the soft white sand in the dawn light, the two families had again – by what unknown chance? – contrived to be in close proximity. And the beach was crowded. No one took the slightest notice of two young people exchanging a few words in the growing light.

'Hello,' he said. 'I saw you in San Marco at Easter.'

'I remember,' was my faltering reply.

'I've been in England since then,' he said. 'At school. But we're on holiday till September.'

'Do you like it there?' I asked.

'It's all right. It's a good thing I speak English well. They don't like foreigners very much, and the boys who look and speak differently are bullied rather badly.'

I regarded his broad shoulders, his confident way of looking and speaking. 'I wouldn't think anyone would bully you,' I said.

He smiled. 'Let them just try.'

We were silent together for a few moments, then – greatly daring – I said: 'My name's Isolda Mazzini-Forsca.'

'I know,' he replied.

He knew! He had taken the trouble to inquire who I was! The very thought of it made my spirits rise like a lark in the high blue sky.

'Your people and the Giolittis don't think much of each other,' he said.

20

'Silly politics,' I said.

'It's a pity,' said Bruno. 'I would like to invite you to my birthday party next Tuesday. We're going across to Murano for a picnic feast and a bathe.'

'I would love to come,' I told him. 'But even if you invited me, my parents would forbid it.'

'What a pity,' he said. 'And I don't suppose I shall have the opportunity of seeing you again before I go back to school.'

I felt tears prickle my eyes, and looked away. 'I don't think so,' I whispered. 'They're very strict with me.'

'Still,' he said more brightly, 'we're together now.'

'Yes,' I said, and met the steady gaze of his serious, rather sad eyes.

Later, when the sun rose above the blue Adriatic, turning each wavelet to silver and gold, and the assembled multitude had eyes for nothing but the glories of the new summer's day, Bruno's hand stole out and imprisoned mine, and I held him fast for what seemed like an eternity of time.

We stood there, hand in hand, not speaking, unnoticed. Just two young people, a boy and a girl in the throes of their first love.

Such was the germination of my love for Bruno Ferrara, and a blighted love it was from the start, for I never set eyes on the object of my affection during the next five years. I learned on the servants' grapevine that Bruno's stepfather had ordered that the boy must spend his school holidays staying at and familiarizing himself with the various properties which the Ferrara family had amassed over the years in England, Scotland, France and elsewhere.

My own education, which was irregular, was in the hands of a succession of governesses, some good, some not so good. My dearest mother's health declined and she passed away. Father decided that a spell in a Swiss finishing school would help me to get over my grief. It did not. As I have said, I ran away twice – and was finally brought home to Venice. It was soon after, just before my sixteenth birthday, that Bruno came back into my life again.

21

'Isolda, you look so beautiful. Oh, I can't wait to be old enough to wear a long dress and go to a grown-ups' ball.'

Julietta had been overseer to my getting ready for my first ball. She had supervised my bath ('Put more of those lovely French bath salts in, Assunta!'), raved over my lace petti-coats, been very dominating about my coiffure ('Not too many curls at the front, you're hiding her brow, which is one of Isolda's best points') and was ecstatic about my ball dress, which was of oyster satin decorated with tiny pink roses at the flounces.

'It will soon be your turn,' I told her.

She pulled a face. 'Yes, in six years' time,' she conceded, pouting. 'Being young is such a bore, and it goes on for so *long*.'

She looked so sweetly forlorn that I could have hugged her – and did. 'Never mind, dear,' I said. 'I'll come into your bed when I'm back, and if you're still awake, I'll tell you all about it.'

'I shall be awake, never fear,' she retorted.

The ball was at the Casa Crispi, one of the most notable great houses on the Grand Canal, once owned by a mistress of King Louis XV of France. I was delivered, along with three girl friends of my own age – all of us chaperoned by a dowager of most stern correctness named Signora di Ventris – at the imposing entrance arch of the Casa Crispi in one of the Mazzini-Forsca gondolas, and shepherded through a courtyard where a trio of marble nymphs poured water from conches into a shallow alabaster basin in which golden carp prowled in and out of candlelight and shade, where miniature cypresses whispered in the night zephyrs; then on up a splendid staircase to the ballroom that spanned the whole width of the building, and where an orchestra was playing a Viennese waltz and all the youth and beauty of Venice was dancing – the ball being essentially for the *jeunesse dorée*, of which my companions and I were by far the youngest – as Signora di Ventris, mindful of her responsibilities, hastened to make us aware.

'You young ladies will sit here, on the balcony with me,' she intoned. 'Should any gentleman approach you to request the pleasure of a dance, he must first present himself to me and I will question him as to his background – if I am not already acquainted with him.'

The girls and I exchanged glances, masking our smiles behind our fans. The signora's reputation as a chaperon was a byword among the young womanhood of Venice. She maintained a strict control over her charges for the first hour or so, but after that the heat of the ballroom and the imbibing of a couple of glasses of champagne usually sent her off to sleep.

Glancing at my reflection in a nearby pier-glass and not entirely disapproving of what I saw there, I then addressed myself to the dancers circling the floor below us, speculating upon the costumes and coiffures of the ladies, sizing up the gentlemen, and picking out those with whom I was acquainted – and there were quite a few. My companions were no doubt similarly occupied, each of them fearful – as I was – that the others would be whisked away on to the dance floor and that she would be left with Signora di Ventris – a wallflower.

The anxious minutes ticked past. The waltz drew to a close. The floor was cleared. Ladies returned to their seats. Gentlemen – tall and short, uniformed and in evening dress, handsome and homely – milled around, sizing up prospective partners and each other, playing out the age-old ritual of gallantry.

Then, as I watched, a tall figure came out of the crowd and approached the short flight of steps leading up to the balcony where we were sitting. He was dark-haired, moustached, and walked with the grace of a panther. I immediately thrilled to the notion that he might be coming to ask one of *us* to dance – but, surely, it would be Zöe whom he would choose – Zöe, who was blonde and very assured for her age. Or, perhaps, Carlotta, bold-eyed Carlotta who never seemed to lack for admiring glances when we were out walking together. Or Edda, who was plump and pretty as a peach, with not a lot to say for herself, but very sweet.

Edda, who was next to me, nudged my elbow. 'Look who's coming,' she whispered. 'He's going to ask me to dance, for sure.'

23

Disappointed beyond belief, I bowed my head so as not to be witness to the inevitable. The next thing I knew, a pair of highly-polished dancing pumps were presented to my vision immediately in front of me. Raising my glance, I took in the whole length of him from feet to head. The head was cocked to one side, rather quizzically, and a slight smile informed those marvellously chiselled lips, now graced with a silky moustache. And the dark eyes regarded me with an intensity that thrilled my heart.

'Hello, Isolda,' he said. 'It has been a long time. . . .'

'Tell me then, Isolda — tell me all!'

I snuggled into bed with Julietta and snuffed the candle. It was nearly four o'clock, and already one could hear the movement of market craft on the canal below our window, and the beginnings of dawn were touching the high ceiling above my sister's canopied bed.

'I danced all night,' I told her. 'Apart from a short break for a buffet supper — and I wasn't one bit hungry, I assure you — I never missed a single one. Not one!'

'And what about Zöe and the others — did they dance all night, too?'

'Oh, I suppose so,' I conceded. 'But not *every* dance. They had to wait from time to time, to be asked, you see. Whilst I — I had one partner all the whole night long.'

'Oh, Isolda, how *thrilling!* Who was he, Isolda, and what was he like? Do tell!'

'We-e-ll, his name wouldn't mean much to you' — I had sufficient prudence, knowing of the family feud, to keep Bruno's name discreetly veiled from even my little sister — 'but he's tremendously tall and distinguished-looking. He's just finished his studies and is going to join the army next month and has promised to write to me.'

'Are you in love with him Isolda?' she probed.

Taken aback by her directness, I could only bluster. 'Oh, Julietta, how can you ask such a thing? Why, I hardly know him and. . . .'

'It wouldn't make any difference to me,' she said firmly. 'Even if I had only just met him, I would know immediately if I had fallen in love with him.'

24

I made no reply to that.

'Well, then, is he in love with *you?*'

'How do I know?' If I had thought that I was to be subjected to this interrogation, I would most certainly have gone straight to my own bed, I told myself.

'Well, did he *say* so?'

'No – not in so many words. . . .' I could have bitten off my tongue for that unguarded reply, upon which she leapt with alacrity.

'You mean, he gave you that sort of *look* – and you knew, in your heart of hearts, that his affections were all for you!' My young sister was widely read in novels of a certain kind, and incurably romantic.

'I knew nothing of the sort, Julietta,' I replied firmly. 'And now, if you don't mind, I should like some sleep, for I have been on my feet all the livelong night.'

I turned over and composed myself, as best as I was able, for sleep, smiling into my pillow. Julietta had probed out my secret and seen me for what I was: a person in love who was loved in return. There was no doubt, no doubt at all. In the long night of the ball at the Casa Crispi – which, as always when one is enjoying oneself to an infinite degree, passed so quickly that one strove desperately to hold back the passing of time, as if every lost moment that could never be recalled was like parting with a piece of one's own heart – I had known the truth of it: I was in love with Bruno, and he with me, and nothing stood between us but the absurd and ridiculous feud between the Mazzini-Forscas and his guardian's family.

Would that be sufficient to keep us apart? I asked myself.

The answer to my question was not long in coming. The following afternoon I was summoned to attend my father in the library. He greeted me with his accustomed grave courtesy, rising upon my entrance and offering me his cheek to kiss. I think this was possibly the first occasion when I noticed how he had grown much older in appearance since my mother's death, how there was a tiredness about his eyes and a slight weariness in his manner. I remembered that, though no longer active in Venetian politics, he still carried a lot of influence in his own party. And he was a man who could never relax.

He motioned me to take the seat beside him and came straight to the point. 'My dear Isolda,' he said, 'it has always been our custom – your mother and I – to speak frankly, and I will do so now.'

'I have today received some rather disturbing information from Signora di Ventris' – he smiled wryly, and I had a brief glimpse of my father as I remembered him in his prime – 'and while I would be the first to concede that the signora is a prime source of Venetian gossip and somewhat given to exaggeration, I must nevertheless take her report with the seriousness that it warrants. Do you follow me so far, Isolda?'

'Yes, Father,' was my dutiful response. I followed him right enough – and I thought I knew what was coming next. Nor was I wrong.

'Signora di Ventris reports that you danced the whole night through,' he continued, taking a cigar from the humidor at his elbow and examining it with quite unneccessary attention. 'Is that correct?'

'Yes, Father,' I breathed.

He made a round, generous gesture. 'You are to be commended, my dear,' he said. 'A young girl at her first grown-up ball – to be so gratifyingly attended is a source of satisfaction both to herself and to her proud parents. Your dear mother, I am sure, would have been as delighted as I am.'

'Thank you, Father,' I murmured, looking down at my hands and discovering, somewhat to my surprise, that they were trembling slightly.

'However,' he said, and repeated himself, 'however. . . .

'The young man who bestowed upon you such flattering attention, my dear Isolda, is quite well known to you by now, of course, by name and by station. Correct?'

'Yes, Father.'

'Count Bruno Ferrara,' intoned my father. 'Son of the late General Count Andreas Ferrara, sometime a member of the Venetian senate and a bitter political opponent of mine. Not, I hasten to add, that his mere opposition would warrant my enmity, were it not for the fact that the Count also allied himself with the Giolittis, who, as you may or may not know, my dear, made determined and scoundrelly attempts to stop my party from voting monies which might prevent Venice from falling into the lagoon by the twenty-first century, or sooner.

'You are following me still, Isolda?'

'Yes, Father,' I replied meekly.

My response seemed to please him. He relaxed sufficiently to light the cigar, nor did he speak again till he had luxuriantly exhaled several mouthfuls of the aromatic smoke.

'So, my dear Isolda, now that I have made the issue plain, you will see that as a dutiful daughter of mine it would be quite out of the question for you to pursue this acquaintance with the young man – even supposing that such a thing were to have entered your mind. Or his.'

I did not reply, my mind was in such a turmoil of mingled anguish, heartbreak, resentment, even anger, that I was incapable of coherent thought. All I resolved – with a maturity of judgement that surprises me when I look back on it – was that I must not at any cost close the door to any hope of my future happiness by quarrelling with my father at that juncture. Like the aspen that bends before the storm and survives, as opposed to the stout oak that resists and is brought down, I resolved to say nothing, in the pious hope that Father would accept my silence as denoting agreement.

And so it was. . . .

Laying aside his cigar, Father stood up and, reaching to take me by the shoulders, gently drew me to my feet and implanted a kiss on both my cheeks. His tired, rheumy eyes glistened with sudden tears as he looked fondly down at me.

'I knew you would understand, my darling Isolda,' he said. 'Indeed, as a true offspring of the Mazzini-Forscas, daughter of a nobleman and an Italian patriot, there was never any doubt in my mind but that you would know that it was out of the question for you to pursue the acquaintance of this young man.

'You have pleased me very much, Isolda, and now you may leave me.'

He patted me on the cheek. I bobbed a curtsy to my parent and left the room.

And that – our first meeting at the Easter Mass, our second encounter on the night of the Redemption Feast, the ball at the Casa Crispi and my interview with Father that followed it – made up one complete strand of my love affair with Bruno Ferrara. Nothing that went before that strand of my memories, not even my mother's death, remained so deeply impressed in my mind, and nothing that came after was untouched by it.

So there was I – years later and bowed by bitter experience – the recluse of the Palazzo Mazzini-Forsca, living alone with the only faithful servant to remain, a ghost in a house of ghosts, condemned to live out my life amidst the crumbling, dusty splendour of days gone by. And one agonizing dread burned in the forefront of my mind – the awful anticipation of my sister's return home from her protracted stay in the Irish convent school to which I had sent her with such immoderate haste. . . .

'Isolda – where are you?'

Assunta called me from the staircase outside the long gallery where I had been walking and thinking.

'I am here,' I called back to her.

She came slowly up the staircase and leaned heavily upon the richly-carved newel post at the top. Strange, I thought, how I had never noticed that my faithful nurse had quite suddenly turned into a very old lady. She had been such a tower of strength all my life, I had supposed her invulnerable to the ravages of age.

'What is it, Assunta?' I asked her.

'Letter for you,' she replied, still struggling to regain her breath. 'Just arrived. And it's from Ireland. From – her. . . .'

Our eyes met, and she must have seen the sudden torment in mine. Hers were all concern for me. She handed me the letter and I broke the seal. The main matter of the contents, written in my young sister's prim and careful convent-school hand, swam before my gaze:

Convent of the Sacred Heart,

28

Dearest Isolda,
I have news for you, wonderful news, tho it brooks misfortune
for others. I will explain. There has been an outbreak of fever
in Castlebar. Two persons have already died, though the convent
has been mercifully spared. However, the Reverend Mother
thinks it prudent that the scholars should leave at once. So, I
depart from Castlebar some time tomorrow. By the time you
receive this, dearest Isolda, I shall be well on my way home, only
twenty-four hours behind this letter.

My kisses to you and to dear Assunta.

Your own loving

Julietta

I looked up from the letter and saw my own concern
mirrored in Assunta's gaze.

'What am I going to do?' I breathed. 'I haven't even made
up my mind if I am going to tell her everything, or how
I am going to tell her – or *anything*. And she'll be here
tomorrow.'

Assunta pursed her lips, as she always used to when I
had done anything particularly stupid and thoughtless in my
childhood.

'Well, you've had plenty of time to make up your mind,
my dear,' she said, 'and now time has caught you by the
apron strings. It's a good thing you thought of taking her to
the villa. There at least, you will have the blessing of a short
respite, to sort a few things out in your mind – if you're
lucky.'

I nodded eagerly. 'We'll leave for the Brenta just as soon
as Julietta arrives,' I cried. 'I'll not even give her time to
unpack. We'll go straight there. Is all in readiness at the
villa?'

'Signora Nevi has been instructed,' she said, referring to
the woman who acted as occasional caretaker and kept an
eye on the property. 'The villa will be clean, aired, and bright
as a pin.'

'Then order a barge to be ready to leave here for the
Brenta at a moment's notice any time after tomorrow
morning, Assunta,' I said. 'And see to it – watch Julietta as

29

I shall be watching her – make sure that she doesn't get into casual conversation with anyone, neither the boatmen, nor anyone we might meet on the way.

'I won't feel easy in my mind, Assunta, till we are safely arrived at the villa, just the three of us. Alone.'

I did not sleep a wink that night, but stalked through the echoing rooms of the palazzo, candlestick in hand, restless and distraught, turning over in my mind all manner of means by which I might divulge my dreadful secret to Julietta without hurting her to the very soul. Selfishly I would also have wished to retain for myself the love she bore for me – but that was a secondary consideration compared with the other.

The long night passed, and still I had no answers. Weary, broken in mind and spirit, I dragged myself to my bedroom and lay down on top of the coverlet, watching with sleepless eyes the unfolding of yet another dawn – one that might be heralding one of the worst days of my life.

Assunta, who almost certainly guessed what I had been about all night, did not bring me my usual pot of coffee at eight o'clock, but left me alone till nearly noon, when she brought – not coffee, but a flask of wine. She poured some for me and firmly placed the glass in my reluctant hand.

'Drink, my darling,' she said. 'There isn't much in this world that a couple of glasses of good Frascati wine won't cure. My father always said that all the ills of this world could be dissolved in a cask of Frascati – and he should have known, with eleven children to feed and clothe on a soldier's pension on Burano.

'And that reminds me, Isolda,' she went on, as I sipped the rich wine, 'do you remember the day that we all – your father and mother, you and Julietta, me and all – went over to Burano for a picnic? And your father rolled up his trouser bottoms and went paddling for mussels among the rocks? And how Julietta was chased by a sheep, and we all laughed ourselves to tears when Pietro the gondolier did his imitation of the woman in the fish market belabouring her husband over the head with a mullet for making eyes at the serving girl? Oh, the good times we had together in the old days. . . .'

'Oh yes, we did,' I concurred. And I lay there, propped up on pillows, sipping my Frascati, and listened eagerly to her recounting tales of the past we had shared together in the golden days at the Palazzo Mazzini-Forsca. It may have been her well-meaning efforts to cheer me, it may have been the wine – or both, but it was not long before my unquiet spirit was calmed, and I became drowsy, presently slipping from drowsiness to sleep. When I woke up the shutters had been drawn and the evening light was seeping thinly through the chinks in their woodwork. I bathed and dressed, and was about to go and seek out Assunta, when I heard a small commotion coming from the canal.

Looking down I saw one of the commercial gondolas pulled in at the water gate of the palazzo. In it, a smartly dressed young woman was instructing the gondolier to unload her luggage on to the steps. This she did with supreme authority and assurance, afterwards paying the man his due, plus a tip, and receiving his fawning thanks with a sublime detachment.

I watched the charade right through with amusement and admiration, and it did not really occur to me, till the episode was closed, that the hugely self-assured young woman who had just arrived at our door was none other than my little sister!

'Julietta, you're so grown up – isn't she become the real young lady, Isolda?'

Assunta's reaction exactly matched my own. She could not believe that the coltish, rather gauche fifteen-year-old who had departed for Ireland two years before could have metamorphosed, like a butterfly from a chrysalis, into the poised and self-confident young person we saw before us.

I smiled. Assunta shook her head, bemused. 'How did she pick up such a high polish in so unworldly a place as a convent?' she inquired of no one in particular.

Julietta laughed. 'Dear Assunta,' she responded, 'convents may be this and nuns may be that, but I can assure you that our Reverend Mother has been far from unworldly in her time. Why, she was once the famous prima donna Marie Dieudonné, performing the principal classical roles at the

31

great opera houses of Europe. She also married a marquis who was killed in the Franco-Prussian war, and it was for that reason she took the veil. When I tell you that. . . .'

It's all right, I thought to myself, watching her. She knows nothing, but when I think that some garrulous gondolier, being ordered to take her to the Palazzo Mazzini-Forsca, might so easily have blurted out the appalling story connected with someone who lives here. It doesn't bear contemplating, the effect it would have had on her.

There's no doubt about it, she'll have to be told. And I shall have to tell her.

But how – *how?* . . .

There was no hope that we could traverse the lagoon, sail up the Brenta and be at the villa before dark. Accordingly Assunta dispatched a message for the barge to be at our water gate by ten in the morning, and we decided to have an early night, especially in view of the long journey that Julietta had made.

By mutual consent she and I shared my bed that night, as we had done so many times in the past – and as often as not talked till the dawn light. We did not fall far short of that long-established custom on this occasion.

'Tell me more about your life at the convent,' I asked her when we had extinguished the candle.

'Later,' she replied. 'It's you I want to hear about, Isolda. I'm worried for you, living in this gloomy barrack of a place, all alone with Assunta. And by the way, why are there no other servants? Don't tell me that we've come up against hard times. Surely all the money didn't run out after Father died.'

'No, no,' I responded hastily. 'It's just that – well – it seems an extravagance to keep the whole place open for two women, so I've shut down everything save my own suite and the housekeeper's quarters where Assunta now lives. And anyhow, it's almost impossible to get servants in Venice nowadays.' My last observation was almost the literal truth: there was not a servant in all the city who would set foot in the Palazzo Mazzini-Forsca – not to work for the woman with the Evil Eye!

32

'Well, Isolda,' she said, 'in that case I think you should close the place down completely – put it up for rent, or something – and move to a smaller house. Leave Venice. Find a place out in the country, on the mainland. There can only be sad memories for you here, when all your hopes for the future died with the man you were to marry. Oh Isolda, dear, how I worry for you sometimes. I really do.'

'Dearest Julietta. . . .' I embraced her, cheek to cheek, and felt her hot tears mingling with mine. 'I'm not the unfortunate creature you make me out to be,' I lied. 'And, do you know, I would take your advice and move out of Venice, were it not for the fact that the place also holds many fond and happy memories. It was not all death and darkness, you know.'

'Of *course* it wasn't,' she cried. 'Oh, we had such happy times together, all of us. Do you remember when the three of us – you, Bruno and I – went riding on the Brenta, and found the gipsy encampment where, for a few lire, they gave us a luncheon of the real gipsy cuisine, with a cabaret of singing and dancing?'

'I remember very well,' I replied.

'And the time when Bruno hired the steamboat and took us to. . . .'

I listened to her while she reminisced happily about times past. And in all her vignettes of those sunny days, one name constantly recurred, being in many cases the principal character and only begetter of these memorable episodes. She spoke that name, always, with a breathless admiration. . . .

'He was so gay, amusing and alive, wasn't he, Isolda? Oh, how you must miss him – oh, there I go again, and I so much didn't want to hurt you, dearest. Please forgive.'

'There's nothing to forgive,' I told her. 'His memory – the memory of those dear dead days – doesn't have the power to hurt, only to lighten the burden of loss. Believe me.

'But now, my dear, enough of me. Tell me all about life in Castlebar. Were things going well with you before the outbreak of fever cut short your summer term?'

'I think so,' she replied. 'My piano playing is greatly improved. In religious instruction, needlework, literature and geography, I'm top of my class – but still have tremendous difficulties with arithmetic since I haven't yet mastered my twelve-times table, would you believe? And at my age!'

We had a laugh about that. Then she became grave again.

'It really wasn't very amusing,' she said. 'The coming of the fever, I mean. One of the first cases was the wife of the convent's daily gardener. She died, and it brought the danger home to us, for it's terribly contagious.'

'Yes,' I said.

'And then, it spares no one,' she said. 'Even Prince Albert, the husband of Queen Victoria, he died of it in Windsor Castle. . . .'

She fell silent. My mind set up a soundless scream – Say it! my mind shrilled to her. Say it and get it over with, for God's sake!

As if in answer to my silent entreaty, she spoke the words that gave me release from the agony of anticipation: 'And then there was poor darling Bruno, of course,' she said quietly.

'Poor darling Bruno' – she still believed the lie. But for how much longer? Till I summoned up the courage to tell her? Or – would she learn the truth of it from other, uncaring lips?

Presently, her steady breathing revealed that the rigours of her long journey had at last taken their toll and she had fallen asleep.

There was no balm of sleep for me; I lay awake, staring up into the dark ceiling and seeing terrible visions there, till morning came at last.

Three

Well before ten o'clock in the morning a trim steam barge was moored at the bottom of the palazzo steps, a thin plume of smoke puffing out of its polished brass funnel. It had scrubbed white decks, a brave flag fluttering at the stern, and three barefoot sailors awaiting our pleasure.

Julietta had scarcely unpacked anything. Assunta and I had been ready to leave since the previous day. We were dressed in travelling costume, with headscarves over our bonnets and thick warm cloaks against a windy passage along the lagoon, and we boarded the barge as the last strokes of San Marco and Santa Maria della Salute died in the busy air of the Grand Canal.

We remained on deck whilst our craft chugged out of the canal, rounded the Dogana into the Guidecca, and set course for Fusina, which is at the mouth of the Brenta Canal.

Once we were clear of the island the lagoon was quite choppy, and the wind grew blustery for all that it was a bright, sunny day. We stayed for a while, watching the sea-gulls wheeling and screaming above our mast. It was then that ill fate nearly brought our whole enterprise to disaster.

One of the sailors – a young fellow with a watchful eye – strolled up to Assunta and, correctly surmising that she was of the servant class, opened a conversation. At the time Julietta and I were on the other side of the deck, but I for one was just within earshot of the other couple.

'You live in Venice, Signora?' asked the sailor of Assunta.

She nodded assent and eyed him watchfully, sensing no doubt that the fellow was a gossip.

'I'm from Padua myself,' said he, 'but work out of Chioggia. We mostly fetch and carry between there and Venice, but don't often get up the Brenta. . . .'

I missed the next part of his discourse because Julietta drew my attention to a beautiful full-rigged ship that was sailing in past the Lido. I caught only a fragment of what the sailor said next, but it was enough to make my heart miss a beat. . . .

'That palazzo,' he said, 'the Mazzini-Forsca, wasn't there some sort of scandal connected with the place a year or so back?'

'Don't know what you're talking about,' was Assunta's swift retort.

'Oh, come now, Signora,' persisted the other. 'Wasn't it the talk of Venice? There was a woman involved. Yes, I remember now. Wasn't she? . . .'

Julietta was still enthusing about the beautiful ship, clutching at my arm and saying how, when she returned to Ireland, she would much prefer to travel by sea, by way of the Adriatic, Mediterranean and the Bay of Biscay, rather than suffer the rigours and delays of ferries and railways followed by a coach journey across the appalling roads of Europe. I listened to her with only half an ear – for the rest, I strained to catch every word of the conversation going on behind me.

'Shame on you for listening to such wicked gossip!' Assunta was saying.

'But it was in the newspapers,' protested the sailor. 'I remember it well, now that I give my mind to it. This woman. . . .'

'I'll listen to no more!' snapped Assunta, but in a low voice. 'Shame on you, fellow,' she went on, 'enough of your idle gossip. Be off and get about your work!'

The sailor departed with many a backward glance. I met Assunta's eye and she mimed an expression of reprieve. To our mutual relief, it was quite clear that Julietta had completely missed the exchange.

'It's getting rather windy, ladies,' said our faithful retainer. 'Don't you think it would be a good idea to shelter in the

36

saloon till we reach the canal? It's nice and snug in there by the look of it.'

And secluded, she could have added – well away from gossiping seamen.

To me the Brenta will always be Venice's quiet back garden, where the age-old canal meanders gently past the lichened stonework of sleeping villas set among whispering cypresses and banks of flowered shrubs whose scent makes the mind grow heavy with languor, a place of ivy-grown statuary quietly gesticulating on overgrown lawns, of bijou domes and miniature, crumbling obelisks, plashing fountains and the humming of honey bees hanging over all.

Our family villa stood apart from the rest, its pillared portico set back from the canal and approached by a curved drive lined with giant rhododendron bushes that gave the casual passer-by no more than a hint of pantiled roofs and the gilded tip of a dome.

We arrived in the early afternoon. The sailors carried our traps to the villa and were paid off by Assunta, who gave her former interrogator a basilisk glance to stifle any last-minute question that might have been teetering on his lips.

We were alone! My relief was immediate and total. Here, hidden behind our ramparts of rhododendron, isolated from all the other villas along the waterfront by a common yearning for privacy – the Brenta villas being owned by Venetians, to escape a city which is as private as a beehive – I could take my time over deciding how I should impart my dreadful secret to Julietta, and then commence to break it to her by easy stages.

Yes, that was the way to do it, I told myself. Oh, how do we deceive ourselves when first we set out to deceive others!

Our first afternoon and evening was taken up by settling in. Julietta and I took adjoining bedchambers at the rear of the villa, their windows overlooking the charmingly unkempt garden with its tiny summerhouse copied after a Roman temple, and a small artificial lake crossed by a humpbacked bridge. We shared a dressing room and bathroom, tiled after the Roman fashion, with high ceilings for coolness, and sparely furnished with exquisite pieces after the eighteenth-century manner. We unpacked and changed into hostess gowns for supper, cooked by Assunta on an up-to-date range which my father had had put into the old kitchen. That night we ate delicious Adriatic prawns cooked in a spicy sauce and served on a bed of saffron rice, enriched with dry white Soave, the wine of Verona, and followed by peaches marinaded in cognac.

After all the fears and anxieties of the last sleepless days and nights, I retired to my room and slept the whole night through, and my dreams were all of the golden days when my love was new, and the only doubts that lay about us, my love and I, were not of our own making, but were imposed upon us from outside, by the stiff-necked stubbornness of our 'elders and betters'. . . .

After the interview with my father, who had indeed assumed that my silence meant that I agreed not to see Bruno again, I certainly kept to the letter, if not to the spirit, of his demand, making no attempt to see Bruno or to communicate with him – though he had earnestly begged me to do so and had promised to do the same.

More aware than I of the fervour of the feud between the two families and their supporters, Bruno had anticipated the difficulties we should encounter in our relationship and had taken steps to cope with it. The next I heard of my beau after the ball at the Casa Crispi was when one of our under-footmen – a youth named Poeta – slipped a note into my hand as I passed him on the stairs. He then went on his way without a word or a backward glance.

The short message set my heart pounding;

Toni's is a discreet coffee house in the Calle dei Fabbri near the Piazza S. Marco. I shall be there between 11 and midday every day this week. I pray that I do not wait in vain.
Yours ever,
B.

At coming on sixteen, I was allowed to walk out in the city unescorted during the daylight hours, a modern custom which was slightly frowned upon by the conservative older generation, of which my father was a typical example. However, on the principle of 'what the eye does not see the heart does not grieve over', I left the palazzo next morning at the stroke of eleven o'clock and took the short walk to the Calle dei Fabbri to meet my beau, with no more than a word to Assunta, informing her that I was going out for a stroll and a coffee – if anyone inquired.

I remember that it had rained the previous night and the streets were clean and sweet-smelling, the air slightly sharp after the languorous heat of the last few days. I walked with a light step. Truth to tell, I seemed to be treading the air, and my heart was singing like a skylark. A few short streets away, one small bridge, and I would be with *him*. The very thought made my knees turn to jelly and inspired me with a feeling that was very near to panic. It should be remembered that I was not quite sixteen, the product of a strict upbringing, and this was the first assignation that I had ever kept with a member of the opposite sex. Furthermore, the whole enterprise was rendered all the more outrageous by being forbidden. And did I feel the slightest guilt or remorse concerning my conduct that summer's morning? I search my conscience as I look back over the years, and can say quite unhesitatingly that I did not!

Toni's coffee house almost literally overhung one of the maze of small canals which run their meandering courses inside the sharp bend of the Grand Canal. One reached it by way of an arch, a small bridge, a shadowed doorway. As Bruno had indicated, it was discreet to a fault. The interior comprised a clutter of tiny rooms leading one from the other, like a Chinese puzzle. Each room was furnished with high-backed pews – like our family pew in San Marco – each with a plain scrubbed table and seating for as many as six. I was addressing myself to the task of peering over into each pew to find Bruno – when I was startled out of my skin to feel a hand gently insinuate itself into mine.

I turned to look into the pair of dark eyes that smouldered down at me.

'I hoped you might come,' he murmured.

'You knew I would come,' was the reply that came to me, unbidden.

39

He took me to a secluded table that occupied a tiny balcony set apart from the rest, where a crazily-wrought medieval window looked down into the canal. The window was open to delicious coolness, and a pair of linnets hung there in a wicker cage.

We sat facing. By unspoken consent, our hands remained joined across the table. We looked at each other for a very long time without speaking, and were only brought back to earth by a motherly body who arrived to ask our wants. Bruno ordered coffee and cakes – and we went back to holding hands.

'My father took me to task about dancing with you all night,' I said.

'I heard about it through the servants' grapevine,' he replied.

'The servants – they know everything!'

'Yes. What did your father say?'

'That it was out of the question for me to see you again.'

'What did you say, Isolda?'

'Nothing. I just let it wash over me. Like fine rain.'

'Shall you be in trouble for meeting me today?'

'Yes, if anyone tells. *I* shan't tell.'

'Nor shall I, Isolda.'

And so it was that, by mutual consent, we became secret lovers. Guiltless – save of flouting the code of our class and the brutal demands of political spite, the lusting for power and an overworked sense of public duty.

The hour we spent together in the secluded coffee house fled like sand between the open fingers – as time always does when one is enjoying oneself to utter perfection. We walked as far as the archway together, and there in the shadow of the ancient stonework he kissed me on both cheeks and then on the lips. We then parted company, promising to meet again soon.

I have no recollection of my walk back to the palazzo. All I know is that the streets were scattered with rose petals, that angels cheered at my passing, and that I was deafened by the sound of joyful trumpets blaring from on high.

The peace of the Brenta villa, the silence broken only by the

40

humming of the bees, laid a balm upon my unquiet mind, so that the days followed in slow succession, with no demands upon me but the rigours of deciding what to wear, approving Assunta's menus each morning, choosing which book to read, gossiping about old times with my two companions, letting time slip past. And scarcely a moment's thought given to the awful problem which I had overlaid with a coverlet of neglect.

Alas for neglect. . . .

About a week after our arrival at the villa, Julietta announced that she was going for a walk along the canal bank, and would I like to go with her? I had a slight headache, which I was nursing on a chaise-longue in a shady part of the garden, and pleaded to remain where I was. She left me – a slight, straight figure in a sprigged cotton frock, wide-brimmed straw, shaded under her parasol – and I had no fears for her departure. The villa owners adhered, by a long-established tradition, to a 'season' for repairing to the quiet of the Brenta which began on the eve of the feast of St Anthony, the 4th of June, and lasted till the end of July. This tradition was seldom broken, and I was quite assured that my sister stood scarcely any chance of encountering, let alone speaking to, anyone on her walk.

In this assumption I was gravely mistaken.

To begin with, she was late back for tea. This in itself did not give me any cause for alarm, for my young sister was known in the family to be notoriously unpunctual over meals. When it came to six o'clock, I did begin to feel restless and consulted with Assunta whether or not to go out and find her. We were still discussing this when Julietta reappeared. And as soon as I set eyes on her, I *knew* that she was quite different from the girl who had passed from out of my sight only a few hours before.

During a belated tea she was strangely silent and withdrawn into herself, answering only when spoken to, and then in monosyllables. Yet she was not moody, there was no hint of unhappiness in her manner – greatly to my relief, for naturally my first thought was that she had met someone who had given her a garbled account of my 'secret'. Instead, she seemed to be nursing a happy experience, guarding it to

41

herself as something too precious, too fragile to be trusted to the ears of outsiders. I bore with her throughout tea, reckoning that, with the kind of loving relationship we enjoyed together – and always had – she would confide her thoughts to me in her own good time. And so it was.

After Assunta had cleared away the tea things and taken them indoors, Julietta stretched herself out in the warm grass at my feet and, reaching up her arms towards the leafy branches of the plane tree under which we sheltered, she said in a radiant voice:

'Isolda, I'm so happy today. I think today's been one of the most perfect I can remember.'

'I'm so glad, dear,' I responded. 'And what has happened to make today so special for you?'

'Well,' she replied, 'firstly, I'm very happy here with you and Assunta. Here, in this little paradise of ours. . . .'

'Yes?' I said encouragingly, guessing that there must be much more. 'And? . . .'

'And I met a most amiable person this afternoon,' she said, and I knew we were coming to the heart of the matter. 'A gentleman. An Englishman. He was riding out, and he drew rein to ask me the way.'

'If lost, then your Englishman must have a very poor sense of direction,' I commented lightly, amused. 'The canal road only goes in two directions – Dolo lies one way, and Mira the other.'

She smiled with a touch of mischief. 'I think he was just trying to scrape an acquaintance,' she said.

'You surprise me,' I retorted, matching her smile. 'And what then?'

'I admired his mount,' she said, 'and complimented him on her condition. She was a black Arab, most beautifully built, with a head like a Greek carving. We fell to talking about horses generally and I told him about our family stable in Treviso, how we always used to go every year to the horse races in the Piazza del Campo in Siena, and how Uncle Roberto was famous for having won there in the sixties.'

I smiled at her fondly, having no inkling of what was to come.

'He's an officer in the British light cavalry,' she continued.

'A lancer. And he's touring Europe during his long furlough. He's already been to France, Prussia, Bavaria, Austria, Romania, Serbia, and now Italy' – she drew a deep breath, her smooth cheeks quite pink with excitement and effort – 'and his name's Rupert St John Forbes,' she concluded. 'Captain Rupert St John Forbes.'

'Why didn't you invite him to tea?' I asked. For what had I to fear from a gallant English officer newly arrived?

'I thought about it,' admitted Julitta, 'but to tell you the truth, Isolda, I didn't want him to think me too forward.'

'Of course not, dear,' was my indulgent reply.

'But he has access to a stable that's well stocked with good riding horses,' she said. 'And he's going to call on me tomorrow, bringing with him what he described as a very nice little dun mare who's a perfect ladies' mount. And we're going to ride together to Padua. Now, what do you think of that?'

'I shall greatly look forward to meeting Captain St John Forbes,' I replied.

'Yes,' she said. 'He was most punctilious about getting himself properly introduced to you, my older sister,' she said.

'Most correct of him,' I said. 'In view of which, he's to be pardoned his rather informal manner of making your acquaintance.' I was quite enjoying my role of indulgent duenna to my young sister. 'Tell me more about your gallant lancer. Has he perhaps rented a villa on the Brenta for the summer season?'

Her answer made my tight little, self-satisfied little world fall apart.

'No,' she replied casually. 'He's a guest of the Marchese and Marchesa di Rollo, at their villa just round the next bend. It's they who own the stables. Do we know them, Isolda?'

'Do we know them?'

Ye gods!

The progress of my love affair with Bruno Ferrara was marked by the infrequency of our meetings and by the ardour which was built up between us – or in my own case, at any rate – during the interminable hours when we were apart.

The coffee house remained our principal trysting place, but during that long memorable summer, we soon found means to meet in secret and alone. Bruno acquired a skiff – a slender rowing boat commodious enough to hold two persons in comfort. We would meet at some fairly unfrequented part of the waterfront – the far end of the Fondamente Nuove near the Church of Santa Maria del Pianto was a favoured spot for Bruno to be waiting for me with the skiff – and he would row us out to one of the islands of the lagoon where neither of us was known by sight.

On many a sun-warmed beach, alone and free, my lover and I shared unimaginable joys, learning to know each other throughout that summer of my sixteenth year, and kept our secret from everyone. My father frequently commented upon my much-improved disposition. No longer did I – in his words – 'moon around the place, bored and inconsolable', but was cheerful, outgoing, and always ready to lend a helping hand. A regular little ray of sunshine – I smile at the thought. If I know Assunta, I am pretty sure that she had some suspicion of the reason for the change in me – though, oddly, she has never admitted as much.

At the end of the summer Bruno was taken from me, and for the next two years I saw him only during his infrequent furloughs from the army cadet school in Bologna. Communication was difficult, but was contrived through the selfsame under-footman Poeta who had carried my lover's first note, acting as postman. Our brief meetings continued to be idyllic. Not the slightest suspicion of a cloud ever appeared on our horizon. Our only fear was that of discovery. We seldom spoke of the future, preferring to live for the here and now. I suppose in our hearts we vaguely hoped that circumstances might alter so that it would some day be possible to face the world, hand in hand, and declare our love. Perhaps when Bruno achieved his legal majority at the age of twenty-five and was no longer answerable to his guardian Giolitti, and when I was similarly placed in relationship to my father – only then, we told ourselves, could we stop living in the shadows.

All that altered when I was nineteen. As on the first, doleful interview with my father after the unforgettable ball at the Casa Crispi, it began with a summons to attend my parent in the library – an event so infrequent as to fill me with foreboding. What could possibly be the matter now? I ran a brush over my hair, checked my fingernails, adjusted my jabot, made myself spruce for the interview. Could it be – and I stared at my suddenly horrified reflection as the notion occurred to me – could it be that Father had learned of my forbidden meetings with Bruno? And was he going to send me away – far away from Venice, for years and years?

Slowly, and with leaden tread, I made my way to the library. On the way there I had assembled the rest of my life in my mind. How, parted from me for so long, Bruno had found himself another girl to love. How, languishing in some Swiss finishing school, or some French convent, I received his letter, telling me that all was over between us and that he and this girl were to be married in San Marco on such and such a date, and he was sure that it was for the best, and that in the generosity of my heart, I would wish him and his bride every happiness for the future. . . .

'Come in, Isolda.'

I entered. My father was seated in his usual chair by the fireplace, a leather-bound volume on his lap. He closed and put aside the book at my appearance, and stood up to receive me formally with his cheek proffered for my kiss. The formality over, I instantly perceived that my parent was distinctly ill at ease. That did nothing to lessen my forebodings.

'Isolda,' he began, 'I would like to talk to you about your future.'

I swallowed hard. 'Yes, Father?' I inflected the response like a question.

He cleared his throat. 'You are – ah – nineteen, are you not?'

'Yes, Father.'

'A very significant age for a young woman,' he said. 'An age when a young woman's thoughts turn very naturally towards her prospects of marriage, children, a home of her own. Indeed, for a girl of the lower classes – those classes which are not bound by family ties and family allegiances, by such concepts as family duty – for such a girl, this question is usually already settled by the time she reaches your age. Indeed, by your age, she is probably a wife, a mother and a housekeeper already.' He stared up at the ceiling, as if in contemplation of such an alien concept.

I watched him in silence, fearful of what could possibly be coming.

'However . . .' He regarded me with a fond smile and – or so it seemed to me – signs of nervousness. 'However, placed as you are, a member of the nobility, daughter of one of Venice's most illustrious houses, no such easy option is open to you, Isolda. Your destiny is dictated by the path of duty. Duty to your family, your family's interests, the upholding of the illustrious line of the Mazzini-Forscas. You are not too young to appreciate such high ideals, are you, Isolda?' He eyed me nervously.

'Nu-no, Father,' I faltered unhappily.

'Good, good.' He sat back in his chair and contemplated me for a full half-minute before he resumed.

'Isolda, you must realize that rank and privilege carry with them certain obligations. This particularly applies in the matter of choosing one's life partner. Take my own case. When it became necessary for dynastic reasons, for political reasons, to join the fortunes of the house of Mazzini-Forsca with those of the Saraccos, I had no hesitation in bowing to my father's wish and taking Angelina Saraccos to be my wedded wife. Nor will you deny, Isolda, that your dear mother, may she rest in peace, was a good wife to me and a loving mother to you girls. In our case, as in so many others, the strict path of duty proved, in the end, to yield a more solid happiness than do many marriages founded on the shifting sands of romantic caprice.

'Are you following the drift of my argument, Isolda?'

I was following him, well enough. So this was it. I was to be sacrificed on the altar of the Mazzini-Forscas. Condemned, like my father before me, and many others before him, to marry to order.

'I understand you perfectly, Father,' I replied. And went on: 'Who is it, pray, that I am obliged to marry?' Not, I added to myself, that I have the slightest intention of so doing.

He was all confusion, mistaking my tart answer for meek acquiescence. 'Oh, Isolda, Isolda,' he said, 'I should have known that you are a true Mazzini-Forsca. My darling girl, you will not regret your decision, I promise you. The gentleman whom I have in mind is a model of noble uprightness, a credit to his high estate and to his country. With our two families joined, our descendants may look forward to generations of felicity. . . .'

'What is his name, Father?' I asked. As well know his name as not.

But my father was not to be deflected from his lecture. 'Strange – is it not? – how the shifting currents of politics present the need for the prudent to seek new allegiances, fresh supporters? How true the saying that necessity makes strange bedfellows. A year ago – less – I would not have believed that I should be making this request of you, my dear Isolda. . . .'

'His *name*, Father!' I persisted.

'When I recall that his family, and that other to which they are so closely bound, were once my bitterest political opponents,' said Father, quite ignoring my demand. 'But there it is. Circumstances alter cases. In the changing climate of affairs, it has suddenly become perfectly plain to all concerned that, by opposing each other, we have been tearing each other apart.

'Er – what did you say, my dear?'

'I said, what is the gentleman's name, Father?'

'Why,' said he, 'I remember now that you and he have met. Wasn't it at some ball or other that the impudent young jackanapes had the temerity to put your reputation to hazard by dancing with you the whole night through?'

'Father – do you mean? . . .' I stared at him, a whole new world of sunlight and glory opening up before me in one blinding realization.

'Young Ferrara,' said my parent. 'Count Bruno, that is. You remember him?'

'Yes, I remember him, Father,' I replied. 'I remember him well.'

'Well, what do you think, hey?'

I turned my back on him, so that he should not see the wonder in my eyes.

'I – I shall have to give the matter some serious thought, Father,' I said.

'Yes, yes, of course, my dear. These matters must not be rushed into. I shall insist upon a long engagement. At least till you are twenty-one. There will be a formal betrothal, naturally, which is as binding as any marriage. I think the betrothal must take place in San Marco before the Cardinal Archbishop. . . .'

I scarcely heard a word he was saying. My whole existence was suffused with a radiance that would have eclipsed the very music of creation.

'Do we know the Marchese and Marchesa di Rollo, Isolda?'

Julietta repeated her artless question.

Did we *not* know them? Did *I*, of all people, not know that dreadful couple?

No, that was unfair. Dreadful by commonplace standards of decent, compassionate behaviour, they only followed the harsh and simple creed of their class with regard to other members of that class who transgressed that creed. And in their eyes I was such a one.

When the terrible blow fell upon me, the di Rollos were among the first to crucify me socially. Upon their lead, I was ostracized by Society as represented by the top twelve families of Venice and their adherents. And since the very beggars in the streets already reviled my name, that meant I was dead and buried in the eyes of all.

'However,' continued Julietta, breaking in upon my bitter thoughts, 'whether we know them or not, it's certain that Captain St John Forbes will present me to them when we return the horses after our ride to Padua tomorrow.'

'Of course,' I replied.

'I think I'm very lucky to have found so personable a beau after only a few days back in Venice, don't you, Isolda? I mean, having been away at school for so long, I am a complete stranger to most of my contemporaries. Oh, I suppose I shall soon be back on the invitation lists for balls and parties again – but Captain St John Forbes, well, he *is* rather special.'

You poor darling, I told her silently. Placed as you are – sister to she of the Evil Eye – there is never any hope of your going back on to the invitation lists again. You might as well shake the dust of Venice from your shoes for ever, and make your life elsewhere, as far away as possible, for, like me, you have joined the ranks of the living dead so far as Venice and the Venetians are concerned.

As for your gallant lancer – you will not see him tomorrow, or any other day. Assuming that you gave him your name, as he gave you his, the die is already cast against you. . . .

They will say, when the gallant captain mentioned that he has met you, 'Julietta Mazzini-Forsca? Not *the* Julietta Mazzini-Forsca, sister of *that woman*. They sent her to some remote convent when the scandal broke. Dear boy, you must put her from your mind, or you will never be able to lift your head in Venice again. And what if news of the acquaintance reached the ears of your colonel, together with the whole dreadful story? Why, it might well put your army career in jeopardy! Forget her, dear boy.'

'I'm so looking forward to tomorrow,' said my sister. 'What a lovely idea it was of yours, Isolda, to come to the villa.'

You poor darling, I thought. Tomorrow, when he doesn't arrive, you are going to suffer one of the first real disappointments of your life.

And that will only be the beginning. What will follow, in the weeks, the months, the years ahead will make your first, small disappointment pale into nothingness.

But that won't lessen the hurt – tomorrow.

Assunta had not witnessed our conversation, and for that I was most grateful, for I feared that she would take me to task and pressure me into making a full revelation to Julietta – a thing I could not bring myself to do there and then.

Julietta went to bed soon after supper that night, the better, no doubt, to face her new admirer on the morrow. Alone in the silent garden with my old nurse working on her embroidery under a lamplit tree, I let my mind dwell upon the problem before me.

How close my darling sister had come, today, to discovering my dreadful secret, and in the cruellest possible manner. What if that young man had taken her back to see the horses and she had met the di Rollos face to face? When I thought of the pleasure that woman – that stiff-necked marchesa – would have had in cruelly snubbing the poor child. Or even blurting out the whole story in front of her. . . .

The young man would not be coming, and it was a blessing in disguise. At the cost of bruised heart – easily healed – Julietta would be spared the horror of learning my secret from hostile lips.

Let tomorrow pass, I told myself. Await the right opportunity to tell her what she has to know, sooner or later. But let it happen here, in this peaceful garden, in the company of people she loves and who love her.

Yes, that was the best course.

'I think I shall go to bed, Assunta,' I said. 'Tomorrow will be rather trying – I imagine.'

If my old retainer felt any surprise at my remark she did not show it. We embraced and wished each other good night as usual.

Strangely, I did not have nightmares, as might have been expected. Instead, I relived the joyous vision of the day that Bruno and I were solemnly betrothed in the golden gloom of the great cathedral, in the presence of the Cardinal Archbishop of Venice; gravely repeating our vows that were as binding as Holy Matrimony. . . .

'I, *Isolda Maria Violetta Mazzini-Forsca, do hereby solemnly plight my troth and promise marriage to you, Bruno Hubertus Ferrara. This I swear by. . . .*'

The promises made, kisses and betrothal rings were exchanged, the marriage contract was approved and provisionally initialled, and the bond was secured. Only the passing of time, or the intervention of death, could now stand between the fulfilment of the contract we had made. Some time after my twenty-first birthday, I should marry Bruno and become the Countess Ferrara.

No need, any longer, for clandestine meetings in coffee houses and secluded beaches of the lagoon. The solemn and binding betrothal permitted a wide degree of freedom concerning the circumstances in which one's courting was carried out. There were still the proprieties to be observed but one could, for instance, dispose of a chaperon between the hours of dawn and dusk; however, holding hands in public was frowned upon, kissing in public was quite out of the question, and to stay in the same residence overnight it was necessary to be in the company of a married couple.

These strictures aside, one was free – free to declare one's love and to flaunt it openly; to kiss and hold hands in private, extending to one another all the sweet tendernesses that lovers have lavished upon each other since time began – but without any guilt.

So it was that, in my dreams that night, on the eve of my beloved sister's first real disillusionment, I relived the brightest, sweetest days of my life that I had known.

A bitter irony.

Julietta was up early and out walking – so Assunta informed me – before we others had awakened. She arrived back for breakfast, which we took beneath the plane tree in the garden as usual.

She was so alive, so gay and scintillating, that I could feel my nerve beginning to falter at the prospect of the bitter disappointment that awaited her.

'The canal banks are so beautiful in the early morning,' she said. 'I can't imagine how one could possibly lie abed and leave all that beauty going to waste. There were kingfishers and house martins swooping low over the water, Isolda, and a heron rose up when I passed by.

'Isolda,' she went on, toying with a buttered oatcake, 'do you know? One day when we were out walking in crocodile near the convent in Castlebar, we came upon a wrinkled old lady – a tinker – who offered to read our palms. Sister Joseph, of course – for she's very straight-laced – wouldn't hear of such a thing, but I took the opportunity to slip back

51

when she wasn't looking and showed my hand to the old lady. And she read my fortune.'

'Did she now?' I said, amused despite myself.

'Yes, and do you know – can you guess – what she saw for me?'

'Tell me.'

'She said that I should be married before I was twenty-one. Now, what do you think of that, Isolda?'

'Isn't that a little early?' I ventured.

'Well, yes,' she conceded. 'And it means that, if I am to have a fairly long engagement, I shall have to meet my future husband quite soon now, don't you see? And isn't that an exciting prospect?'

'Very,' I agreed.

A pause, and then . . .

'Isolda, I suppose soldiering's a very dangerous occupation,' she mused.

'Yes,' I replied, guessing which way her thoughts were moving and fervently wishing that I had the ready wit and agility of mind to deflect them along other paths. 'In times of war, at least,' I added.

There followed another pause.

'Are the British often at war?' she asked.

'Well, yes, they seem to be,' I replied. 'Rather like the Romans of old, they have a very large empire, and their subject peoples sometimes grow troublesome and revolt against their rule.'

'Oh yes, I've done that in history,' she responded. 'Africa, India, Canada, Australia – all over the world. And I suppose the officers' wives are allowed to travel with their husbands?'

'I – I suppose they might,' I faltered. By this time I was being led helplessly along a path that I did not want to tread under any circumstances. But how to prevent her wild, enthusiastic imaginings, her building of castles in the air?

'I love travel,' she said dreamily. 'The lure of far-off places is very strong with me.

'I think I should make a good soldier's wife, don't you, Isolda?'

I could not but agree – for she undoubtedly would.

Captain St John Forbes was due to arrive with the horses at ten o'clock. Long before then, I was convinced that my sister had comfortably married him in her imagination.

By ten minutes past ten she was becoming restless. At the half-hour, she grumbled a little about her admirer's lateness and went out to the end of the drive to – as she no doubt hoped – espy him from afar.

Alas for her vain hopes.

By eleven – such is the optimism of the young and unspoiled heart – she had decided that he must have had a slight accident with the horses: one of them had cast a shoe, or lamed itself on the rough road. At a quarter to midday, she had fallen silent. When noon came, she left me without a word and went up to her room.

Assunta came out to me soon afterwards.

'What's happened to Julietta?' she asked, much concerned. 'The poor little thing was in tears when she ran past me upstairs.'

Sadly, I told her the whole story. About the handsome young officer, the di Rollos, the admirer's non-appearance, everything. She also was in tears by the time I had finished.

'You simply have to tell her, Isolda,' she said. 'Soon. Tomorrow. Before it's too late and she hears about it from the likes of the di Rollos.'

'I know, I know,' was my reply. 'Don't you think I've been saying this to myself ever since I heard about the young man and his connection with the di Rollos? But after what has happened today, I can't possibly add to her hurt any more. Now I have to let a little more time go by, time for her to recover from this small hurt before she's brought face to face with the greater hurt that might destroy her utterly in her present state.'

The old retainer's work-worn hands reached out and took mine.

'You're right, Isolda,' she said. 'Leave it till she's forgotten this young man. Time enough, then, to break the news to her. You'll do it then, I know. You've shrunk away from it for long enough, and I don't blame you, my darling girl. But now at last you see clearly what must be done. I shall pray for you tonight, my Isolda, that you will find the strength to go through with it when the time comes.'

'Thank you, Assunta,' I replied. 'But better pray that Julietta will find it in her heart to have pity on me when the time comes, and not cast me out into darkness like all the rest. All the rest that is, save you, dearest, dearest Assunta.'

We embraced. And neither our respective ages, nor the disparity of what is stupidly called 'class', stood between us. We were simply two women bound together by a common hurt, a shared outrage.

Four

Of course, Captain Rupert St John Forbes never came, neither that day nor any other day. Nor did the gallant young gentleman even send a message with the most transparent of excuses; no doubt the di Rollos persuaded him – supposing he needed to be persuaded – that even such slight civility was not required in the case of a sister to That Woman.

Julietta kept to her room the day after her great disappointment and kept herself to herself for more than a week after that. But her naturally buoyant nature presently reasserted itself.

One evening, she confided in me – and not for the first time.

'Captain St John Forbes was a great disappointment,' she declared.

'I can understand that, dear,' I rejoined.

'He was so handsome – so gallant.'

'It was a great pity,' I said, 'but you've got over it. Men – handsome and gallant men in particular – are not always to be relied upon.'

Then she said a very strange thing that made me pause in the act of threading my embroidery needle to cast her a swift glance.

'He wasn't fit to fasten Bruno's shoes,' she declared.

'Bruno?' I said. 'Do you mean – *my* Bruno?'

'Of course, who else?' she replied, surprised. 'You agree, don't you, that Bruno was quite the most marvellous person ever?'

'Well, yes,' I replied. 'He was my fiancé. We were to

be married. It goes without question that I thought him marvellous.'

I almost added: 'But my feelings for him could scarcely be compared with yours, surely' – but I decided against it.

'There was no one like him,' she said in a dreamy tone of voice. 'He was a man with whom every other man I shall ever meet will have to bear comparison – and to the newcomer's disadvantage.

'I expect it's the same with you, Isolda,' she added.

'There have not been any newcomers in my life, Julietta,' I replied in a very small voice.

'Of course not,' she said. 'How could there be, after Bruno?' She laughed, and with more than a touch of bitterness. 'With no one else to bear comparison with him, I expect we shall both end up as old maids, Isolda. So much for my being married before I'm twenty-one.'

She rose from her chair and went out of the room without another word or backward glance.

Curiously disturbed and uneasy after the encounter, I went over to the window of the sitting room and looked out. Beyond the stately columns of the portico I could see the swifts and house martins flying high above the concealing rhododendrons and stooping down out of sight towards the still waters of the canal. Julietta's slight figure was flitting in the evening light along the shadowy path, and was soon gone.

I gave a sigh. One had always supposed that the young Julietta had idolized Bruno, for had he not been everything that a child looks for in a favourite brother? That she had also loved him after her girlish fashion was really no surprise.

Nor, considering the ordeal I was condemned to go through when I told Julietta my secret, was it any consolation, either.

What she had revealed to me could only make the ordeal a thousand times worse!

My birthday fell a few days later. As a family we had always made a small ritual of present-giving, and this day was no exception. Not entirely to my surprise, the piece of embroidery that Assunta had been working on since we came

56

to the Brenta had been intended for me. She pressed it into my hands at breakfast time and kissed me on both cheeks.

'A happy birthday, my darling girl,' she said. 'And may you find the happiness you deserve in your coming year.' With that she broke into a flood of tears and fled indoors.

Julietta rummaged in her reticule and produced a paper-wrapped cube which she laid on the table by my plate.

'Happy birthday, dear,' she said. 'I bought this little thing from a gipsy girl I met on the canal bank the other day.'

I thanked her and unwrapped the small object, which proved to be a quite pretty fancy box stuck all over with tiny sea shells – a thoughtful and useful present, and I told her so.

'It's nothing,' she said. 'But it will serve to keep pins and needles in, and as a memento of our lovely days on the Brenta.'

Touched by her kind thought, I found myself on the point of tears, and to cover my confusion I made a small play of smoothing out the piece of paper in which the gipsy had wrapped my sister's purchase. I vaguely registered that it was, in fact, a sheet of newspaper, yellowed with age, but perfectly clean.

There was printing upon it, dominated by huge declarations that screamed up at me.

I must have cried out, for Julietta overturned her chair in her haste to see what had so disturbed me.

There was no hiding it from her.

My terrible secret was there – written plain. . . .

THE TIMES OF VENICE – Thursday, 14 February 1878

MURDER AND SACRILEGE!
****
VENETIAN NOBLEMAN'S DAUGHTER ACCUSED OF MOST FOUL KILLING OF HER BETROTHED!

Officers of the Venetian Judicial Police yesterday made the dramatic arrest of SIGNORINA ISOLDA MAZZINI-FORSCA, aged 22, after the interment of her betrothed, the murdered

COUNT BRUNO FERRARA, aged 24, whose body was found lying on the despoiled altar of the family chapel at the Palazzo Mazzini-Forsca last week.

TAKEN FOR QUESTIONING

Signorina Mazzini-Forsca was apprehended at the close of the interment on S. Michele and taken to the office of the Judicial Police, where she remained for some time. It is understood that, following her questioning, the young woman signed a written confession of her guilt and was formally arrested and charged. The murder trial is expected to take place...

So they took me away with them, that rain-soaked day of Bruno's funeral at San Michele. They took me in the police barge, and the mourners in the funeral gondolas watched me go, blank faces and cold eyes staring at me from behind thick black veils, from under tall hats. Only Assunta gave any sign of sympathy. She raised her hand to sketch a gesture that might have denoted encouragement, or even farewell – but it earned her such outraged glances from her companions that the impulse died in the making.

My captors never addressed a word to me till I was taken ashore at the Molo and escorted, through a watching crowd that had mysteriously gathered, to the Office of the Judicial Police which lies behind the ducal palace. There I was ushered into a small, bare room and bidden to wait till I could be interviewed.

My state of mind may well be imagined, being compounded of fear, affront, mystification and despair. I think that if one single member of the funeral party had stepped forward and demanded to know the reason for my arrest, I might have assembled a spark of fortitude. As it was, I felt – save for Assunta's well-meant but futile little gesture – so utterly abandoned and alone that I was weaponless against any assault that might have been made against me.

'Come this way, Signorina.' The summons was delivered by a uniformed functionary, who stood aside and let me pass through the door. He guided me by the arm through interminable corridors and up flights of narrow stairs, to a door at the top of the building, upon which he knocked. Receiving an answer, he opened up and gestured me inside.

'Take a seat, Signorina.' The instruction – order – was delivered by a man seated behind a roll-top desk in the centre of a small room that was – or so it seemed to me – otherwise entirely furnished by rows upon rows of shelves, stretching from floor to ceiling, and all crammed with musty-looking books and folders bulging with yellowed papers. The man at the desk did not look up from writing in a slow and deliberate hand with a scratchy pen. He was of late middle years, thick-set, bloated of face and figure, nearly bald, grossly untidy, and dressed in a seedy frock coat with armlets of black crepe. His neckcloth was crumpled and none too clean.

I sat down. In the silence broken only by the slow progress of his pen, I took the opportunity to glance about me. The only other item of solid furnishing in the room was a small table set against the wall to my right. There was nothing upon it save – to my instant alarm – a pair of handcuffs! The sight of this sinister article brought me very forcibly to the gravity of my situation. I – formerly the highly respected daughter of a prince of the nobility – had been brought under duress to an establishment where no one had had the thought to make a decent concealment of an instrument for restraining troublesome criminals. Or was this a hint of the sort of treatment I could expect if I became – *unmanageable?*

Time passed. The man came to the end of his page and read it through with tantalizing slowness. This done, he scratched what looked like a signature at the foot, scattered sand from a shaker on to wet ink, blew it off, placed the piece of paper precisely squared off to a corner of his desk, and looked up at me.

His eyes were like those of a vicious dog. I have seen captive wolves with just such eyes: red-rimmed, close set, angry, given to avoiding a steady gaze – as if to conceal the thoughts that lie behind them. He opened his mouth to speak, disclosing yellowed teeth.

'You are Isolda Maria Violetta Mazzini-Forsca?'

'Yes, I am, and . . .' I began.

'Confine yourself to answering the questions!' he snapped, and made a note upon a clean sheet of paper. 'Parents living?'

I felt my hackles rise. Everyone in Venice – and surely he, a functionary of the Judicial Police – knew full well that I was now an orphan. But I answered him straight. 'Both deceased. My father passed away last year.'

He next demanded my age, place of residence, next of kin, whether I was suffering from any infectious disease or other illness. At the end of it he sat back in his chair and fixed his shifty gaze upon a spot somewhere above my left shoulder.

'Why did you kill Count Bruno Ferrara?' he demanded.

I struggled for words and came out with some such phrase as: 'Why should you think that I? . . .'

'Answer directly!' he interposed. 'Why did you murder your affianced?'

I shook my head – violently – so that my hair fell down and the loose ends lashed my cheeks.

'I did not murder my fiancé!' I cried.

He made no reply to this. Instead, he scribbled a few lines on the paper. Presently he returned to the attack, and I was thrown off balance by the unexpectedness of the question.

'You are – or were – acquainted with a certain Carlotta Salvatorelli?'

'Yes,' I replied.

'She was a friend of yours?'

I shrugged. 'We were of the same age, moved in the same social circles. I wouldn't put it as high as friendship. More – as you said – an acquaintance.'

'And Bruno Ferrara, he was also an – acquaintance – of this young woman?'

'He knew her – yes.'

'And admired her greatly.' The angry dog's eyes met my gaze briefly, then sped away.

'I – I wouldn't say that,' I replied.

'Admired her so much that on at least one occasion, after your betrothal, you felt it necessary to take Bruno Ferrara to task for paying open court to this young woman.'

'That's not true!' I blazed in outrage.

'There are witnesses who testify that you publicly admonished Ferrara for flirting with Salvatorelli on the dance floor, and then slapped his face.'

I nearly laughed aloud. 'But that's ridiculous!' I cried. 'I teased him for responding to Carlotta's rather heavy coquetry, while knowing all the time that it was all a joke. And then I gave him a light, admonishing tap on the cheek – also in jest.'

'After which, you called for your gondola and went home – alone,' said my interrogator flatly.

I drew breath sharply. 'I can explain . . .' I began.

'You will have plenty of opportunity for that, Signorina,' was his response. 'Let us now pass to the occasion when you received the news of Carlotta Salvatorelli's tragic death. You recall this occasion?'

'Yes,' I responded soberly. 'My fiancé was with me at the time. We were at Florian's. A newspaper seller came in with an extra edition. Bruno – my fiancé – bought a paper and we read that Carlotta had been found drowned in the Grand Canal.'

'And what was Ferrara's comment upon reading this news?'

'I – don't remember.'

'I think you remember very well, Signorina. His comment – and there are witnesses to testify to it – was, "The poor darling must have drowned herself out of love for me." Correct?'

I drew a deep breath. 'Well, yes,' I said, assembling every ounce of patience at my disposal. 'He may have made some such comment. But, if you had known Bruno, you would appreciate that, with his rather sardonic sense of humour, it's just the sort of idiotic thing he *would* say. But it meant – nothing!'

'Just another light-hearted jest,' was the other's sneering response.

I made no reply.

He scratched another couple of lines on the sheet of paper and sat back again.

Presently he said: 'Let us move on to an occurrence that took place only a few days before Bruno Ferrara's murder. You had been to Verona on some business connected with

61

the apportionment of your father's estate between you and your sister. You had announced to your fiancé that the business with the lawyers might take two days. In the event, you returned unexpectedly after spending only the single day in Verona. Correct?'

'Yes.'

'Upon your arrival back in Venice that evening, you sought out Ferrara at his residence. Correct?'

'Yes.'

'And where was Ferrara living at the time?'

'In a bachelor apartment near the Campo Morosini, close by the Ponte dell' Accademia.'

'Not with the Giolitti family?'

'He had moved from the Casa Giolitti shortly after our engagement,' I replied.

'In order that he could more discreetly rendezvous with yourself. . . .'

I did not deign to answer.

'And – *others?*'

'That is an outrageous insinuation!' I cried, half rising to my feet upon a compulsion to fling out of the room and slam the door behind me.

'Do not raise your voice to me, Signorina!' he said quietly and with a reptilian menace. 'And sit down!'

I obeyed him, and found that I was trembling from head to foot.

He took from a folder a sheaf of notes and consulted them. 'I have here a deposition from the caretaker of the apartment house where Ferrara resided up to the time of his murder,' he said. 'In which she states that, on the eve upon which you returned from Verona, she heard you and the dead man in violent argument, during which you cried out – among other things – "If I find that woman here again, I'll kill you!" '

'That's not true!' I cried. 'I said nothing of the kind. What I said was . . .'

'You will have ample opportunity to give your version of what happened and what you claim to have said, Signorina,' interposed my tormentor. 'For the present, you will listen to the facts as they have been presented, and you will hear my interpretation of those facts.'

Numb with horror, hideously aware that I was caught up in a web of lies and grotesque distortion, I could only sit and stare.

'I am suggesting to you,' he said, 'that upon your arrival at Ferrara's apartment that evening, you surprised your affianced in the act of entertaining a woman who was known to you, and that after this woman had made a hasty departure, you and Ferrara had a violent quarrel, during which you threatened his life. . . .

'No – do not interrupt me!

'I suggest that Ferrara laughed in your face – I have the deposition of the caretaker that she heard this – and that you then left the apartment, slamming the door behind you.' My tormentor then rose to his feet and stalked, soft-footed, towards where I was sitting, and his eyes remained fixed upon a point above my head. 'I suggest that you returned home, nursing the jealous hatred that Ferrara's conduct had inspired in you. I suggest that you lived with this for two more days and nights – at the end of which, you sought out the man whom you were pledged to marry, and having lured him to the solitude of your family chapel on some pretext or other – *you stabbed him to the heart with this knife!*' So saying, he produced from behind his back a knife with a narrow, tapering blade of blued steel that was ominously discoloured with rusty-looking stains.

I screamed in his face and shrank away, overcome with a paroxysm of trembling that I could not have checked to save my soul.

He fixed me for a moment with the wolfish eyes that now blazed with an unholy triumph. A moment's pause, and then he turned and strode swiftly to the door. Opening it wide, he turned to regard me.

'Wait here!' he said flatly.

And then he was gone.

I have no recollection of how long I remained alone in that accursed room. The overcast sky turned from daylight to

63

dusk, and from dusk to night. And still I sat there, nursing my terrors in darkness.

After an eternity of bleak solitude I heard footsteps approaching up the staircase. A loom of light appeared under the door and presently it opened to disclose the stooping figure of a man with a pale face and a mane of silvery hair that fell over the collar of his coat. He limped heavily on a walking-stick. The rosy candlelight picked out the lineaments of his face and revealed a mild and pleasing expression. When he addressed me it was in a voice that matched his looks:

'How could they have left you sitting here all alone in the dark?'

I watched him, fascinated, as he crossed the room and took the seat that had been vacated by the other man.

'Would you care for some refreshment?' he asked.

I shook my head.

'A cup of coffee – some cognac?'

'No thank you,' I replied. 'Please? . . .'

'Yes?'

'Have I been arrested?' I asked him.

'Strictly speaking, Signorina, you have not,' he replied.

'Then can I go home?' I begged him.

He slowly shook his head. 'Unfortunately, you can not,' he said. 'Not until we have a few matters settled between us, at any rate.' He smiled, and it was a blessed relief to have someone seated at that desk who actually looked straight at me. Unwaveringly.

He said, 'My colleague has been explaining things to you, I believe?'

'He has accused me of murdering my fiancé!' I cried. 'This he did after spinning a tissue of lies, in order to prove – or so it seemed – that Bruno Ferrara was a philanderer, or worse!'

The man stroked his chin and nodded understandingly and, I thought, with a certain sympathy.

'My colleague arrived at a hasty conclusion,' he said. 'Supposing, Signorina, we again go through the points that he raised.' And he glanced down at the papers which still littered the desk top. 'Beginning with the quarrel – shall we

64

call it the small tiff? – that you and your fiancé had over Carlotta Salvatorelli. Now, as a contemporary of Signorina Salvatorelli, you knew her quite well, did you not? Even though she was no more than – I think you described her as an acquaintance – you must nevertheless have formed an opinion of the young lady's character. Yes?' He gazed at me encouragingly, head on one side.

I felt emboldened to be frank with him. 'Not to speak ill of the dead,' I said, 'but poor Carlotta was a shameless flirt!'

He nodded. 'Ah, and is that so? Tell me, then – was this generally known, and discussed, amongst your other acquaintances and friends?'

'Everyone knew,' I replied. 'And Carlotta herself made no secret of the fact that men – flirtations – coquetry – were all her life.'

'I see. Then it was in this spirit of coquetry – flirtatiousness – that she set her cap at your fiancé – if I may use the phrase?'

'Yes,' I admitted. 'She did just that.'

'In front of you. Quite shamelessly.'

'Yes. While they were dancing together.'

'And in plain view of your friends and acquaintances.'

'Yes.'

'Like you, these others knew of her reputation. They saw her flirting with your fiancé. And they saw him respond in a positive manner – A moment, please, let me continue, Signorina! – but, as you said, only in jest.'

'Yes,' I replied. 'Only in jest.'

'Nevertheless,' he said, 'people being what they are – and, believe me, I sympathize with the way you must have felt at the time – some of those present and looking on may have misinterpreted Count Ferrara's response to Signorina Salvatorelli's advances. Yes?'

I nodded. With such a reasonable person as this man, there was no point in being other than candid and straightforward. 'Some people see the worst in everything. One person at least – Zöe Bonomi – made a most improper remark, just to hurt me.'

'And you were hurt.'

'Yes, I was.'

65

'And angry.'

'Yes – angry.'

'Not only with Carlotta and with this Zöe Bonomi – but also with your fiancé, whose jesting behaviour led to you being subjected to ridicule and embarrassment.'

'To be honest, I was furious with him.'

'And you quarrelled – and you smacked his face. Quite hard?'

I nodded. 'Well, yes. Hard enough.'

'And then,' said my interrogator, 'you called for your gondola and went home – still angry.'

'Frankly – yes,' I admitted. 'But, you see. . . .'

He spread his hands and smiled at me. And that smile was just a little too honey-sweet, the eyes a shade over-friendly.

'I see it quite plainly,' he said. 'How *well* we have progressed in so short a time! The truth is beginning to emerge, is it not, Signorina?'

I caught my breath, and it seemed to me that a trap had opened up beneath my feet, and I – all unaware – had fallen into it.

That awful moment of revelation, when Julietta saw the horror in the old newspaper, has long been a far-off memory, but one that will burn away in a corner of my mind, a fiery brand, for so long as I live.

I seldom speak of it now, but it is sometimes a curious relief to take it out and tell someone. I think that if I did not do this occasionally – and it will be no more than three or four times in my life, no more – the memory would burn into my soul and destroy me.

Julietta's first reaction was of disbelief, as if someone – I, for instance – had composed the thing as some sort of cruel practical joke to alarm her.

'What – what does it mean, Isolda?' she faltered.

'My dear, I can explain. . . .' I began, and reached out a hand to make physical contact – just that.

She shook me off, her eyes suddenly wide and wild, her nether lip trembling uncontrollably.

'No, leave me be!' she cried. 'It's not all a dream, it's true, isn't it? I can see it in your face, your eyes. It's all written there, just like in the newspaper.

'Here' – she snatched at the scrap of paper that had destroyed me – 'let me read it again – right through!'

I watched, as she read, wide-eyed and pale of countenance, her lips moving slightly to the words, a curiously endearing habit that she had kept since childhood.

Suddenly she looked up – and her eyes were like those of my interrogator – the first interrogator.

'They say that you signed a written confession to murdering Bruno,' she hissed. 'Is that correct?'

'Yes, Julietta,' I replied. 'But. . . .'

She had no time for 'buts', she returned to her reading. When she had finished she carefully folded up the paper and put it in her reticule. That done, she rounded on me.

'You admitted to killing him,' she said slowly. 'You told all in every detail. True?'

I nodded. No more 'buts'. . . .

'You admitted in the confession that you did that awful thing of your own free will, knowing what you were doing. And no one to help you. Just you, yourself. . . .'

I bowed my head and said nothing.

'You said it was because of Bruno's infidelities. His – I think the word was "flouting" – flouting of his betrothal vows.

'You said that this confession was given of your own free will and without – what was the word? . . .'

'*Coercion*,' I breathed. 'Without coercion – that means without being forced.'

'Thank you, my sister,' she sneered.

There was silence between us for a few moments – and then the denunciation began – the wild, cutting, searing condemnation that admitted of no protest, asked no questions and delivered verdict, sentence and execution in one single act of crucifixion. . . .

'*Why are you still alive and free?*' she blazed.

I did not reply.

'Why are you still standing here, after what you did?' she continued implacably. 'You, who deserve to die twice over – more, a score of times – for killing such a person as Bruno.

'To think of it – that you could have destroyed such a life!

'I – I loved him, you know that, don't you?' her voice grew quiet. Tender, even. 'I told you the other day that I loved him and that no other man will ever match up to him – not ever!

'You killed him out of jealousy. In sheer jealous spite, you ended that beautiful life the way wicked children squash flies!'

She flung away from me, then. Crossed over to the other end of the garden, from where she eyed me with distant loathing, as if she could not bear to be near to me, as if I had become a leper to her.

'And why did you commit a mortal sin by defiling the altar?' she cried. 'Tell me that!'

I did not answer.

She watched me from afar for a few more moments, then, turning on her heel she walked quickly back into the villa. A door slammed behind her. I thought I heard her footsteps mounting the stairs to her room. And then – silence.

Silence, save for a slight whimpering sound that grew in its intensity till it became the heart-felt sobbing of a child.

It was I. . . .

'Where is she, Assunta – where is Julietta?'

'She packed her things and left, Isolda,' replied my dear old nurse, whose eyes were swollen from the bitter tears she had been shedding. 'Wouldn't let me fetch her a carriage, but set out to walk all the way to Dolo. She'll be half way to Venice by now. Heaven knows what she'll do then. She wouldn't say – not that she was in any state to make decisions, poor child.'

I closed my eyes. 'Oh, dear God,' I murmured.

'Tell me what happened, dearest,' said Assunta. 'Let me share your hurt. What happened after she saw that piece of old newspaper you told me about?'

'At first, she didn't believe it,' I said. 'Then she saw the guilt written all over me. And she probed into my shame.'

'And then,' prompted the old woman, 'she started asking questions, yes?'

'Oddly, no,' I responded. 'At least, she waited for no

68

explanations. She read the newspaper article through. And when she came to the piece about my confession. . . .' I choked on the word, and Assunta's toil-worn hand was laid on my shoulder in support. 'When she had read my confession, she then – *destroyed me with words!*'

The grip on my shoulder tightened. 'But, my darling girl,' breathed Assunta, 'didn't you tell her what *really* happened?'

'She didn't ask me,' I replied. 'No, that's not quite true. She did want to know why I had committed mortal sin by defiling the chapel altar – but, of course, I had no explanation for her. It was then she turned and left me. And that was what hurt most of all, Assunta. My own sister condemned me unheard. She didn't even ask: "You *did* kill Bruno, didn't you?"

'I wasn't even given the chance to lie – as she might have thought.'

'Then you should have spoken out!' she cried.

I rounded on her – as near to being angry as made no difference. 'Don't you understand?' I shouted. 'I was too hurt. Too stricken. Too damned proud, if you like, to tell her the truth of it!

'I stood condemned in Julietta's eyes as I do in the eyes of all Venice.

'Well, then – let it be so. *Let it be so!*'

It was then that the events of that day – beginning with the fatal scrap of newspaper, Julietta's headlong flight to her room, followed by my own, and ending with the news of her departure and Assunta's well-meant probings – seemed to take the form of a pointed stake which, driven home by the blows of cruel Fate, was plunged into my very soul, and I collapsed as a person and became a mindless, heedless mass of nothing.

From far off I heard Assunta's voice – soothing, consoling, and frightened by turns – as she somehow helped me to my feet and guided me up to my room, where I collapsed on my bed and sought oblivion.

PART TWO

A Time of Trial

Five

It was a long time before I became fully aware of how long the brain fever had laid me low, and out of delicacy Assunta was always very vague about it.

By the time I was able to sit up in bed and feed myself, I had shed a lot of weight, my cheeks had lost their former roundness and displayed the bone structure that now characterizes my appearance. Outside my window, furthermore, the rhododendron walk had dropped its glorious blooms and the flowers of late summer were in full abundance.

It was some time before Assunta could bring herself to tell me that the summer flowers were those of the following year. I had been in a dark night of the soul for more than a year!

Presently I was well enough to get up and sit in the garden, where I passed the time in reading, sewing, and quiet contemplation. Michou the kitten, now a full-grown cat of a gentle and philosophical nature, shared my days. Assunta was always on call, but prudently left me be as much as possible, in order that I might find myself again – as indeed I eventually did.

The first thing I wanted to know as soon as I was able to take stock of the world around me was – what had happened to Julietta?

My old nurse did not tell me the whole story at once, but gradually let things drop here and there, so as not to shock me unduly. In short terms, my sister appeared to have completely disappeared. Assunta had learned from the servants' grapevine of Venice that she had let herself into the palazzo, presumably to pick up a few of her treasured

73

belongings, I suppose, and was seen to leave by train – the Paris train – the following day.

She had not returned to the convent, for Assunta wrote immediately to the Reverend Mother to ask.

I was determined to continue her excellent attempts to trace my sister. In the meantime I had plans for myself. . . .

'Assunta, it's time for me to return to Venice,' I said. 'Doctor Dami agrees that it would be the best thing for me in the circumstances – to try to pick up the threads of my life as they existed before – before it all happened.'

Dr Dami was the local physician from Dolo, a genial old man who had never in his long career been brought face to face with such a malady as mine, but who had very sensibly done nothing to worsen my condition, relying instead upon the healing hand of nature and a few reassuring words to work the cure. Which proved to be the right course.

'Do you mean? . . .' began Assunta.

'I mean my life as it was before Bruno was – before Bruno's death,' I said. 'I shall steel myself to go out into the streets and on the canals. I shall attend Mass, drink coffee and aperitifs at Florian's like I used to do. I shall address people I know, and if they cut me dead, I shall again bid them "good day" next time we pass in the street. Sooner or later, I'm convinced, they will grow tired of insulting me. Who knows? – one day someone might say "good day" back to me!'

Our return from the disastrous sojourn on the Brenta was marked by a tremendous downpour of almost tropical rain that lasted two days and nights. We went back to Venice by road, arriving at the Palazzo Mazzini-Forsca to find the place awash on the upper floors. The roof beams had rotted beneath the tiles and the rainwater was coming in unchecked. A fine picture gallery on the third floor was drenched from top to bottom, and many fine paintings of the seventeenth and eighteenth centuries, including unique portraits of notable Mazzini-Forscas, were quite ruined by the filthy water. Worse still, on the floor below, the *piano nobile*, an entire ceiling by the great G.B. Tiepolo depicting the apotheosis of my great-great-grandfather, the Admiral Prince Maximilien Mazzini-Forsca, was utterly destroyed. My own

74

suite was rendered uninhabitable, so I moved into the former housekeeper's quarters with Assunta and took the bedroom next to hers. Worse was to follow. My frantic application to the three principal building contractors in the city to come in and carry out repairs brought the same result: they refused even to answer my letters, and I was reduced to bringing in a jobbing builder who, for a grossly inflated price, condescended to apply to one of the finest sixteenth-century buildings in Venice the kind of workmanship he was used to giving slum hovels in the old ghetto. Nevertheless I persevered with him, and by gentle cajolery managed to make him extend his talents further than even he would have believed. But nothing could replace the Tiepolo, the Titians and Tintorettos, the Carpaccios, Giorgionis and Crivellis.

Having brought my family home into something like habitable shape again, I next addressed myself to the task of rehabilitating myself as a person rather than remaining society's outcast.

It was not easy. As on the memorable occasion when I first ventured out into the streets, I was insulted and shunned; people crossed themselves and made the sign against the Evil Eye, while children called after me and dogs snapped at my heels. I was cheated and overcharged in shops and by gondoliers. At Florian's the waiters pretended that I did not exist, and when I demanded their service, would bring me cold coffee, overcharge me on the bill, give me incorrect change.

I faced all these vicissitudes with a fortitude that astounded me. Where, I sometimes asked myself, is the mild and gentle Isolda of old? From whence came this hard-headed woman whom I found myself not liking very much?

What had happened, of course, is that my experiences had hardened me. The terrible break with my beloved Julietta had resulted in my forming a shield around myself against the world and its works. What other defence did I have? I could either steel myself to survive, or go under. I preferred to survive.

And then, one fine day, everything changed. . . .

It happened this way: I had taken a commercial gondola

75

from the water gate of the palazzo to the square of San Marco – this in preference to walking there by way of the side streets, which usually teemed with children and dogs – my worst and most vociferous opponents. Upon reaching the Molo, my gondolier – who had been eyeing me in such a manner during the short voyage that I should have been forewarned – named a sum for his services which was little short of an insult. I paid him what I considered to be his due, and a bit more. This was not enough for the rogue. He seized my arm and would not let me go, he said, till he had the full fare. And then proceeded to insult me in a most vile manner.

A sizeable crowd swiftly began to collect, and they added their support to the wretched scoundrel who was abusing me.

Then came – a happy intervention.

'Take your hands off that lady, you dog!' The command was delivered in perfect, idiomatic, but heavily-accented Italian, and couched in such commanding terms that the gondolier immediately obeyed and proceeded to whine that he had been cheated, that I had insulted him, and a lot more.

My rescuer – a tall man in a dramatic cloak and a slouch hat, who carried with him an air of authority lightly borne – tossed a coin into the bottom of the gondola and ordered the fellow to be off. He then extended his hand to me, helped me up the step and led me through the gawping crowd.

'Let me take you away from here, Signorina,' he murmured. 'And the further the better.'

We proceeded in silence, he with his hand on my arm, into the great square. It was then I paused, and confronting my rescuer I said: 'Signor, I cannot begin to tell you how deeply grateful I am for what you did. My name is Isolda Mazzini-Forsca. Whom, pray, do I have the honour to address?'

He took off his hat, revealing a shock of raven-black hair that was shot with grey flecks at the temple and above his exceedingly well-shaped ears. His eyes – deep blue and lively – regarded me keenly, and his firm lips sketched a grave smile when he replied. 'My name is Delamere, Signorina.

76

Colonel Jamie Delamere, and glad to have been of some small service.'

'You are English, Sir?' I ventured, addressing him in that tongue, which I took a pride in speaking fluently.

'American, Ma'am,' he responded. 'Of the State of Massachusetts. And most happy to make your acquaintance.' His manner was grave and courteous, his countenance most arresting, and suggestive – with its lean, aquiline modelling – of certain piratical characteristics that went with the dramatic cloak, the slouch hat with its broad and curly brim. I took to Colonel Jamie Delamere on sight. To me he seemed the very epitome of strength allied to gallantry. I detected also, beneath the piratical façade, a person of considerable inner gentleness and sensibility. Events were to prove that I was correct in this summation.

I made a gesture as if to part company from my rescuer.

'Well, Colonel,' I said, 'it has been most . . .'

'Wait, Ma'am,' he interposed. 'Now that we have met, let's not pass on our way like ships in the night. Will you not do me the honour of joining me for some refreshment? Might I suggest Florian's?'

I was so grateful to him, and so taken by his manner, that nothing on earth could have prevented me from accepting his invitation. Even when we entered Florian's, and I became as uncomfortably aware – as ever – of the hostile glances, the muttered asides, the tossing of heads and the lookings away with which the habitués were accustomed to greet my entry, I was not so put out as usual – being borne as I was on the arm of such a man as my new-found friend.

He directed us to a seat in a corner, casually signalled a waiter and regarded me with a heartening smile.

'What's it to be, Ma'am? For myself, I've a fancy for a half-bottle of your excellent local Merlot red wine.'

'I will join you, Sir,' I responded. And, settling myself in my seat, and feeling more at ease than I had felt for a very long time, I launched into light conversation with my companion.

'Are you in Venice, indeed in Europe, for long, Colonel?' I asked.

'For as long as the spirit moves me, Ma'am,' was his

response. 'For I'm free to roam as I please, and the world is my oyster in a manner of speaking. After I left the army, I went to Paris and augmented my scant education by taking a degree at the Sorbonne University. Next, I did some work on my specialist subject at Trinity College, Cambridge. I think, when I have visited all the places I want to see in Italy and the Balkans, I shall hie me to China and learn a smattering of Mandarin.'

I was intrigued and amused by my companion's unselfconscious manner of delivering his astonishing, brief itinerary, and pressed him further. Nothing loth, he was about to launch into a dissertation upon what he had described as his 'specialist subject', when a thought struck him – and he glanced round with a frown.

'What's happened to the service in this place?' he said. 'We've been here for five minutes and more, and those idle fellows' – he indicated three waiters who were lolled, gossiping, by the serving counter – 'are discussing their social arrangements.

'You there, waiter!' he called out in a deep, commanding growl that brought every gaze in the room upon him, the waiters' included. 'The one with the beard, you'll do – come and take my order and look sharp about it.'

In no great hurry, his addressee strolled over to our table and stood there, notebook and pencil poised, looking down at Colonel Delamere, but casting occasional, sneering glances in my direction.

'We would like a bottle of red Merlot, please,' said my companion. 'And something to nibble. A few pistachio nuts will do.'

'No pistachio nuts,' responded the waiter.

'Very well – almonds.'

'No almonds,' came the reply – delivered with a sidelong sneer in my direction.

Delamere fixed the fellow with a flat stare that would have put a more discerning person than the waiter completely out of countenance, and then said quietly, pointing, 'But you have just served that gentleman over there with a dish of almonds.'

78

'That was the last of the almonds,' was the brazen response.

Silence. Everyone in the café was agog, and I saw some of the customers – particularly those whom I had long earmarked as my more determined detractors – nudging and raising eyebrows at each other. Our waiter's two colleagues over by the serving counter were grinning openly. I stole an anxious glance at Colonel Delamere, wondering what he was going to do, fearful that even a man of his impressive bearing might be at a loss in dealing with a creature so insolent, so stupid and insensitive.

I need have had no fears on that score. . . .

'Ask the manager to come and see me, waiter,' he said quietly.

'The manager?' The other knew – or thought he knew – how to deal with bumptious foreigners who demanded to see the manager. 'He's busy.'

'I am glad to hear that Signor Rossi is busy,' responded the Colonel suavely. 'It indicates to me that my investment is being well attended to. Nevertheless, you will present my compliments and tell Signor Rossi that Colonel Delamere would like a word with him . . .

'*At once!*' The last injunction was delivered like a blast of icy wind in the arctic wastes.

The waiter sped away. He was back in no time with a swallow-tailed functionary whom I had always assumed to be the manager – and this was indeed the case. He was quite clearly uncertain in his mind, and regarded my companion with an air of guarded respect and suspicion.

'Er – you are Colonel Delamere, Signor?' he asked.

'I am,' responded the other.

Rossi slid a glance towards the waiter, who stood at his elbow, displaying signs of a man who sees his livlihood at stake. He returned his glance to my companion. 'Er – you know me by name, Signor Colonel.'

'I make it my business to know you by name, Rossi,' replied Delamere. He smiled – but it was a chilly salutation. 'The establishment appears to be in good shape, Rossi,' he went on. 'One could wish for a certain amount of re-decoration here and there. The furniture will need to be renewed next season. See to it, will you?'

The manager swallowed hard. 'Er – yes, Signor Colonel,' he replied in a strangled tone.

'That will be all, Rossi,' said the astonishing American. 'You may go now.'

'Th-thank you, Signor Colonel,' breathed the other.

'Oh, one thing more,' said Delamere. 'This waiter fellow here' – he indicated the now shrinking wretch in question, 'is of the mistaken belief that the café has run out of both pistachio nuts and almonds. Correct his misconception and have a supply of both sent to this table immediately, please. Thank you.'

The red Merlot was remarkably good. The almonds and pistachios likewise.

'Are you really a shareholder of this place?' I asked my companion.

He smiled. 'Do *you* think I am, Signorina Mazzini-Forsca?'

'I don't know. Not for sure.'

'Neither does Signor Rossi,' he said. 'And that's all that matters.'

'But – you knew his name.'

'His name – as manager and licensee – is indicated in small lettering over the door,' said my remarkable friend.

'Well,' I said, 'whether you are, or whether you are not, your performance certainly extricated both of us from a most embarrassing scene. And I have to tell you,' I added, looking down at my hands to avoid his gaze, 'that it is my presence here with you which prompted the waiter to be gratuitously insolent.'

He said: 'This would be something to do, also, with the way the gondolier treated you?'

I faced him squarely. 'Yes.'

'Want to confide in me?'

'I don't know you,' I replied.

'You didn't know anyone in that crowd of folks who gathered to hear what the gondolier was calling you, Ma'am,' he responded, 'but, sure as hell, they know plenty about *you* by now!'

I closed my eyes in an agony of remembrance. 'You – heard what that man called me?' I whispered.

'Sure. He called you a murderess, and sacrilegious to boot,' replied Delamere. 'That was a pretty sweeping denunciation. Is it widely applied to you in Venice?'

'It is said by – everyone!' I breathed. '*Everyone!*'

'I see,' he said. 'And I repeat, do you want to confide in me?'

'You're very kind, I'm sure, Colonel Delamere,' I told him. 'But what use could it possibly be for me to confide in you – and of what interest to you, save to satisfy your curiosity? I hope I have not offended you.'

'As to that, you've not offended me in the least,' he replied. 'As regards what use it could be – I might, I just might, be able to help you.'

I looked at him keenly, and saw nothing in his countenance that I did not like. Nothing was there but good will, honesty, sincerity – plus another quality which I could not quite define, but was akin to – what? Integrity?

'I think I will confide in you, Colonel Delamere,' I said at length.

Florian's was not the place for confidences. The atmosphere – notwithstanding that my friend had set his firm stamp upon it – was not conducive to baring one's soul to a comparative stranger. Nor was there anywhere we could sit without being stared at by passers-by, many of whom might recognize me. In the event, I proposed that we walk – and keep walking.

So it was that I unburdened myself to Colonel Jamie Delamere, that summer's evening, in the course of walking along the waterfronts of Venice: along the Slavonian quay, over the Ponte del Vin, across the narrow neck of the city to the Fondamente Nuove and on to the bay called Misericordia, with the building known as the House of the Ghosts guarding its far entrance. As we walked I gave my companion the history of my misfortunes, beginning with my first encounters with Bruno Ferrara, our reunion on the night of the ball at the Casa Crispi years later, our secret meetings culminating in the seeming miracle of our betrothal – and what came after; though at that stage of our relationship I could not

81

bring myself to speak of the circumstances leading up to Bruno's terrible death.

I told him, then, of my experiences at the hands of the Judicial Police. Including the final interrogations. . . .

'Wake up and come with me, Signorina!' ordered the gaoler.

I had not been to sleep, for how could I with two lamps burning in the narrow room that served as my cell? Nor had I slept for a long time, so long that I had lost count of the passing hours, and, there being no windows in the room, I had no way of telling night from day.

Wearily I stood up from the narrow bunk which, with its straw mattress, none too clean blanket and hard pillow, was the only item of furniture in my tiny cell – and followed my gaoler.

There was the usual endless traipse along dank corridors and up dangerously steep stone stairways, to the room which, by then, had become sickeningly familiar.

My interrogator – he whom I have come to think of as Number One – was seated behind the desk and writing, as usual. Nor did he look up till he had finished the page he was engaged upon. He then gestured me towards the seat facing him and treated me to one of his gliding, evasive glances. I instinctively reached up to make a futile attempt to straighten my hair, which had remained unbrushed and combed since I had been taken from the cemetery. Uneasily aware, also, that I had been given no provision to wash and clean my teeth, I already felt like some wretched outcast. I was also hungry and – what was worse – terribly thirsty.

'We will continue where we left off this morning, Signorina Mazzini-Forsca,' said my interrogator, lowering his wolfish eyes to the paper before him.

'Please, may I first have a glass of water?' I begged.

He made a brusque gesture. 'Later, later,' he said. 'All that can wait. First – to work. . . .

'We have already established that there was bad blood between you and your betrothed some weeks, if not months, before you murdered him. Correct?'

I had long since ceased to deny my guilt at every turn. The brief nod of agreement was simply to prevent further wearisome and repetitive argument. But I still did not let him have it all his own way.

'Not really bad blood,' I corrected him. 'We had a few lovers' tiffs.'

'I have written "bad blood" in my report,' he said savagely, baring yellowed teeth. 'And so it will remain. You are in no position to quibble!'

I closed my eyes and tried to hang on to the few remaining rags of my sanity.

'We will return to the incidents that took place at the apartment near the Campo Morosini two days before you murdered Ferrara,' he said. 'Upon your arrival back in Venice from Verona, you went to the apartment. Correct?'

I nodded.

'Give me your verbal agreement!' he grated.

'Yes. Yes, I went to the apartment.'

'Because you heard that Ferrara was entertaining a female person there at that time. Correct?'

'That is not true!' I cried. 'I went to see my fiancé simply to let him know that I was back in Venice . . .'

'Enough!' he interposed. 'You will have ample opportunity to make your own lying explanations in court.

'To resume, you went along to the apartment fully prepared to surprise Ferrara and this female person – and to make as much trouble as you were able. Correct?'

'That wasn't my intention!' I cried. 'I only . . .'

'You are lying!'

'*No!*'

'I have an affidavit here,' he said, 'from a witness who is willing to testify that you said – among other things – "I am going round there, and that creature will be sorry".'

'That is an absolute lie!' I cried.

'You will have ample opportunity to deny the witness's evidence!'

It was always the same. First the accusation, and then, when I made a denial, it was brushed aside with this old pretext. I was tired, heavy-eyed, with a raging thirst and hunger pangs. I was also very, very frightened. And this treatment was sapping my will.

He droned on, every so often stopping to demand my

agreement to some outrageous accusation or other – always supported by what he described as irreproachable witnesses who were willing to testify under oath. Past caring, I simply sat there, eyes closed, and nodded to his every question. This seemed to satisfy him.

Presently – it must have been three hours or more after I came into the room – he abruptly stood up and left me alone.

I huddled in the chair, and someone started quietly keening to herself. It was a shock to discover that the noise was coming from me.

'Signora Mazzini-Forsca, you are not looking well. Are they not taking proper care of you?'

The over-anxious question, put to me in such gentle tones, quite removed the slightest suggestion of sarcasm from the speaker's reaction upon seeing me as I was: unwashed, unkempt, tear-streaked and frightened.

It was my Number Two interrogator. The mere sight of him, the sound of his voice, made me hope anew. Passing my dry tongue over my cracked lips, I whispered to him that I was very thirsty.

'A glass of white wine will set you up nicely,' he said. 'I, myself, always take a glass at this time of day. No, I'll listen to no protests. Wine it shall be.' Whereupon, unlocking a wall cupboard, he took out a carafe and two tulip glasses. My hand trembled with anticipation as I took from him a brimming glass.

'Your very good health, Signorina,' he purred. 'And a swift and happy conclusion to our deliberations.'

I did not respond, but let the paper-dry wine pass over my tongue. In all my life, I had never known such instant bliss, such complete release from anguish. In a trice I was able to swallow in comfort and to utter a word or two of thanks.

He replenished my glass from the carafe and took his seat behind the desk, smiling at me with that gentle, benign curve of the lips, the good-natured crinkling at the corners of the lively eyes.

'I have been reading through the transcript of my colleague's discussions with you, Signorina,' he said. 'All in all, I would say that we are making some progress. Don't you agree?' He waited politely for my reply, his finely-sculpted head cocked a little to one side.

'All of the witnesses are lying about me,' I said.

Spreading his beautifully manicured hands in a gesture of sweet reasonableness, he said: 'My dear lady, is it not always thus? Speaking as a man of the law, I would say that no two witnesses can be found to give exactly similar versions of the same event.'

'But it's lies – all lies!' I cried.

He allowed my outburst to pass without comment, merely smiled indulgently and took a sip of his wine.

'Let us have a look at one issue that my colleague has pursued with some diligence,' he said at length. 'It concerns your visit to your fiancé's apartment upon your return from Verona. You remember the occasion?'

'Of course.'

'Upon your arrival there, you found that Count Ferrara was entertaining a certain lady . . .'

'Entertaining!' I cried. 'Always that word. Your colleague used that word. The reason for her being there was quite . . .'

He gently waved me to silence. 'Let us leave the reason aside for the time being,' he said. 'Let us say that such a visit, from a lady, at such an hour of the evening, might have been interpreted by you as being – shall we say – indiscreet? Come now, Signorina, be reasonable. Don't make my task any more difficult by splitting hairs. A lady – a personable young lady, I am presuming – visits your fiancé at his apart-ment on an evening when he thinks you are staying in Verona. What more natural than that you should experience a certain – disfavour?'

'Well, I was surprised, certainly,' I conceded. 'But . . .'

Again he waved me to silence. 'Dear lady, let us consider what happened. I will set the scene. Picture yourself. You have just returned from Verona – and we all know the dusty road from Verona, the interminable waits at the posting inns, the rapacious café owners – all the hardships of our modern society which make us long for the days of universal railway service to come. Notwithstanding your tiredness, you yearn

85

to see your lover, from whom you had expected to be parted for two whole days. Do I have it right so far, Signorina?'

I nodded.

'So – you are about to call upon him. On the way there you are told that he is entertaining a lady . . .'

'That is not true!' I cried. 'As I told your colleague . . .'

'Forget what you told my colleague, Signorina,' he responded. 'I am re-stating the case. Out of concern for your sensibilities, I will not dwell unduly upon the painful circumstances in which this information was passed on to you by an ill-wisher: the falsely-pitying smile, the knowing aside. Let us say that, tired, travel-worn, you arrive at the apartment to find – *her* . . .'

'Please!' I cried. 'You don't understand. . . .'

Again that gentle, compassionate smile. 'Signorina, I understand very well,' he responded. 'You are very happy to discuss this matter quite fully and frankly with me – whom you trust. What you cannot abide is the thought that all this is going to come out in open court, with all Venice, all the world, to look on and snigger.'

'Yes – that's it,' I breathed.

He sat back in his chair and, setting his wine glass before him, he took from his breast pocket a fold of paper – not very large.

'Discretion is the privilege of the court,' he said. 'This paper bears the name of the other lady who was involved in that evening's events. One word from you, Signorina, that you will co-operate with me in getting at the truth, and all the unnecessary details of that evening – the lady's name included – will be glossed over. Do you agree – will you co-operate fully?'

I nodded.

'Very well,' he said, and, smiling, held out the folded piece of paper towards the candelabrum that stood on the corner of his desk. The paper blackened, took fire, burned away to ashes, which he crushed into fine dust with a fingertip – and then wiped himself clean on a lawn handkerchief.

'That symbolic gesture,' he said, still smiling, 'denotes that the name of the lady in question is erased from the memory of the court.

'And now, dear lady, to business. . . .

'More wine? No? As you wish.

'Now. Following upon Count Ferrara's frequent and undisguised affairs with various women, named and unnamed, you were so brought to desperation and anguish of mind that, scarcely knowing what you were doing, you drove a dagger into your lover's heart in a fit of jealous rage. . . .'

I listened numbly, with only half an ear, to the same tissue of lies and half-truths that my first interrogator had been drumming into my weary mind, night and day, for what seemed like an eternity of time. Only, now it was different. My second interrogator had offered kindness instead of brutality. He had slaked my thirst. Within the limitations of his calling, I had come to trust him, and believed that he trusted me in return.

Most of all, he had relieved me of a nagging worry. With the memory of the candle flame eating up that scrap of paper, my tired mind was willing to listen – if only with half an ear.

'And how long did they hold you before you were formally charged with the murder?' asked Colonel Delamere.

'Three days,' I replied. 'And I was questioned for six hours or more, day and night, by one or the other of my interrogators in turn.'

'Three days – my God!' He drove a fist into the palm of the other hand and made some angry mention of democracy, habeas corpus and Magna Carta. 'And then you signed a written confession,' he said. 'Now, what in Hades made you want to do a thing like that?'

I tried to explain. . . .

'They were so clever,' I said. 'The first interrogator – the one who treated me as if I were already found guilty, sentenced and condemned – worked to break my spirit. His colleague took over from him at the times when I was near to despair, willing to listen to anyone, agree to any suggestion that held out hope of relief and release. He was clever, that one. He played me the way an angler plays a fish – giving a bit, so that the victim thinks that with a little yielding he might win his freedom – and then entrapping him again and drawing him even further into the net.

'In the end,' I said, 'it indeed became like being trapped underwater, so that I was willing to say anything, do anything, in order to be allowed just to breathe and stay alive. They were very clever, both of them. The first one planted in my mind the notion that I was guilty despite the evidence of my own experience, my own senses. The second let me know that he understood my agony of mind and wanted only to help me. After that, it was just a short step to agreeing that some of the awful things which the first interrogator was putting into my mind might – just might – have a few grains of truth.

'And then I made a sort of confession. And signed it. After that, I was formally arrested and allowed to sleep for as long as I liked, undisturbed.'

'There's only one thing that puzzles me,' he said at length. I raised my eyebrows questioningly.

'Why did you never leave and start life afresh elsewhere?' he asked.

It was a question I had often put to myself, and I had the answer for him. . . .

'I am a Venetian born and bred,' I said, 'A Venetian to my fingertips and proud of my ancestry. In love with the palazzo that has housed the Mazzini-Forscas for four hundred years, mindful of the happiness I knew there as a child. The city where I met my first love, so cruelly taken away from me.

'Was I to be driven away from Venice by the stiff-necked bigots who shunned me, or by the ignorant creatures who crossed themselves or made the sign against the Evil Eye?

'No – damn them all!' I cried. 'Here I am, and here I stay – and one day they'll all eat their words!'

We were silent for a very long time. A slight wind from the north ruffled the still waters of the Misericordia. I shivered. My companion took my hand in his. With his other hand, he took my chin, gently, between finger and thumb, and turned my face to regard him.

'Isolda Mazzini-Forsca,' he said. 'I think that I was possibly sent by fate to help you. And it so happens that, quite by chance, I am singularly well-equipped to do just that.' He paused, and his deep blue eyes seemed to search me and find me out in my most hidden places.

'Do you want my help?' he asked.

There was no doubt, no hesitation in my mind, any longer.

'Yes,' I said simply. And, in saying this, I seemed to hear the voice of the old woman in the strange shop in the back street – on that disastrous evening of my first venture out.

'*He who will come to you from over the sea . . . your only hope of salvation may lie in him. . . .*'

Six

We parted company on the Molo, for Jamie Delamere was staying at the nearby Danieli hotel. He himself handed me into a gondola, having picked out a gondolier whom he liked the look of, and paid him in advance. It was arranged that he call upon me the following morning in order – and the very thought of it had the power to kindle a flame of hope in my heart – in order to commence his task of, as he put it, 'reopening your case'.

I arrived back at the palazzo without incident and was anxiously greeted by Assunta, who knew full well that my forays in the city were seldom without incident, for did I not arrive back as often as not white-faced with anguish and red-eyed from weeping? Too tired and overwrought to dwell upon my adventures, I contented myself by mentioning that I had made a useful acquaintance and that he would be coming to the palazzo in the morning. I then ate my supper in silence and went to bed – leaving Assunta to her speculations.

That night I dreamed about Jamie Delamere. He appeared to me as a knight in burnished armour, like Verrocchio's splendid equestrian statue of the *condottiere* Bartelomeo Colleoni. In my dream he performed various unspecified knightly services for me, but then departed without saying goodbye. I awoke with a vague feeling of disenchantment at about four in the morning, and remained awake listening to the market craft moving down the Grand Canal till it was time to rise.

The American's gondola arrived at our water gate on the stroke of eleven, just as Assunta was heating the water for coffee. I greeted him in the yard which, as with so many of Venice's great houses, was cloistered by the four sides of the building and open to the sky, and served as an ornamental garden, with semi-tropical palms, flowering bushes, statuary, running water and a fountain.

He took my proffered hand.

'Have you changed your mind about employing my specialist subject in solving your problem?' he asked.

'If anything, I have reinforced my decision after much thought,' I responded.

'I'm glad,' he said.

He had exchanged his cloak and slouch hat for more formal attire of a dove-grey frock coat and a tall hat. Faultlessly tailored, with immaculate linen and expensive accessories, he was every inch the gentleman cosmopolite.

'I thought we would take coffee here,' I ventured, seeking for a commonplace to bridge a moment of – for me, at least – embarrassed silence as we regarded each other and measured the reality against a brief recollection of yesterday.

'That will be splendid,' he responded, and we took facing seats at a small table set close by the fountain, in the refreshingly cool shade. Assunta appeared almost immediately with coffee and cakes, and I introduced them. I was amused and pleased to see that my new friend made an instant and favourable impression upon my old nurse – and my observation was confirmed when she gave me a covert nod of approval as she departed upstairs.

I poured coffee and we sipped in silence for a minute or so. It was the American who gave the lead to our deliberations.

'Regarding your sister,' he said. 'You told me how, after the grotesque mischance of that scrap of newspaper, she reviled you and afterwards fled back to Venice and beyond.' He eyed me reflectively. 'Do you miss her?'

'Do I miss her?' I closed my eyes and felt a treacherous tightness of the throat. 'Colonel Delamere, not a day, not an hour passes, but I think of Julietta with bitter regret. Regret that I didn't have the courage to tell her everything in good time, to shield her from the awful shock that, as it turned out, also accompanied the hurt. You see, in my weakness, I nursed the vain and foolish hope that it might never be necessary to tell her. May heaven forgive me – for I shall never be able to forgive myself.'

He nodded gravely. 'What steps did you take to find out where she went, and where she is now?' he asked. 'You see, it may very well be that – due to my methods of inquiry – I shall almost certainly have to interview her sooner or later.'

The idea of this very impressive man seeking out poor Julietta and questioning her disturbed me slightly, but I told him all I knew.

'I wrote many times to the Reverend Mother of the convent in Ireland where Julietta was due to return,' I said. 'When it was clear that she had gone into hiding somewhere, I instructed an international private inquiry agency in Paris to make a search for her. So far neither they – nor anyone – has had a sign of her. It's almost as if – as if she'd vanished from the face of the earth.'

'You've not heard from her yourself – at any time?'

'Not a line since she left. No message by word of mouth. Nothing.'

We sat in silence for a while as I refilled our cups. My companion appeared to be deep in thought, but I was prompted to break in with a question that had remained unanswered during our brief acquaintance, though the subject had been raised several times. . . .

'Colonel Delamere . . .' I began.

'Signorina Mazzini-Forsca?' he responded, with the ghost of a smile.

'I'm very grateful for your very generous offer of help,' I said. 'I'm also rather puzzled, and can only suppose that you are a most generous and compassionate person, or why else would you stoop to assist a complete stranger to you – even if she has had the misfortune to be tried for the murder of her betrothed, thereby earning the hatred of her native city. You've spoken of what you describe as your "specialist subject". Does this subject have anything to do with clearing my name? I mean – will it help you?'

He leaned back in his seat and folded his arms, nodding as if in approval of my straight speaking.

'I'm glad you asked that, dear lady,' he said. 'And I will enlighten you.

'The story begins in Paris five or so years ago. As I told you, I was belatedly attending to my higher formal education after an adulthood in the military profession. I had served in the French army during the Franco-Prussian War and been invalided out. Three years at the Sorbonne studying the natural sciences led me to think that there might be a life's work for me in this direction. It took a chance attendance at a lecture given by the noted neurologist Charcot to point me in the general direction I should take. Now Charcot's clinical work on hysteria in relationship to hypnotism – the subject of that particular lecture – was only of passing interest to me, but it fired my interest in the wider aspects of the human mind. I followed the work of the Englishman Sir Francis Galton in his mental tests and psychological questionnaires. I delved into the findings of the Austrian school, notably Stumpf and Lipps. . . .

'I am afraid, dear lady, that I am boring you.'

I hastened to assure him that this was far from the case, but that I was totally ignorant of these matters, and how, I asked him, did they concern my particular problem?

'Psychology – the study of the workings of the human mind – is my specialist subject, Ma'am,' said the American. 'It is my belief that psychology provides the key to all human activities. And among these activities, I include man's age-old addiction to – murder!

'It is my belief that the real murderer of Count Bruno Ferrara will only be unmasked – at this late stage – by the science of psychology.'

Delamere's astonishing declaration, and the utter conviction with which he delivered it, impressed me greatly, while at the same time filling me with puzzlement. In my heart I knew that my hope of lifting the dark shadow that lay across my life was merely clutching at straws – but what more promising straw lay to hand than this most convincing American?

One more thing, however, had to be settled between us. I raised the subject with some embarrassment.

'Colonel,' I began. 'A rather delicate matter. When you offered to help me, I took it as a generous and gallant act on your part towards a woman in distress. Now it seems that, by taking up your offer, I've secured the services of a professional scientist. . . .'

He smiled. 'Dear lady, if you're asking me to name a fee for my services, please put it right out of your mind.'

'Sir,' I protested, 'I assure you that I'm a woman of ample means. No figure you could mention would embarrass me.'

Again that smile, which extended to the wise, all-seeing blue eyes. Here was a man who looked beyond a person's impulses and saw the truth that lay behind. He guessed that, though I obviously liked and admired him (for who could not have?) I was also wary of being beholden to him, and much preferred to keep our association on a businesslike basis.

'Very well, Ma'am,' he said at length. 'I, too, will lay my cards on the table. I am, like you, a person of considerable means. I practise my specialist subject of applied psychology for principally my own interest, and with no thought of profit. However, if you feel happier with a more formal arrangement, may I suggest that, when I've completed my inquiries to your satisfation, we arrive at a mutually agreed sum by way of my fee – and that you donate it to my favourite charity? Agreed?'

'Agreed, Colonel Delamere,' I replied without hesitation. I offered him my hand to seal the agreement and, taking it in his, he shook it with considerable vigour. Given the circumstances, some men might have retained hold of it for a shade longer than was strictly necessary, perhaps even have indulged in hand-kissing. Not he. No boudoir gallant, Colonel Jamie Delamere.

'And now,' I said, 'where do we begin?'

His face grew stern. 'If it's possible,' he said, 'I should like to view the private chapel where the murdered man was found.'

The private chapel of the Palazzo Mazzini-Forsca was added to the main building in the mid-seventeenth century and consecrated by the then Cardinal Archbishop of Venice. It had been in constant use by our family, friends, visitors, servants and others since that time, and the chaplainship, which was a sinecure in the gift of the head of the family, was currently held by an aged canon of the nearby Church of Santa Maria Zobenigo. But, as I explained to my companion as we wended our way to the chapel, a very unhappy situation had arisen. . . .

'After the discovery of the body, the See of Venice ordained that, sacrilege having been committed, the chapel must be de-consecrated till the sin is purged. So the place is now, spiritually, an empty shell.'

'But an extremely beautiful shell, nevertheless,' said Jamie Delamere as I opened the carved oak door and admitted us both into the mysterious gloom of the Baroque interior. Smaller than the *piano nobile* of the palazzo, but most beautifully proportioned, so that it appeared longer, wider and more lofty than it really was, the chapel possessed several notable works of art, including a crucifixion by Titian and an unfinished Pietà sculpted by the master hand of Bernini.

'And there,' said my companion, his voice strangely sonorous in the echoing emptiness about us, 'is the fateful altar.'

'Yes,' I whispered, and shuddered as if someone had just walked over my grave.

We walked up the aisle, side by side, towards the flamboyant altar backed by its reredos depicting the Ascension in a convoluted surge of swirling, gesticulating figures rendered in paint and in carved marble. The table of the altar itself was of basalt inlaid with plaques and cartouches of marble and alabaster, carved and gilded in the Baroque manner and bearing the Holy cypher and the arms of the Mazzini-Forsca family. Six tall candlesticks flanked the empty tabernacle and the lamp that burned no longer.

'And it was here that Count Bruno was discovered?' murmured my companion. 'Lying on the table of the altar.'

'Yes.'

'Face upwards, with a dagger in his heart.'

I nodded, being unable to frame the answer.

'What manner of man was your betrothed?' he asked. 'As to build, I mean. Was he, perhaps, a tall man? Compared with me, for instance.'

I looked at my companion. 'I would say he was about

your height,' I replied. 'Perhaps an inch or so shorter. No more.'

'And as regards weight?'

Again, I appraised the American. 'Rather more heavily built than you, I think.' I smiled wryly – sadly. 'Poor Bruno, if he had lived, would undoubtedly have put on weight in middle age, like so many Italians.'

'Mmmm.' Delamere ran his hand along the altar top, as if gauging its height, the smoothness of the stonework. He remained for a few moments deep in thought. And then, turning to regard me, he said, 'Signorina Mazzini-Forsca, would you be willing to take part in a small experiment – here and now?'

I shrugged. 'But of course,' I replied. 'Anything you ask. But what? . . .'

For answer, he did a most surprising thing. Disregarding the dusty floor (which to my knowledge had not been swept since the scandal of my fiancé's murder and my own arrest drove every member of the palazzo staff save Assunta to quit in a body) and his dove-grey suiting, he calmly laid himself down full length, beside the altar and looked up at me from this supine position, his face set and serious.

'And now, Ma'am,' he said, 'I want you to pick me up in your arms – as awkwardly and slovenly as you please, don't spare my comfort – and lay me on the altar table.'

'But I . . .' I began.

'Yes?'

'I don't think – no, I'm sure that I couldn't possibly lift you on my own,' I protested.

'You could try,' was his cold response.

'Very well.' And, stooping, I attempted to lift him by sliding my hands under his armpits and raising his head and the upper part of his trunk. This I managed to do adequately well. But I could get no further.

'Lift me up a little higher,' advised Delamere, 'and try to prop me up against the edge of the altar.'

With some difficulty I managed to carry out his instruction – though he cheated by taking some of his weight on his elbows when I had him lying against the altar.

'Now take hold of my ankles and lift me on to the table,' he said.

I tried. I tried repeatedly – but it was no use.

Presently he relaxed and stood up.

'Well then,' he said. 'I think we have conclusively proved one thing to our satisfaction, Ma'am. Even with my giving you a little assistance, you are incapable of lifting a living man my height and weight on to that altar unaided. With a dead weight, you would have got nowhere at all.'

It was cool, quiet and curiously peaceful in the chapel. By unspoken, mutual agreement we went and sat in the family pew under the ornate pulpit. We sat in silence for a while, and it was Jamie Delamere who spoke first.

'The point about your lifting the body on to the altar,' he said. 'Was it raised at the trial?'

'No.'

'Or during the interrogations?'

'No.'

He muttered something under his breath about 'criminal incompetence' and 'judicial manipulation of truth'.

'Who discovered the body?' he asked.

'One of the under-footmen, a youth named Poeta – Poeta Longhi.'

'When was this?'

'Early morning. It was Poeta's duty to open up the chapel, and in winter to light the wood-burning stove, in case anyone wished to perform their devotions before breakfast. Oh – and by the way, it was he – Poeta – who used to act as messenger between Bruno and me, during the time when we met only in secret.'

'Did he give his evidence at the trial, this Poeta?'

'Yes, he was among the first to do so,' I replied. 'I remember it well. . . .

'As if I could ever forget. . . .'

'I call Signor Poeta Longhi.'

The prosecuting counsel was a floridly handsome, tall and heavily built man in his late forties. He was reputed to have

97

his eye on a seat in the Senate, and was merciless in pursuit of convictions.

'Call Poeta Longhi!' echoed the clerk of the court.

From my seat in the dock between two hard-eyed wardresses, I looked out over the rows of heads that were all turned to stare at the door at the rear of the court through which the witness would enter. Many of then took the opportunity, also, to steal a glance in my direction. I knew some of them by sight. The Marchese and Marchesa di Rollo were there in the front row of the spectators.

The di Rollos and others had had to travel from Venice to witness what they undoubtedly hoped would be the ultimate downfall and degradation of my sentence following a verdict of guilty. Upon the application of my counsel, the venue of the trial had been shifted to Verona, on the ground that public feeling against me was running so high in Venice that an unbiased jury could not be got together in the whole of my native city. Small hope, I thought, of my faring any better in the city of Romeo and Juliet – if the hate-filled glances from the public galleries were anything to go by.

There was a small stir in the rear of the courtroom and Poeta Longhi came in, escorted by a uniformed constable, and took his place in the witness stand to be sworn in. Poeta, a thin, pale-faced youth with a hank of fair hair hanging down over his narrow brow, was dressed in his Sunday-best black, and looked frightened. Being illiterate, he was obliged to repeat the written words of the oath after the clerk. He was then addressed by the prosecutor, and gave his name, status and home address. Since the administration of justice in Italy was based on a similar system to that of the French, the presiding judge then took over the questioning.

'Did you discover the body of Baron Ferrara?'

'Yes, Your Honour,' replied Poeta nervously.

'Speak up when you address the learned judge!' snapped the prosecutor.

'Tell the court how it happened,' demanded the judge.

'Your Honour, I went across the yard to open up the outer door of the chapel,' replied the wretched youth, who was overawed and visibly trembling.

98

'Outer door? What does he mean by the outer door?' demanded the judge testily.

'Your Honour,' replied the prosecutor, rising, 'I should explain that the chapel is separate from the main building and connected by a short corridor lined with windows. Admission to the chapel by this entrance is confined to the family and their guests, since the corridor leads from their drawing room. Servants and others enter the chapel by an outer door from the yard.'

The judge nodded sourly. He was a man of advanced years and totally unknown to me. It struck me, then, that I had never seen so evil a countenance on any living being. He had never been comely, even in his salad days I would have imagined; a lifetime of malice and hatred had left its indelible mark on his ashen-grey features.

'The witness will continue,' he growled. 'What did you see upon entering the chapel?'

'There was this figure – I saw it almost at once, right after I had opened up the stove,' responded Poeta. 'Up there on the altar – murdered!'

'Your Honour. . . .' My counsel rose to his feet, displaying the world-weary smile of a man who has grown cynical from dealing with fools. 'How could the witness possibly have arrived at such a conclusion? According to the plan, the wood-burning stove is right at the far end of the centre aisle from the altar.'

The judge scowled. 'Signor Rispoli, you are splitting hairs again,' he snarled. 'I am accepting that the witness arrived at his conclusion upon closer examination of the body. Kindly take your seat again. Carry on, witness. You have done well so far.'

Visibly heartened by this commendation, Poeta swallowed and resumed his testimony. 'Your Honour, when I went closer, I saw that the man was dead. There was a knife sticking out of his chest, you see? And blood everywhere.'

'Did you recognize the victim?'

'Yes, Your Honour, it was Count Bruno.'

'You knew him well?'

'Why, yes, Your Honour.' Poeta cast a sidelong glance in my direction, and I clearly detected an aura of fear in the youth's manner – and the fear, or so it seemed, was directed towards me, and because of me. 'It was me who carried secret messages from Count Bruno's valet back to Signorina Isolda,' he added.

The judge leaned forward, eyes narrowed. 'You say you used to carry secret messages?' he demanded. 'Why was that?'

Poeta explained that these exchanges had taken place when the relationship between Bruno and me was not only secret but also forbidden. This brought my counsel to his feet again.

'Your Honour,' he said, 'I submit that this evidence is irrelevant. At the time of the murder, my client and the deceased were properly affianced, and with the approval of both families.'

'Nothing in my court is irrelevant, Signor Rispoli,' responded the judge, close-set, evil eyes narrowed. 'I consider the fact that the couple once carried on a clandestine relationship most significant.'

'As you say, Your Honour,' replied Rispoli, abashed. He sat down again – having been snubbed for the second time. Fearful that his no doubt well-intentioned efforts were doing nothing to assist my case – rather the reverse, it seemed to me – I prayed that he would be more prudent with his interruptions.

At the Judge's prompting, Poeta then told how he had run to fetch his immediate superior, the head footman. The latter had summoned the police, and by this time the whole household was in turmoil.

I listened to this testimony with an anguished mind, particularly when it touched upon the details of my fiancé's tragic end, but I had already wept all the tears that lay within me, and grieved my soul dry. Dry-eyed, then, I waited, like a lamb for the slaughter, for whatever they next had in store for me.

The prosecutor was on his feet again. 'Your Honour,' he said, 'this witness, Longhi, still has further evidence to impart to the court. I would ask Your Honour to question him regarding what he saw before he actually *entered* the chapel that early morning.'

The judge turned his sour gaze upon the shrinking youth

100

on the stand. 'Think back to what you saw on your way to the chapel,' he demanded. 'And remember that you are on your sacred oath.'

Poeta shuffled his feet and bowed his head. When he next spoke, his delivery was barely audible.

'The witness will speak up!' shouted the judge.

'As I walked across the yard,' faltered the unhappy youth. 'I saw – I saw. . . .'

'Yes, what did you see?' demanded his tormentor.

'I – I saw the light of a candle moving down the corridor from the chapel to the palazzo. I saw it plain – through the windows.'

'Did you see who was bearing the candle?'

'Not at first, Your Honour. But when she drew abreast of the window nearest to me. . . .'

'Ha! So it was a woman, hey?'

'Yes, Your Honour.'

I tensed myself. This piece of evidence was new to me. Produced at the eleventh hour, was this the revelation which would point to the true perpetrator of the ghastly crime and release me from the torment into which I had been plunged? I listened, spellbound, for what was to come next.

The judge uttered the very words that burned in the forefront of my mind: 'Did you see this woman clearly?'

'Yes, Your Honour,' came the reply.

'Would you know this woman if you saw her again?'

'Yes, I would know her.'

'Is she present in this courtroom?'

'Yes.'

I drew a swift intake of breath. *She was here – the murderess was here – a witness to my degradation!*

'Point her out to the court.'

Poeta Longhi turned. I met his gaze with a tremulous smile, thinking that he was about to offer me a look of reassurance before denouncing my lover's killer.

But – no. . . .

He was pointing at me!

'That was the woman I saw!' said the wretched perjurer. 'Signorina Mazzini-Forsca!'

101

Then someone was screaming – frantically proclaiming that it was lies, all lies – and that she was innocent.

I did not immediately realize that this hysterical creature was me!

I finished the account of that appalling scene in the court-room at Verona, and my voice died away in the domed ceiling of the chapel.

Delamere made no comment but remained seated beside me, staring at the pillared nave and stroking the angle of his jaw.

Presently he stirred. 'This testimony of Poeta Longhi,' he said at length. 'You had never heard it mentioned before – the story of the woman with the candle coming away from here down the corridor?'

'No,' I replied.

'You were never confronted with it during the interrogations?'

'No.'

'Your counsel never alluded to it during your consultations with him?'

I glanced at him in surprise. 'Consultations?' I repeated. 'There were no consultations worth mentioning. I saw him briefly – once – when I was being held on remand in the prison at Verona two days before my trial.'

Delamere returned my stare. 'Are you telling me that that was the only contact you had with the advocate appointed to defend you?'

'Yes.'

'And what did you talk about on this single occasion?'

I searched my mind, for there was not much to tell. 'Well,' I began, 'he told me not to worry, but to put myself completely in his hands. He said that my written confession could be discounted because it was obtained under duress, and that the evidence against me was entirely circumstantial and would not stand up to close examination before the court. And I believed him.'

He nodded, and his blue eyes were very far away in thought.

'What was the name of this advocate?' he asked.

'Rispoli.'

'Who appointed him to defend you?'

'I don't know,' I admitted. 'I suppose it was my lawyer in Verona.'

'Was Rispoli a Venetian, or from Verona?'

'Neither, I think. I'm almost certain he was from Milan. Yes, I'm sure I heard the jailers mention that he was Milanese.'

We fell silent again, I with my bitter memories of that appalling ordeal of the trial – which I had only begun to touch upon to my companion. I glanced sidelong at him. He was gazing up at the ceiling, deep in thought.

In order to attract his attention, I said: 'After Poeta Longhi's denunciation, the courtroom was in a complete uproar, with me trying to make myself heard above the din, and the judge banging his hammer on the desk and shouting to the police to clear the court. The two awful harridans who were guarding me dragged me down to the cells and gave me bread and water. That was my luncheon.'

I looked down at my fingers and willed them to stop trembling.

Jamie Delamere's lean brown hands came out and took hold of mine. 'No more for this morning,' he said. 'You've had enough. More than enough. And speaking of luncheon, I'm going to take you out and give you a treat.'

The 'treat' was a trip by steam ferry to the Lido, to the Grand Hôtel des Bains, where I had not set foot for longer than I cared to remember. Jamie Delamere was obviously well known there. It was 'Good day, Signor Colonel' and 'How are you, Colonel Delamere? We have not had the pleasure of your company for a long time.'

We were bowed to a quiet corner table in the palm court, where a three-piece ensemble was playing selections from the Strausses. The head waiter brought menus. My companion ordered hock and seltzer as aperitifs for us both. I felt pampered, cosseted and a whole woman again – a pleasant change from the hunted, frightened creature who had lived out a half-existence for so long in the shuttered and dust-sheeted fastness of the Palazzo Mazzini-Forsca.

The luncheon chosen, the wine poured, my companion raised his hock glass and offered me a toast. 'To the success of our enterprise,' he said. 'The road may be long and hard, Ma'am, but I am convinced that we shall find the truth at its end.'

I pledged him in return and raised the glass to my lips. As I did so, I saw a shadow move across the tinted glass of the large window slightly to my right – one of the many in the palm court that looked out upon a view of the hotel's semi-tropical gardens, the beach beyond, and the shimmering Adriatic that stretched, wave after wave, to the violet-blue horizon.

The glass fell from my suddenly limp fingers and was shattered into a hundred pieces on the tiled floor by my feet.

'Oh, my God!' I breathed.

'What is it, Ma'am – what's amiss?' said Jamie Delamere, rising to his feet as waiters came running to attend me.

It was on the tip of my tongue to tell him what had alarmed me, but the waiters' presence, as they fussed around clearing up the mess, prompted me to the caution that I had practised during the long months of my agony.

The clearing-up done, another glass provided and fresh wine poured, my companion reached across the table and touched my hand reassuringly.

'Something upset you. I'm here, if you want to talk about it. Take your time,' he said.

I drew a deep breath. 'It's silly, I know, but – someone was watching us – me – through that window,' I faltered.

'Someone you know?'

'I'm not sure,' I said. 'I only saw him for an instant – it was a man – and there wasn't enough time for me to recognize him properly. But I had a very strong feeling that I've seen him before.'

He nodded thoughtfully. 'Are you well known on the Lido?'

'Less well than almost anywhere in and around Venice,' I said. 'My parents sometimes brought us here to bathe when Julietta and I were young, but Mother much preferred some of the smaller islands of the lagoon than having to mix with the cosmopolitan set here on the Lido.'

Jamie Delamere raised his glass and peered at the light through the pale wine. 'So it's unlikely that the person who took such an interest in you – or both of us – lives on the Lido.'

'Very unlikely,' I replied. 'I simply don't know anyone well enough here to have recognized them, however imperfectly, at a fleeting view.'

'Then it's probable that the man in question followed us here, from Venice,' he said.

I was turning this disturbing thought over in my mind when the head waiter came to inform us that luncheon was ready, and would the Signorina and the Signor Colonel be pleased to take their seats at table?

Over the tortellini, whose richness was totally wasted on me, so that I pushed the stuffed dumplings around the plate and tried to hide them under their cream and Parmesan sauce, Jamie Delamere worked manfully to revive the holiday spirit that had inspired the earlier part of my 'treat' by telling me amusing stories of his student days in Paris and Cambridge. But it was no use. Presently he also laid his fork aside and sat back.

'We can't get away from it, can we, Isolda?' he said.

Not unaware that this was the first time he had addressed me by my given name, I answered him soberly. 'I'm afraid we can't, because this affair has become the whole of my life, overshadowing everything – my peace of mind, my hopes for the future – my all.'

He refilled his wine glass. 'Do you mind if I put a thought to you which might – just might – hurt you and possibly make you angry with me?' he asked.

'If it's a constructive thought and likely to lead us somewhere, I would gladly welcome it,' I replied.

'Well,' he said, 'I can't help noticing that, when you get around to it – which isn't very often – you sometimes speak of your late fiancé with a certain – how to put it? – *detachment*, that hardly speaks of undying love. Or am I being unfair?'

I was shocked, but tried not to show it. 'Is that how it

strikes you?' I asked. 'Well, I suppose your psychology provides you with a ready-made explanation for it.'

He looked contrite. 'I *have* hurt you,' he said, 'and you *are* angry with me.'

'Forget that,' I replied. 'Supposing you are right – why, do you think, has my love for Bruno died with him?'

'Well,' he said, 'speaking as a psychologist, you could be the sort of woman who might be less concerned over the loss of her beloved than she is about saving her reputation – or her own precious skin.'

'Do you think I'm that sort of woman?' I asked.

'No,' he replied.

'So – what other explanation?'

His response was delayed by the arrival of a squad of waiters, two of whom took away our unfinished plates with many rueful glances, while the others served the second course.

When they had left us, he said: 'Perhaps, some time before Bruno's death, you fell out of love with him for some good reason. Or, the way things often are between lovers, for no good reason at all.'

'Go on,' I said. 'Don't stop.'

'On the other hand, some time *after* his death, you stumbled over evidence of some activity on his part – infidelity, for instance – that changed your whole attitude to his memory.'

'Any more?' I asked.

'It's possible,' he said, 'that your concern for Julietta has become the most important thing in your life – outweighing your fears for yourself, your love for Bruno, his precious memory – everything.'

I could remember times in my life when I had been brought face to face with unexpected truths about myself – fads and foibles, prejudices and aversions which were so much a part of me that I scarcely noticed I had them. But never was a truth about myself so forcibly drawn to my attention as this one that the American psychologist had unearthed.

I stared at Jamie Delamere with a dawning realization.

'I see it all now,' I said. 'When I had done all the weeping there was in me, when I had grieved for Bruno till there was nothing left in me to grieve with – it was then that I laid my dead love to rest along with my memories and turned to the living.

'You are quite right. My principal concern after the murder was for Julietta and what it would do to her when she learned that her beloved sister was arrested and tried for the murder of a man whom she – my sister – looked upon as a beloved brother.'

'Your feelings do you justice,' said my companion. 'But, surely, if you had explained everything to Julietta in good time, she would have understood and lavished all her love and sympathy on you.

'After all, Isolda – you were found to be "Not Guilty" and set free!'

I stared at him with momentary surprise. And then I realized that we had been talking at cross purposes. . . .

'Oh, but I thought you *knew!*' I cried, appalled. 'I thought I had told you that I was *not* cleared of Bruno's murder!'

My trial dragged on for eleven days, and they were eleven days of hell that have scarred my soul for ever.

My counsel had decided that I should not give evidence on my own behalf, since, he said, by retracting my written confession and pleading 'Not Guilty', I had destroyed my credibility with the court. 'Leave it to me, Signorina,' he advised me during one of our brief meetings in the cell beneath the courthouse, 'and I will concentrate on securing your release on the ground that all the evidence against you is circumstantial.'

So for nine days I was obliged to listen as, one after another, a stream of men and women – many of them totally unknown to me – went up on the witness stand and gave evidence of Bruno's infidelities, his cavalier conduct and total disregard for my feelings. That was bad enough, but when many of them lied under solemn oath about my terrible jealousy, my violent responses to my fiancé's behaviour and my repeated threats to kill both him and his paramours, I frequently gave way to my feelings and screamed aloud that it was all lies. For this the judge always sent me down to the cells – and the trial continued without me. It may be that, for this reason, I missed some of the more appalling untruths.

107

On the tenth day my counsel and the prosecutor made their speeches to the jury of scowling Veronese citizens, from whom – by the looks they constantly threw in my direction – I could surely expect no mercy. The prosecutor suggested to them that the vast accumulation of evidence greatly outweighed its circumstantial nature, and he constantly repeated the saying 'Where there's smoke, there's fire' – demolishing my counsel's plea that none of the evidence proved that in the end it was I – Isolda Mazzini-Forsca – whose hand had driven the dagger into the heart of my betrothed.

On the eleventh day (a whole weekend had intervened, which I spent alone in my narrow cell, eaten alive by my fears for myself and hideous anxieties about Julietta – blessedly unaware at her convent school in Ireland), the judge gave his summation to the jury.

If I live to be a very old woman, I shall remember the words of his short and devastating denunciation when I am dying – every word, every harsh and sarcastic inflection, every twisted phrase another nail in the coffin of my hopes. . . .

'Signors of the jury,' he began, 'it is your duty to give your verdict on this woman. Counsel for the defence has argued that the evidence against her is entirely circumstantial. The prosecutor has countered this by pointing out that the *sheer weight and the mass of evidence* against this woman lends it the quality of truth. I do not direct you to accept the prosecution argument – but I order you to bear it in mind.

'You have three alternative verdicts.

'You can bring a verdict of "Not Guilty" – in which case this woman, guilty or not, can go free from this court and can never be tried again on the same charge. Even though she goes on to commit another murder, and another, and another – she will remain innocent of this murder, in the eyes of the law, for ever.

'Or you can bring in a verdict of "Guilty". What may happen in this eventuality? I will tell you. This woman is rich and influential in our society, with rich and powerful friends. In no time at all, influence will be exerted to have your verdict overthrown upon appeal to a higher court. If that fails, the case will be taken to the Italian Senate. Appeals will be made to the Crown. The very force and persistence which wealth and influence are able to exert in our society will be brought to bear to overturn your verdict, Signors of the jury.

'What alternative remains? Ha! There remains one more course open to you, Signors. And, in my opinion, it not only best suits the evidence which has been offered, but also provides the best postscript to this appalling crime. The verdict "Not Proven" is exactly what it says. The prosecution has not proved its case up to the hilt; on the other hand, the accused has not satisfied this court beyond all reasonable doubt of her innocence. She can go free, and – save in most rare and exceptional circumstances – cannot be tried again on the same charge.

'Signors of the jury, I direct you – nay, I *order* you – to bring in the verdict of "Not Proven" against this woman.

'To do any other would be to invite cries of fury from the very heavens!'

'That old man,' I said when I had recounted this to my companion, 'that evil, malicious old man condemned me to a lifetime in the shadow of a punishment that can never be lifted. In the eyes of the law and in the eyes of the people of Venice I have never been cleared of the murder of my betrothed. Nor ever will be!'

Again, Jamie Delamere's hand sought mine, and his fine eyes gleamed with the hard cutting edge of resolution.

'Yes, you will, Isolda!' he promised me. 'If I have to round up every so-called witness who perjured himself or herself and wring the truth out of them, if I have to take each and every one of those signors of the jury and rub their faces in the real facts, if I have to unmask that so-called judge as a rogue and a scoundrel and a shame to his high calling. . . .'

He drew breath, and went on: 'If I have to move all Venice across the lagoon and sink it into the Adriatic, I'll clear your name before all men, Isolda Mazzini-Forsca, so help me God!'

I stared at him, inspired by his ardour, his utter conviction.

'Yes, you will, Jamie!' I breathed. 'I think you *will!*'

Seven

I left the luncheon table with a lighter heart than I would have believed possible at the start of it. We returned to the palm court and my escort smoked a cigar while I sipped coffee and listened to what he called his 'plan of campaign'.

'Tomorrow, perhaps even this evening,' he said, 'I shall get down to the business of interviewing all the witnesses at your trial. Their names and addresses will of course be available from the Judicial Police.

'I wonder,' he mused on reflection, 'if it would be prudent to alert the police, at this stage, that I am inquiring into the case? Perhaps not, for if they were as deeply involved in devising this travesty of justice as the court appeared to be, I might find obstacles placed in my way.

'No – the information I need will be available in the archives of the Veronese Hall of Justice. I will seek it there – discreetly and anonymously.'

A thought came to me. 'I can help you with the caretaker of the apartment house where Bruno lodged,' I said. 'She is Signora Agatha Bellini, and the address is fifteen, Calle di Mezzo.'

'Fifteen, Calle di Mezzo.' Jamie took a stub of pencil from his pocket and scribbled down my information upon his starched shirt-cuff. 'I will call upon Signora Bellini this evening,' he said. 'And I fancy that she will long remember my passing. It was she, was it not, who testified that you surprised Bruno with an unnamed lady friend, whom you sent packing – afterwards threatening to kill your fiancé if he ever entertained her again?'

110

'Yes,' I said. 'And Signora Bellini's testimony was a curious parody of what really happened.'

'What did *really* happen, Isolda?' he asked, eyeing me through his aromatic cigar smoke.

'Well Bruno, who lived very modestly in spite of being one of the richest young men in Venice, had some trouble in finding a daily woman to cook and clean for him in that small apartment,' I said. 'When I returned from Verona, I called to see him and found that he had at last managed to secure the services of a most unsuitable person. As I remember, she was in the act of washing the hall floor when I arrived. This she did by the classic, slatternly method of swamping the tiles with water, swooshing it around and hoping for the dirt miraculously to disappear. But that wasn't all. Bruno had just finished a meal. I say "finished" – he had hardly touched it, and it still remained on the table. Tagliatelli, it was supposed to be – but the pasta was burned, the sauce over-salted, and one wouldn't have given it to the cat.

'When the woman had gone, I advised him to pay her off. I said, "My darling Bruno, if you keep that woman in your employ, her cooking will kill you as sure as you're born!" We laughed loud and long about it.'

'What manner of woman was this person?' asked Jamie. 'Was she young – beautiful, perhaps?'

'Young? Beautiful? Oh, dear me, no,' I said. 'She was a toothless old harridan with a most impossible squint, poor thing. I felt really sorry for her and begged Bruno to pay her off generously.'

'And it was this conversation that Signora Bellini overheard,' said Jamie. 'And afterwards altered into a very different version of her own – a parody, as you said.'

'But why – *why?*' I cried. 'Why should this woman have lied, and what induced her to tell those lies on oath in court, in order to destroy me?' I felt my voice taking on the edge of hysteria, as I seemed to sense the evil closing in upon me again. 'Jamie, what could I have done in my life to have earned the hatred of so many people?'

He laid a hand on my shoulder, to steady me. 'Don't torture yourself with vague imaginings, Isolda,' he said. 'You are innocent – keep that idea in the forefront of your mind.

111

As to why Signora Bellini and the others gave false witness against you – just you leave that to me to discover.'

It wanted an hour before the next steam ferry left the Lido for Venice, so we went for a walk along the Adriatic shore, arm in arm, braving the quite brisk breeze that blew from seaward and sent children's kites scudding up on high. There were very few people on the beach, for the weather was too boisterous to sit out. I found myself looking back over my shoulder, fearful that I might see our secret watcher again, but there were only the children with the kites, and one grave-faced little boy in a sailor suit, who was being walked by his nursemaid and who looked wistfully at the kite-flyers.

Conscious that my companion and I, by adopting the use of each other's given names, had crossed a certain threshold of intimacy, I had the impulse to learn more about the man whom I had come to accept as a friend, the more to understand the manner of person whom I had taken – almost completely, *but not entirely* – into my confidence, and upon whose broad shoulders rested all my hopes.

'Tell me more about yourself,' I asked him. 'I know you were a soldier, a student of the sciences. What else? What about your boyhood, your family?'

'I was born and bred in Boston, Massachusetts,' replied Jamie. 'My family was in shipping, grandfather having made a fortune in the coastal trade before, during and after the Civil War. Shipping or no, my inclination was towards a military career, so I enlisted as a private soldier and prospered in my chosen line. And all the time I had this scientific bent, which led me into the engineering branch of the army. Later, before I resigned my commission and went to France, I patented an improved breech-screw for field artillery pieces which brought me in a fortune.' He gave a wry smile. 'You might say that I became rich in my own right by devising a more efficient means to increase the worldwide population of widows and orphans.'

I made no response to the slight bitterness and self-hatred that had entered his voice, and we had walked quite a way further along the beach before he resumed his tale.

'It was maybe on account of this, and what I experienced

112

during the Franco-Prussian war,' he said, 'that I turned from military engineering to the more peaceful applications of science. This led me, by the paths I've told you about, to the study of the human mind with a view to unravelling the mystery of what makes people behave the way they do. I don't lay claim to have got all that far in my quest, but I've been privileged to see a little light ahead at the end of a dark tunnel, and such knowledge as I've gained is at your disposal in the solving of your problems, Isolda.'

'Thank you, Jamie,' I said.

It was in sober mood that we retraced our steps to the ferry. Neither of us spoke as we were borne across the choppy waters of the great lagoon towards the towers, domes and pinnacles of the city of the Doges that lay shimmering in the sun. It was not till I looked back towards the low line of the Lido that I saw a small steam launch following in our wake. There was the dark figure of a cloaked man standing alone in the bows. He was too far away for me to discern his features, but he was clearly looking in our direction. I drew Jamie's attention to the stranger, and saw his eyes narrow dangerously.

'Do you think? . . .' I began.

'He might be our mysterious watcher,' came his reponse. 'Well, we can also watch *him* and see what he's up to.'

When the ferry came alongside the Molo and the passengers disembarked, we saw that the steam launch had stopped some distance offshore and that the watcher still remained in the bows, apparently still looking in our direction. When we were ashore and going on our way across the Piazetta, we looked back again and saw the launch start up again and glide out of sight in the direction of the Arsenal.

Jamie escorted me on foot to the street entrance of the palazzo, but did not come in. He promised to call, or write to me, as soon as his inquiries had borne fruit. I thanked him for my 'treat', while expressing the regret that it had been marred by the presence of the mysterious watcher. It was upon this note that we parted company.

Assunta greeted me with the air of someone who has been waiting on tenterhooks for longer than she could bear.

'A letter for you, my darling!' she cried, thrusting it into my hand. 'And the postmark is Paris!'

The writing of the address was unfamiliar to me, but the contents explained it all.

'It's from the inquiry agents in Paris,' I said. 'The people I instructed to trace Julietta's whereabouts. This is their latest report.'

'Ah, yes,' replied Assunta, adding with impatience, 'do they have news of our darling girl? Tell me swiftly, Isolda, for I am dying of suspense!'

I read the letter aloud – and with ever-growing despair . . .

' . . . *We have continued to make widespread inquiries throughout the Paris region, and beyond. In addition, we have instructed our associates in Belgium and Holland, Germany, Scandinavia and England, to pursue these inquiries into the whereabouts of Signorina Mazzini-Forsca. All to no avail. We can only surmise, dear Signorina, that your sister is beyond the reach of our inquiries, and regretfully state that we must consider the said inquiries to be closed. . . . '*

I met Assunta's horrified stare.

'Isolda, what does it mean?' she faltered.

'I think it means that they reckon Julietta to be dead,' I said flatly, 'and beyond the expertise of their agency to find. I suppose they must know their business.' I bowed my head and closed my eyes, but the tears found their way through and spilled down my cheeks.

'We mustn't despair, Isolda,' said the old woman. 'Our darling must be somewhere. She'll turn up, never fear.' Her frightened eyes betrayed the forced optimism.

'These people are experts, Assunta,' I said. 'They enlist the full co-operation of the local police forces. If they can't find Julietta, no one can.' I paused, and was prompted to add: 'Except perhaps Colonel Delamere.'

'Ah, that Colonel Delamere,' cried Assunta. 'He's a fine man, Isolda. You can trust him, mark my words. A tower of strength. Puts me in mind of my brother Aldo. God rest his soul.'

This was praise indeed, for dear old Assunta – a lifelong spinster whose only children had been Julietta and me –

114

had hero-worshipped her older brother Aldo, a fisherman drowned out in the lagoon on a night of storm.

I retired early that night, and it was just light enough to see clearly across the Grand Canal from my dressing-room window. Moored at the foot of a flight of steps was a small steam launch, the same as – or similar to – the one which I swore had followed us from the Lido to the Molo. And there, his face obscured from my clear view in the twilight, was surely the same cloaked figure of the mystery watcher, standing on the deck and looking straight across the canal towards my lighted window.

With trembling fingers I extinguished my light and drew the shutters. I then put my eye to the slats of the shutters and peered through.

The unknown watcher remained for a while, still regarding the dark window behind which his quarry lurked; but presently he moved away down the deck and entered a small wheelhouse behind the funnel. A few minutes later another man – a seaman I supposed – came out and unfastened the mooring lines.

The launch then slid away down the canal towards the point where the gilded sphere atop the Dogana marked the exit to the lagoon.

Three anxious days passed before I saw Jamie Delamere again. He arrived at the palazzo unannounced, bringing a nosegay of flowers for me and a box of French chocolates which he presented to Assunta with real old-world gallantry, kissing her hand and addressing her as 'gracious Signorina'. Dear Assunta blushed like a girl and retired to the kitchen with cheeks aflame. I rounded on Jamie with mock severity.

'I'll not have you suborning my staff, Sir,' I declared. 'Servants are hard enough to get, in all conscience – but to have one's own friends trying to entice them away. . . .

'Oh, Jamie,' I concluded, very near to breaking down, 'I am so glad, so very glad, to see you.'

'Trouble?' he asked.

I told him about the letter from the Paris inquiry agents.

He understood its import, well enough, but he was tactful.

'She may have gone to ground somewhere,' he said. 'Taken employment in some remote farmstead. Emigrated overseas, perhaps.'

'Or have died,' I said.

He must have gauged the depth of my misery, for he did not probe further. Instead, he changed the subject and asked me if I had seen any more of my mysterious watcher. I told him that I had.

'And I'm afraid he's beginning to get on my nerves,' I added.

'That's quite understandable,' he said. 'And psychologically quite normal – healthy, even. For a person *not* to react with the appropriate amount of controlled fear would suggest a mental abnormality. I well recall a case where. . . .'

His words did something to reassure me, but I was spared any clinical details by the arrival of Assunta with coffee. The dear old lady had also put a plate containing a selection of her French chocolates on the tray. We thanked her and she departed again.

'And what have you been doing these last three days, Jamie?' I asked him as I poured the coffee. 'And do you have any other news for me – good or bad?'

'I've been busy, as you'll hear, Isolda,' he replied. 'As to the news, some of it is bad, some of it intriguing, and some of it I can only describe as – sensational!'

'Then tell me, I beg you!' I cried. 'You can't imagine how my imagination has been running riot since we parted.'

He settled back in his seat, produced a cigar case, requested and received my permission, and proceeded to light a sizeable smoke. I watched him with ill-controlled impatience.

Presently he said, drawing upon the cigar in between phrases: 'My first visit was to . . . the caretaker Signora Agatha Bellini, whose highly imaginative . . . version of your conversation with Bruno . . . no doubt did much to . . . secure the verdict of . . . "Not Proven".'

'And how did you find her?' I demanded excitedly. 'And did she deny everything?'

By then he had got his cigar well alight and to his satisfaction. He regarded the glowing tip and frowned. 'I found that the bird had flown,' he said. 'Gone. Packed and gone, bag and baggage, her crippled husband with her — so her successor informed me.'

'Gone — to where?' I asked.

'I ran her to earth, with a little assistance from her successor,' he replied. 'Signora Bellini has greatly improved in fortune recently. From being an underpaid and overworked caretaker with a crippled husband to look after, she is now the owner of an exceedingly well-stocked grocery emporium in the vicinity of the Campo San Polo. And her husband is cared for by a living-in nursemaid.'

'But, Jamie,' I said, 'where did *she* get the money to set herself up in such style?'

'You may well ask, Isolda,' he replied. 'I put the question to the lady myself — and she threatened to call the police and have me thrown out. And she had no comment to make regarding the testimony that she gave at the trial of Isolda Mazzini-Forsca. On that subject, her lips are sealed. *Or have been sealed!*'

I closed my eyes and looked around inside my head. In sheer desperation, I called out: 'Jamie, what am I going to do? Who — *who* — is my secret enemy?'

He had no answer for me. Only a chill comfort.

'We'll come to the end of the road, never fear,' he said. 'And meanwhile, it's a stony road we tread, Isolda.

'After Signora Bellini, I sought out Poeta Longhi, formerly under-footman, who gave evidence of your leaving the chapel some time after the murder. His family, I learned, comes from Chioggia and like most folks there they are fishermen. When they learned that I was seeking Poeta, there was a discernible lowering of my welcome, despite the fact that I had taken along a bottle of *grappa* as a present and to loosen a few tongues. I had already discovered, you see, that Poeta had left Venice and its environs.

'It was with some difficulty that I got them to admit that he has emigrated to America.'

'*America?*' I echoed.

'He sailed from Genoa for New York less than a week after your trial,' said Jamie. 'Questioned as to how he had raised the fare money, they muttered something about him having saved it up. What used you to pay under-footmen in the old days, Isolda? Not a lot, I don't suppose.'

'He was bribed,' I murmured. 'Bribed to bear false witness against me.'

'Undoubtedly. And in a very convenient manner,' said my companion. 'For who's going to take the trouble to seek out and find one insignificant Italian boy in all of teeming New York?'

He took a long pull at his cigar and watched the exhaled smoke ascend to the ceiling of my sitting room. 'Do you want to hear more, Isolda?' he asked.

'I want to hear it all,' I replied. 'No matter how bad, I can't evade anything. I am not a very brave person, Jamie, but this I am beginning to learn – the moment I cease to endure, this thing will destroy me.'

As I said that, I seemed to hear again the words of the strange woman in the eerie shop, on my first excursion into the streets. . . .

' . . . *your only hope is to endure. That way only lies your salvation. If you give in, you are lost for ever and the grass will grow over your grave untended.* . . . '

Jamie nodded sombre agreement to my comment and said: 'After those two witnesses, I turned my attention to the men of the law. The prosecuting counsel I disregarded, for though he pursued you mercilessly, he remained within the limits of what a prosecutor may do to secure his conviction. Your own counsel was a different matter, for not only did he fall short in large matters, such as not introducing the fact that you are demonstrably physically incapable of lifting a grown man on to a high altar, and also made not the slightest attempt to search out the witnesses as to their credibility, but in small matters he antagonized the judge with his trifling interjections, and was remiss on several minor points of law. All this I checked, you see, from the transcript of the trial in the Veronese archives.'

'But, surely,' I said, 'no advocate would accept a bribe to deliberately conduct his client's defence so that he couldn't win?'

Jamie stroked his jaw in the manner which I was coming

to know so well – a sign that he was tussling with an unpalatable truth.

'I have not rejected the possibility,' he said at length.

'Oh, come, come!' I exclaimed, accompanying my words with a mirthless laugh that teetered on the edge of hysteria. 'Don't tell me that the eminent Signor Rispoli has also been set up in a prosperous grocery emporium!' I could have bitten off my tongue as soon as the gibe had left my lips. 'I'm sorry, Jamie,' I added with contrition. 'That remark was unworthy of us both.'

'You have every reason to be bitter, my dear,' was his mild response. 'As to Rispoli, it may well be that, like so many others, he also has his price. . . .' He paused.

'Yes?' I prompted him.

'I paid a flying visit to Milan yesterday,' he said, 'and sought an interview with the man in question – only to discover that the advocate is now a high court judge.'

'Oh, no!' I cried.

'And as such,' continued Jamie, 'is now beyond all criticism. Despite my applications for an interview, I was able to get no nearer the Honourable Signor Judge Rispoli than his secretary's assistant, who showed me the door after I was obliged to state the nature of my business with His Honour.'

I clenched my hands so tightly that the fingernails bit deeply into the palms – but I held on, and endured.

'I also made inquiries about your trial judge,' continued Jamie, 'more as a matter of course than in any hope that I would be allowed to see him. That evil old man, however, has passed beyond the compass of my questioning, and must now plead his innocence before a higher court than any of our devising. He died last month.'

Trapped! Trapped . . .

I paced the floor of my sitting room, back and forth, back and forth, with Jamie Delamere watching me in silent sympathy that was as warm and tangible as a cosy fire on a freezing cold day.

Trapped in a web of deceit, by a faceless enemy – or enemies. Tied hand and foot, by a concerted tissue of lies, in a verdict which set me apart for the rest of my life as an outcast. Scorned and shunned by my beloved sister as the murderer of the man who, by her own admission, she had loved as the brother she had never had.

And my only hope was this man, this stranger from over the sea, whose first, determined attempts to chart a path through the lies to the truth had met with such a disastrous response.

All things pass. Even my sudden mood of black despair subsided into mere irritation. I paused in mid-stride and smiled down at him as he remained seated there, smoking the last of his cigar.

'Don't think for one minute, Jamie, that I don't appreciate what you've done,' I told him. 'In my saner moments – and I have now thought myself into one of my saner moments – I realize that a lot of dead wood has to be cut away before we shall arrive at the truth.

'But tell me squarely, my friend,' I added, 'from where you are sitting now, can you put your finger on the motives behind Bruno's murder and my persecution? Can you give a name to the crime that has been committed?'

He shook his head. 'No I can't, Isolda,' he replied. 'At first, I had guessed it to be a crime of passion, but the more I hear of Bruno's character, the more he comes through to me as a charming, life-loving individual with a taste for mild flirtation, but an unswerving love for you. I don't think that the incident with Carlotta Salvatorelli and your supposed jealous reaction is the stuff of which crimes of passion are made, nor do I think that girls like poor little Carlotta drown themselves for a caprice.

'And that, Isolda,' he went on, 'brings me to a piece of information that came my way only last evening. And I believe it will totally demolish any suggestion that you murdered your fiancé in a jealous passion – at least, not over Carlotta.'

'And what is this piece of information, Jamie?' I asked eagerly.

'I thought back to a quartette of young girls who went together to their first grown-up ball,' he said.

'Carlotta, Zöe, Edda, and me,' I supplied.

'And all four chaperoned by Signora di Ventris.'

'Dear old Signora di Ventris,' I said. 'What a handful she must have thought us.'

'The signora is more capable, more shrewd, than you girls imagined,' said Jamie. 'I thought to go and visit her in her crumbling old family house on the Guidecca, where she lives all alone. It occurred to me that she might be able to shed a little light in a few dark corners. And so it was.

'For instance, she pooh-poohs the idea that you could possibly have killed Bruno. Says she, "That couple were as in love as any young couple could be – and if Bruno enjoyed the sight of a pretty face he never let it turn his head." '

'Good for her,' I said.

'If she spoke well of you,' said Jamie, 'she was less complimentary about Carlotta. According to her, that tragic girl gave birth to an unwanted child. The matter was hushed up by her family, the birth concealed, and the infant put out to foster parents.'

'Then who was the father? – Oh!' I faltered. 'It couldn't have been Bruno!' I stared at him, willing the answer I craved. . . .

I need not have doubted. He smiled and shook his head. 'No. Signora di Ventris was adamant that it was not Bruno,' he said, 'though she did admit that she could not put a name to the man. But, she added: "That flibbertigibbet Zöe Bonomi knows the father, for didn't Zöe act as go-between with them, arranging their rendezvous?"'

'You see what this means don't you, Isolda?' he said, seizing hold of my hands and eyeing me earnestly. 'Once we have established the truth of Signora di Ventris's story, the whole tissue of so-called evidence that the inquisitors of the Judicial Police fabricated against you concerning Bruno and Carlotta, your supposed jealousy, the interpretation that was put upon his so-called callous reaction to her drowning – all that is demolished!'

'I see it clearly,' I replied. 'So what next?'

'Zöe is in Rome at the moment,' he said, 'so an interview with her will have to wait. What I do have – and I got it out of Signora di Ventris on the promise that I would use the information only to help clear your name – is the identity of the woman who fostered Carlotta's unwanted child.'

121

Night. And a high moon over the lagoon.

Jamie had selected a gondolier known well to him, one who could be trusted in any eventuality. Our goal was the isle of Burano, which lies at the eastern end of the lagoon. Jamie had not wanted me to accompany him, but I had insisted. We sat together in the moonlight, with no sound but the gentle splash of the oar and the hiss of water under the craft's sharp stem. To our left, the lights of Murano, all ahead the humped shapes of the other islets of the archipelago: San Erasmo, San Francisco del Deserto, Mazzoroba, Torcello. A dog's bark from somewhere far off carried clearly over the still waters. I shivered and drew my grey cloak more warmly about my shoulders. It was a long row and most of it against the incoming tide that tended to carry us northwards. Our gondolier was flagging visibly by the time one was able to pick out the church of San Martino and scent the tang of the fishing nets hung out to dry along the dark harbour walls.

A last, deft flourish of his oar, and the gondolier brought us neatly alongside the jetty. Jamie handed me ashore.

'Which way, then, to Signora Gucci's house?' he demanded of the gondolier.

'Third turning on the left along the canal, Signor,' responded the other. 'Signora Gucci's is painted yellow, so you can't miss it. You want me to wait here, heh?'

'Yes, we shouldn't be long.'

'Be as long as you like, Signor.' The gondolier struck a light for his pipe and settled down in the seat. He obviously knew Jamie as a good payer.

Arm in arm my companion and I walked along the side of a narrow canal that cut into the island from the lagoon. Since Burano is given over almost entirely to the fishing occupation, the canal banks and the roadways above were lined with boats of all sizes, and the reek of the sea hung over all. We found the yellow-washed house down the third turning easily enough. Like the rest of the habitations to be seen, the place was in utter darkness, nor had we encountered a single living thing since we quit the gondola. Fisher-folk go to bed early.

Facing a low door set under an archway, Jamie muttered

in my ear. 'The signora will undoubtedly be in bed and none too pleased to be woken,' he said. 'You had better speak to her. A foreign-sounding voice will only convince her that she is about to be assaulted and robbed.' With that, he knocked briskly on the door.

Presently there came a voice from behind the shuttered window above. 'Who's there – what do you want?'

'It's a friend from Venice, Signora Gucci,' I replied. 'I've something important to ask you, and there's quite a lot of money involved.' This was the tempting formula which we had devised for persuading the woman to open up for us.

'Wait there,' came the reply. The formula appeared to have worked.

Minutes later the drawing of bolts and the grating of a key in a lock heralded the opening of the door – to disclose a woman of late middle age, dressed in what looked like a gunny sack, with her thin, grey hair in an untidy plait.

'Oh, there's two of you,' she said, with an eye to Jamie's height and bulk, and seemed to hesitate about letting us in.

'I have been instructed to pay you for your assistance, Signora,' said Jamie smoothly. And he mentioned a figure which would have kept a Burano fishing family for a year.

'Come in,' responded the woman.

By the light of the candle she carried we made our way down a narrow passage and into a vaulted, stone-built room that must once have served as living quarters for a large family. Our information was that the woman now lived alone and took in occasional foster infants. Well beyond the loom of the candle we could pick out an enormous open fireplace flanked by bread ovens, and a long refectory table occupied the centre of the room.

The woman set down the candle and motioned us to take seats, which we did.

'What's this help you're seeking, then?' she demanded, with more than a touch of suspicion.

Jamie was all suavity. 'Signora, you have been recommended to our friends as a lady to be entrusted with the care of a new-born baby,' he said. 'Is that so?'

'Aye, I've fostered a few in my time,' she replied. 'After my husband was lost at sea and all my lot had left to get

123

married. So your – *friends* – want me to foster their baby, eh?' And she cast me a sidelong glance that was all speculation.

'That is so,' replied Jamie, 'and they are willing to pay handsomely for the service. However. . . .' he paused.

'What's the catch, then?' demanded the woman sourly. 'There's always a catch when it comes to talking about big money.' She gave me another penetrating look, taking in my silk-lined cloak, my Paris-made gloves.

'There is no – catch – Signora,' replied Jamie. 'It's just that our friends, being of the very highest social standing in Venice, naturally want the very best for the child, and are willing to pay accordingly.'

The candlelight mercilessly revealed the flash of avarice that illuminated the woman's uncomely countenance, and her close-set eyes narrowed. 'For the right money, I provide a child with all the care and attention it could find in its own mother's arms,' she said. 'Why, haven't I fostered infants from some of the best people in Venice and all around?'

'I'm pleased to hear you say that, Signora,' purred Jamie. 'And our friends will be pleased also. However. . . .'

'Yes? . . .' The suspicious look came into the woman's face again.

'Our friends would be happier if they could have some kind of assurance,' said Jamie. 'Some form of recommendation, perhaps. . . .' he sketched a vague shape in the air.

'I've told you that I've taken in babies from some of the very best people,' snapped the woman. 'But I'm naming no names!'

'That is a pity,' said the other. 'I would have thought that, for a promise of complete discretion, plus a handsome fee . . .' and he named a figure that was in advance of the previous offer.

The woman softened at once. One felt that her protests of discretion were somewhat over-stated. 'I'll give you one name as a recommend,' she said. 'No more.'

'From a high-born family,' prompted Jamie. 'None of your merchants' or shopkeepers' offsprings – but a child of the nobility.'

124

'You shall have a name,' said the woman. 'First – the money.'

Jamie counted out a handful of coins and gave them to the woman, who examined each and every one, and then hid them somewhere in her voluminous apparel.

'Is it new-born, this babe?' she asked. 'The one I'm to foster, I mean.'

'It's not yet born,' said Jamie – with some truth.

'Ah,' muttered she, and cast another speculative glance in my direction.

'If I might please have the name in question – to reassure our friends,' he prompted her.

'The mother's name I never knew,' said Signora Gucci. 'The father of the infant, when he brought it here, gave me his name and an address where I was to send a message if the babe lacked for anything.'

Jamie and I exchanged a swift glance. The moment was upon us!

'I had use for the same,' went on the woman, 'for, by Our Lady, didn't the little creature fall ill within the week, and die that same day.'

'The baby's dead?' I exclaimed. And was this, indeed, Carlotta's unwanted infant?

The woman gave me a hostile, defensive stare. 'It was not for lack of care and attention that the little mite departed,' she cried. 'And I informed the father straightway. Though I'm no scholar, and had to get my friend Signora Tossi to write a note, which I had delivered to the signor in the care of a certain number at the postal office in Venice. But I had no reply. Still, I was well paid, and there was enough to bury the poor mite, and a bit over for a Mass.'

'And the man to whom you sent the note, Signora?' demanded Jamie.

'I remember it well, now that I come to think,' said Signora Gucci slowly. 'Number fifteen, it was. Box fifteen, the Postal Office, Venice. . . .'

'And the name?'

'Such a gentleman he was, sir,' said the woman. 'The likes of yourself, though not a foreigner like yourself – no offence intended. And younger than you by ten years, I shouldn't

125

wonder. Such fine clothes. Handsome as the picture of the Blessed San Sebastiano in our church.'

'His name, woman!' barked Jamie.

'The name he gave me was – Signor Bruno,' said she.

'Signor *Bruno?*'

We were silent for most of the way back to Venice. Not till we had rounded the point, and the light of the Dogana came into view, did Jamie lay a gentle arm across my shoulders. He may, or may not, have been aware that I had been quietly weeping all the way from Burano, but he had not imposed upon my misery till then – for which I was profoundly grateful.

'It may be all a mistake, Isolda,' he said. 'We have only the word of a grasping woman, or that of a man who was only out to deceive, and hide his tracks.'

'I've told myself that a hundred times in the last hour or so, Jamie,' I replied. 'But it makes no difference. Don't you see? I'm tired of living on hope. Hope, like apples stored too long in a loft, grows stale. Ever since Bruno's murder, I've been telling myself that what they have been trying to prove about me is all lies, and what they have been saying about Bruno is all lies. I have lived in hope of the truth all this time – save for when they broke my spirit for a short while and I gave way and signed that confession. But now I think that I've been wrong all this while. You know the saying – "Where there's smoke there's fire." The prosecutor quoted it at my trial. Perhaps they've been right all this time. Perhaps Bruno was more than just flirtatious. Perhaps my jealousy was more powerful than I have led myself to believe. I just don't know!

'But, don't you see? – I'm tired of hoping!

'Now it seems to have been proved at last. Don't make me hope any more, Jamie. I don't want to be a case history in your psychological inquiries!

'Let the dead rest in peace!

'And let me be!'

He escorted me to the water gate of the palazzo, but did not offer to come in, nor did I invite him. We parted company without a word.

The next day and the day following passed like a dream from which there was no awakening. Assunta's eyes followed me everywhere with an expression of anguish, but she said nothing. No probing. No attempts to cheer me up. I was grateful to her.

For sleepless nights and timeless days, I wandered through the desolate rooms of the palazzo, so redolent of memories from days gone past and never to return. And ate my heart out.

On the evening of the second day, when the market boats were coming back down the Grand Canal after a hard day's work, empty now save for the tired vendors and their families, their dogs and their full purses – I had a visitor.

'Such a nice gentleman,' said Assunta. 'He says his name is Signor Lippi, and that you and he are old acquaintances.'

'I know no one by that name, Assunta,' I replied. 'And I really don't want to see anyone today. Please give him my compliments and tell him I'm indisposed.'

She took my hand. 'My girl,' she said, 'I haven't interfered with you, nor pushed myself forward, these last couple of days, but I can guess – knowing you as I do – that something very much out of the ordinary is disturbing you, and I don't doubt but that you'll confide it to your old Assunta when you feel ready. Meantime, why not see Signor Lippi? He strikes me as being just the sort of kindly gentleman who might take you out of yourself, as the saying goes. How about it?' And she patted my cheek, as she had done for as long as I can remember.

'All right, I'll receive your Signor Lippi,' I told her indulgently.

She went out the door and was soon back, with the figure of a man silhouetted against the light coming from beyond.

'Signor Lippi, Signorina,' intoned Assunta formally.

He came into the room. His smile was just as I remembered it. 'Good day, Signorina,' he purred. 'It has been so long.'

It was my second interrogator. He who had twisted my mind and seduced me into signing the false confession which, later, I had found the strength of will to renounce. The same splendid profile, the mane of silvery hair, the academic stoop that hinted at long hours spent in scholarly pursuits, but, most of all, there was that voice – warm and gentle, caressing, like that of a wise and beloved counsellor.

'Thank you, Assunta. You can go,' I said coldly. And I regretted the order and the manner of its delivery as soon as I saw the sudden puzzled hurt in her dear face. How could she – with her simple, uncomplicated trust – have discerned the viper that was hidden behind the mask of the sweet-faced cripple?

Alone with him, I leapt to the attack as the best form of defence against – whatever he might have in store for me.

'Why have you come here?' I demanded. 'Haven't you had enough? My trial is over and my reputation destroyed. There's no more you can do. Say what you have to say – be brief about it – and then go!'

He smiled – again that mild and gentle smile. 'Certainly, Signorina. But first, if only out of regard for my infirmity, won't you invite me to sit down?'

In one phrase, he had put me at a moral disadvantage. Quietly cursing myself for having fallen into the trap of discourtesy, I motioned him to a seat – well away from the one which I took for myself.

He watched me for a while, his head on one side, a slight smile playing upon his exceedingly mobile lips. Waiting for me to make the first move, as, presently, I was driven to do out of sheer suspense.

'Well?' I said. 'Why are you here, Signor?'

The finely-modelled face with its overtones of suffering sketched a brief, sad smile. 'I had hoped for a better reception from you, Signorina,' he said. 'After all, a very considerable degree of mutual sympathy and understanding grew up during our talks together, did it not?'

My hackles rose at that. 'How can you be so hypocritical?' I cried. 'You deceived me into trusting you and took advantage of my anguish, my sleeplessness, and the fact that I was half out of my mind with anxiety, to bend my will the way you wanted it to go. Can you call *that* sympathy and understanding?'

He made a dismissive gesture with his slim and elegant hand.

'My dear Signorina Mazzini-Forsca,' he said, 'I was only doing my duty, and the outcome of our discussions finally led to your verdict of "Not Proven" – which was the right and proper verdict. In every sense you were responsible for the death of your affianced. The only doubt remaining is the *degree* to which you were responsible.'

'*How* was I responsible?' I demanded.

'By your insane jealousy,' he replied.

I caught my breath. 'Jealous, you mean, of my fiancé's conduct?' I demanded. And I felt myself to be treading on shifting ground, remembering what Jamie and I had learned from the woman on Burano.

'Jealous of the conduct of a libertine,' said Lippi. 'A man whose degenerate life was given over to the pursuit of fleshly delights, and who found the perfect partner in the late Signorina Carlotta Salvatorelli – mother of his child.'

I drew a sharp breath. My thoughts must have been plainly written all over my face for him to read.

Again that smile. 'Yes, Signorina,' he purred, 'thanks to the lead given us by the excellent Colonel Delamere, we also now know of the infant that was once fostered by Signora Gucci of Burano!'

I watched, unable to speak, as he smoothly explained. . . .

'Our attention was drawn to the excellent colonel from the very first. You must know, Signorina, that you have seldom been out of our surveillance since the trial. Your meeting on the Molo, when the American gallantly rescued you from a most embarrassing situation, the charade he played out in Florian's, early signs that he was appointing himself your knight-errant – all these events were witnessed by our agents.

'Delamere's futile attempts to discredit the witnesses at your trial – that was sheer folly. But, when upon no more than a vague intuition that you would lead us to something, I authorized that you were to be followed across the lagoon that night, we had cause to bless the American's shrewdness.

'Yes, Signorina. It was through him that, like you, we learned of the child and its parentage.

'And I should tell you' – here his voice, usually so smooth, took on a harsh, unaccustomed edge – 'I should point out that, if we had had this proof of Ferrara's behaviour at your trial, the prosecutor would have had no difficulty in persuading the jury it was your jealousy that guided the hand which drove the dagger into his heart.

'And there could have been only one verdict possible . . . '*Guilty!*'

Eight

Signor Lippi of the Judicial Police regarded me keenly for a while, no doubt weighing up, in his subtle and twisted mind, what exact effect his words had had upon me. I suffered his attention with as calm a manner as I was able to put on. Presently, when I had collected myself, I faced him squarely.

'What possible use is it for you to keep on persecuting me?' I demanded. 'I remember the judge's words at my trial. The verdict allowed me to go free, yet carrying the taint of guilt for the rest of my life. Isn't that enough – can't you be satisfied with ruining me? Must you hound me, day and night, for as long as I live?'

The tired, gentle face took on a smile that was almost loving when he replied. 'Signorina, I am concerned for justice,' he said. 'And justice demands that you must pay for the taking of a life – as I believe to be the case, and as I was once able to convince you, yourself, however briefly.

'You say that you remember the judge's words. Do you not remember that he said you could not be tried again – *save in most exceptional circumstances?*'

Fascinated by his searching eyes, as a rabbit is allured by a snake's unwavering stare, I nodded. Yes, I recalled the words, if with some difficulty – but they had meant nothing to me at the time.

'The most exceptional circumstances,' continued Lippi, 'might include a case where the accused person's guilt later came to light in additional evidence so overwhelming as to scream out for a re-trial. In which case the intervention of the Italian Senate with an Order in Council would enable

131

justice to be seen to be done: A re-trial by order of the Senate!'

Could this happen to me? Could the whole grisly business be gone through all over again? The crowded courtroom, with the di Rollos and their like crowding the favoured seats in the public gallery, the mumbling clerks, the judge and advocates in their flowing gowns, the reek of excited humanity, the endless questions, the eternal lies. . . .

'No!' I cried out aloud. 'No – they couldn't do that!'

'That's how it will be,' purred Lippi of the Judicial Police. 'You and your friend will not rest till you have dug out every piece of evidence relating to the murder of Count Bruno Ferrara, and we shall be following in your footsteps. Piece by piece, we together will unravel the tangled web surrounding the life and death of your fiancé.'

'And discover the truth!' I cried.

He smiled. 'We'll all discover the truth,' he said. '*And the truth will destroy you!*'

With that he rose to his feet. Leaning heavily upon his walking-stick, he regarded me, head on one side, a smile on his face that one could have sworn denoted only benevolence.

'Why did you not stand by your written confession?' he asked gently. 'Why now, even at this late stage, do you not confess all and throw yourself upon the mercy of the court, repenting your crime before God and before man?'

'Never!' I cried. 'Signor, I am glad you came here today. Before you came, my spirits were at their very lowest. I had quite given up hope and wanted only to creep into a dark corner and cover my head with sacking. Thanks for your visit. You've given me the will to fight back again.' I faced him out, confident and triumphant. Inspired by the return of my courage.

If Lippi was dismayed by the effect that his visit had had upon me, he did not show it. The gentle smile remained, likewise the mild-eyed gaze that was half-pity, half-affection.

'I am sorry for you, Signorina,' he said. 'You are doomed to destruction. You rush towards it as a bride to her wedding. If only I could convince you that your only hope of peace in this world and the next is to confess everything, all my efforts would not be in vain.'

132

The man's hypocrisy, knowing it as I did, had no power to persuade me. Though his very persistence earned my grudging respect.

'Goodbye, Signor Lippi,' I said. 'Again, I thank you for coming to see me. But – I beg you – don't bother to come again.'

He bowed to me, and the smile never left his face.

'Good night to you, Signorina Mazzini-Forsca,' he said. 'Pray don't trouble to rise. I will see myself out, or your excellent Assunta will perform that service.' He went to the door and opened it. On the threshold he turned to regard me again. I had the sudden premonition that he was about to deliver a parting shot. I was not mistaken.

'Speaking of Assunta,' he murmured, 'are you aware that your faithful servant and former nursemaid knows all about the baby who was fostered by Signora Gucci, and has known all the time?

'You look surprised. But you must remember that Assunta comes from Burano, and the fisher-folk of Burano have no secrets from each other. They are all related, anyhow, one side of the blanket or the other.

'Good night again, Signorina.'

He left me.

'Is it true, Assunta – have you known all this while without saying a word to me?'

There was something in her eyes that I had never seen before. Defiance? I could not tell. She was certainly near to tears, and her voice was close to breaking as she answered me.

'Isolda, my dearest . . .' she began.

'I think,' I interposed, 'that I should prefer you to address me correctly as "Signorina" till you have properly explained yourself.'

The tears now fell fast down her wrinkled cheeks. 'It's true,' she said brokenly. 'Alicia Gucci told my cousin Isadora, who passed it on to my niece Maria, who told me. Yes, Count Bruno it was, who brought the babe one night to Alicia Gucci, admitted that he was the father of the child, gave her much money, and never came near again.'

133

'And when was this?' I demanded, and could scarcely believe that it was I who was so calmly conducting this harsh interrogation. 'Was it before our betrothal ceremony?'

'It was after the ceremony – ah – Signorina,' she whispered.

'*After!*'

I closed my eyes and saw again the image of the two of us – Bruno and me – in the candle-lit, incense-laden gloom of the great cathedral, with the Cardinal Archbishop's sonorous voice intoning the sacred vows for us to repeat. . . .

'I, Bruno Hubertus Ferrara, do hereby solemnly plight my troth and promise marriage to you, Isolda Maria Violetta. . . .'

'How *long* after?' I demanded, shattering the image.

'It was – a few weeks only after the betrothal, Signorina,' whispered Assunta.

A few weeks only. Then Carlotta must have been carrying the child – *his* child – at the time when he stood before the high altar of San Marco and vowed in chastity to the promise of marriage.

'Why didn't you tell me?' I asked her. 'Why – even after he was murdered?

'Was it because? . . .' I stared at her in dawning horror of realization. '*Because you thought that I had, indeed, killed him?*'

The woman's guilty conscience was written all over her countenance, streaming tears as she was, heartbroken as she so very clearly was.

'You pretended to believe that I was innocent,' I said. 'You kept from me the fact that you, yourself, knew why I might well have murdered my betrothed out of jealous fury!

'Why, oh, why, Assunta?'

She fell on her knees before me, took the hem of my dress between her toil-roughened fingers and pressed it to her lips.

'I would have done anything for you,' she whispered. 'When I found out that he – Count Bruno – had done that cruel, evil thing and made his vow before God with the sin on his soul, I would have lied, and lied, and lied for you. Even if you had killed and I know in my heart, now, that you hadn't – I would have given my all to protect you.'

134

'Oh, Assunta – Assunta, my dearest!' Stooping, I helped her back to her feet and embraced her. The skinny old arms wrapped themselves round my shoulders and the thin, tear-streaked cheek was pressed against my cheek. 'I'm sorry I was so harsh with you.'

'That wicked, wicked man,' she whispered against my ear. 'I wouldn't have blamed you if you *had* killed him.

'If I had known then what I know now,' she added – and her voice took on an edge of violence that I would never have believed her to be capable of – 'if I had known then, I would have killed him with my own hand for what he did to my darling girl!'

Looking over her shoulder, I met my own reflection in the mirror opposite, and saw the look of sudden, horrified thought that sprang to my mind at her astonishing declaration.

'Do you *really* think that Assunta killed Bruno out of love for you?'

Jamie was with me. I had summoned him in a brief note by hand of messenger to the Danieli, and told him of Lippi's visit and what had come after.

'No, I don't,' I replied. 'Not really. We know that it would have been physically impossible for her to have carried it out. But, Jamie, the will was there – she would have done it, given the opportunity. And that's what worries me – the hatred and violence which surrounds this whole terrible affair.'

He looked at me in that thoughtful, piercing way he had. 'But you no longer want to sweep the whole thing under the carpet and forget about it,' he said. And it was not a question. 'That's why you sent for me, I guess. What changed your mind? Was it what Assunta said?'

'That was the last straw,' I admitted. 'But Lippi really shocked me out of my apathy. His sneering announcement that if you and I carried on searching for the truth we should end up by providing him with the certain evidence of my guilt – that's why I asked you to come.'

He smiled. 'And I'm glad you did, Isolda,' he said. 'Bully for you, lady!'

I thought for a moment, and said: 'Jamie, I'm entirely in your hands. You are in charge. What do we do now? And I will go anywhere, do anything, to settle this thing. Clear my name. Make my peace with Julietta if she still lives. Confound Lippi, the Judicial Police, all Venice, the di Rollos and all.'

He walked away to the balcony window and looked out across the Grand Canal. I watched him: a four-square figure, broad of shoulder and tall of frame. The sort of man, half way between the oak who stands against the storm and the aspen who yields a little against its fury.

'The child is the key,' he said at length.

'Carlotta's baby.'

'Yes, Isolda. This thing will be solved only when the paternity of the baby has been proved. I'm convinced of it. Yes, I once scorned the idea that Bruno's murder was a crime of passion. I'm not so sure now. It now looks to me as if the murder was either a crime of passion – committed, say, by another of Carlotta's lovers who found out about the baby. Or, it was a crime of revenge, carried out by a member of the girl's family. And, by the way, the Salvatorellis originally hailed from Sicily – and you know about the Sicilian code of vendetta. . . .'

He had not turned round as he spoke, but still continued to look out across the canal and down to the lights that bent towards the lagoon.

'So?' I said. 'What next?'

'The key to the child's paternity is Zöe Bonomi,' he said. 'According to Signora di Ventris, Zöe and Carlotta were inseparable throughout the time that Carlotta was carrying the baby, so it's inconceivable that the poor girl – no doubt alienated from her family and not knowing what was going to happen to her – didn't confide everything in her friend.'

'Including the name of the father,' I said.

'Exactly.' He turned to face me. 'Isolda, we must go and question Zöe,' he said. 'If she gives us a name other than Bruno's, we have the name of the man who impersonated Bruno when he took the baby to Burano. We also have a name which will lead us to the conspiracy surrounding Bruno's murder. Or so I believe.'

136

'Zöe is in Rome,' I said.

'Then Rome it is,' he said. 'Could you leave at short notice?'

'I can leave now – tonight!' I replied without hesitation.

He smiled. 'That won't be necessary. Tomorrow will do. Tomorrow early, and, if we can catch the connections, we should be in Rome by late afternoon.'

'You have Zöe's address, of course.'

'Yes, she's staying on the Appian Way with her family.' His eager eyes sought mine, and if ever I had any doubt, I knew then that this man could not have been more involved in my troubles if they had been his own. 'Think of it, Isolda – within a day or so, we may well have a name – and the key to the mystery of Bruno's murder.'

'Yes!' I sensed the anticipation of blessed release.

'But – Isolda. . . .' His expressive countenance took on a more sombre look.

'Yes?'

'While anticipating the best, you must be ready to accept the worst,' he said. 'If Zöe declares Bruno to have been the father of the child after all – shall you be able to bear it?'

I searched my mind, took stock of what I had – and could only reach a compromise with myself.

'I don't know, Jamie,' I replied slowly. 'The knowledge that Bruno deceived me might hurt me very deeply. I shall just have to wait and see, shan't I?

'But whatever happens, I am going to Rome.'

It was mid-morning. Bologna and the great plain of northern Italy were behind us. Florence was only two hours' journey ahead, and the train was climbing the foothills of the lordly Apennines. The marshes and rice fields of the plain had given way to barren hill farms, where whitewashed hovels clung to the steep slopes, their chimneys trailing thin plumes of smoke to the cerulean sky. And the far peaks were tipped with whiteness against the summer sun.

We had a carriage to ourselves. Jamie was seated opposite me, looking more like an Englishman in his London tweeds, a silk necktie banding his muscular throat and secured through a gold ring.

'Do you know Florence?' he asked.

'In fact, I lived there,' I replied. 'My father served in the army during the unrest that led up to the unification of Italy, and he was military commander of the city. We had an apartment in the Lungàrno Acciaioli overlooking the river. Assunta used to wheel me in my bassinet to the gardens of the Pitti Palace.'

'The Acciaioli, I knew it well,' he said. 'By the Ponte Vecchio. Has it changed much, I wonder?'

'Florence will never change.'

'I suppose not. If it outlived the Renaissance and the Borgias, it will survive the unification.'

Small talk . . . small talk. . . .

'Do you think we were followed?' I blurted out the thought that had been uppermost in my mind since we left Venice.

'We took great precautions against it,' he reminded me. 'Remember that we left separately and never met up till we were well clear of the city. Your heavy veiling, the fact that you discarded that conspicuous pink duster coat in the lounge of the Danieli and left there all in grey. As for me – what flatfoot would recognize an honest son of Boston, Massachusetts behind a Harris tweed suit, a deerstalker hat, and a monocle stuck in his eye?'

He reached across and squeezed my hands. I smiled at his reassurances, and felt more secure, even though the image of Signor Lippi was not so easily dismissed.

'Florence – this is Florence. All change for Pisa, Rome and the south!'

We alighted in the busy station yard, carrying only our light hand-luggage. While Jamie was seeking out a cab I looked about me at the crowds bustling to and fro in the busy concourse. Any one of them could have been an agent of the Venetian Judicial Police: the countryman in his blue smock carrying the squeaking piglet under one arm, the tall-hatted city gentleman on his way to the Stock Exchange, the straw-hatted young *flâneur* with his whangee walking-cane – which of these was in the pay of Lippi?

Jamie came back with a one-horse cab, which he directed to take us to the Piazza Signoria where good restaurants

138

abound. We had three hours to wait for our connection for Rome, and the leisure to enjoy a protracted meal outdoors in the sunshine of Europe's loveliest city. Disregarding the poigant errand upon which we were bound, and the added fear that we were being followed all the way, I was in a situation in which most women would have envied me. All this – and with a most attractive male for escort.

We selected a restaurant just off the square that had tables set in sunshine and shade. We chose one that partook of both, under a spreading lime tree. Jamie selected our menu. I recall it still – spaghetti with tomato sauce, ribs of beef in the Florentine manner, followed by cheeses, and a strawberry and orange dessert.

It was during the second course that I became uneasily aware of a pair of eyes that drifted every so often in my direction, and remained looking at me for longer than mere chance or curiosity warranted. I bore with it for a little while, not wanting to appear over-emotional to my companion, but presently I whispered to him: 'There's a man sitting alone two tables away, behind you and to your right – don't look now! – I think he's watching us.'

Jamie waited a while till I alerted him, and gave a swift glance behind when the object of my fears had turned his head to address a waiter.

'Powerful-looking fellow,' was his comment. 'If he is one of Lippi's agents and it ever came to a fight between us, he would give me a hard tussle, I reckon. Keep half an eye on him, Isolda. But don't let him see that you're worried.'

Thanks to the presence of the staring stranger, the meal, which should have been a delight and a blessed respite from the constant pressures of my plight, was sadly spoilt. I found myself hurrying through the dessert, anxious to be away from that brooding stare and in the train to Rome.

'Is he still looking this way?' murmured Jamie as he settled the bill.

'Yes, he has been for the last five minutes,' I murmured.

'We'll fire a shot across his bows when we leave,' was my companion's cryptic comment.

The mystery watcher had made no preparations to follow us, though it must have been apparent that we were about to go. When Jamie rose and presented me with his arm, the man continued to fork food into his mouth.

Our exit into the square took us past his table, and my heart missed a beat when Jamie slowed down close by the man's chair and addressed him with forced affability.

'Do be so good as to give our kind regards to Signor Lippi when you send in your report,' he said.

'Signor?' The man turned his head towards us, puzzlement written all over his face.

'Get a good look at us, did you?' said my companion with a heavy overtone of menace.

The reply, when it came, struck us both to confusion:

'I would find the greatest difficulty in so doing, Signor,' responded the stranger in mild tones. 'You see, I am almost totally blind.'

We departed in considerable embarrassment.

But we had not heard the last of the blind man of the Piazza Signoria. . . .

It may have been the warmth of the sun, the wine I had had at luncheon, or maybe the feeling of release after the suspenseful circumstances of our meal, but I nodded off to sleep shortly after our train steamed out of Florence, and I woke up with my head on Jamie's shoulder.

'Oh, I'm so sorry,' I apologized. 'Have I been asleep? It must have been terribly uncomfortable for you.'

'It was,' he replied, grave-faced, 'but I bore it with my usual fortitude. They breed hard men in Massachusetts.' He looked out of the window and I could have sworn he smiled. 'Won't be long now,' he said. 'I suggest we go straight to the hotel, have some tea, and then plan the rest of the evening. There is no point in seeking out Zöe tonight. Best leave it till the morning.'

'Where shall we stay?' I asked.

'There's the Hotel Barberini, which is in the Piazza Colonna, near the Quirinale,' he replied. 'I have a suite permanently booked there while I'm in Italy. You can have it, Isolda, and I'll have them fix me up with a room and a bath. We'll be arriving in ten minutes.'

Having said that, he turned his gaze to the passing scenery

140

of the Roman campagna, with its lush pastures, tidy farm-steads, broad parklands and elegant villas. I studied his averted profile and wondered, not for the first time, about this man of such independent means that he was able to wander the world at will, reserving suites for himself in the smart hotels of Europe, turning his mind to whatever whim took his fancy.

Playing knight-errant to damsels in distress. . . .

Presently we were steaming into the Eternal City, drawn by our iron chariot past the crumbling monuments of a civilization that had once held the known world to ransom.

'Rome! This is Rome! End of the line!'

The Hotel Barberini was all one might have imagined an establishment patronized by Jamie Delamere to be. Our arrival at its plate-glass door was a signal for the entire staff of the front hall, the manager, under manager and their acolytes to gather in welcome.

'Good afternoon, Colonel Delamere. How are you, Signor? Your suite is ready, as always. . . .'

At Jamie's instructions I was escorted to a splendid suite comprising bedroom and dressing room, lounge and bath-room. My companion also instructed a page to attend outside my door and, when I was ready, to show me the way to the roof garden for tea.

He was waiting for me when I arrived up there, and rose to his feet at my appearance.

'Like it, Isolda?' he asked, gesturing at the view over the balustraded parapet, which embraced a magnificent vista of the River Tiber from the church of Santa Maria del Popolo to the north, along the curving sweep past Castel Sant' Angelo, Saint Peter's and the Vatican, down to the pantiled roofs of Trastevere to the south.

'It's wonderful!' I enthused. 'Wonderful. And this garden, Jamie, what a delight.'

It was indeed. The entire flat roof of the hotel was set out as a replica of a Renaissance garden, reminiscent of Tivoli, with fountains playing and pale statuary gesticulating amongst the drifting spray. Mature trees and bushes aflame with semi-tropical blooms bedazzled the eyes, and grapes as

141

black as night hung in profusion from subtle trellis-work above our heads.

'Here comes the tea,' said my companion. 'Afterwards, I suggest we separate for a couple of hours. I have some business – not connected with our present enterprise – with my lawyer in the city. You would probably like to take the opportunity for a rest after the long journey, Isolda. Shall we meet up here for a pre-dinner aperitif at, say, eight o'clock exactly?'

I agreed. Eight o'clock it should be. We then had tea – cucumber sandwiches, scones and cream, cakes – after the English manner which was considered to be so smart in Rome.

We spoke of this and that, making no mention of the quest which had brought us to the Eternal City, but simply taking a quiet delight in each other's company.

In view of what was to follow, that tea-time was especially memorable to me. Everything that goes before that time has been altered out of all recognition in my mind, and I see everything that has come after through new eyes.

I bathed in a sunken pool set in the middle of the marble floor of my bathroom. The taps were of gold and the tiles were Etruscan, I think. It was the kind of luxury which I – who had lived almost all my life in a crumbling Venetian palazzo – had seldom experienced. We boasted a Tiepolo ceiling at the Palazzo Mazzini-Forsca, but all the bath water had to be heated in the kitchens and carried upstairs by hand to a vast, portable copper bathtub, which did daily service in everyone's dressing room.

Bathed, I changed into a *tissu d'or* dinner gown and a shawl of silver thread. Long used to dressing my hair myself, I bound it into a chignon with a silver fillet which had belonged to my grandmother. The French clock on the chimneypiece in the sitting room rang the hour of eight when I took a last look at myself in a pier-glass and went up to the roof garden.

One look, a few strides across the tiled floor of the roof garden, told me that my assignation with Jamie had been

142

badly chosen. To begin with, there was no one else to be seen. The fountains were silent, and a stillness lay over all.

It was also quite cold. I had forgotten that, due to my illness on the Brenta, much of the summer had passed me by unregarded. The touch of autumnal chill hung in the night air. Small wonder that the clientele of the luxurious Barberini Hotel preferred to take their aperitifs in the comfort of the heated rooms below. Furthermore, though dusk was giving way to night, the Chinese lanterns that were strung between the trees and along the overhead trellis-work had not been lit.

I shivered, drew my shawl more closely about my shoulders, and hoped that my companion would not be long in coming to join me and escort me downstairs.

Some minutes passed. No sign of Jamie. I had decided that my best course was to go downstairs and perhaps wait for him in the front hall when I distinctly heard footfalls at the far end of the garden, coming from behind a high yew hedge that lined the centre pathway.

By his sound, the unseen newcomer was clearly a man – and he whistled quietly between his teeth.

'Who's that?' I called out in a voice that sounded quite unlike my own, being sharp, and inflected with a note of anxiety.

There was no answer – but the footsteps ceased.

I forced myself to stay calm. It was possibly a waiter, I told myself, come up to the roof garden on some errand, and as surprised as I to encounter an unseen someone from out of the darkness.

Then why did he not respond?

It seemed to me the most prudent course was to walk quickly and unconcernedly towards the door at the head of the stairs leading down from the roof. Then I realized that to do so I should have to walk down the centre pathway beyond the yew hedge – and that meant I would most certainly encounter the whistling man who had not answered my call. Who, moreover, was now not only silent, but standing still. . . .

I suppose that, in a state of fear, one's natural instinct is to shrink back against something, some bastion to have at one's back as a protection of attack from the rear. I found myself pressed against the balustraded parapet and looking back into the dark garden for the first sign – if any – of the intruder.

I was posed like this, tense and still and straining my eyes to pierce the by now quite considerable darkness, when from out of the shadows to my left there burst a hurtling figure!

Before I had time to draw breath for a scream, he was upon me. An explosion of impact, and I was reeling back with the creature's hands about my throat and his warm breath fanning my face.

I struggled for my life, as I felt those powerful hands bearing me back against the balustrade, forcing my head and shoulders over the rough stonework towards the abyss beyond. At first, my instinct led me to try to pull away the hands that were choking out my life, but I quickly sensed that this was futile – so I reached out instead and raked the dark face looming above me, and felt my fingernails scoring skin and flesh. The man screamed like a wounded animal, momentarily relaxed his grip on my throat and enabled me to gulp a life-giving mouthful of air, just as I was beginning to slip away into unconsciousness.

The respite was brief. Pain and fury adding power to his resolve, my would-be murderer released my throat and, taking a grip about my waist, commenced to lift me bodily over the balustrade.

Five storeys below, the granite pavement of the Piazza Colonna beckoned me to my tomb.

I screamed. His hand came over my mouth, choking off the sound.

And then – blessedly, from out of the darkness of the garden, someone was calling my name. . . .

'Isolda – *where are you?*'

Instantly, the death grip was relaxed. My assailant backed away from me. I saw his dark profile raised to listen.

The call was repeated. . . .

'Isolda – answer me!'

'Jamie, I'm here!' I cried.

Next moment, the man who would have killed me was

gone – vanished back into the silent darkness from which he had come.

I stood upright, just as Jamie Delamere's tall figure came towards me round the hedge. He moved quickly enough to catch me before I fell.

I could have been unconscious for only a few seconds. When I swam back into the world of reality Jamie was laying me down on a seat which stood only a few feet from the scene of my assault. He chafed my hands and softly patted my cheek – it was these gentle ministrations which had aroused me.

'Are you all right, Isolda – in pain – anything?'

I supposed that he was concerned in case my attacker had employed some kind of weapon against me. I shook my head.

'No – all he – all he tried to do was to throw me over the balustrade. And, if you hadn't come when you did. . . .' Relief giving way to sudden realization, I was choked to silence at the awfulness of it.

'Thank God I arrived in the nick of time,' he said. 'I was late, you see, because my cab was held up by a religious procession in the square.

'A few moments later – or less! . . .'

We exchanged glances in the shadowy light of a newly-risen moon.

'I'll take you below,' said Jamie, helping me to my feet. 'A stiff cognac will set you up, but I don't suppose you'll be equal to dinner in a crowded restaurant. However, we'll see how . . .

'Hell!' he exclaimed. 'Look what's here. . . .'

Stooping, he picked up an object which was lying close by the place of my recent assault, and held it out in his hand. It appeared to be a semi-circle of dull metal pierced with what I took to be four finger-holes.

'What – what *is* it, Jamie?' I faltered. The thing had an indefinable look of menace.

He drew a deep breath and exhaled slowly before he replied.

'In the part of the Boston dockland where sensible folk

145

don't wander around alone after dark,' he said, 'they call this devilish little weapon a knuckle-duster, for which I wouldn't know the equivalent Italian term. It's otherwise known as an "equalizer" – that's to say you take one along if you went to knock the hell out of a bigger fellow than yourself.

'And that means. . . .'

We both knew, in the instant, what that meant.

'He must have got word – somehow – that we had this assignation up here at eight o'clock,' said Jamie. 'He was here and waiting. And since he'd hardly need an equalizer against you, it follows that he was planning to tackle the both of us.'

I saw it well enough. If Jamie had arrived early, or I had been late, it was he who would have borne the first brunt of the assault. Whatever happened to me – he – Jamie, my self-appointed knight-errant – could have been lying down there in the Piazza Colonna, after having been bludgeoned to unconsciousness with the cruel equalizer. . . .

I was in the sitting room of my suite, comfortably settled in a chaise-longue with my feet up and a glass of cognac scarcely touched at my elbow, listening to Jamie *and trying to assemble my thoughts and bring into focus a new and disturbing notion which had crept, all unbidden, into my puzzled mind. . . .*

'The manager had the answer,' Jamie was saying. He and the manager had been speaking together in the hallway outside the sitting room and I had heard their muttered voices. 'It seems that, shortly after we arrived this afternoon, a fellow came to the staff entrance, said he was a *commis* waiter looking for work and was there anything going? By some trick or other, he managed to be one of the fellows who served us with tea in the roof garden. And overheard us planning our rendezvous – which he must have regarded as an unexpected stroke of luck. Needless to say, he is now nowhere to be found.

'Are you all right, Isolda?' he asked anxiously. 'Am I tiring you? Do you want to be left alone to sleep?'

'No, no, I'm all right thanks, Jamie,' I assured him. 'But what I don't understand is – who was behind the man who

146

tried to kill us this evening? For, surely, that's what he intended to do.'

'Not Lippi, that's for sure,' replied my companion. 'Not even the Venetian Judicial Police would go *that* far. No, Isolda, it's quite clear that we – the both of us – are in this thing – this conspiracy, call it what you like – up to our necks. Not only do we know too much for our own good, but – and this is the important part – we're likely to find a helluva lot more. And the fellow who was waiting for us up there was a paid killer. His method, and the equalizer – they both smack of the professional assassin.

'Do you follow me, Isolda?'

I nodded. 'Whoever's behind the man who was waiting up there was also responsible for Bruno's murder . . .'

' . . . or is protecting Bruno's murderer,' completed Jamie. 'We're thinking along the same lines, Isolda.'

Are we, Jamie? Are we really both thinking along the same lines at this moment, my dear?

Can it be that you, also, saw a great light up there on the roof garden, when it came to me – all unawares – that if you had been killed, everything would have gone out of my life? . . .

And now he was striding up and down the room, hands behind his back, occasionally gesturing as he spoke – a mannerism which I had come to recognize as Jamie Delamere sorting out a difficult problem.

'Whichever way you look at it,' he said, 'this business has become confoundedly dangerous, and is likely to get worse. So I'm going to ask you, Isolda, to back away from the inquiries and leave everything to me. . . .'

'But . . .' I began.

He would bear no interruptions. 'What's more, I figure that the situation has become so dangerous already that you'd better get lost somewhere. I have excellent connections in Paris. My idea is that you leave for Paris tomorrow morning, on the first train out of Rome. And you'll be escorted by someone who can handle the sort of fellow we met up with tonight. The hiring of professional thugs is not restricted to the criminal classes.' He gave a mirthless laugh. 'With you safe in Paris, I can carry on with the inquiries unimpeded. I shall start tomorrow by calling on Zöe Bonomi, of course. . . .'

'And I shall come with you – as we arranged originally!' I interposed.

He paused in his striding. His face was a picture. I could have hugged him.

'Er – what was that you said, Isolda?' he asked.

'I said that I am coming with you tomorrow,' I replied. 'Because I am not running away to Paris, or anywhere else.'

He frowned. 'Isolda, I must insist!'

'Insist away,' I responded. 'It will make no difference.'

'But, after what happened tonight,' he said, 'you know full well the risks you run. I can't possibly allow you to . . .'

'You can't stop me,' I told him. And, in a curious sort of way, I was thoroughly enjoying the argument. I had always been an independent sort of person, yet here was this man – this self-appointed knight-errant of mine – actually caring enough about me to lavish me with protection.

He didn't love me, of course. To him I was just a part of his psychological researching. A 'subject' – no more. But he might get around to loving me one day – or so I devoutly hoped. And meanwhile, it was bliss simply to have someone around who cared enough to want to protect me. And at the risk of his own safety.

He fixed me with a very cross expression. 'Is that your last word?' he demanded.

'Yes,' I said. 'If you can't accept it – ah – Colonel Delamere, I ask you to withdraw from the situation and leave me to carry on the inquiries myself.'

Oh, don't let him agree to that! That was much too sharp of me. A man has his pride – what if he walks out on me?

'I see,' he responded. 'Well, in that case . . .' He paused.

'In that case?' I repeated, my heart in my mouth.

'I shall just have to accept your terms,' he said, 'for having – as they say – set my hand to the plough in this enterprise. . . .'

'Or – as they say – put your shoulder to the wheel,' I supplied. For now my imprisoned heart had risen like a lark to the high blue sky and I wanted to laugh and cry together.

He looked severe. 'This is no time for – ah – levity, Isolda,' he said.

'Of course not, Jamie,' I replied contritely. 'I'm very sorry. Please continue.'

'Having started this inquiry,' he said, 'I shall go on till it's completed. You can stay with me if you insist, but I must also insist that you obey me in all things. Keep out of trouble when I order you. Make no ill-considered moves on your own. And, most of all, trust me implicitly. Do you agree?'

'Yes, Jamie,' I murmured. I would have agreed to anything at that moment. Gladly.

'So tomorrow,' he went on, 'we will take a carriage and drive out along the Appian Way. Not too early, for we don't want to impose upon Signorina Bonami and her family before mid-morning. Speaking of the young lady's family, they might pose certain obstructions. . . .'

I was only half-listening. All that mattered was that he had passed the first, stern test I had subjected him to. Despite all, he was staying with me.

That was all that mattered at this stage. Everything else – my sudden yearnings for a whole new future which had so unexpectedly opened up before me – all that could wait for the time being. Despite all, despite the intensity of the revelation, the earth did not shake for me, nor did the skies open.

Nor was it like it had been with Bruno – a calf-love which had grown into an obsession that had been nurtured and fed upon parental opposition (for I now clearly saw it as such).

I had no appetite for dinner. Jamie left me soon after, and I bathed again – feeling defiled by the touch of my would-be murderer's hands – and went to bed. Sleep came upon me almost immediately.

And so – in a wonderful sense of peace and security that was quite at odds with my true plight – ended my first evening of being in love with Jamie Delamere.

Nine

Morning dawned with the sort of day that is essentially Roman, as I know it. Though close enough to the sea to be classed as more or less maritime, the Eternal City is so different in climate from the ancient seaport of my upbringing that it could almost belong to a different continent from Venice.

Late summer in Venice is all light and shade, with shifting clouds, occasional high winds and rain. Rome at this time takes on the gentle languor of the south, revealing all the differences between the Mediterranean and the Adriatic. That morning, when I went out on to the balcony of my bedroom and looked across the Tiber to the Vatican City, the very air seemed to be filled with sunbeams and a heady stillness broken only by the distant cries of street traders and the echoing bark of a sleepy dog.

Mindful of Jamie's order not to make any ill-considered move on my own, I nevertheless decided to take a short walk before breakfast, to sort out my thoughts. So I put on a light cotton frock and a broad-brimmed straw tied under the chin with a silk scarf, took up my parasol and went out into the piazza, where early-morning traffic was rattling over the cobblestones and the first part of the working population was busying its way to another day of toil.

Free as a bird, light of heart in my new-found delight, I wended my way, leaving the Quirinale palace on my right, towards the object of my venture. The great Baroque fountain very soon came into view – most preposterously splendid in its swaggering display of posturing statuary and elaborate conceits of water sculpture. It was just as I remembered it from the very early days when my father's coachman had carried me there – a little girl – on the last morning of that, my first, stay in the Eternal City.

'Here's a lire piece, Signorina Isolda,' he said to me. 'Throw it into the fountain and you will always return again to Rome, no matter what.' I had thrown my coin into the Trevi fountain – as I have done so many times since – and fate has always brought me back.

There was a beggar seated by the fountain's bowl, a merry-eyed fellow with a wooden leg and a crutch, who munched at a stick of bread and, wishing me a good morning, asked me for alms. I felt in my reticule and took out a ten-lire piece to give to him, for which he thanked me civilly.

Moments later I stood irresolutely in front of the hissing fountains and the swirling surface of the great bowl, in whose shallow depths uncounted and uncountable coins winked in the shifting sunlight and shadow.

'What's the matter, Signorina?' asked my beggar. 'Forgotten how to make your wish?'

'No,' I replied. 'It's just that – I gave you the only coin I possess!'

'Ah,' he said, and looked wise. 'It's a lucky thing you came across a man like me, a man of substance, who's able to be at your service in a time of misfortune.'

So saying, he took from somewhere out of his picturesque rags a one-lire piece and gravely presented it to me. I thanked him.

'Glad to be of help, Signorina,' he said with considerable grace. 'It's always gratifying to be able to assist someone less fortunate than oneself.'

I threw in the coin and made my wish, and then went on my way, much amused by my curious encounter, which had seemed to contain within itself a nugget of philosophy. Upon reaching the hotel I went straight to the breakfast room, where I found Jamie already at table.

He put down his newspaper, rose and took my hand. I had a strong compulsion – instantly quenched – to reach out and touch his cheek.

'Did you sleep well, Isolda?' he asked me.

151

'Very well indeed,' I replied. 'And you?'

'Never better,' he said. 'I woke at six and went out for a walk as far as the Trevi fountain.' He looked serious. 'You know, Isolda, all Rome is full of the most scoundrelly-looking characters. I tell you, I saw scores who might have played the role of the fellow on the roof garden last night. Rogues and vagabonds abound. Mark you don't go out alone, I beg you.'

I thought of my philosophical beggar, smiled to myself, but said nothing.

The brilliant late summer weather held as, seated side by side in an open carriage, we were carried out of the city by way of the Gate of San Sebastiano and down the ruler-straight Roman road known to fame as the Appian Way. Our driver, who had introduced himself as Augustino and who appeared to take us both for tourists and foreigners, had intimated that he would keep us supplied with incidental information along the way, and for no extra charge.

'The Villa Tortoni, I know it well,' declared Augustino, naming the destination that Jamie had given him. 'It is not far. Just beyond the temple of Mars and close by the old cemetery of Sant' Ambroglio. We should be there in good time.'

'Thank you,' said my companion, and raised an eyebrow at me.

I was not for having the conversation monopolized by the no-doubt garrulous coachman, for since last evening I had become impatient to learn all I could about the man who had so unexpectedly turned all my life and my thinking upside down.

'What do you plan to do when your business – our business – is finished in Italy, Jamie?' I asked, switching very firmly from Italian to English, and thereby excluding Augustino. 'I take it that your talk of going to China to learn Mandarin – or was it Manchu? – was merely a figure of speech.'

'Maybe so, Isolda,' he replied with a smile. 'But I shall go to the Orient one day, never fear.'

Augustino interposed – in very good English: 'My brother

152

Giacomo, who was a seaman, he travelled to the Orient. Singapore and Shanghai, many places. He was drowned in the China Sea. Very sad. We are now passing over a stretch of the original lava paving of the Appian Way, which was begun by Appius Claudius Caecus in 312 BC. On your right is the ruin of a temple to Jupiter, not much of it left.'

A private conversation in a foreign language clearly being out of the question, I reverted to Italian and changed the subject to the matter in hand.

'After we gain the information from the lady in question,' I said, 'what then?'

'If the lady is forthcoming,' replied Jamie, 'clearly we must then return to Venice and make what use of it we can. But so much depends upon her answer.' He searched my face, his deep blue eyes clouded with gravity. 'And are you now prepared for the worst, Isolda?'

Prepared for the worst – prepared for the revelation that Bruno was, after all, the father of tragic Carlotta's dead child! The revelation about my own self that had so recently been granted to me made a very great deal of difference, of course. So far as Bruno was concerned, I had buried my dead, and though my earnest wish was to find him to have been free of faithlessness, I could now face the alternative. What was more important than finding him innocent or guilty of betraying his vow was to bring his murderer or murderers to justice and to clear my own name.

I answered Jamie with complete honesty. 'One way or the other,' I said, 'the truth must bring us nearer to the solution.'

The foregoing exchange had been carried out in low tones so that our driver should not overhear. Being rather pointedly excluded from our conversation did not however seem to trouble the garrulous Augustino, who very soon resumed his conducted tour of the Appian Way.

'In Roman times,' he said, 'the road was lined with many taverns which were notorious for their orgies and such immoralities. Yonder is the remains of the temple of Mars, and beyond that the cemetery. I hope the signor and signora will not be too late.'

'Too late?' Jamie and I stared at each other in puzzlement.

'Carriages have been leaving for the Villa Tortoni all

morning,' said Augustino. 'The signor and signora are lucky to have hired me. Five minutes later and they could have been out of luck. All very sad. In the midst of life we are in death.'

'What *is* he talking about?' I whispered.

'And here is the villa,' said the strange coachman as the pantiled roofs of a long, low building came into sight over an ancient wall topped with still cypresses. 'Signor and signora may not be too late, after all.'

Before we had time to question Augustino about his obscure references to lateness, death in life and so forth, we came to the entrance of the property, which comprised a large ornamental gateway opening on to a weed-grown drive that led up to the pillared façade of the villa. And coming up the drive towards us was a procession of carriages led by a hearse drawn by four black horses with sable plumes nodding on their heads. The glass-enclosed hearse was similarly beplumed and the four mutes who trudged forlornly along beside it had long streamers of black crêpe trailing from their tall hats. Behind the hearse came a long column of carriages. As Augustino had observed to us, most of the available carriages in Rome appeared to be there.

Instinctively my hand reached out towards Jamie and he took it in his. Halted by the gateway, we had a close view of the procession as it passed before us and proceeded on down the Appian Way towards the cemetery. First the hearse, with the pall-draped coffin set with masses of flowers; next, closed coaches with drawn blinds – these would be the mourning family. After them came the open carriages, at the tail of which, without a word of instruction from us, Augustino urged his horses to follow.

'And who is dead in the Bonomi family, I wonder?' murmured Jamie.

I did not answer, nor did I speculate to myself. But an awful premonition was shaping in my mind.

The slow procession to the cemetery was soon over. The hearse passed under a funerary arch with a carved frieze representing swags of myrtle hung between horned rams' skulls, and we followed after, down an avenue of time-worn tombs overhung with sentinel cypresses, to an open grave that stood by a ruined chapel at the far end. There the mourners alighted, and followed the coffin as it was carried by the mutes to its place of rest.

Arm in arm with Jamie I numbly took my place at the outskirts of the crowd, where several mourners of the lower classes were grouped – servants, farm workers and the like, dressed in their seedy black Sunday clothes.

Jamie tapped one of these on the elbow. 'Excuse me, but who has died?' he asked.

The other – he looked to be some kind of indoor servant, perhaps a scullion or cellarman – glanced at the questioner in surprise, and noticing that neither of us was in mourning, seemingly took us to be passing strangers.

'Why, it's the daughter of the house,' he said.

'What name, then?' asked Jamie.

I clenched my hands tightly and waited.

'Signorina Zöe Bonomi.'

Zoe – dead! . . .

But had I not sensed as much – as soon as I saw the hearse coming down the drive towards me – that the blonde beauty with the sulky, shifty eyes was no more?

If Jamie was as shocked and bewildered as I, he did not show it, but questioned the fellow with the kind of ghoulish gravity that mildly interested hangers-on display at funerals.

'Was she ailing for long, the young lady?' he asked.

'Bless me, no,' responded the other, who seemed only too willing to communicate. 'For didn't she have an accident only the day before yesterday?'

'An accident, was it – what happened?'

'It was me who found her,' said Jamie's informant with some relish. 'Her mare came back alone, you see? So I says to the groom, "Ten to one the signorina's had a fall, broken a few bones or lying stunned, like as not." So I saddled the cob and rode out the way the mare had come. Others came after me, but it was me who found her. I rode an hour in all directions – north, south, east and west. It was near sundown before I espied her lying down there in the old Roman quarry, her neck broken like a stick.'

I closed my eyes and tried to will away the image of the

155

blonde beauty with the sulky eyes staring dead and skywards. . . .

'And that was – when, you say?' persisted Jamie.

'Like I told you, the day before yesterday,' said his informant. 'They don't keep them long in this sultry weather, you see. . . .'

Jamie took my hand and walked me away.

'How awful!' I whispered. 'I feel that I should go over and offer my condolences to her parents, but they wouldn't remember me.'

'And it could be dangerous,' he said. 'In the circumstances. . . .'

I met his eye. It was cold and stern. 'Jamie, you mean? . . .' I faltered.

'It's too much of a coincidence,' he said. 'Think about it. I had the information from Signora di Ventris three – four – days ago. If someone else also got hold of that information – by following me there, for instance – they would have had time to travel to Rome the same night, and. . . .'

'And silence Zöe!' I finished for him, and clasped a hand across my mouth to stifle a gasp of horror. 'Do you think it happened like that, Jamie?'

He looked at me long and steadily, as if making up his mind to tell me the very worst, and finally deciding upon it.

'Yes I do, Isolda,' he said quietly. 'I think we are dealing with a person – or persons – who will stop at nothing to keep us from the truth. Everything that has happened so far confirms me in that view.'

I could not but agree with him. The hideous event of the previous night only went to prove it. He, or I – or both of us – could have ended up like Zöe!

We journeyed back to Rome in silence, and even the talkative Augustino was sensitive enough not to intrude upon our thoughts.

How I wished I could frame the few simple words that could draw us together, the man I loved and I. When I thought of how much he had done for me, the risks he was taking, and surely not all in the interests of psychological

156

inquiry, it seemed wrong that a yawning gulf of silence could separate us.

But there it was. I did not have the words to span the gulf, and the brooding figure at my side gave no sign of sharing his thoughts with me.

We arrived back at the hotel. Jamie paid off the coachman, adding a generous tip.

As we parted in the hall he said that he would call upon me in my suite later in the day, and advised me to order a light luncheon to be sent up.

'That and a rest would be advisable,' he said. 'We can then decide upon our next move.'

Leaving me upon this inconclusive note, he went on his way and I on mine. As I entered my suite I saw that the sky was dark, with storm clouds beginning to mass over the heights across the Tiber. All at once the sky was rent by a tremendous flash of lightning beyond the dome of St Peter's, followed by a crash of thunder. I hastened to close the shutters – just as a sudden downpour of rain hammered upon the windows. A stark and depressing ending, I thought, to our tragic excursion.

It was then I saw – the note. . . .

The folded sheet of paper was lying on a silver salver set upon the occasional table by the door. I picked it up, broke the seal and read the brief contents with mounting alarm:

Ask yourself why it was that Colonel Delamere conveniently managed to be a quarter of an hour late for your rendezvous on the roof garden last evening? He must be regretting that he arrived just a little too early after all. Think about it.
 – A Friend

The note was written in a sprawling hand that was quite unknown to me. The intent of the message was perfectly clear. I was to gather from it that either Jamie was in league with my last night's assailant, or, having some prior knowledge that such an attack was to take place, had deliberately delayed his arrival at the rendezvous.

A moment's thought was sufficient for me to dismiss both ideas out of hand. The very notion that the man I loved had been playing me false all this time was totally unacceptable and an insult to my intelligence and to his obvious integrity. The only explanation for the communication was that my unknown enemies were trying to drive a wedge of suspicion between my helper and me. They thought that, if I doubted him, I would cease to open my heart and give him my complete confidence in all things.

How little they knew about me – how could they guess that I was in love with him?

But, I next asked myself, what would Jamie think of the note? Not being in love with me, nor knowing of my feelings for him, might he not think that a maggot of suspicion – however tiny – had been implanted in my mind? Next time we were in danger, when my trust in him would be stretched to the limit and beyond, he might think that I would fail him.

What to do?

The answer came to me: tell Jamie nothing!

Why worry him with what was, after all, no more than a crude attempt to drive us apart? Best destroy the hateful note and its revolting insinuations. The mutual trust that existed between the two of us – reinforced, on my part, by the love I bore for him – would continue as before. And the evil force that was trying to destroy me would be thwarted, its latest attempt strangled at birth.

That was my reasoning, born of love and trust.

Alas for the reasoning of a woman in love. . . .

I had no appetite for food, nor did I feel like taking Jamie's advice to rest myself. All I wanted was to see him again, and longed for his knock upon my door, when he came to tell me his plans – after his deeply analytical mind had tussled with the problems that beset us. When I had burnt the hateful note in the grate and scattered the ashes, I stalked around the suite – as, in the past, I had spent nights uncounted in haunting the empty rooms of the Palazzo Mazzini-Forsca. The hours slipped by, the storm raged over Rome, and dusk began to fall. But still no sign from the man I loved.

I had just decided to summon a page to take a message to Jamie – for despite my customary self-assurance, I shrank

158

from the idea of thrusting myself forward by going to his room — when there came the double knock on the door which was our pre-arranged signal announcing him.

Joyfully I let him in, and it was as if we were meeting again after an age of separation. I looked away, so that he should not see the glory that must have shone from my eyes.

'I thought you were never coming,' I said.

'It's taken me a while to sort out in my mind what should be our next, best move,' he explained. 'Did you rest?' he added.

'No. I didn't feel tired.'

'But you had some luncheon?'

'Didn't feel hungry.'

'Isolda, you must look after yourself,' he said gently. 'The events you are passing through take a heavy toll of one's nervous energy. The best way to cope is to live as closely as possible to a normal everyday existence. Regular meals, regular hours of sleep. And no feeding off your nerve ends. Do you follow me?'

'Yes, Jamie,' I replied with a docility that I would never have believed myself capable of so short a while ago. 'I'll try to remember that.'

'Good,' he said. 'Who was the note from, by the way?'

'What note?' I replied — immediately, upon a reflex, without an instant's thought.

'You didn't receive a note?' he said. 'That's odd. The waiter who brought up my luncheon asked me if you had also returned to the hotel, because he'd left a note in your suite which had been delivered by hand. He wondered if it might be important.'

I gazed at him in awful fascination, speechless, irresolute.

'That's very odd,' he said. 'The fellow was quite insistent that he'd delivered it.' He turned towards the door. 'I'd better make inquiries. . . .'

'Jamie — wait!' I cried.

He turned with a look of surprise. 'Yes, Isolda?'

'Jamie, I lied to you,' I said. 'That's to say, I wasn't honest with you. I did receive a note. It was here when I came in.'

His face — the face that I had come to love — took on an expression that I had never seen there before.

159

'You say you – *lied* to me, Isolda?' he demanded. 'Whatever for?'

I avoided his stare and looked down at my hands, which, not to my surprise, were trembling.

'To – spare you,' I whispered.

'To spare me – *what?*' he countered. 'Where is the note? – if I might ask.'

'I – I burnt it.'

'*Burnt* it?'

'Yes.'

'Can you remember what was in this note?'

'Every word!' I cried. 'Every word is imprinted on my mind. If you must hear them, I'll tell you. . . .

'It said . . .' and I repeated the hateful message, just as I so clearly remembered it.

When I had finished he made no immediate reply but remained where he was, just looking at me with an expression that I could not fathom.

'Well – say something!' I cried.

'What is there to say?' he responded. 'You tell me that you concealed the message from your – friend – in order to spare me. . . .'

'I did – I *did!*' My voice rose uncontrollably.

'What you mean is – you destroyed the note because you decided you couldn't trust me.'

'But I *do* trust you!' I protested, desperately trying to make him understand. 'Don't you see? That's why I was able to burn the hateful thing and shut it out of my mind. It meant *nothing!*'

'I'm sorry, Isolda,' he said, with the heavy patience that one uses to explain things to rather dull children, 'but I don't follow your argument. If you trusted me, you would have shown me the note. We would have discussed it sensibly, rationally, and arrived at the conclusion that this – friend – was merely trying to make mischief between us.'

(And has – and *has!* I screamed inside my mind. How very cleverly he's made mischief between us!)

A new expression flitted across his face when I did not reply.

160

'Or perhaps,' he said, 'the answer simply is this – you don't trust me to trust *you*.'

'Yes – perhaps,' I replied. The admission came reluctantly, but it had to be said, because it was the simple truth.

'Why, Isolda?' he asked quietly.

(*Because I love you, but you don't love me!* – that was the soundless scream which I could not even have whispered aloud to him for my soul's salvation.)

'That's – just the way it is,' I said at last.

'I see.' He nodded gravely. 'Well that, I think, is all there is to say. Your unknown friend has indeed searched us out and found us wanting. I'm sorry.'

'What are you going to do now?' I asked, remembering, even in my moment of agony, that I was a daughter of the Venetian aristocracy and must not in any circumstances be seen to give way, but must hold my head high in adversity.

'There's nothing left for me to do but to bow out of this association,' he replied. 'With great reluctance, I have to say that I can do no more for you under the circumstances.'

'Very well, Colonel Delamere,' I said, fighting hard to keep my voice steady. 'I am sorry that it had to end like this, but I thank you for all you have done.'

He bowed. 'Goodbye, Signorina Isolda,' he said.

'Goodbye.'

He turned, and was gone from me without a backward glance.

'Fool! Little fool!'

I shouted the words at my reflection in the long mirror. The sound of his footfalls had barely faded away down the hall outside.

'You're all pride!' I said. 'Daughter of the Venetian aristocracy, when will you *learn*? You lost your sister because you were too damned proud to proclaim your innocence to her. Oh, no – she was expected to accept it unhesitatingly, unquestioningly – and unspoken. That poor girl must be chiding you for being a fool, somewhere in her unknown grave!

'And now you've made the same mistake with Jamie, and thrown away your last chance of happiness.

161

'Why couldn't you have debased yourself? What did you have to lose, fool? You could have said, "I don't trust you to trust me because you don't love me the way I love you." He might have spurned me, but he's human enough to have accepted my explanation.

'He might have stayed. . . .

'God – he might even have stayed long enough to learn to love me a little!'

Then I was running – out of the suite and into the corridor. Taking the steps down to the front hall, three at a time. Rushing across the open space to where the duty under manager sat behind his ornate desk – and leapt to his feet to see an honoured lady guest in such an obvious state of distress.

'Colonel Delamere,' I panted. 'His room number – please!'

'The colonel – ah – that will be number – ah – but the Signor Colonel has just gone out, Signorina.'

'Gone out – *where?*' I cried, and the note of hysteria must have been painfully apparent.

The man hunched his shoulders in a gesture of helplessness.

'Signorina, how should *I*? . . .'

I turned on my heels and raced to the plate-glass doors, flung myself through them and went out into the rain-soaked night.

Which way? . . .

An instant's irresolution in the teeming darkness of the empty square, and I set off in the first direction that presented itself – towards a lighted archway at the far corner. This, at least, offered a promise of shelter where I might pause and take stock of the problem before me – to find the man I loved in all of storm-racked Rome.

I reached the archway, soaked to the skin beneath the thin grey gown that I wore, my shoes sodden wet and useless; and looked about me, left and right, to where three broad boulevards stretched away into infinities of rain and darkness punctuated only with a few flickering lights.

'Hello, little lady – going somewhere?'

A hand pawed at my arm. Turning, I screamed into the

162

raddled face of an old roué in tall hat and opera cloak; broke from his grasp and ran – anywhere, to be free.

My delicate silk shoes were cut to rags by the uneven cobblestones and their heels wrenched away. I kicked them off without stopping in my headlong flight, and went on my way barefoot, my stockings ripped to ribbons. Choking for breath, I stumbled to a halt at the next crossing – and thereby saved myself from running right beneath the flying hooves of a passing cab-horse. The driver's shrill curses were hurled back at me as they clattered on into the darkness.

On, on I ran again. Peering ahead of me with rain-blinded eyes for the glimpse of a figure that I knew and loved so dearly, but encountering only the creatures of the night, who reached out and clutched at me, whispered unspeakable things, pursued me till they wearied of the sport. And still I went on, even though every stumbling step only brought nearer the conviction that I should never find the man I sought – till, finally, I decided that he had gone from me for ever.

That thought, and that alone, made me pause.

Yes, that must be the answer. Jamie had not thrown himself irresolutely out into the night, but had left the hotel for good, taking with him only the light hold-all that he had brought from Venice. Perhaps, even at that moment, he was seated in a north-bound express train, thinking back with relief to his parting from the hysterical, wayward creature who had made so many demands upon his good nature and then spurned his trust at the first testing-time.

Gone for ever! Not to Venice, that was for sure. Never again would he set foot in the city where he might meet up with that thankless creature, that stupid, demanding woman whose constant protestations of innocence sounded ever less convincing with each repetition.

Borne down with the burden of grief and guilt, bitterness and remorse, I sank to my knees on the streaming cobblestones and bowed my head in tears of anguish.

A long time passed.

When I looked up, the rain seemed to have slackened. I was kneeling in a darkened square, at the far end of which the well-remembered writhing forms and bombastic façades of the Trevi fountain stood as a background to a theatrical stage upon which I – the kneeling figure – was not the only player.

Someone else shared the scene. Standing by the bowl of the now still and silent fountain was the tall figure of a man. His back was turned to me, his head bowed as if deep in thought. The whole posture – the droop of the broad shoulders, the arms hanging limply – spoke of a sadness and despair that matched my own. And I knew him at a glance.

Then I was running, joyous and unashamed in my love, calling his name, thrilling to the sound of it.

He turned at the sound of my voice, but his face was in deep shadow, so that his expression was hidden from me.

But his voice told me all . . .

'I went back to the hotel. They said that you had come out after me. I've searched everywhere. Oh, thank God – thank God!'

I was enveloped in his waiting arms. As he stooped to gather me to him, a fitful light touched his face and I saw my own love mirrored in his eyes.

'It doesn't matter, my darling,' I whispered against his lips. 'Nothing matters now – *nothing!*'

'But, my dearest, why didn't you tell me? After all, it's the man's place to make the declarations of love. Or, at least, that's what I've always gathered from reading novels. I'm afraid I only have a rather limited first-hand experience.' Having said that, I had an impulse – instantly obeyed – to reach out and lightly touch his cheek.

Light of heart with our new-found knowledge of each other's feelings, we sat together in my suite at the hotel, exchanging confidences – like lovers since time immemorial.

Jamie imprisoned my hand and, transferring it to his lips, implanted a kiss there. He then became very serious.

'Isolda, darling, I loved you since I first saw this beautiful and tragic creature growing pale at the insults of a boorish gondolier and a sniggering crowd,' he said. 'From that moment on, I've never ceased to love you.'

'Correction!' I said. 'When you thought that I had

destroyed the note through lack of trust, you cooled to me considerably. You even deserted me.'

'I bow to the accusation,' he replied. 'My pride was bruised, I admit it. I flung out of the hotel and got no further than the corner of the square, where I went into a café, ordered a cognac at the bar and took stock of myself. I had scarcely put the glass to my lips when I knew what I must do – which was to swallow my damned pride, rush back to you, declare my feelings and beg your forgiveness. When I got back, they told me you'd also raced out into the night. The rest you know.'

We embraced. This was a protracted pause to our conversation, and wholly delightful.

'As to why I didn't declare my feelings earlier,' he said at length, 'I simply didn't think it right to take advantage of your troubled state. After all, you were badly in need of a shoulder to cry on – that was pretty obvious. I was happy enough to provide the shoulder. As to the way I felt about you – I decided that would have to wait till you were a whole woman again. Freed of suspicion, free of your own sense of guilt. Free to make your own choice about everything. About me, for instance.'

'And you arrived at that conclusion through your study of psychology?' I asked.

'Um – more or less,' he admitted.

'Then, my dearest,' I replied, 'your precious psychology has very little regard for the heart of a woman. And you may tell that to Messieurs Charcot, Stumpf, Lipps and the rest.'

'Yes, Ma'am,' he replied. And silenced my further declarations by possessing himself of my lips.

'But what do we do, Jamie?' I asked him. 'What next – after Zöe?'

We had had a late supper sent up to my suite. The gentle dalliance of two lovers newly-declared had turned into a council of war with serious overtones of life and death.

'I spent the entire afternoon and most of the evening thinking out our next move,' he replied. 'And you are not going to like my solution, Isolda.'

165

'Tell me, then,' I responded, 'and let me be the judge of that.'

'You must cut loose of this whole thing,' he said.

'Wha-a-at?' I cried. 'You mean, give up? Let myself be forever branded in Venice as a sacrilegious murderess who got away with it?'

'Crudely put,' he responded, 'and psychologically unsound because based upon emotion and not upon logic.' And when I tried to intervene he laid a finger gently on my lips to silence me. 'Consider, dearest,' he said. 'Bruno is dead and Julietta is gone. Nothing you can ever do will bring them back to life. Add to that: Carlotta may or may not have destroyed herself, and Zöe's supposed accident was almost certainly contrived. What's to be gained by adding yourself to the list of the slain? And if you are in any doubts about the person – or persons – behind all this devilry, be assured that they are utterly determined to prevent the truth about Bruno's murder being known. They are also tremendously powerful. Remember how your trial was rigged from top to bottom – witnesses for certain, defending advocate a strong probability, even the judge was not above suspicion.

'I would help you all I could – and will still do so if you insist upon continuing. But, dear Isolda, what profit for me if you were to meet the fate of the others?'

I looked at him for a long time, this brave, good man who had not thought to include his own peril in the balance.

'So what do you propose that I do, Jamie?' I asked him. 'Run away from Venice for ever?'

'Yes,' he said. 'Come away with me. Be my wife. The whole wide world is open to us, my Isolda.'

Returning to Venice. And for the last time. A brief stay at the Palazzo Mazzini-Forsca to settle my affairs, arrange for the sale of the place and its contents, make lifelong provision for faithful Assunta, pack a few of my most treasured belongings to take away with me as the only mementoes of my life in Venice (not too many of these, because from here on I was going to look forward, and no backward glances to what might have been) – and then to take the wings of the morning and fly away with my love to the uttermost ends of the earth, leaving behind a question mark to lie across the memory of Isolda Mazzini-Forsca for ever.

We took the express train, my love and I, and were in Florence by noon of the next day. There was no need for us to change trains on that particular journey, for the express was carrying on to Venice after only a short wait to pick up passengers. Food and drink were not provided aboard, so Jamie went off to find bread and cheese and a bottle of wine on the station. I sat back, relaxed, and let my thoughts drift pleasurably to the prospect of becoming Mrs Jamie Delamere, nominal resident of Boston, Massachusetts and citizen of the world. We had sat up late the previous night, planning our travel itinerary. Naturally, the Orient figured largely in our plans. We had spoken of China, Japan, the isles of the Pacific and the China seas, the Antipodes, India, the long journey to the Himalayas, the fabled trek to the Golden Gates of Samarkand. . . .

So enrapt was I in my daydreams that I did not at first notice the man watching me from outside the carriage window. He was leaning against a pillar a few feet away, hat pulled down low over his brow, coat collar turned up, though the weather was seasonably warm. But it was the manner in which he turned his head away – quickly, guiltily, when I glanced in his direction – that struck me as odd. Prompted by a curious premonition, I remained watching him – to see if, after a discreet pause, he looked back towards me.

And he did. I glimpsed his face for only a second or two, before he turned and sped away as fast as his legs would carry him – to be lost almost immediately in the scurrying crowds.

In that brief time I had a very clear view of his face. Truth to tell, I gained no clear impression of the features, nor could I ever have recognized the man again – but for one peculiarity.

Scored down one side of his face were the scarlet furrows of four fingernails – where I had raked him in my dying desperation two nights before on the roof garden of the Hotel Barberini, with the iron-hard cobblestones of the Piazza Colonna waiting to receive me far below!

167

'It was him – you're quite sure, Isolda?'

We were on our way again. Florence was behind, and with it, I hoped, our would-be murderer. Jamie had listened soberly to my account of the brief confrontation.

'Quite sure,' I said. 'Not merely because of the nail-marks, but he was definitely *spying* on me, Jamie. And when he met my eye again, he ran like a hare.

'But – oh!' An awful thought struck me. 'Do you suppose that he might have doubled back and rejoined the train?'

'After having been spotted,' said Jamie, 'it's hardly likely that he'd take the risk. However – if he shows himself again. . . .'

My beloved took from the pocket of his overnight bag a small pistol which he then concealed about his person. I had had no idea that Jamie went armed, and found that I had decidedly mixed feelings about it.

The incident of the man with the nail-clawed face had had a depressing effect upon me, and I only toyed with the delicious fresh bread and tasty cheese that Jamie had bought, and took no more than a sip of the wine.

Of course he noticed my preoccupation. 'A dime for your thoughts, Isolda,' he said. 'Still worried about our friend with the scratch-marks?'

'We can't escape it, can we, Jamie?' I put to him. 'Last night – even only half an hour ago – it all seemed so easy. The roads to Samarkand and Trebizond were just around the corner. But, my dear, this thing, these people, are not going to let us slip through their fingers so easily. We both know too much now. And they are obviously convinced that we are as determined as they are to stay in the game.'

'Then,' he said, 'we have to find some way to let them know that we've had enough, that we don't think the game's worth the candle. That we want to get away. To stay alive.'

'But how can we possibly do that?' I demanded. 'They're not talking to us. They just want us dead. Even the note that was delivered to me was no more than an attempt to split us apart so that we could be destroyed separately.'

He thought for a few moments and then he snapped finger and thumb. 'Tell you what,' he said. 'There *is* a way of making known the way we now feel to our unknown enemy – or enemies.'

'How, Jamie?' I demanded.

'Isolda, you are a Venetian,' he said. 'Did you ever hear tell of a well-kept secret in Venice?'

Rather irritably I replied: 'There is no such thing as a secret of any kind in Venice, Jamie. But what has that to do with our problem?'

'If I were to rise to my feet in, say, Florian's café, and announce that I and the Signorina Isolda Mazzini-Forsca were leaving the city, Italy, and all Europe for good, never to return. What would be the effect?'

'The effect?' I echoed. 'Well, the news would be all over the city in no time. It would be whispered during the Stations of the Cross in every church in the city before the hour was out. Every gondolier on the Grand Canal would have had it much earlier. . . .

'Oh, Jamie,' I said with sudden revelation, 'I think I get what you're driving at.'

He reached out and took my hands.

'That's what we'll do,' he said. 'Once back in Venice, I'll let it publicly be known – in Florian's or elsewhere – that Isolda and her new bridegroom-to-be are quitting the city for ever. The Woman in Grey, the Fair Untouchable, will no longer defile the city with her presence. And we, my darling, can hope to be allowed to leave unmolested.'

'Yes, Jamie – yes!' I cried. 'Let's do that! And they'll surely let us go in peace, won't they? What would be the point for them – whoever *they* are, or he is, or she is – to draw further attention to their crimes by destroying us unnecessarily?'

We joined hands and kissed. It was a pledge of our intention.

Later, Jamie slept, but there was no respite for me. I stayed awake and restless in my mind while the train rumbled on through the Apennines, out of the last, long tunnel and on to Bologna, with the wide river delta and Venice not far ahead.

I contemplated his sleeping profile. If I ever saw strength in a man's face, it was written plainly on my love's broad brow, his firm jaw, the strong bone structure, the firmly-moulded mouth.

Is this the face of the man, I asked myself, who proposed that we run away and hide ourselves in the wide world beyond Venice, leaving behind the unsolved mystery, the unavenged dead, the triumph of evil?

And then I answered myself that the question was ill-founded. It was not for his own safety that he proposed to run away, for that was against his natural instincts. It was for my sake, and mine alone, that he was acting against those instincts.

And why had I so readily agreed to his plan?

Why, for the same reason. Because I feared more for his safety than for the triumph of good over evil. Because of my love for him I was willing to shut my ears to the cries of the unavenged dead. For that, I would let evil go unpunished – asking only for the life and well-being of my beloved.

So, by following the desires of our hearts, both of us had proved ourselves unworthy, not only of each other, but of ourselves as people.

It was an uneasy thought to carry with me as our train steamed across the broad delta and the towers and domes of Venice appeared like sentinels beyond the skyline of waving reed and sedge.

Ten

We took a covered gondola to the palazzo, a wise move because the rain clouds that had been gathering over the lagoon at our approach unburdened themselves as soon as we embarked upon the Grand Canal. By the time we were abreast of San Geremia the surface of the water was pockmarked with the first droplets; when we passed under the Rialto bridge and glimpsed the first sight of my ancestral home it was drumming on the cabin roof and lying in a fine mist upon the still air inside where we sat, hand in hand.

There was no one to greet us at the water gate, but I carried in my reticule a key to the iron-barred doors leading into the yard.

At the sound of our footfalls on the steps, Assunta came running.

'Isolda, my darling girl!' she cried, throwing her arms about me. 'I've been half out of my wits for the worry of you.' She stepped back to regard me, still holding me. 'Oh, but you look so tired. Haven't you been sleeping well?' And, to Jamie: 'Haven't you been looking after my precious girl, Signor? Shame on you for neglecting my lovey!'

Jamie and I exchanged a smile as my devoted old nurse conducted me up to her sitting room, established me in a comfortable armchair and put on the kettle for a cup of English tea, chattering all the while. Even for the effusive Assunta, she seemed more gushing than usual – almost as if, by prattling on about complete inessentials, she could avoid touching upon something that was really uppermost in her mind. Something – distasteful. . . .

'The weather has been so bad,' she said, 'rain every day, and San Marco knee-deep in water they say, though I've not been out, never a step further than the Rialto markets. How was Rome? I haven't been there, you know, since your mother the Principessa passed on, God rest her soul. Have you had anything to eat? There's plenty in the larder. I can do you a pasta and some fish, how would you like that? Oh, Isolda my darling, you look so tired, you really do. . . .' And she began to cry.

I comforted her as well as I was able. The kettle boiled and I made a pot of tea for the three of us and gave a cup to the poor old darling.

'You worry about me too much, Assunta,' I told her. 'Drink up your tea, and I'll tell you the new and exciting news.' I was alluding to the plans of our marriage and departure from Venice, and while I knew that she would delight in the former, the idea of my never coming back to my native city in the foreseeable future would be a terrible blow to her.

Taking my cup, I sat down again – and looked about me.

'By the way, where's Michou?' I asked. 'He's usually purring on my knee within minutes of my coming into a room.'

The crash of Assunta's cup and saucer on the marble floor was accompanied by an outburst of anguish from the old woman. Disregarding the damage, she buried her face in the skirts of her apron and gave way to most piteous sobbing, nor could I comfort her, try as I might.

I glanced towards Jamie for guidance. He shrugged and spread his hands in a gesture of helplessness. 'Would you like me to leave you two alone together?' he whispered.

'No, stay with me, please,' I replied. 'Something terrible's happened. I know her so well, and I sensed it as soon as I set eyes on her.'

Kneeling by my old nurse's chair, I put my arms round her shoulders. 'Tell Isolda, dearest,' I said to her. 'Don't keep it to yourself. That's what loving friends are for – to share with.'

She presently conquered her heart-rending sobs and dried her eyes. The expression in those sad, peasant's eyes struck me to the heart when she turned her gaze upon me; it told

172

of all the misery and puzzlement that old age can encounter in a harsh and unthinking world.

'What is it then, dear?' I persisted.

'Mi-Michou,' she whispered.

I gave a sharp, involuntary intake of breath, and knew a sudden dread to which I could not give a name.

'Michou the cat?' I cried. 'What – what's happened to him, Assunta?'

And then she told me.

'Darling Jamie, we can't run away now. If whoever's behind all this can do such things to a little cat, what might they not do to people?'

He and I had retired up to my own sitting room, after I had put Assunta to bed with a sleeping draught. It was another council of war, but in greatly different circumstances, and with a whole new viewpoint of our problems.

The fate of Michou the little cat can – *must* – be told briefly. Briefly, then, Assunta had been summoned to the back gate in the kitchen yard by a frenzied knocking just after dark the previous evening. There was no one there when she opened up, but Michou the cat – or what remained of him – was hung on the knocker. The effect which this experience had upon a person of her gentle disposition can only be imagined, as can the mentality of the ogre – or ogres – who perpetrated the outrage. And the intention of the obscene gesture was clearly spelled out – in English, no doubt in deference to Jamie – which was attached to the small corpse:

You will be next!

Somehow, out of her desire to shield me from the sight, the old lady had taken down the pathetic remains and given them a decent interment in the garden of the palazzo. She had then spent a hideous night and most of the following day awaiting my return.

I had delivered my comment whilst staring out of the window on to the canal. Jamie did not immediately answer,

173

but his hands closed upon my shoulders, and I felt the strength of him, the warm assurance.

'You're right, Isolda,' he said. 'I think I've known all along that we'd never stick to our notion of running away. It isn't in us, my darling. We're made of sterner stuff – heaven help us.'

I turned to face him. Those beloved, deep blue eyes – much deeper and bluer than mine – matched the firmness that was revealed in his voice.

'So what now, my love?' I asked.

'First, I propose – with your permission – to move here, into the palazzo,' he said. 'Unity is strength, and I don't intend to let you far from my sight till this whole dreadful business is cleared up. So, if you'll apportion me suitable bachelor quarters, Ma'am, I'll send round to the Danieli for the rest of my traps and move in.' Now he was all action, the soldier of fortune instead of the psychologist. Bright-eyed, devil-may-care and ready for anything. It was yet another facet of the strange man to whom I had given my heart – Jamie Delamere the happy warrior.

'I see,' he said, looking out across the canal to the steps opposite, 'that our policeman friend is still watching from his launch.'

'He's been there ever since we returned,' I said.

'So Lippi must have been informed of our arrival back from Rome,' said Jamie. 'That probably means that one of his agents was travelling with us on the train.'

'The man whose face I clawed?' I ventured.

'I don't think so, my darling,' he replied. 'Not even the Judicial Police descend to taking the roles of judge, jury and executioner upon themselves, no matter how convinced they may be of the guilt of the accused person. No, I think we may still assume that our would-be killer is in the employ of our enemy, or enemies.

'But the sight of our watcher gives me an idea. . . .'

'And what's that?' I asked him.

'We'll go and see Lippi,' he declared, to my surprise. 'Beard the lion in his own den. I've a notion that he may be inter-ested to learn of poor little Zöe Bonomi's untimely end, if he hasn't heard about it already. That, and the attempt upon you on the roof garden, plus the horrible killing of the cat, might go some way to convincing him that he's barking up the wrong tree by persisting in believing you're the guilty party, my love.'

I had my doubt and fears. 'The prospect of voluntarily presenting oneself at the office of the Judicial Police – where I spent those hideous days and nights under interrogation – doesn't appeal very much,' I said ruefully.

Jamie stared at me in a surprise that I could have sworn to be simulated. 'Oh, I'd not intended that you should go, darling,' he said hastily. 'This is something I'd rather tackle on my own.'

'You said "we" would go and see Lippi, and we it is,' I told him with as much firmness as I could muster – and seeing the real concern in those beloved eyes, it was not a lot.

I put Jamie in a set of rooms that had once been my father's, on the second floor facing the canal. He had a gondolier bring his gear from the Danieli, and so my love spent his first night under the roof of my family home.

Next morning he was out early, for I heard his footsteps crossing the yard at the back, and the sound of the gate being opened. Though it was broad daylight, I did not rest till he returned.

He did not return alone. . . .

'This is Giuseppe,' he said, by way of introduction.

I was taking a light breakfast of coffee and toast in the garden, when Jamie put in his surprise appearance with quite the most forbidding male creature I had ever set eyes on. He towered over Jamie by a head and a half, and was broader in the same proportion. A narrow, beetling brow under a shaven skull was augmented by beady blue eyes of a sullen malevolence, and a slash of a mouth that opened to disclose a set of surprisingly white and even teeth. He could not have been much older than Jamie, but – the teeth apart – he looked appallingly ill-used. The ultimate shock came when, upon offering him my hand by way of greeting, he presented me with a mangled stump.

'Giuseppe was once a gondolier,' explained Jamie, 'and

175

several times winner of the races at the Historic Regattas. The loss of his right hand meant the loss of his livelihood on the water – but he will make an excellent companion for you, my dear.'

'Companion?' I stared at him blankly.

'To be exact – bodyguard,' he explained. 'I shall not always be at hand to protect you, either here in the palazzo or out in the streets. Giuseppe will be always close at hand, yet discreetly apart. He's had his instructions and he understands them perfectly. Correct, Giuseppe?'

The giant nodded, fixing me with an expressionless gaze which told one nothing of what was going on in that bullet head, behind those cold eyes.

Later that morning we went by gondola to the Molo, where we disembarked and walked to the dread Office of Venice's feared Judicial Police. Giuseppe had been awaiting our arrival. As we crossed the piazzetta his massive figure straightened up from leaning against the wall of the Doge's Palace, put away a newspaper that he had been appearing to read, and followed after us at a discreet distance. For once – perhaps for the first time since I appreciated the very real danger in which Jamie and I stood – I felt comparatively safe.

'Wait here. Signor Inspector Lippi will see you presently.'

A functionary had taken our particulars and requirements at the entrance desk. A half-hour wait had followed, and then another minion had escorted us to a room – the selfsame room where I had suffered the appalling interrogations – and left us to cool our heels even further. Or so we supposed. However, scarcely a minute passed before Lippi entered, crossed over to the desk and bowed most civilly to us both before motioning us to be seated.

The handsome head, the academic stoop, the gentle smile – they were all a piece of the man as I knew him so well and had latterly come to detest him so much.

His first words were enough to make my hackles rise.

'Did you both greatly enjoy your excursion to Rome?' he asked with a bland smile. 'My own agent, who accompanied you there, spoke of torrential rain – far worse than we experienced here in Venice.' The question and its attendant comment were directed to me, but his eyes slid sidelong, calculatingly, to Jamie.

It was Jamie who answered. 'Can we dismiss the question of the weather, Signor Inspector,' he growled, 'and address ourselves instead to the issue that brought Signorina Mazzini-Forsca here today?'

Not one bit put out, Lippi made a gesture with an elegant hand that suggested his favourite attitude of sweet reasonableness.

'By all means, Colonel Delamere,' he replied. 'It *is* the eminent Colonel Delamere, inventor and patentee of the Delamere reciprocating breech-loading mechanism, later author of distinguished papers on the practical applications of clinical and analytical psychology to the problems of everyday life, and of published works including the highly applauded *After Psychology – What?* and *Healing the Mind?*'

'You're well informed about me, Signor,' said Jamie, without any noticeable show of surprise.

'It is my business to be so, Signor,' came the reply. 'But you were wishing to come to the point about the reason for your visit. Please proceed.'

'To begin,' said Jamie, indicating me, 'I hope – we both hope – to be able to free Signorina Mazzini-Forsca of any lingering suspicion that she was responsible for the death of her late betrothed, the noble Count Bruno Ferrara.'

Lippi smiled sadly. 'Signor, you will have to try very hard, and produce some very hard evidence, to convince me that the verdict of "Not Proven" was not well given in this case.'

'I will try,' replied Jamie. 'And when I've done so, I hope you'll bend all your efforts, which you've so far spent in persecuting Signorina Mazzino-Forsca, to bring the real murderer – or murderers – to justice.'

For the first time ever, I saw Lippi put out of countenance. At my beloved's accusation, twin spots of high colour appeared in his pale cheeks.

'Please continue, Signor,' he breathed.

'You may or may not know,' said Jamie, 'that we went to Rome to contact Signorina Zöe Bonomi, whom we believed to have some private information concerning the true parentage of the child who was fostered by a Signora Gucci of Burano. Upon our arrival at the girl's residence, we found that she had died – been killed – in most suspicious circumstances.'

Lippi shook his head. 'The Bonomi girl died from a fall while riding out,' he said. 'My agent investigated the accident most thoroughly and found it indeed to have been – an accident.'

'Your agent must be a most valiant and expert gentleman,' said Jamie.

'He was sufficiently expert to have kept you both under close surveillance,' replied the other. 'Both on the train, while at luncheon in Florence – and onwards.'

'Florence!' I exclaimed. 'You mean – the blind man in the restaurant?'

Lippi smiled his patronizing smile, treating me with the sort of look you would expect from someone who had unexpectedly found himself in possession of a talking dog.

'Not really blind,' he explained. 'But practising a subtle deception that he learned at the police academy. The young officers are always susceptible to exotic new ideas.

'But please continue, Colonel.'

Now it was Jamie's turn to look out of countenance. But with no obvious lack of assurance he returned to the fray.

'On the night of our arrival in Rome,' he declared, 'the signorina was attacked and nearly thrown to her death at the Hotel Barberini. Account for that if you can!'

Lippi's smile was growing rather tired, the smile of a man of delicate constitution who is easily wearied. Not for the first time, I wondered how he had managed to stand up to the intense interrogations to which he had subjected me.

'Very simple, Colonel,' he replied. 'Petty theft, with or without violence, is rife in Rome. Signorina Mazzini-Forsca, though she dresses tastefully and modestly in her grey, and does not flaunt her jewellery with ostentation, is nevertheless wearing an exquisite pearl and emerald ring at this very moment. . . .'

I glanced down at my finger and realized with a guilty start that I was scarcely aware of the ring in question, much less of what must have been its considerable worth.

'For one hundredth part of that ring's value,' continued Lippi, 'any Roman *borsaiuolo* would risk his own neck – let alone the signorina's.'

'Not a convincing explanation, Signor,' was Jamie's retort to that. 'For, taken in conjunction with everything else, I reckon that a good case can be made for the signorina's life to be in danger.'

'An attempt by a sneak thief,' said Lippi contemptuously, 'some loose talk about another lady dying in suspicious circumstances. What else do you have to back up your case, Colonel?'

Jamie told him about the treatment meted out to Michou the cat, and the message that had accompanied the outrage. But Lippi only sneered.

'It has to be remembered that the lower classes of the city are given to expressing their hatreds rather crudely,' he said. 'As an unacquitted murderess given to the mortal sin of sacrilege, the signorina has aroused much hatred in Venice, particularly among those – the ignorant and superstitious – who believe in the Evil Eye. The sacrifice of the cat – for so they regard it – serves not only as a warning, but also to fend off the Evil Eye.

'Is that all you have to support your case that Signorina Mazzini-Forsca is more sinned against than sinning, Colonel?'

For answer, Jamie stood up and took my hand. I rose also and stood beside him. By the telling glance of Lippi's clever eyes, I could see that the gesture of intimacy between us was not lost on him.

'It's obvious that my evidence has been wasted on you, Signor Lippi,' said Jamie, 'so we'll take up no more of your time.'

'My time has not been wasted, Signor,' responded the other smoothly. He also stood up. 'For so long as you both pursue the truth of this case, you are also helping the Judicial Police.

'Sooner or later, with or without your help, I hope to see the signorina back on trial again – by order of the Italian Senate.

'Good day to you both.'

He bowed us out.

179

There was a disturbing footnote to our ill-fated visit to the office of the Judicial Police which, in view of what came after, remains fixed in my memory. When we emerged into the narrow alleyway behind the great square – a gloomy hole in the corner where the Venetian authorities rightly see fit to hide away the headquarters of that sinister force – we espied a dark figure shambling towards us. Head bowed beneath a seedy black hat, a caped coat thrown carelessly over the shoulders, and pounding the pavement with a stout walking-cane, the man came on at a great pace, looking neither to left nor right. When he drew nearly abreast of us – and we had only just emerged from the door of the office – he met my eyes and I instantly remembered him. Indeed, there was a moment of mutual recognition and the other's brutish mouth narrowed in a forbidding grimace at the sight of me. A moment's pause as his savage eyes sped to take in my companion from head to foot, and he darted in through the doorway of the office.

'By heaven, he's a nasty-looking individual!' exclaimed Jamie. 'And going to the right place, by his looks. One of *them*, I shouldn't wonder.'

'Indeed he is,' I replied. 'That, Jamie, is the creature I knew as my Number One interrogator. He was the brute who broke my spirit and left it to Lippi to piece together after his own fashion. I never knew him by name, but of one thing I'm sure. . . .'

'And what's that, my dearest?' he asked.

'He's the creature I saw peering through the window at us for a brief instant at the Grand Hôtel des Bains on the Lido,' I said. 'Only, I didn't recognize him then. It was the first time I had seen him wearing a hat.'

'Well,' said my beloved. 'That's one mystery cleared up.'

Giuseppe the bodyguard was given the former butler's quarters at the rear of the palazzo, with windows that looked out on to the yard and the south wall of the chapel. As Jamie pointed out, this was the most advantageous place in the building, since no one could leave or enter without passing our bodyguard's forbidding gaze. The double doors by the water gate were henceforth barred and padlocked, and the Palazzo Mazzini-Forsca became again what it had been during the tumultuous days of the Renaissance, when the assassin's sharp dagger and the poisoner's tainted goblet held sway in love and politics: a luxurious fortress against all comers.

The failure of our mission to Lippi left us with few remaining options save to wait for our opponent – or opponents – to make the next move. We did not have long to wait. The following morning a note was brought by hand to the back door. Delivered by a youth of transparent honesty, who had braved the portals of the Woman of the Evil Eye for the sake of a no-doubt generous tip, and who swore he had never seen the party who gave it to him, nor would he know him again, the note was properly sealed and addressed to me in a tolerably educated hand.

The contents were straightforward, but unnerving:

Let the game of cat-and-mouse end without further delay. If the Signorina Mazzini-Forsca will meet me at the gate of the Arsenal tonight at midnight, I will make myself known and tell all. She can then walk free and live no more under a shadow.

'This is interesting,' said Jamie. 'Note how he acknowledges that he's been playing cat-and-mouse with us. *And* he baits the trap with just the inducement we need – the clearing of your name. Look at the tempting way he phrases it – "Walk free and live no more under a shadow". Why, Isolda, that exactly expresses how you feel, doesn't it? I've heard you say the same, or similar, many times.'

'Then what do we do, darling?' I asked. 'Ignore it?'

'No,' he replied. 'We fall for the bait and walk into the trap.' And when I stared at him in astonishment: 'This is the move we've been waiting for, isn't it, my love? Agreed, it's not very attractive, but what else could one expect?

'It's a trap – but we'll see who's the one to be caught. The mouse – or the cat!'

Eleven o'clock. The chimes of half a dozen nearby basilicas

tolled out the hour. The three of us looked at each other — Jamie, the bodyguard Giuseppe, and myself.

'Time to go,' murmured Jamie. 'And I'm still of the opinion, Isolda, that you should have allowed Giuseppe here to have got hold of one of his more slightly-built brethren, dress him in your clothes and take your place.'

'No,' I replied. 'The mind we are up against is too subtle to be taken in by a trick like that. I shall be expected to appear. If I don't turn up, nothing will happen. If I do. . . .' I left the remark unfinished.

'If you do,' Jamie completed it for me. 'If you do, there may be all hell to pay. Fortunately, we're prepared. You are armed, Giuseppe.'

The giant nodded. His hand vanished beneath the heavy cloak he wore, and reappeared holding a short fowling piece, a large-bore musket that peasants of the lagoon and its surroundings use to shoot wildfowl in their dozens. I shuddered to think of the havoc such a terrible weapon could wreak upon a man at close range.

'Good,' said Jamie grimly. 'And I have my pistol. You, Isolda, my dear, have no other weapon than your ready wit — and I'd have you carry no other. If the shooting begins, if there's any sign of physical danger, I beg you to throw yourself to the ground — preferably somewhere in a dark corner out of sight — and stay there till the trouble has subsided. It's a pity,' he added, 'that we're not able to call upon the assistance of the police in this affair — but there it is.

'And now — as to the plan for tonight. . . .'

Jamie produced a rough sketch map of the Arsenal and its surroundings, which he laid out on the table in my sitting room where we were gathered. He was a good draftsman, and one could clearly pick out the narrow, eastern end of the island city and the vicinity of the Arsenal, together with the maze of small canals and water basins around it.

'We'll approach from the Mola and proceed along the waterfront,' said Jamie. 'For if we're being followed — as likely we shall be — there's no point in being fanciful and taking to the back-doubles. However — here' — and he pointed to a spot where one of the minor canals joined the main waters of the lagoon – 'I shall simply disappear.' He smiled at me – that devil-may-care, buccaneering smile that I had lately come to know and love, and which had the power to still all my fears. 'When the bell tower of San Martino comes in sight, Giuseppe will similarly disappear, and you, Isolda, will carry straight on to the rendezvous, approaching it from *this* side of the Arsenal Canal. . . .'

He laid a hand on my shoulder, no doubt seeing the look of sudden alarm that I could not keep out of my eyes. 'It will be an unpleasant five minutes' walk for you, darling. You'll feel very alone and vulnerable. But I shall be close by you, watching your every move and ready to give protection. On the other hand, Giuseppe will be making for the other side of the canal, ready to give you support from that end. By the time you reach the gates of the Arsenal, we shall both be in position. Do you follow me?'

I thought I saw it all very clearly. . . .

'So, we are setting a counter-trap,' I said, 'in which I'm to be the bait, and you two are the jaws of the trap.'

'You've got it right, Isolda,' said Jamie grimly. 'And it's a man-trap!'

We made our final preparations to leave. I was dressed in my grey serge, with a cape to match and a substantial bonnet that tied under the chin. Giuseppe wore the heavy cloak and slouch hat that gondoliers seem to favour when off duty. Jamie had reverted to *le style Anglais*, in a Norfolk jacket, knickerbockers and a flat tweed cap. One last glance at the sketch map, and we departed by way of the back yard and headed as straight for the Piazza San Marco as the narrow, twisting streets allowed us.

There was no moon. No one was about in the darkness, and a chill wind blew off the water, dampening the air. I shivered – and Jamie must have taken the gesture for a touch of fear, for he put one arm round my shoulders and gave me a reassuring squeeze.

'With luck we'll have this thing cleared up tonight, my love,' he murmured. 'Be strong – be my Isolda.'

Emerging from the piazza to the waterfront and keeping the Doge's Palace to our left, we walked swiftly on, our footfalls resounding hollowly from the eyeless buildings, and the water lapping among the gondolas on their mooring posts to the right. Far off, across the lagoon, the lights of an anchored ship stood out against the dark mass of the Lido.

At the third humpbacked bridge from the piazza, Jamie kissed me briefly – and simply disappeared, darting behind the balustrade of the bridge and melting into the darkness. My heart went after him.

I walked on, with Giuseppe trailing slightly behind. The giant's bullet head constantly turned from side to side and behind him, searching out every dark shadow, investigating each splash of water as it touched the foreshore, suspicious of the slightest movement.

Presently the bell tower of the church of San Martino came in sight, darkly silhouetted above the roofs of its quarter. A stone's throw from the ornate entrance to the Arsenal, it was our marker and the signal for Giuseppe to make himself scarce. Indeed, I half-turned my head to give him a nod of farewell and good luck – but he had already gone.

I was on my own!

Alone in the night, where heaven knows what unknown forces of evil were massed against me. From then on, my footfalls sounded much louder, my presence ever more obtrusive in the empty streets, my unguarded back hideously vulnerable.

I checked myself from quickening my step, for there lay the seeds of panic. Likewise, though my every nerve end screamed for me to do it, I resisted the constant, nagging impulse to look behind me – in the fear that some frightful apparition, some nightmare face, might be hovering close by my shoulder and matching its footfalls, step for step, with mine.

The bells rang out the hour of a quarter before midnight, and I was very close. Only one more bridge, and the triumphant archway of the Arsenal loomed into sight, guarded on each side by massive stone lions. My time of trial was fast approaching.

I came to the entrance and took my stand at the foot of a flight of steps leading up into the darkness. Nothing stirred.

No sound but the ever-present plash of wavelets against ancient stone.

I waited, straining my ears into the night of the sleeping city (for Venetians are early to bed and early to rise), probing at the darkness, fearful of seeing anything, yet praying for a sign that my waiting and wondering might soon be over.

I had no watch with me, and took to the notion of counting seconds in my mind. I must have counted out ten minutes, but still the bells did not toll the hour, and nobody came.

Who would come? . . .

That was the next thought to occupy my teeming mind. Would it be someone known to me? A member of the Venetian aristocracy, perhaps? One of the di Rollos, or any of their ilk who had taken the trouble to journey to Verona and witness my downfall in court? Surely, my unknown enemy, or enemies, must be familiar to me – or why else would my destruction be pursued with such frenzy? One does not strike without reason, nor vent one's loathing on a stranger.

Time passed. . . .

I thought I heard something move in the darkness of the great archway behind me, but it could have been a cat, or even a seabird roosting up in the ancient carvings of the frieze. The noise was not repeated.

The first toll of a midnight bell shocked me out of my taut reveries. The bell, instantly followed by all the bells from out of every campanile and dome lantern in Venice, occupied all my attention while the sound lasted. And when the last stroke of midnight sounded from the final bell, and all was silence again, I took stock of myself, knowing that the fateful hour had come.

Was that a figure moving down there, by the humpbacked bridge leading over to San Martino? Did someone give a low whistle from the opposite direction – a signal? Was that someone breathing quite close to me – or was it me?

Suddenly – a shout! . . .

It came from the San Martino direction – so what I saw must have been a living figure. I instinctively backed away into the shadows.

185

And felt myself touching warm flesh!

My mouth opened in a scream, but the sound was checked by a hand that came from behind and wrapped itself roughly across my open mouth. Next instant, I was struggling in a vice-like grip, and a deep voice hissed in my ear:

'Silence, Signorina! Be still!'

It was Giuseppe.

'What's happening?' I whispered when he had released me.

For answer he shook his massive head and, laying a finger on his lips, continued to look out into the darkness in the direction of the bridge leading over the narrow canal to the Church of San Martino, where all was now silent.

But not for long. . . .

There came the crack of a gunshot – and then another. With the second one, I distinctly saw a flare of orange flame, quickly gone. And then there came the sound of running footfalls – going away into the background. A few moments later, the sounds had faded.

'Come, Signorina. Follow behind me,' muttered my companion.

He strode forward, out of the deep shadow, and I saw that he was holding his deadly fowling piece loosely by his side, its wicked muzzle pointing ahead. I crept after him, fearful of what might lie ahead, but glad of the giant's reassuring presence. I would not have stayed alone at the gate of the Arsenal for all the world.

We had not gone more than half way to the humpbacked bridge when I saw – *it*. . . .

A still form lay close by the bridge, half in and half out of shadow. At the sight of it I gave a cry of alarm and ran forward. Brushing aside Giuseppe's restraining hand I went on, and falling on my knees beside the prostrate figure, turned the face sideways to my gaze. And found myself staring down into the unconscious features of the man I loved.

'Jamie – oh, my dearest! What have they done to you? How could they, how *could* they?'

Keening, I held his limp head against my breast and felt

186

the sticky blood well upon my fingers. His dark hair was matted with blood.

I almost fought Giuseppe when, with an unbelievable gentleness, he detached me from poor stricken Jamie and examined him closely about the head and neck.

'Has he been – shot?' I faltered.

'Hit over the head, I think,' was the giant's response. 'Better get him to a doctor. Take this, Signorina. It's safe.' And he passed me his fowling piece.

I watched, suffering every movement for Jamie's sake as massive Giuseppe slowly and carefully picked up the limp form in his massive arms as if it had been a sleeping babe.

As I moved to follow him, my foot knocked against something lying in the shadows. It was a pistol – Jamie's pistol. It smelt of hot powder, and I knew that he must have fired at least one of the shots I had heard.

We slowly directed our footsteps back the way we had come. As I trailed sadly behind Giuseppe and his unconscious burden, I had the clear realization of how badly our carefully-laid plans had come to nothing.

We had set a trap with me as bait, but the cunning enemy had ignored the bait and taken out one jaw of the intended trap. And that, clearly, had been the intent – to deprive me of my aid and my love, my life, my everything – leaving me alone, bereft and helpless.

The good sisters were loving charity itself. They took in poor Jamie without question and laid him on a bed in a quiet, high-ceilinged room. The doctor arrived soon after: a bustling little man with a beaming smile that hardly faltered as he bent over my Jamie and examined the cruel wound at the back of his head. He then indicated to the sisters to remove me from the ward.

I sat by myself on a hard chair in a long, echoing chamber in the heart of the hospital, waiting. As if reluctant to impose upon my misery, Giuseppe distanced himself at the far end, leaning against the wall, narrow-eyed and watchful – searching out the face of each nun who bustled past on her night's business, for the hospital never sleeps. Still performing his duty as guardian, the former gondolier gave me great comfort, and I realized that I was not totally alone.

The first grey light of dawn was seeping in through the high windows set in the whitewashed stone walls when the doctor came out to speak to me. I saw, by the weariness and expression of defeat in his face, and by the leaden dragging of his tired feet, that his night's work had not been crowned with success.

'Is he? . . .' I prompted him.

'He lives,' was the response.

'Thank God!'

'But he is very poorly — very poorly indeed.'

'Is he going to die, Doctor?'

'I don't know, Signorina.'

'May I see him, please?'

'He is deeply unconscious, dear lady. In a coma, from which he may never emerge.'

'Oh, no-o-o!' I breathed.

'In fact, if he were to depart this life without waking, it might well be deemed to be a blessing.'

'But why — why?' I cried. 'To have him alive and awake, even if injured, still, that would be something. . . .'

I paused when I saw the look in his kindly face. It was compounded of pity, sorrow — and embarrassment.

It was then, slowly, haltingly, he managed to bring himself to tell me the whole truth in its stark brutality. The savage blow that Jamie had received to the back of the head had caused severe damage to the brain — so severe that it put him beyond the skills of medical science, which could only spell out the options open to him. . . .

He could recover consciousness, sooner or later, and be as right as he had ever been.

Or he could remain in a coma for an hour, a day, a year, or for his whole lifetime. Or pass at any time from unconsciousness to death.

The last alternative — the one which the doctor had spoken of so grimly as a bad alternative to merciful death — was that he could emerge from the coma, no longer as my Jamie Delamere, but as a thing with the superficial likeness of a human being. Mindless. Condemned to eke out the rest of his life as a non-person.

Eleven

'The monsignor will see you now, Signorina Mazzini-Forsca.'

The smooth cleric moved aside to let me pass. I had waited half an hour in an unheated room of the Cardinal Archbishop's palace, and with commendable patience. I had learned patience, and come to embrace it as a friend during the last three months.

The Cardinal Archbishop's chaplain rose from his seat — none too quickly — upon my entrance. He had scarcely changed since the day he had officiated at Bruno's funeral on San Michele: the unlined face with its self-regarding blandness that could be so easily mistaken for youth, the tendency not to meet one's eye.

He was courtesy itself, motioning me to a seat and inquiring after my health and that of 'the American gentleman'. Taking everything into account — for, of course, he knew all about me, and had probably guessed at the time, as I had, that I was certain to be arrested soon after the funeral was safely over — he was presenting himself as a model of Christian charity. I was much heartened.

'Now, Signorina,' he said at length, making what was surely a quite unneccessary protraction of studying a paper before him, 'to the matter of the petition that you have submitted to His Eminence.'

'Yes. The petition begging to be allowed to marry my fiancé Colonel Delamere,' I supplied.

'Who is at present in a state of — ah, where did I put the medical report? . . .' He rifled amongst his papers.

'A state of deep coma,' I interposed. 'And has been so

190

for three months since his accid . . . since he was savagely attacked.'

'Quite so,' said the chaplain. 'I have the report here. A few brief moments, if you please, while I refresh my memory as to details. . . .' He was soon immersed in a many-paged report, a copy of which had also been sent to me and which I could have recited to him from memory – every word and phrase burnt on my mind in letters of bitter fire.

But it was going to be all right, I told myself. The Cardinal Archbishop, in his well-known compassion, would certainly permit me to marry the poor, unconscious man who had plighted his troth to me, and to whom I was joined by the ties of a love that knew no bounds, so that I felt as close to the poor imprisoned mind in that injured head as I had ever done in his brilliant wakefulness.

The chaplain presently laid aside the report, placed his hands together, as if in prayer and, resting his elbows on the desk, touched his lips with the tips of his beautifully-tended fingernails.

'A very grave condition,' he mused. 'The doctors do not hold out any great hope of complete recovery.'

'But there is always hope!' I blurted out.

'Quite so, quite so!' he responded, and his youthful-looking face was suffused with a sudden radiance. 'There is always room for hope. And prayer,' he added.

'However. . . .'

'What was His Eminence's reaction to my request?' I cried, adding in more subdued tones, 'And has he come to any decision?'

The chaplain made more play of re-reading the paper before him.

'To take a few points,' he said at length. 'Colonel Delamere is a member of the Faith, so you declare.'

'Yes.'

'At what church does he worship – I should say, *did* he worship – while in the See of Venice?' The eyes met mine blandly, without any guile.

'I – don't know,' I replied truthfully.

'But he did worship during his time here – when he was well. Before his affliction?'

'I don't know,' I admitted.

'That raises difficulties in one's mind,' said the chaplain. He returned his gaze to the paper.

'You say that you are affianced to this unfortunate gentleman?' he said. 'Then, presumably, you either took part in a ceremony of betrothal, or gave proper notice to the incumbent priest at the church of your choice that you wished to participate in such a ceremony?'

'No,' I whispered in a voice that sounded very unlike my own.

'You did not?' He looked surprised – shocked, even.

'We – we didn't have time,' I explained.

'You didn't have time?' he stared at me in blank disbelief. 'You *didn't* find time to plight your troth in the proper manner, taking solemn vows regarding your intent?'

'No,' I said. 'We met. After a while, we fell in love. Within days, before we could do anything about it, he was – taken from me. . . .' I felt my resolve crumbling, and fumbled in my reticule for a handkerchief.

'Very well, very well,' said the chaplain briskly. 'Let us pursue the point. Did this gentleman intimate to a third party, or in any letter, of his intention to marry you?'

I thought for a moment. 'Well,' I said, 'we were on the point of confiding in Assunta – that's my old nurse – but something intervened. Something rather – serious.'

'Something more serious intervened,' repeated the man behind the desk. 'Very well, Signorina. I think I have the picture in my mind.' He returned to the paper, and I stared at his bowed head with its beautifully-tended hair – and smouldered inside me.

Little fool, I told myself. You're losing the day. He doesn't even believe that Jamie asked you to marry him. But why – why should he imagine that you'd make it all up? For what reason would I be telling him a tissue of lies, does he think?

I soon had my answer. . . .

He looked up, and his gaze was now directed to a spot somewhere above my left shoulder.

'Ah, it appears that the gentleman in question possessed – indeed still possesses – considerable financial means,' he said. 'Do I have my facts aright, Signorina?'

'I believe so, Monsignor,' I replied. 'But I don't really know, for, you see. . . .'

'According to an affidavit from the United States Consulate,' said the other, 'Colonel Delamere is a very rich man indeed. Rich and distinguished as soldier, inventor, scientist. . . .'

His eyes upon the affidavit in question, his voice droned on, and I knew what the outcome was going to be. My petition to be joined in matrimony to the man I loved and who loved me was going to be refused on doctrinal grounds. That was reasonable. Outrageous, but reasonable within its lights.

But the other reason – the insinuation that I was taking advantage of a poor, stricken and possibly fatally brain-damaged man, deeply unconscious and unable to speak out for himself, to falsely claim that he had asked for my hand in marriage, in order to enlist the aid of the Church in a fraudulent attempt to steal that man's fortune for myself (for what else was the chaplain implying?) – that was more than I could bear.

By the time the chaplain had finished commenting upon the United States Consulate's affidavit, I had risen to my feet. When he saw this, the monsignor looked up with an expression of mild surprise.

'Pray don't get up, Signorina,' he said. 'I must now tell you that, taking your case carefully into consideration, I find no grounds for submitting your petition to His Eminence. No – please don't go – I would further add that, should the unfortunate gentleman be recovered to full health in his mind, so that he expresses a wish to be joined with you in Holy Matrimony with the blessing of the Mother Church, I can foresee no impediment. . . .

'What – are you leaving, Signorina?' He seemed quite put out by my unceremonious departure.

'Thank you, Monsignor,' I said over my shoulder. 'I take your point. And I'm sorry to have wasted so much of your valuable time.'

Assunta was appalled. Of course I had told her of my intention, and she had been waiting on tenterhooks for news of my audience at the Cardinal Archbishop's palace. When I told her what had happened, her mouth fell open in dismay.

'I can scarcely believe it, my darling,' she declared. 'Why, I'm sure, quite sure that this decision cannot have been the wish of Our Blessed Lady, let alone that of His Eminence – who always looks such a kindly man.'

'I don't think Our Blessed Lady was consulted in the matter,' I retorted tartly. 'His Eminence certainly wasn't. The rejection of my petition to be allowed to marry the man I love and who loves me got no further than the desk of that upstart chaplain!'

Poor devout Assunta may have been gravely dismayed by my irreverence, and certainly looked it. She covered her head with her apron after her fashion, and wept bitterly.

A few weeks after Jamie's injury, when it became apparent that a quick return to consciousness was out of the question, I had had another visit from – of all people – Inspector Lippi.

He came unannounced, and Assunta showed him into my sitting room, where I received him – so eager and restless was I for activity, any sort of activity – without hesitation.

He limped in, bowed deeply to me, and took the seat I indicated. I thought immediately that I discerned in him a very marked change of attitude towards me. There was a certain guarded watchfulness in his manner, where formerly he had dominated me by smooth condescension and soft words. Now, he seemed at a loss to express himself.

'Signorina,' he began, avoiding my eye, 'I think I may owe you an apology.'

'Indeed, Signor?' I replied. Apologies in plenty, I thought, but which of the many owed to me do you have in mind?

The fine-looking head was bowed. He appeared to be busily engaged upon examining the crook of his walking-stick.

'I think that we – that is the Judicial Police – may, after all, have been mistaken in judging you to be guilty of Count Bruno's murder,' he said quietly.

I drew a deep breath and slowly exhaled it before I could trust myself to respond to this astonishing statement.

194

'Signor Inspector,' I said, 'are you telling me that all the torments you and your colleague put me through in an attempt to pin upon me the guilt for a crime I never committed – were all to no purpose whatever?'

He nodded. 'I think so,' he replied. 'Circumstantial evidence – particularly of the sort that surrounded you and your doings – can be very damning. But circumstances also cut both ways. I think that all that has happened to you since – culminating in the brutal attack upon Colonel Delamere – and, by the way, how is the colonel? . . .'

'No change in his condition,' I replied.

'Oh, I am so sorry,' he said. And he looked sorry. 'As I was saying, the savage injuries received by Colonel Delamere have convinced me – that's to say, the Judicial Police – that there are forces ranged against you and the colonel which are more likely to have brought about the death of Count Bruno than you, yourself. That, Signorina, is what I have come to tell you today.'

'Thank you, Signor Inspector,' I responded in a very tight, small voice that I was trying desperately to keep under control. 'You'll forgive me if I say that your apology and retraction come too late to be of any use to me. I have been tried on tainted evidence and branded for life as a murderess who got away with it. You'll also forgive me, Signor Inspector, if I don't fall upon my knees and give thanks to you for your apology. If it had come earlier – for instance, when Colonel Delamere and I came to plead with you – he might not now be lying at death's door, and worse. Even earlier, and my beloved sister – now missing, perhaps dead – might still be here.'

I got to my feet, hinting that I wanted rid of him. He took the hint. As he turned to leave me, I had a wayward thought. . . .

'How is your colleague, the one with the unfortunate manner, who also interrogated me?' I asked. 'I never knew his name, but we met him outside your headquarters that day.'

'You mean Sub-Inspector Minghetti,' he replied. 'He is well enough. Why do you ask, Signorina?'

'Well, at that time, I realized that it was he who followed

the colonel and me to the Lido, after you decided to have us spied on everywhere we went,' I said.

A puzzled look flitted across his sensitive, clever face.

'Indeed?' he replied, adding, half to himself, 'The Lido, eh? I had quite forgotten.'

On that inconclusive note, he left me.

All during those three hideous months of Jamie's deep coma I visited him daily, sitting by his bedside for most of the daylight hours, watching over him, talking to him constantly in the – as it proved to be – vain hope of some response, helping the hard-pressed nuns by tending to his few and simple needs. Feeding him was the most difficult function. This we did by the technique of introducing a rubber tube through the nostril and down the oesophagus, so that liquid nourishment such as beef broth could be admitted.

Apart from Jamie, my life was an empty desert. I made constant and fruitless attempts to trace Julietta, employing inquiry agents in the main European centres – and becoming ever more convinced of her untimely death. During the period of her absence there had been several virulent influenza epidemics throughout the continent, not counting the fatal fevers which were prevalent in the sprawling and polluted cities. Always a rather delicate child, she might well have fallen victim to any such scourges as these. In any event, I mourned her for dead, and tenderly consigned her to my memories of golden days past and the regrets of what might have been.

It was soon after my disastrous audience at the Cardinal Archbishop's palace – no more than a week – that I had yet another of the cryptic communications from the unknown and faceless enemy. As before, it was delivered by an innocent hand. As before, it was brief, and carried overtones of menace:

You have learned your lesson. Let the dead lie in peace and you will suffer no more. Make some clear public announcement that you agree to this suggestion and the rest will be forgotten. After all, you really have no choice in the matter. I have beaten you, but you may crawl away to die in bed in your own good time.

196

I put the wretched thing away in my bureau, thinking to give the so-called suggestion of a surrender to my unknown enemy – or, at best, a truce – some further thought. After all, I told myself, the real damage was done to me. Bruno gone, Julietta gone, my reputation in shreds and – most poignantly of all – Jamie reduced to a comatose vegetable. What else was left for me? Revenge? When Jamie was well and whole, I had yearned for revenge – and in following that yearning, my loved one had suffered most appallingly.

Might it not be better to let things slide? Provide my unknown enemy with the sign he called for – a word, a gesture, that I had given up the quest for revenge and the clearing of my name?

Perhaps. I would give it some thought. The choice, in any event, was all mine. No one else was involved any more – only Jamie, and he was beyond caring about vengeance.

Or so I told myself. But, as so often happens, the choice was virtually taken from out of my hands, and I was shocked out of my placid acceptance by a most poignantly dramatic incident.

It happened a day or so later at the hospital. I arrived there as usual at six o'clock in the morning, when the patients were being washed and fed in preparation for the morning's rounds of the Reverend Mother, the doctors and surgeons, and such visiting dignitaries as the Mother General of the Order, envoys, legates, ambassadors and suchlike. There I found little Sister Agatha, the nun who had special care of Jamie, in a tizzy of excitement.

'Signorina Mazzini-Forsca, Signorina Mazzini-Forsca!' cried Sister Agatha – she was scarcely more than a child and years away from her final vows. 'The colonel opened his eyes and spoke just a short while ago. He spoke, Signorina! He *spoke!*'

Naturally my heart leapt, and I rushed with her into the quiet room where Jamie was kept all alone. He was just as I had left him the evening before: lying on his back, arms held limply at his sides, eyes closed as if in sleep, mouth slightly open. And I experienced an immediate pang of disappointment.

'How long ago was it that he opened his eyes and spoke,

Sister?' I asked, eyeing the child doubtfully, for though a dear, sweet person, she was given to her over-enthusiasms that sometimes led her along paths of fancy.

Only, this time she was oddly convincing, and the first excitement of greeting me with the news over, quite rational and calm.

'It was just over half an hour ago, Signorina,' she said. 'I had come in to draw the shutters and put out the night-light, when I suddenly heard a sound from the bed, here. I went over to the colonel, and there he lay – looking at me. Truth to tell, I was rather disappointed when he didn't smile, or anything, but then I remembered that he didn't know me from Adam, nor could he have had the slightest idea where he was.'

'But he spoke?' I demanded of her. 'He spoke to you, you told me. What did he say? Sister Agatha – tell me quickly, I beg you. Did he – did he speak my name?'

'No-o-o, I don't think so,' said the girl, 'but then, I didn't really catch anything he said at all, for by the time he'd opened his mouth to speak, I was half way over to the door to fetch Sister Mary Joseph and show her the miracle. Then, by the time I reached his bedside again, his eyes were closed and he was unconscious.'

'But – if it happened once, it could happen again!' I cried. 'And, next time, he might come round for good.

'Oh, Sister Agatha!' I turned to her and saw her eyes dancing for joy and surely mirroring mine. 'Perhaps he will be sitting up by luncheon and demanding his favourite dishes, and complaining if they aren't cooked just so, and. . . .'

I realized, without any shame, that I was crying like a babe. And little Sister Agatha was crying too.

Sister Mary Joseph, in charge of the wards, was told of the great event and gave it as her opinion that Jamie would most certainly become conscious again. It was, she said – and she had had considerable experience of head injuries – part of a familiar pattern of recovery. But, she warned me – and her saintly old countenance grew grave when she did so – it would be unwise to expect too much, too soon.

'Be thankful, my dear, for any improvement from what he

198

is now,' she said. 'And we'll see what our prayers can do to help nature along.'

All visitors and nursing staff were forbidden to enter the room on Sister Mary Joseph's orders. She said that she would even exclude the morning rounds – an almost unheard-of thing. I was to stay with the colonel on my own, she said. Sit with him. Talk quietly to him, and wait. Wait and hope.

She left me. They all left me. I was alone with the man I loved – and a whole bushel of hopes.

I talked to him all that morning. Beginning with the earliest memories of my life, I recounted every event I could remember, I told him of the dreary succession of governesses whose lives I had plagued in the little schoolroom on the third floor back of the Palazzo Mazzini-Forsca, about my adventures at finishing school, how I ran away and came home. On a sadder and more serious note, I touched upon how my mother's last illness had tarnished the brilliance of our happiness as a family, and then of the awful pall which had fallen upon us at her passing. All that morning, as I chattered on, passing from smiles to tears, from sunshine to shadow, I never for one moment let my eyes stray from the beloved face, and every so often reached down to brush aside a stray lock of hair and smooth the pillow by his cheek. During his three months' absence into the unknown world of the inner mind, Sister Agatha and I had mutually taken the decision to allow him to go unshaven as an alternative to submitting him to the hospital barber every day. Accordingly, his face was now framed with a most handsome naval-style beard, which I personally kept scissor-trimmed to sleek perfection, permitting the finial at the chin to grow out in a rather rakish point – like some proud Spanish conquistador of old.

The morning passed. The afternoon shadows crept over the tiled floor of the room. In a day marked by the sound of the nuns singing the Canonical hours down in the chapel, I lived through an agony of waiting. Matins, Prime, Tierce and Sext, Nones and Vespers – I suffered through them all. Compline I never heard, for sheer weariness overtook me then, and I drifted away to sleep sitting up – only to be shocked into sudden and shattering wakefulness by the movement of the hand which I had held in mine throughout the livelong day.

He was stirring! Jamie was coming back to me!

'Jamie, my darling!' I whispered urgently, close by his ear, and those dear lips moved slightly as if in response. 'Jamie, it's me – Isolda. Your Isolda!'

Something like a sigh issued from those lips, and I thought his eyelids flickered. I gently chafed his hand and continued to talk to him, calling his name and my own, straining to make some contact with him in the dark recesses of his emerging mind, reaching out to touch a phantom hand which, it seemed to me, was blindly striving to touch mine.

'Is all well?'

The whispered question shocked me to reality. It came from Sister Mary Joseph, who, entering the room without my hearing her, was standing behind me and, like me, peering down into the silent face on the pillow.

'His hand moved just now,' I whispered. 'And I'm sure he tried to say something.'

'And look!' I pointed. 'He's trying to open his eyes!'

'Bless us all, so he is!' murmured the old nun. 'Yes, the poor dear man's coming round, there's no doubt of it. Our prayers are to be answered!'

Sister lit a night-light, and its rosy glow threw the still face into the perfection of some martyred saint in a canvas by one of the old Venetian masters – but, to my bitter disappointment, also served to show that the slight movements of the eyes had now ceased again.

My companion squeezed my shoulder comfortingly. 'Have patience, my dear child,' she whispered. 'He is coming back to you. I feel it. I will stay with you, and we'll pray together.' So saying, the old lady knelt by the bedside, and her saintly, lined face took on a seraphic stillness.

I remained where I was, crouched, holding the still hand, gazing down into the expressionless countenance of the man who was my only reason for living.

The hours of the night slipped past, marked by the tolling of the city bells.

Sleep never had another chance to win me. Not any longer.
Stillness.

A sense of peace.

And then. . . .

He awoke!

His eyelids flickered, flashed open to disclose those brilliantly dark blue eyes. The fingers tensed against mine – tightly, so that I called out with the shock of sudden pain. His whole body stirred. His mouth opened for a violent intake of breath, which he then exhaled in an explosion of sound. But no words.

The words came afterwards. . . .

For as long as I live and breathe, I shall never be able to shut out the sound of that voice arising from the inner mind. It blasts at my ears in the dark hours of sleeplessness, in lonely places where one sometimes strays, in desolate graveyards and empty churches, unlit city streets and other places of unease.

I have tried to write it down many times, in the hope, perhaps, of exorcizing the sounds from my memory – but nothing comes but a jumble of mixed vowels and consonants, giving not the slightest interpretation of what I heard and what poor, shocked Sister Mary Joseph heard as she looked up from her prayers in awful surmise.

It was not so much the jumble of barbaric sound as the tones in which the gibberish was delivered. I should explain that my darling Jamie's normal voice was a well-modulated baritone, deeply shaded in the lower registers, lightly overladen with the accents of his country of origin, and entirely pleasant to the ear.

I knew an old lady who lived all alone, poor soul, in a tumbledown mansion at the slum end of the Grand Canal. As an act of charity I used to visit her when I was a girl, along with Assunta, and take her a few goodies, sit with her a while and try to cheer her up. She owned an old parrot – a cross, complaining thing with most of its feathers gone. It would jump up and down on its perch at the sight of strangers and shriek in a shrill, high-pitched cackle.

The gibberish that issued from the lips of my beloved was delivered at me in the selfsame, shrill and inhuman screech of that old, mad parrot!

201

Sister Mary Joseph called urgently for Anselmo. Anselmo was a crippled ex-porter, a man, nevertheless, of considerable strength, who lived in a hovel within the covent walls and was kept to do the rough work around the place – as well as to be on call to help with any of the patients who might become unruly. He it was who dragged me away from the screeching figure in the bed, freed my hand and arm from a grip that had the power and frenzy of insanity. I cowered and watched as he then held the writhing form imprisoned while the doctor forced heavy draughts of laudanum between those foam-flecked lips, till all motion ceased and my Jamie was lying unconscious again – once more the martyred saint from a painting.

Sister Mary Joseph embraced me. 'Have peace, my dear,' she said. 'This is just a phase he is passing through. The healing process has not yet properly begun, but things are moving. We must continue to hope and pray.'

I did not answer her, for my own faith was not equal to the task of accepting that the thing which had manifested itself inside the outer shell of the man I had known as Jamie Delamere was going to be exorcized so easily. Not all the faith in the world, surely, could accomplish so much.

A great bitterness had entered my heart – and with it a savage determination.

The hour between midday and luncheon is the time when the smart set of Venice promenades in the great square in front of the cathedral and inevitably is attracted towards Florian's for an aperitif.

I chose my time very carefully, just as I chose the costume I should wear for the occasion: a two-piece in dove-grey, with a cloak in a contrasting darker shade, and a Cossack-style fur hat in the same colour. I, too, promenaded with the smart set, and won many glances – scandalized, appraising, hate-filled, wistful, lustful, affronted, depending upon the subject's age and sex. I, too, went into the famous café when I judged that all the best people, the influential people, would be gathered there and chattering away like parakeets. It was a pity, in a way, that summer was not with us, so that tables would have been laid outside and the orchestra playing light

202

pieces from the popular repertoire. But, on the other hand, the crowded interior would provide me with a better platform.

The chatter ceased as soon as I entered the glass doors. All heads turned to regard me as I remained poised there. A few – the more sensitive – quickly looked away again, but the majority continued to feast their eyes upon That Woman with unconcealed malevolence.

The manager, seeing me standing there, came fussing up. He was the same Signor Rossi whom Jamie had lately made a fool of, and he clearly remembered the occasion. This, and his understandable wish to rid his establishment of That Woman, dictated his approach.

'No more room, Signorina!' he snapped.

'There is ample room, Signor,' I responded in a quiet voice which, because of the utter silence that had fallen upon the watchers, penetrated to the furthest corners of the café.

'However,' I added, 'what I have to say may best be said standing up.'

This remark reduced Rossi to silence with the rest. I let my eye drift over the watching faces – recognizing many of them from the balls and parties, the soirées and salons that my mother had held in our Golden Days – and waited till I thought I had each and every one of them literally sitting on the very edge of his chair with sheer suspense, breathless, waiting for me to speak again.

I spoke. . . .

'You know me,' I said. 'Most of you know me by name. For those who do not, I am Isolda Mazzini-Forsca, daughter of the Principe and Principessa di Mazzini-Forsca, betrothed of the late Count Bruno Ferrara, whose murdered body was found on the altar of our family chapel.'

I paused to gauge my audience. Not a sound. Not by so much as the flicker of an eyelash was anyone going to disturb the atmosphere which I had created. I had them in the palm of my hand. I then proceeded to flagellate them. . . .

'Some of you were present at my trial for the murder of my fiancé. You came in your gaudiest clothes and your richest jewels to see a woman crucified for a crime she did not commit. I do not think you were disappointed, for instead of

203

being put away, I was released to your tender mercies – to your snubs and insults, to the scandalmongering and the petty cruelties which you have heaped upon me since that day.

'Along with those who put me in the dock and gave me a mockery of a trial, you are also responsible for the fate of my beloved sister, who fled from the horror of life with me and is lost to me for ever.

'You will be pleased to know, Signors and Signoras, that, so far as I am concerned, your guilt ends there. Furthermore, if you would wish to absolve yourselves from that guilt, you should all do me a small service.'

I paused and drew a deep breath. This was the moment that I had been awaiting for so long – my opportunityy to strike back at the faceless creature, or creatures, who had brought me to the state in which I stood – and by whose hand my beloved Jamie had been reduced to the condition he was now in.

'Signors and Signoras,' I continued. 'The murderer, or murderers, of my late fiancé are still at large and persecuting me. Having brought me and my loved ones to our knees – *or so they think* – they are willing to leave me be. The expression used was: "You may crawl away and die in bed."

'Do this for me, my friends, and you will earn my forgiveness. . . .

'Tell it in the streets and canals of our city. Declare it in the churches, have your priests proclaim it from their pulpits – that Isolda Mazzini-Forsca has not learned her lesson, is not beaten, and will not crawl away to die!

'If you should know the face or faces of my enemy, or enemies, speak out loud, eye to eye. Say that Isolda Mazzini-Forsca will neither slumber nor sleep till she has ripped the mask from the face of evil.'

One last blast of denunciation and I would be finished. . . .

'If you are in this room, listening to me, Face of Evil – Remember!

'*Remember!*'

With that, I turned and swept out of the café. Half way across the great square, the silence which I had left behind me erupted into a sudden welling of tumultuous sound, the sound of many voices raised in excitement, speculation, affront and heaven knows what else. I smiled tightly to myself, regarding the hubbub as a sign that my outburst had struck home. Like an actor on the stage when the curtain comes down on his performance, I had won myself a sort of applause.

'I hope I did it right, Jamie,' I murmured aloud. 'The idea was yours in the first place.'

PART THREE

The Quest

Twelve

Spring came and went, and after it the year's roundelay.
Winter arrived, and my life continued unchanged.

I went daily to the hospital. In the interminable months
since his terrible injury, Jamie had showed no signs of the
living mind that lay entrapped in darkness, save on that one
terrible occasion when someone – or something – else had
briefly appeared to us. Blessedly, there was no recurrence of
that. He simply remained comatose and serene. The passing
months wrought some change upon his features, slendering
and refining them and bringing them closer to the image of
a martyred saint. His thick pelt of dark hair became shot
with flecks of grey. He lost a considerable amount of weight,
but – the very notion would seem ridiculous if it were not
true – the physicians declared that, taking all considerations
into account, the patient was physically in quite excellent
health!

Following upon my declamation in Florian's café, the attitude of the Venetians generally underwent a subtle change
towards me. I was treated to no special civilities, no one
ever wished me 'good day', or nodded to me in the streets.
Nevertheless I no longer seemed to be regarded as a social
outcast and pariah. Urchins did not shout after me in the
alleyways any more. Mothers did not drag their infants away
from my path, nor did the more superstitious avoid walking
in my shadow. People did not cross themselves in my presence, nor make the sign to avert the Evil Eye. I never overheard myself being spoken of as 'That Woman', 'The
Mazzini-Forsca Woman', 'The Murderess', or 'The Sacri-

legious One'. Because of the semi-mourning that I had worn ever since my trial, I was simply referred to as 'The Woman in Grey'.

This grudging consideration that I received was undoubtedly the result of my 'speech' at Florian's, which certainly must have been passed around the city in no time at all. But my daily attendance at the hospital, where I not only assisted with Jamie, but also gave a little of my spare time to helping with some of the other patients, undoubtedly won me an entirely undeserved reputation for piety and charity of the sort usually reserved for penitents. All the world respects a penitent!

Nor was I troubled any more by the force that I had come to call the Face of Evil. Whoever was behind the tragedies of my life must certainly have heard my challenge, and had taken note of it. Perhaps for fear of drawing further attention to itself, the Face of Evil had decided to take no further action against me.

It was as if peace had returned to my life at last – except for the thought of Jamie lying there in the silent room at the hospital, and the conviction that I would never know the whereabouts of Julietta's grave.

And so we continued some sort of untrammelled existence at the Palazzo Mazzini-Forsca. Assunta's health gave me cause for worry. The poor old dear now suffered cruelly from rheumatism and seldom ventured out of her sitting room. It still being impossible for me to find a servant – even if I had wanted one – it was left to me to act as cook and housekeeper for the both of us. Naturally, I closed down even more of the splendid rooms, leaving us only our two small suites, plus the old housekeeper's kitchen in which I did all the cooking.

Apart from our own, one set of rooms remained untouched since the day they had been vacated. They comprised the suite – my father's old suite – that Jamie had used for the short time he had lived under my family roof. In imitation of poor Queen Victoria of England after the untimely death of her beloved Prince-Consort Albert, I kept those rooms exactly as he had left them, and went to them every day, to dust and polish, to run my hands over his suits in the ward-

210

robe, his neckties and shoes, the pieces of personal jewellery, shaving tackle, watch and chain, cufflinks, and so forth. Unlike poor Victoria, I was not driven to the extreme of causing hot water and clean towels to be placed in the dressing room every morning and eve – but I prayed for the day when it would be necessary for me to do so.

It was for Jamie's sake, above all, that I did not give up the palazzo, despite the inconvenience of the great establishment, never mind the financial advantage I could have gained from renting or leasing out the old place. And yet, in the last resort, my home was full of so many dear memories that I don't suppose I would have quit it under any circumstances.

The place was full of ghosts. Some of them, at least, made their presence felt – and heard. . . .

The footsteps in the upstairs corridor had begun to manifest themselves in the autumn of the previous year. I heard them during a sleepless night, and put the sounds down to the rattling of a loose window frame upstairs. The giant ex-gondolier, who no longer lived in the palazzo, but had moved back with his widowed mother on the Giudecca and still worked for me as an odd-job man, went up to investigate the source of the noise next day and reported that a faulty window was, in fact, the culprit. Nevertheless I continued to hear these manifestations. One night I woke to hear *whispering* on the stairwell. I should explain that the main staircase of the building – a most sumptuous structure, wide enough to take a carriage and horses, as an ancestor of mine had once demonstrated – had the knack of so enlarging sounds that the merest whisper at the top of its four flights could be heard quite clearly at the bottom. For this reason, it was not surprisingly known as 'The Whispering Stair'. Be that as it may, one does not expect to hear muttered voices in an establishment housing only one other person, and she almost bed-ridden, at two o'clock in the morning!

Though considerably uneasy, I lit a candle and went to investigate, commencing at the landing outside my door. I listened. The sounds had ceased. Taking courage, I mounted the broad stairs, the sound of my slippered footfalls entirely muffled by the thick Persian carpeting. Nothing on the landing above. I went on. The floor above that, which had been largely given over to my mother's personal apartment, was also quiet.

At least – for a moment or so, while I stood still and listened.

But then, as I turned to move on up to the next and last flight, I distinctly heard a door close behind me – *inside my mother's apartment!*

Much alarmed, my first impulse was to flee back the way I had come, but common curiosity and a loving familiarity with the old palazzo won over my fears. I decided to investigate more closely.

The door into the apartment was unlocked, with the key on the outside, and it was certainly not that door which I had heard. I went on in, to a small hallway where four doors led off – as I knew – to my mother's sitting room, bedroom, dressing room and bathroom. They were the only remaining doors in the apartment – *and they were all wide open!*

I remained transfixed there for some few minutes, trying to come to terms with this curious puzzle – how someone, or something, had quite quietly and deliberately closed a door that did not exist?

'Assunta, tell me – why are the inner doors left wide open in my mother's apartment?'

I was serving her a breakfast tray in bed the following morning, for the poor creature was racked with rheumatism. She glanced up at me in some surprise at my question.

'Why, dear, to allow a free circulation of air,' she replied, 'so as to prevent the dry rot from attacking the panelling.'

'I see. And the outer door is always kept unlocked?'

'Of course, Isolda,' she replied, still puzzled, 'for anything that might have attracted a burglar was put away in the safe long since. Why do you want to know?'

I told her. . . .

'Ghosts?' she said when I had finished my tale. 'Well, I've heard tell of the place being haunted in your grandfather's day, but that was natural. He was married to an English-woman, and they're an odd lot, the English. My mother was in service when that Lord Byron was in Venice, you know.

Wild, ungovernable creature, he was. *And* all his lady friends. They'd go racing horses in the sands at the Lido during low tide. There are some on the Lido who claim to see the bad, mad Lord Byron riding out on the foreshore when the moon is full. I well remember hearing . . .'

Cutting short her reminiscences, I said: 'What was the haunting in my grandfather's day, Assunta?'

'Well,' she said, 'it all began with the coming of the English woman. No sooner had she moved in than she was complaining about noises in the apartment and on the stair.'

'Noises – what kind of noises?' I demanded.

'Same as you're talking about, dear,' came the answer. 'Footsteps in the night, banging doors, mutterings on the stair. As to the mutterings, the Englishwoman was shown how even a breath of wind made that kind of sound on the Whispering Stair, but she would have it that the place was haunted – or so I've always been told.'

I let the matter rest there, convinced that we were talking at cross purposes. Assunta did not take seriously my tale of footsteps, whisperings and closing doors; I set my face firmly against any question of there being a supernatural explanation for the sounds. So I changed the subject to that of her health.

'Assunta, there's a clinic in Treviso,' I told her, 'that treats elderly people with your complaint. I understand it's run by a famous German doctor who once had a practice in Baden-Baden – that's where Uncle Tommaso went to recoup after his accident, you know. So I thought . . .'

'You're not sending me off to an old people's home!' she cried. 'I'm not for the scrap-heap yet, my girl, and don't you think I am!'

Astonished at her outburst, even though I had foreseen certain difficulties, I could only bluster a reply. 'But there is no question of sending you to a scrap-heap, as you put it. The clinic gives a course of treatment to rheumatic patients. Just that. When you've completed the treatment, they send you home, and . . .'

'Completed the treatment?' she echoed, holding out her gnarled and work-worn hands that were knotted and twisted by her malady. 'What clever German doctor's going to cure

213

these? And my legs? And my hips? Send me home – ha! – that's a laugh. Once they get me in that place, I shall be there to the end of my days, and it won't be long.'

I sighed. 'All right, Assunta,' I conceded. 'Forget I raised the idea. It's just that I can't bear to see you in that state, and thought you might agree to. . . .'

She reached out and touched my hands. There was naked appeal in her rheumy old eyes, and they were flooding with tears.

'Don't send me away, Isolda,' she begged. 'I know I've become a burden to you. What with the colonel, and this great place to look after, heaven knows you've troubles enough. But I'll pull myself together and be more of a help to you, Isolda, I swear it. I. . . .'

I squeezed her hand. 'Forget I said anything,' I told her. 'We'll stick together, you and I. Where would I be without you?'

She clung to me, sobbing with relief and release. And I thought of the tragedy of old age and the vulnerability of the poor, who are so helpless against the tides of illness and misfortune, reliant upon charity and the whims of their benefactors. All of a sudden I felt ashamed of my role of benefactor – for though I had told myself that my motives were pure, I knew in my heart that it would be a relief to have someone else look after Assunta and make her well.

Something else had been preying on my mind during the previous weeks, something that I had managed to evade for several successive years, and always at great cost to my conscience. I think it was the growing conviction that Jamie would never recover that brought me to the awareness of life's fragility – and made me remember the other love of mine who was cut off so short in his young manhood.

Since that awful day of his interment and my arrest on San Michele, I had never once visited Bruno's last resting place. In the years between I had never dared set foot on the isle of the dead, for fear of the calumny – indeed violence – that such an act might have brought down upon my head. But now that the people of Venice had mellowed towards me, though well short of forgiveness, I felt that I could dare

214

to follow my conscience and pay some tribute on the next anniversary of his death – which was a week hence, on February the fourth.

Having made up my mind, it was still no easy matter to go through with the plan. Two days before the anniversary I went into the best florist shop in the city – Orlando's in the great square – and made my wants known. . . .

'A funeral wreath, Signorina?' responded the assistant, eyeing me up in my grey habit, yet, I think, not recognizing me. 'What flowers have you in mind? At this time of the year, I can offer early spring blooms specially shipped from North Africa. We have daffodils, tulips, primroses, violets. . . .'

Recalling that the Ferrara coat of arms was mostly coloured violet and gold, I decided upon a wreath of daffodils and violets – a makeshift choice, for I could not recall my late fiancé ever expressing any preference in the way of flowers. The assistant wrote down my order and asked for my name and address.

'Mazzini-Forsca,' I told him, 'and I will call for the wreath myself on Saturday,'

'Mazzini-Forsca,' he exclaimed, and looked away.

I had witnessed the enlightenment of he who was surely the last person in Venice to know me by sight!

And one thing was certain. By nightfall, everyone in the city would have added two and two together and realized what I was planning to do on Saturday.

It was cold, overcast, and threatening rain when I stood on the Fondamente Nuove and sought out a gondola to take me to San Michele, which lay in a blanket of mist offshore, but there was not a craft in sight, nor, when it began to rain, was there a soul moving along the entire long quayside. Huddled under my umbrella and clutching my wreath to me, I took what additional shelter I was able to find under a stunted pine tree that overhung a low wall, and had half-decided that my enterprise was doomed to failure, when I espied a solitary gondola emerging from one of the small canals that enter the lagoon along that part of the quay, and shape course in my direction.

215

I ran to the water's edge and waved to the man with the oar. He acknowledged my summons and soon brought his craft alongside me.

'San Michele and wait there.'

He nodded acknowledgement. In defence against the rain he wore a grain sack over his head, with one of the corners pointing upwards above his crown, like a monk's hood. It hid most of his face.

The short journey across to the isle of the dead brought back memories of previous doleful occasions when I had made that mourning voyage – notably Bruno's funeral cortège, when the gondoliers had had the row of their lives against a half-gale. Today, the waters were glassy still and pock-marked with rain droplets.

We reached the small quay and I stepped ashore on the island.

'You will remember to wait?' I reminded my gondolier. He nodded his head without turning to look at me.

I passed under dripping trees, between rows of marbled tombs topped with sad-faced angels, under a funerary arch, and into the cloister of the ancient church. The massive door opened to my touch and I tiptoed nervously into the silent church, where the faint scent of long-burnt incense hung upon the air.

I had hoped to find people there, perhaps some of the good Franciscans who tended the cemetery isle and its place of worship. The emptiness, the eerie silence, came as something of a shock. It was all so – terribly *still*. . . .

The Ferrara family monument stood close by the wall on the northern aisle. It was of stark white Carrara marble and sculpted by a minor Roman master in the previous century. Representing a father, mother and trio of children – ancestors of the man I might have married – it stood as a symbol of pride and arrogance that I had never been able to associate with Bruno, who had been nothing if not – I would hardly say 'modest', but certainly unassuming in his cheerful, matter-of-fact way.

And somewhere in the crypt that lay behind and below the monument, the same Bruno slept his eternal sleep within the bronze coffin that I had seen being lowered down there.

Another realization of mortality – I had been experiencing them a lot lately – and I remembered that it had been ordained for me to join him, as wife and countess, in that eternal sleep below.

I shuddered, as if someone had walked over the grave that I must some day inhabit.

There were no other floral offerings on view on this, the anniversary of the murder. The last of the Ferraras remained unhonoured and forgotten by all save the woman over whom he had cast his own particular spell of charm all those years ago in the cathedral of San Marco.

'Goodbye again, Bruno,' I whispered. 'Sleep peacefully in your grand tomb.' And I laid the wreath at the foot of the monument and walked quickly out of the silent building.

The rain was still coming down with a sullen persistence. Despite my umbrella, I was half-drenched by the time I regained the quay, with my soaked skirts flapping most uncomfortably.

Looking down on to the quay, I drew a sharp and horrified breath. . . .

The gondola had gone!

And well gone. The wretched creature must have set off back to the Fondamente as soon as my back was turned, for there was no sign of any craft between there and where I stood.

What to do? That was the question. No use standing about and getting wet, in the vain hope of hailing a passing gondola, for there are not many clients who choose to go sightseeing on the lagoon on a wet Saturday late afternoon, and public conveyances to and from Venice, San Michele and the islands beyond were few and far between. It struck me that my best option was to seek help from the Franciscans in the monastery adjoining the basilica.

I found the ornate door to the monastery. There was a bell hung there in the porch. I pulled the rope. The notes clanged out, tunelessly, across the stillness of the cloister. Nothing happened. I rang again. After a few minutes' wait I heard shuffling footfalls, followed by the drawing of bolts, and the door creaked open – to disclose one round, watery eye and a patch of white beard.

'What do you want?'

I explained that I was seeking help. This brought a dusty response:

'No visitors!'

'I'm not a visitor,' I explained. 'I simply want to get back to Venice. Do you have a boat?'

'Visitors Tuesdays and Fridays. And no women!'

The door had by now swung open sufficiently for me to see that he was not wearing Franciscan habit, but a seedy black cassock that suggested he might be a sacristan, or perhaps merely a doorkeeper.

'Can I speak with one of the brothers, please?' I asked, seeing that I was getting nowhere with my present companion.

'No woman allowed – go away!' he snapped, and made to shut the door – a move which I made some attempt to resist, which added more fuel to the old man's fury.

'Please. . . .' I begged, hoping that my expression would melt him, since he was obviously deaf, and my words were wasted.

'No visitors! No women! Go away!' he cried, and wrenching my hand from the edge of the door, he slammed the heavy woodwork in my face.

My spirits profoundly depressed by the encounter, I retraced my steps through the cloister and took stock of my situation. Here I was, marooned on an islet inhabited only by the dead and a handful of monks who were heavily guarded from contamination by the outside world – particularly its women – by a deaf old curmudgeon. Against all odds, my best option now remained the slender chance of hailing a passing boat. Meanwhile I had the rain to contend with and – I cast a rueful glance skywards – night was beginning to fall.

After some searching along the perimeter of the graveyard, which took scarcely any time at all since the whole of San Michele could comfortably be accommodated inside St Mark's Square and its surrounding buildings, I decided that my best vantage point was the shelter of a willow tree that overhung a tomb close enough to the enclosing wall for me to peer over and espy any craft passing down that, the western side, of the isle. And it was there, quelling my impatience, and pushing to the back of my mind the natural aversion I had to death and its incidentals, that I settled myself to wait.

There was not much to see – only the still waters of the lagoon to one side, the small forest of tombs and gravestones on the other, the rain-dripping cypresses and willows, the bell tower of the basilica etched against the dying daylight.

And an open grave quite close by me, with a grave-digger's spade stuck upright in the pile of newly-turned earth.

I remembered the grisly detail I had once overheard years before, in the staff parlour at the palazzo. The story went that, apart from the very rich who can afford to purchase mausoleums and crypts for perpetuity, the tiny island is unable to contain the remains of all Venice's dead. So the poor are allowed to rest for only twelve years – no more – before their humble graves are opened up, the bones removed to one of the uninhabited islands of the lagoon, and the empty graves reoccupied for another twelve years.

I shuddered. . . .

It was soon after that, when darkness had truly fallen and the cemetery had become a place of deep shadow relieved only by the dimmed whiteness of marble, that I became aware – as sure as if I could reach out and touch the watcher – that a pair of eyes were regarding me from out among the gravestones.

It is possible that I had seen a movement out of the corner of my eye, or my ear could have picked up a slight sound. I had no proof, no recollection of either. With nothing but intuition to go upon, I was quite sure I was being watched – and nothing on earth would have convinced me otherwise.

That being the case, what to do? . . .

My instinct – or whatever it was that had put the idea in my mind – told me that the watcher was quite close and standing somewhere beyond the open grave. I decided, then, to make a dash for the perimeter wall, to bolt through an archway almost immediately in front of where I crouched, and thus put the wall between me and the unseen menace.

No sooner said, no sooner done. Carefully furling my

umbrella (which might serve as a useful weapon if it came to the emergency!) I poised myself for flight. Three deep breaths – and I took to my heels.

The damp earth and wet grass made the going difficult in my high-heeled button boots, but I gained the archway in a dozen swift strides, turned sharply to my left and continued on my way along the outer side of the wall, down a path that ran above the waterfront. Reaching the south-west corner of the roughly square islet, I paused, panting, and espied both ways along the wall – ahead, along the southern side, and back the way I had come. Both paths were deeply shadowed as far as I could see – but quite empty.

I breathed a sigh of relief, but was almost immediately shocked to a new awareness. . . .

Someone – the watcher? – was walking past quite close to me – on the other side of the wall.

And, to pile frightfulness upon dismay, *he was whistling tunelessly through his teeth!*

Then I was back again in the dark roof garden of the Hotel Barberini in Rome, with my killer stalking me behind the yew hedge. In just such a situation, I had almost immediately been assaulted and come within an ace of ending my life by being hurled over the parapet. What might be my fate now? The dark waters of the lagoon? In the centuries of Venice's bloody, tumultuous history, countless hundreds had met such a fate in private vendettas, crimes of passion and political squabbles, the victims being carried out into the Adriatic by the tide which scours out the lagoon, leaving it sweetly clean, twice in every twenty-four hours.

Would that be my fate? Or – a most appalling thought came to me – *what if that freshly-prepared grave was intended to be mine?*

I thought I saw it all quite plainly. My purchase of the wreath had not passed unnoticed – that went without saying. News had undoubtedly reached the Face of Evil, and a plan had been set afoot to waylay me on the isle of the dead and dispose of me for good.

But – why? Why, after leaving me in peace ever since my public declaration in Florian's, was I suddenly to be marked down again as a victim? Despite my bold words on that occasion, I had made no move against the enemy since that day. How *could* I, without Jamie by my side to guide me in everything I did, and to take the lion's share of the risks? Why was I again the victim?

These thoughts flashed through my mind in less time than it takes to imagine, and were only fleshed out in later tranquillity. At the time my overriding impulse was to escape, and my instincts told me that my best defence lay in silence and concealment. So I stood stock still, and let the tuneless whistling move on, which it did – till it faded into silence along the other side of the wall.

So far as our relative positions were concerned, my would-be killer (and surely he was the same creature who had made the attempt in Rome all that time ago – and did he still bear the marks of my claws?) had now put me between himself and the buildings. Might I not make another attempt to summon the monastery doorkeeper and beg sanctuary from the good Franciscans? I examined the thought – till I had a vision of being trapped on the brothers' doorstep, the bell unanswered, with my killer lurching towards me across the enclosing cloister, his hands extended, fingers splayed – and thrust the idea out of my mind.

What about the church? Was there nowhere inside the roomy basilica – a vestry with a door to lock and bolt, or a dark cupboard where I might hide? The trouble with putting myself beyond a door was that it served also as a means for my assailant to enter, and once inside, I was trapped. Yes, far better to enjoy the advantages of the open space – however restricted.

I had settled my mind on this, and turned my head to see if the coast was clear behind my back – when I found myself looking straight into the grinning, triumphant face of my stalker!

I have heard of a small animal being fascinated by the fixed stare of the snake that intends its destruction. In such a way I found myself totally incapable of thought or movement – and for how long there is no telling. Furthermore, something of this awful fascination seemed to communicate itself to the

221

other, for he neither moved nor uttered a sound, but continued to stare into my eyes, his shadowed face not half an arm's length from mine, so close, indeed, that I could feel his breath fanning my face, and caught the reek of strong spirits upon it.

My first movement, when the initial, appalling shock was over, was an involuntary clenching of my fists. In doing this, I became forcibly aware again of the umbrella that I still held in my right hand. It felt hard in my grasp. Hard — and useful.

With no more than blind instinct to inspire me, and some primeval, forgotten skill to guide my aim, I brought the umbrella up — point first — and drove the steel ferrule full into the face before me. I felt the shaft jar in my hand. I heard his scream. I saw him fall back, hands pressed to his face.

Then I ran. A headlong, breathless pell-mell flight along the path, with no thought but to put as much space as possible between me and the killer's certain and savage vengeance.

The cemetery of San Michele is set out in a chessboard of square plots — fifteen or more — each bounded by a wall or a cypress-lined walk. At the next archway in the perimeter wall I darted through and into one of the square plots, ducking in and out of the gravestones, leaving row upon row of them behind me to mask my position and confuse my pursuer — if pursuing me he was, if I had not left him incapable, half-blinded perhaps, poor wretch.

I could have spared myself the charitable thought. The first time I felt secure enough to cast a backward glance, I saw his plunging figure not twenty yards behind me and coming on fast. Too far away to see his face in the darkness, I had no way of telling the extent of the damage I had wrought, but it had certainly not impeded him for more than a few moments.

I raced on, a cold fear in my heart turning dangerously to blind panic, knowing that it was only a matter of time before I, hindered as I was by my ankle-length skirts, must fall victim to a powerful and faster-moving pursuer. This onset of panic, dulling my wits, led me to lose my way and take a wrong turn. I stumbled through an archway – to find myself looking down into the dark waters of the lagoon. And there was no way to left or right – only back the way I had come – straight into the arms of my vengeful killer!

It was then I saw the lights moving through the darkness across my front – that and the sounds of voices coming to me across the water. I called out for help – and was answered. I looked back over my shoulder, to see my pursuer coming towards the arch. I saw his sagging mouth, his blood-streaked face, the hate-filled eyes. Clearly, like me, he was nearing the end of his tether, for he paused and supported himself against the arch, chest heaving, laboured of breath. But the eyes never left me. '*It is only a short rest,*' he seemed to be saying. '*After that, when my strength is back, I shall come and get you. . . .* '

The voices were calling to me from over the water. The lights had changed direction and were moving towards me. With the eye of faith, I could just pick out the shape of a boat coming from the darkness. My would-be assassin must have seen and heard also, for with a snarl of fury, he drew himself upright and began to move towards me, hands extended.

I turned away from him, fearful to see his face again. Below me lapped the chill waters. There might be sharp rocks below, stakes pointing upright just beneath the surface to impale the unwary. Nothing mattered – except to put myself beyond those clutching hands.

I leapt. . . .

The shock of immersion caused me to draw a deep, involuntary breath – and with it went a large quantity of near-freezing water. Choking, flailing, borne down by my water-logged skirts, drowning – I sank lower and lower, with the certain knowledge that I should never be able to fight my way to the surface.

And then a hand was wound about my hair, and I was being lifted up – up – up into the God-given air. As my mouth broke surface, I gulped in the blessed life-force.

'Only a young thing,' I heard a voice declare. 'Tried to drown herself, I shouldn't wonder. Best get her ashore.'

There followed a nightmare time of half-consciousness, of being moved from place to place, of many voices. Several times I tried to rouse myself and speak up, to assure my rescuers that I was not as half-drowned and helpless as they supposed, but – oddly – I found myself without the strength even to open my eyes, and the words simply would not come.

The experience culminated in a sudden cosseting warmth, and after that – oblivion. After an interminable lapse of time largely given over to dreams of the most bizarre nature, I opened my eyes to find myself in a bare, whitewashed room that instantly put me in mind of Jamie's room at the hospital. And there, bending over me, was a smiling woman, her face framed in a nun's coif.

'How are you feeling, my child?' she murmured.

'I – I'm well enough, Sister,' I faltered.

I was in a hospital – a different one from Jamie's – and the crew of a fishing boat had brought me in the previous night after having picked me up by San Michele, where they supposed I had tried to drown myself!

'Young and beautiful as you are,' mused the nun, 'how could you have wished to throw away the good God's gift of life?'

I hastened to assure her that such had not been the case, but that I had fallen into the water – a white lie deliberately offered because I had no wish to involve her and her *consoeurs* in the appalling events of the previous night.

'What is your name, child?' she asked. 'We undressed you to put you to bed, but there was nothing on you to say who you were or where you came from. Is there someone – a relation or friend – whom we should inform?'

I gave my name – and to my relief, this unworldly woman had never heard of me, for which I was grateful. I told her where I lived and begged that Assunta be informed that I was safe and well. She promised to send word round to the Palazzo Mazzini-Forsca immediately. And she had something to add. . . .

'In the case of suicides, or attempted suicides,' she said, 'it is the law that we must inform the police. I am afraid that this has already been done, my child, and an officer has been waiting outside since dawn, to interview you as soon as you are well enough to be seen. It will be necessary for you to tell him what you have told me.

'Do you mind – are you feeling well enough?' she added anxiously.

I assured her that I was perfectly able to meet the police. With great thoughtfulness she then brushed my hair and made me look tidy to receive my 'guest' – as she called him. Then went out to fetch the police officer.

'Good morning, Signorina Mazzini-Forsca. And what has brought you to this sorry state, might one ask?' came a voice from the door.

My 'guest' was none other than Inspector Lippi of the Judicial Police!

He limped over and took a seat at the foot of my bed. The clever, sensitive face mirrored his thoughts as he regarded me, head on one side.

'I would not have thought suicide was your style, Signorina,' he said. 'Which only goes to show how wrong one can be about people.'

'*You* are quite wrong, Signor Inspector,' I responded. And I told him, briefly and unsparingly, about my ordeal on San Michele. He listened without either comment or facial expression, but merely regarded me evenly, as if estimating the truth or falsehood of what I was telling him.

When I had finished he said: 'This man – your assailant – is the same person whom you and Colonel Delamere claim to have made the attempt upon you in Rome – correct?'

I nodded. 'Yes, and not only because he whistles between his teeth. Both times, I came very close to this man, and though I never saw his face plainly – even on the station in Florence – I *sensed* his identity. One never forgets one's attacker, Signor Inspector!'

He stroked his smooth cheek. 'It is odd, is it not,' he mused, 'that these attacks upon you have been resumed after quite a long interval?'

'The thought had occurred to me,' I replied.

'Have you, perhaps, been pursuing a new line of private inquiry?' he asked. 'Have you stumbled over something – a

225

damning clue – that points to the identity of your enemy – or enemies?'

'No, I have not,' I told him truthfully. 'But I wish I had!'

After a moment's silence he got up and limped across the room, leaning heavily upon his stick, his white-maned head bowed, a frown of concentration upon his pale, scholarly countenance.

Presently he paused and looked at me. 'Signorina, I shall have to help you,' he said. 'Strictly speaking, such a routine inquiry should first be carried out by regular police, but it so closely concerns the Ferrara murder that we of the judicial department must take the initiative.'

'Thank you, Inspector,' I said coldly, mindful of the notable lack of help one had received from him in the past. 'And what do you propose to do?'

'First, we shall trace the gondolier who took you over to San Michele,' he said. 'The man was clearly employed to pick you out, transport you there and leave you stranded for the assassin to dispose of you. . . .'

Yes, that was how I had imagined it. The entire plot had been hatched upon the news that Isolda Mazzini-Forsca was going to lay a wreath on the tomb of her dead fiancé on the anniversary of his murder. It could be said that I, myself, had been a party to conniving at my own killing!

But Lippi was addressing me. . . .

'I'm sorry, Inspector,' I said. 'Did you ask me something?'

'Two things,' he responded. 'First, can you describe the gondolier? Second, have you any notion of the wound that you inflicted upon the assassin?'

I explained how – with hindsight – it was obvious that, by wearing the sack on his head, the former had deliberately concealed his identity. 'As for the wound,' I continued, 'it was too dark to see what damage I did to him, but I drove the point of the umbrella with all my force, and he screamed like a stuck pig.'

Lippi nodded. 'Then we shall inquire of all the doctors and hospitals in the city,' he said, 'to find if any man has called upon them with a serious face or eye injury.

'And now, Signorina, I will leave you,' he said. 'And,

226

believe me, I am more delighted than I can express to see you alive and well after your terrifying experience.'

He bowed and limped to the door. When it had closed behind him I speculated about that strange man, once an enemy, now a self-declared ally. In his way, a personable man. Devastatingly intelligent. His sincerity spoilt only by a fatal smoothness of manner.

I found myself beginning to trust him.

A physician arrived at noon, examined me and announced that I was well enough to be sent home, though he stipulated that I should rest up till the following morning. Heartily glad to be given leave to go, I agreed to his terms and was presently taken by the hospital's private launch to the palazzo.

Assunta and Giuseppe were there to greet me. The old lady had been brought the news, though fortunately she had retired to bed early the previous night without seeking me out, and had not even been aware I was missing till the message came from the hospital. She was beside herself with concern for me, covered me with kisses and demanded to know what had happened, how I had come to end up in hospital – everything. Out of concern for her fears, I dismissed the entire episode lightly – with a tissue of half-truths about my falling in a canal. That much I was obliged to admit, or how else explain the fact that I was wearing a reach-me-down frock that they had lent me in hospital?

Assunta took command. 'Giuseppe!' she ordered. 'Pick up the signorina and carry her to her sitting room. Put her on the chaise-longue there, and I'll be up presently with a hot toddy for my poor darling.'

And that was the pattern of my day. I longed to go and see Jamie, but Assunta would have none of it. Instead, she dispatched Giuseppe to the hospital for any news of Jamie, and condemned me to rest with my feet up.

The day slipped past uneventfully. I lay and wondered how Lippi was faring with his inquiries, and – disturbing thought – if I could now expect a continuous repetition of attempts upon my life. Not a very brave person, I think I would have quit Venice there and then if it had not been for

227

leaving Jamie – who, as Giuseppe reported – was predictably showing no change.

I fell asleep at dusk with Jamie's dear, unconscious face in the forefront of my mind, and dreamed of him as he was in the prime of his strength: Jamie the smiling buccaneer, my knight-errant and the joy and delight of those tragically few days when we had shared our mutual love.

I was woken in the dark hours – still on the chaise-longue in my sitting room – by the sounds of footfalls ascending a staircase. Shocked to sudden alertness, I sat up and strained my ears. The footfalls were light, rapid and quite clearly resounding upon stonework. A few moments later, they were silent.

Had I imagined them? I asked myself. Or was this yet another inexplicable happening, like the whispers, the closing doors, the footfalls that proved to be a faulty window frame?

Uneasily I drew the coverlet up to my chin, too shocked by my recent ordeal to venture out and search out the source of this new occurrence. Still speculating, still listening, I was blessed with sleep.

I woke to a scream from along the passage – followed by a crash!

It was broad daylight. The sun streamed in between the slats of the window shutters, and the clock on the chimney-piece told the hour of nine. I was off the chaise-longue and half way across the sitting room in my bare feet when I heard an anguished sobbing. I wrenched open the door and rushed out.

'Assunta – oh, you poor dear!'

My old nurse was sprawled on the floor at the foot of a small flight of stairs leading from the former servants' kitchen that we both shared. A fallen tray and the remains of a simple breakfast of coffee and rolls scattered around her told their own tale. In the loving kindness of her heart, and despite her infirmities, the faithful old servant had made me some breakfast and fallen down on the way to deliver it.

'Assunta, are you hurt?' I asked her.

She did not reply, nor look up, but remained where she was, in a crouched position, her legs sprawled out before her, sobbing as if her heart would break. I fell on my knees beside her, put my arm round her shoulders and gently lifted her chin between my finger and thumb.

'Are you hurt?' I repeated.

'I'm nothing but a burden to you, aren't I, my Isolda?' she said piteously.

'No you're not, Assunta,' I answered. 'For where would I be without you?'

'I can't manage any longer,' she whispered, and the tears began again. 'You know that, don't you?'

I had to nod agreement.

'I should go into that clinic, like you said, shouldn't I?'

Again, I nodded.

'You're right,' she said, and appeared more happy in her mind now that the decision was made. 'But what shall you do – how will you cope – all alone in this place?'

I shrugged. 'I shall muddle through. Don't worry about me.'

'Well, at least you'll have Giuseppe to look in,' she said.

I nodded.

And, apart from Giuseppe, I thought – and it was a sudden, numbing and terrifying thought – there'll only be me. . . .

And the ghosts who haunt this place.

Thirteen

I arranged for Assunta to go by carriage to Treviso, for the roads were very good and the weather fine. I also opted to accompany her to the clinic, having written to Doctor Haussman and secured a place for her. Haussman was the director of the clinic, with a very fine reputation in the treatment of rheumatic conditions by the most modern techniques of applied heat and running water, together with the intake of mineral salts bottled and imported from the famous spa resorts of Europe. Far from being what poor Assunta had described as 'a scrap-heap', the Haussman Clinic was patronized by the wealthy and distinguished of northern Italy. Even His Majesty King Vittorio Emmanuel himself had been there to 'take the waters'.

A week after my dreadful experience at San Michele, the two of us set off in a hired carriage and pair for the busy market town of Treviso.

Both of us had improved in spirits: Assunta for the usual reason that one is always relieved to have made up one's mind, one way or the other, on a difficult issue. Having assured herself that I was perfectly capable of coping alone in my modest quarters, she was looking forward with great eagerness to benefiting from the Haussman treatment, which I had carefully explained to her as well as I understood it. For my part, it seemed to me that, notwithstanding the inactivity since the events on San Michele, matters were moving to a climax in that direction. The fact that Lippi was now my ally might certainly speed things along. My only regret was that I seemed unable to help solve the mystery

230

which surrounded me. Now – if only Jamie were well! If only his brilliant plan to entrap the would-be trappers at the Arsenal that fateful night had been successful.

Vain regrets, vain regrets. . . .

Perhaps Lippi would succeed where we had failed. But if only there was something I could do to help.

'Your father the Principe was very fond of Treviso in the old days,' commented Assunta, breaking in upon my thoughts. 'Soon after he married your dear mother, before you came along, they rented a very fine villa just outside Treviso, at Istriana, to get away from the summer heat and smells of Venice. I went with your mama as lady's maid. The villa was on a hill and surrounded by a belt of trees, and your mother and I used to sit under the shade and work on our embroidery while your father fished in the river that flowed past below.

'He was a great fisherman, your father,' she went on, now well absorbed into her memories of yesterday – the Golden Years. 'Your father kept a record of every fish he caught with his line. The date of the catch, the sort of fish, and its weight. All this he put down in his daily journal. Ah, he was never without that daily journal of his, your father. . . .'

I let her drift on, happy in her reminiscences and really needing no other audience save a silent sounding-board.

Something she said, though, touched off a recollection of my own. . . .

Two weeks before my ceremony of betrothal I had one of those summonses to attend Father in the library. I went with a light heart, for my conscience was clear of all fault so far as my parent was concerned. Was I not the apple of his eye? Had I not consented to be married to the man of his choice? What self-sacrifice on my part!

To tell the truth, though I had not thoroughly confessed my secret meetings with Bruno during the period when I had been expressly forbidden even to communicate with him, Father – no fool, he, but very shrewd – had almost certainly gleaned something of what had been going on between Bruno and me. From time to time, at meals and such, he would let drop some such remark as: 'You and Bruno appear to get

231

along very well – on such short acquaintance', and 'There are not many modern daughters who would bow to their fathers' choice of a life partner' – delivered with a wry, sidelong glance and a twinkle in his clear blue eyes that recalled stories I had overheard about his youthful reputation as a notable man-about-town and Venetian gallant.

He was waiting for me in the library and greeted me with a fond kiss, handing me to a seat beside him.

'Dear Isolda, I have good news,' he said. 'As you know, there were difficulties in the way of the Cardinal Archbishop officiating at your betrothal ceremony because he had been summoned to Rome that particular week to attend an extra-ordinary meeting of the Holy Office. However, I now learn from his chaplain that the meeting has been indefinitely post-poned and that His Eminence will be here to bless you both. Now, isn't that splendid news?'

I agreed with my father, whilst being perfectly aware that my parent was as much concerned – if not more so – with the social and political advantages of having his daughter's betrothal ceremony presided over by the Cardinal Arch-bishop as he was spiritually uplifted by its religious aspects.

'And after the betrothal – the wedding,' said Father. 'And after not much delay.' And when he saw the surprise – not to say the joy – in my eyes, he explained: 'Oh, yes, I know I had intended a long betrothal, Isolda, but circumstances have changed. It would now be prudent – safer, even – to settle this dynastic marriage as speedily as possible.'

With this surprising statement, my father opened the drawer of the bureau and took out a thick, calf-bound volume which I knew to be his daily journal. Twenty volumes of this journal, all similarly bound, stood in line on a shelf in the library, and represented twenty years of this distinguished man's adult life as Venetian nobleman and Italian patriot. He opened the current volume, dipped his pen in the inkwell, and wrote the following entry, which, as nearly as I could recall on the road to Treviso, went something like this – for he spoke it aloud as he wrote:

'Friday the seventeenth – comes news from the office of His Eminence's chaplain that H.E. will not be attending the meeting in Rome and will officiate at Isolda's betrothal.

Greatly pleased. Informed my darling girl, and she is pleased also. Must push forward plans for the wedding. Time is running short. . . .'

'*Time is running short*' – his very words. And how was it that I had totally forgotten that significant phrase, and never recalled it till that day on the road to Treviso?

The answer is simple. That interview in the library was the last human contact I ever had with my father. The following morning he was found dead at the bottom of the Whispering Stair with a broken neck. The doctors said that he had suffered a massive heart attack at the top of the landing and had fallen. In the tragic surroundings of his funeral, with the betrothal ceremony coming so soon after, the curious statements he had made concerning my forthcoming marriage became overlaid with more pressingly urgent events.

The Haussman Clinic was everything that one had expected it to be. The doctor himself was extremely pleasant and radiated confidence in himself and his treatment. The nursing sisters were also German and most kind to old Assunta. With commendable tact, she was given a small villa of her own apart from the main house, with her own sitting room. As a member of the servant classes, it would have been unbearably embarrassing for her to mix freely with the kind of patients for whom the clinic normally catered. Indeed, for all his charm, it is probable that the good doctor would not have accepted my old nurse had it not been for my rank and wealth.

It seemed that he knew nothing of my trial for murder. . . .

'I will write to you twice weekly, Assunta,' I told her, 'and you must ask one of the sisters to read my letters aloud to you and have them pen a few lines to me at your dictation.' Like most women of her age and class, Assunta was illiterate.

I stayed to have tea with her in her quarters, then took my leave, for I had a new and pressing need to return home as soon as possible. We parted company at the carriage. For one of the few times in my life I was going to spend a night under a different roof from that of my faithful old nurse.

We had not progressed far out of Treviso when the

coachman turned to address me. He was a stranger to me, hired by the day from a rank in the city.

'Excuse me, Signorina, but it seems you have an admirer – if you don't mind me mentioning it.'

'Indeed?' I responded, amused. 'And what makes you say that?'

'Why, there's this coach following behind us,' he said, and jerked his thumb behind.

Peering down the road over the rear of the carriage, I saw indeed that a covered coach and pair were following along behind, though by no means closely. I turned back to my driver.

'You have a romantic disposition,' I chided him. 'There's no earthly reason to suppose that every other conveyance on the road today is following after *me!*' And I smiled.

'That's as may be, Signorina,' responded the driver, 'but yonder coach followed us all the way *from* Venice, also. I thought nothing of it at the time, for the reason you just gave. But perhaps you can explain to me why he pulled out of a side turning as we came out of the drive of the clinic and came on after us!'

'Oh,' I said, and again: 'Oh!'

Mindful of my perilous circumstances, I was very uneasy about the follower, and grew increasingly more so. However, as we drew nearer Venice and the covered coach gave no sign of coming up to overtake or intercept us, I plucked up my courage and addressed my driver again.

'When we come to a suitable bend in the road,' I said, 'would you please pull up at the verge to allow the coach to pass by us?' I smiled with a coquetry I certainly did not feel. 'I should like to get a glimpse of my secret admirer,' I added.

'Right you are, Signorina,' grinned the man. 'And I hope for your sake that he's a fine young fellow with a fortune – if you'll forgive the liberty, Signorina.'

A little further on we came to a bend that was also masked by a clump of trees that gave good cover. Round the bend and beside the trees, my driver brought his horses to a halt at the side of the road. I sat forward in my seat, tense with suspense. Watched and waited.

Moments later the covered coach swept round the bend

into sight, with its driver up on the box. The fellow gave us a stare of what looked like surprise as he flashed past, but my eyes were all for the interior of the coach.

I was doomed to disappointment. The carriage window was drawn up and the blind drawn down. Whoever my secret follower, he was not for disclosing his identity.

'Drive on,' I said.

My coachman smiled down at me. 'Don't take it too badly, Signorina,' he said. 'There's plenty of fish in the sea.'

Followed all the way to Treviso and back.

But by whom? By orders of Lippi, for my protection? Or was my every move being covered by the forces against me – awaiting another such golden opportunity as I had provided at San Michele?

Arriving back at the palazzo, I let myself into the empty house that seemed so unfamiliar now. Apart from our stay on the Brenta, this was the first time the place had been unoccupied for as much as half a day. Even when the entire family was absent from Venice, the palazzo had always teemed with servants in the old days.

For the present, I turned my mind to the task before me. . . .

The recollection of my father's strange remarks about the importance of speeding up my wedding to Bruno had taken on a special significance. At the back of my mind there was also the thought that my father's sudden and inopportune death was also not without significance – but for the present I thrust the notion behind me, since it opened up possibilities which I did not even care to contemplate.

Without even removing my bonnet I went straight up to the library. The room had hardly been used since Father's death. I pulled off the dust covers and looked about me.

Clearly, my search began with the bookshelves. I looked up at the shelf in question and saw the long row of calf-bound volumes containing the day-by-day account of my father's twenty years as a public figure.

I counted – eighteen volumes. The year of his death – which was 1877 – and the volume for the previous year were missing.

The last volume – the one he was using at the time of his death – presented no problem. It was almost certainly still in the bureau drawer. The whereabouts of the one for 1876 was a different matter. . . .

I tried the bureau drawer. It was locked.

Down in the kitchen quarters I rummaged in a toolbox that had been used by a long-gone handyman, and found a strong-looking chisel with which I applied my inexpert attentions to the inlaid mahogany and rich ormolu embellishments of the antique bureau. Presently I had forced the lock and was able to open the drawer.

It was empty.

'Doctor Mancini will be with you in a few moments, Signorina. Would you like to make yourself comfortable in the waiting room?'

The doctor's wife was a petite, bird-like creature whom I once remembered seeing on the outskirts of some reception or other at the ducal palace. She gave me a nervous smile.

'We have followed all your troubles, Signorina,' she said, 'and my husband and I feel the greatest sympathy towards you and always remember you in our prayers.'

This, the first unsolicited gesture of kindness from any Venetian since my troubles started – and a comparative stranger at that – heartened me immensely, particularly in view of the reason for my calling on the woman's husband.

'Ah, here is the doctor. Arturo – you'll remember Signorina Mazzini-Forsca.'

'Good day, Signorina.'

If the wife was shyly outgoing, the husband was quite different. I detected in him a certain – not shiftiness, but a vague aura of restraint. He seemed uneasy at my presence, and had difficulty in meeting my eye. When his spouse had left us I decided that the best approach would be to come straight to the point – so I did.

'Doctor,' I began, 'I want to know the full details surrounding my father's death!'

The effect on Doctor Mancini was most marked. In his late fifties at a guess, pale of complexion, with thinning grey hair, he seemed to be the kind of man that the world of fame

236

and fortune has left far behind, and to his deep regret. The lines of defeat that strongly marked his sunken cheeks were accented by twin spots of colour that appeared on the cheekbones when I made my announcement.

'Well, Doctor?' I said when he made no reply.

'I – I don't understand, Signorina,' he stammered. 'Your father the Principe met with an accidental death. My partner and I were called in to examine the deceased. The cause of death you must know. What else is there to add?'

'The cause of the fall, as I understand, was a heart attack,' I said. 'I don't recall if you attended my father before his death, but can you tell me if this had been his only attack? I may add that I don't remember hearing of any such thing.'

The uneasy eyes avoided mine when he replied. 'Ah – that question were more easily answered by my partner, Signorina. As a specialist in diseases of the heart and lungs, it was he who diagnosed the attack as the cause of your father's fatal fall.'

'Can I speak to your partner, Doctor?' I asked.

'He emigrated – er – to America some few years ago. To – I believe Baltimore, where he took up a practice.'

'Can I correspond with him?'

'I – I'm afraid I don't have his address, Signorina,' came the reply.

'Does anyone in Venice have his Baltimore address?'

The eyes flared with sudden alarm. 'I think not,' he said. 'Doctor Nitti – er – had no relations in Venice.'

'But, surely,' I persisted, 'I could simply write to him addressed to Doctor Nitti, care of Baltimore general hospital. There must be a general hospital in a major American city – and they must have heard of a Doctor Nitti, emigrant from Italy, and practising locally.'

I thought for a moment that my companion was going to faint. He opened his mouth to speak, but thought better of it. He then closed his eyes. 'The – the last I heard,' he said at length, 'the last I heard was that Doctor Nitti had died. I may have been misinformed. The source of the information was not – reliable. But there it is.' He opened his eyes and looked down at his hands.

'I see,' was my response. And I thought I saw very well.

'Now, Doctor, tell me – my father's heart condition aside, would you say that the fall would have been sufficient on its own to cause his death?'

'Oh, undoubtedly!' Mancini clearly felt himself to be on safer ground, and answered most readily. 'The neck was broken at the fourth and fifth cervical vertebrae. . . .

'Ah, pardon me, Signorina, for the indelicacy.'

'Don't bother to spare my feelings, Doctor,' I replied tartly. 'I have been immunized against the harsh things of life – and death – in a hard school of experience.

'You were saying. . . .'

'Yes, Signorina. Quite simply, your father fell the length of the great staircase and that was more than sufficient to cause death by the means I have – er – indicated.'

'All the way down the staircase, you say?'

'Yes, Signorina. He was found lying at the foot.'

I drew a deep breath. 'Doctor Mancini,' I said, 'those stairs are very wide, and the risers are very low, forming what might be described as a gentle slope. An ancestor of mine once drove a carriage and horses up that staircase for a wager. It is not an easy matter to fall down that staircase, Doctor – not from top to bottom. . . .

'Not unless one were pushed – *hard!*'

There was no more to be gained from the frightened Doctor Mancini. Quite clearly, he was concealing something – something that he had piously hoped to have been swept away under the carpet and forgotten years ago. It must have been a shock to have some meddlesome woman probing into matters that – save for when his bad conscience got in the way – he had conveniently forgotten.

I came out of the doctor's house and wandered across the great square before the cathedral. Some children were playing ball, and a man was feeding the pigeons; they perched all over him as if he had been a tree.

My father had been murdered – I was certain of it. His killing was part of the complex skein of events of which my own tragedy was only a thread. His remark to me the last time we met should have been the starting point of my probings into the identity of the Face of Evil, but passing

238

events had driven it from my mind – to be rediscovered only after Assunta's chance remark on the road to Treviso.

I walked to the end of the Piazzetta and looked out across the basin of San Marco to the island Church of San Giorgio Maggiore under the wintry sun.

What next? I asked myself.

Should I tell my suspicions to Lippi? Say to him: 'Inspector, it happened like this – someone won his way into our house and killed my father by throwing him violently down the staircase. A strange pair of doctors were summoned in a panic, and both testified that he died of his fall following a heart attack. One of these doctors is now heaven knows where and the other is frightened out of his wits – but nothing on earth will ever make him tell, because he was probably very well paid, but that's *all* he has because he's a failure in life and such people cling on to the things they possess with more courage and tenacity than you'd believe. . . .

'How do I know all this, Inspector? Because of something my father said the last time I saw him – something which he obviously confided to his daily journal, because someone has taken the trouble to steal the two volumes of the journal that probably tell the whole story if one knows what to look for. . . .

'What's that you said, Inspector? Find the two missing volumes and you'll believe me?

'Naturally – who wouldn't?'

Giuseppe was chopping firewood in the kitchen yard when I let myself in at the back gate. The giant paused in his labours and jerked his thumb towards the kitchen entrance.

'Woman came to see you, Signorina,' he said. 'Said she believed you wanted to speak to her. It was cold out here, so I put her in the kitchen.'

'Thank you, Giuseppe,' I said. 'Did she give her name?'

'No, Signorina. Wouldn't tell me.'

I nodded, puzzled. On my way to the door, I paused as he called after me.

'If she gives you any trouble, just let me know, Signorina.'

I smiled. 'Very well, Giuseppe,' I replied.

The woman was sitting with her back to me when I entered the kitchen – sitting at the kitchen table, one hand and arm resting on the scrubbed table top, looking out of the window at seagulls wheeling over distant rooftops. She turned to regard me, and I knew her on the instant. The close-set, avaricious eyes, the uncomely looks. She was the foster mother from Burano – not much changed after nearly two years.

'Well, Signora Gucci,' I said. 'This is a surprise.'

'I wonder you can say that,' she replied. 'From what I hear, you've been inquiring after me.'

Puzzled by her remark, I decided to let it pass. 'Well, now you're here,' I said, 'why don't we talk? Coffee? A glass of wine?'

'I'll take a glass of wine,' said the woman. 'As to talking, I suppose you're still interested in that babe you came to see me about, eh?'

I gave her a guarded reply. 'Perhaps,' I said.

She looked cunning. 'That story you gave me – about the babe your friend wanted me to foster – that was all lies, wasn't it? You were after the names of the father and mother of the other child – the one who died – weren't you?'

'Perhaps,' I repeated, pouring her a bumper glass of Chianti, but myself abstaining.

'And still interested, eh?' she said. 'Or so I hear.'

'I might be.'

'Well,' she said, obviously not taken in by my non-committal responses, but accepting them as the currency of the half-world of semi-crime in which she lived, 'I can tell you all you want to know – and more. But it will cost you money, Signorina. Oh, yes, it will cost you.'

'How much?' I asked, trying hard to quench my eagerness and playing the role of hard bargainer.

'Plenty,' she said. 'Enough to pay my fare over to America to join my son and his family – and enough to keep me for life.

'Shall we say . . .' And she mentioned a figure that must have seemed a fortune to her and was, indeed, far more than I ever kept about me in cash.

'That's a lot of money,' I said, continuing to pursue my role. 'I should want to know a lot for that.'

'You'll learn all you want to know,' said she. 'And when I've told it I'll not feel safe till there's a whole wide ocean between me and Venice.'

I paused in silence to absorb the implications of that grim remark, and then I nodded.

'Done,' I said. 'But I shall have to go to a bank for that amount. I simply don't have so much in the place.'

'How long?' The cunning eyes narrowed with suspicion.

'Today,' I said, as eager as she to complete the business. 'Shall we say late this afternoon?'

'I can't come here again!' she cried, looking over her shoulder as if she imagined some menace lurking in the shadows of our kitchen. 'Too risky to be seen coming here again.'

'Then – where?' I asked.

She thought for a moment. 'Do you know the square at Santa Maria Formosa? It's not far from here.'

'Of course.'

'Meet me by the bridge opposite the church door,' she said. 'At – six o'clock. And come alone. If you bring anyone with you' – she glanced towards the door, and by implication to Giuseppe busily chopping wood in the yard – 'bring anyone else, and you won't find me there.'

'Six o'clock opposite the church,' I repeated. 'I'll be there – and alone.'

I saw her off the premises, closing and locking the yard gate behind her. Giuseppe had paused in his labours to watch the woman's departure. When he met my eye he slowly looked away.

By the time I left the Palazzo Mazzini-Forsca to keep my appointment with Signora Gucci, it was quite dark and a thin drifting of snow was descending, like confetti, through the night sky.

Well wrapped in a thick grey woollen cloak and with the money securely bundled in a leather bag, I locked the yard gate behind me and set off in the direction of the rendezvous, which was only about ten minutes' walk across three small canals and in and out of twisting alleyways.

The snow and the biting cold had emptied the streets. Through lighted windows, as yet unshuttered, I could see families gathered about warm fires in the candlelight, and there were one or two shops still open, their wares scarcely visible behind the ice-frosted panes of glass.

Over the first of the canals, I looked down from the bridge and saw that the snowflakes were now so large that they survived for some seconds on the surface before they became part of the dark water. I shivered and went on my way.

By the time I reached the ancient Church of Santa Maria Formosa the square surrounding the building was covered in a thin carpet of snow, across which there ran the rutted trail of a single hand-cart and the footprints to go with it. There was no one in sight.

'Signora Gucci!' I called softly into the shadowy darkness cast by the high-walled church and its tall bell tower.

There was no answer. Nor did the woman put in an appearance when six o'clock struck, nor in the quarter-hour that followed. By then, the snow was coming thickly and my head and shoulders were being covered, standing as I was in the open by the bridge.

Shelter commended itself, and what better than the deeply-recessed church porch, which commanded a view of the bridge, its approaches, and a fair piece of the square?

It was quite dark under the arched porch, and I huddled there in my cloak, grateful to be out of the wind and the swirling whiteness.

Waiting. . . .

By the half-hour, I had convinced myself that the woman was not coming. Next, my fancy moved to the thought that the position in which I found myself was not unlike the fateful night when I had acted as bait at the gates of the Arsenal. Except that I was now alone. Yes – Signora Gucci had stressed very forcibly that I must come alone. And then there was her talk of hearing that I had been inquiring after her, that I was still interested in Carlotta's baby – I had let that pass at the time, but what did it mean?

Treachery? . . .

Had I walked into yet another trap – and this time unpre-
pared and unguarded? The very thought made me recoil in
horror, back against the iron-studded door behind me.

And, as I did this, my foot touched against something that
gently yielded to its pressure.

With pounding heart, I stooped to see what it was, and
felt a cold face beneath my hands, a hank of limp hair, an
open mouth. No need for me to look into that face. A touch
of the coarse-woven clothing that she wore completed the
picture in my mind's eye.

I leapt to my feet, ran out into the snow, towards the
bridge, and only an imp of prudence prevented me from
screaming out loud.

It was a prudence that served me ill. My headlong flight
was enough to betray me. From out of the corner of my eye
I saw a dark figure detach itself from the shadowed wall of
the church to my right, and another from the left. The bridge
was close at hand. I scurried over it, sliding and slipping in
the yielding snow, dropping the money bag and leaving it
where it fell.

Terrified and confused though I was, I had sufficient
reasoning left in me to appreciate that I was leaving behind
me a trail of footprints that my pursuers could have no
difficulty in following. However, at the next corner, there
was an alleyway leading sharply off that was so narrow,
with overhanging roofs so nearly touching in the middle, that
no snow had reached the cobblestones underfoot. Thankfully
seizing the opportunity offered, I darted into the alleyway
and took the next turn, and the next, and the one after, till
– breathless and spent – I found myself a dark corner of a
wall against which to crouch, watching and waiting for signs
of my pursuers.

They came soon after. Two of them, silhouetted figures
only. They paused for a few moments at the entrance to the
alley in which I was hidden. Hesitant, irresolute, they
muttered to each other for a few instants, then went on their
way. I waited till I reckoned they must be far from me –
then waited as long again.

All was still as I listened at the end of the alley, then turned back the way I had come, and returned home by the most circuitous route I could devise.

Weary, frozen to the bones, frightened out of my wits, I closed and locked the yard door and felt safe for the first time since my hands had passed, trembling, over the dead face of Signora Gucci. But a feeling of safety may soon pass – given even the most favourable surroundings. As I turned, I caught sight of a light – a fitful loom of light caused by a passing candle – in the upstairs window that I knew to be my mother's sitting room.

Who – or what – was up there? I was determined to know. The idea that my own home – and I, the last of the Mazzini-Forscas – was being violated by an alien presence, cast out all fear. In a trice I was inside the palazzo and bounding up the dark staircase down which my father had reputedly fallen to his death. Reaching the landing outside my mother's apartment, I wrenched open the outer door and stormed in through to the sitting room, ready to face anyone – or any thing – that had dared to defile a habitation that had been sanctified by the presence of my beloved mother.

The room was empty. A single candle burned on the writing table opposite the fireplace. Lying on the table, also, were two large books. As I approached I saw that they were indentically bound in calf leather. Tooled in gold leaf on the front of each were the dates 1876 and 1877. And I knew that I was being introduced to my father's missing – *stolen* – journals!

I sat down at the writing table and, drawing the candle closer, opened the journal dated 1876. This comprised the year leading up to the writer's last months. I decided to begin at the beginning and work my way through all three hundred and sixty-five days.

The month of January told of post Christmas and New Year activities. Julietta's birthday, Father's projected visit to Rome, the death of an old friend in Paris, some trivia about local politics, worries about his eyesight.

I skip-read the blandness, rifling through the pages for the whole of the spring and early summer of that year till I came to an entry that, despite my present state of mind and the circumstances in which I sat, brought a smile of recollection to my lips.

Sunday, July 8th – I—grows into a very charming young woman. Image of her mother. Cheerful and helpful. Much improved in manner compared with J—. May be the growing-up process. Must soon address myself to thoughts of her marrying. But whom? . . .

It was that particular summer when Bruno bought the skiff and we were having our stolen voyages to the remote islands of the lagoon. No wonder I was 'much improved in manner'. I was ecstatically happy at the time, with all the joys of first love.

I sighed and went on with my task.

The remainder of the year was blandness itself, but was enlivened towards its close by the following entry:

Wednesday, December 9th – After much soul-searching, put to I— the many advantages of marrying young Ferrara, and delighted at her ready agreement. With a daughter such as she allied to the Ferrara dynasty, the house of Mazzini-Forsca will prosper. . . .

Dear father and his concern about the family fortunes. How little had he known that such a consideration had never entered my besotted, lovelorn mind.

There was more about my forthcoming betrothal and marriage early in the year of 1877, which I did not read in full. Instead, my eye was taken by a disturbing note which entered into Father's life.

It began with the following, cryptic entry:

Tuesday, February 6th – Such insolence. Anonymous letter delivered by hand. Am threatened with dire consequences for various unspecified shortcomings. . . .

There was more later. . . .

Sunday, 4th March – Most astonishing. Imagine, when I opened my prayer book in S. Marco this morning, there was a cryptic, scurrilous note inside. Made no mention of it to Isolda and Bruno, who were with me. . . .

And again, as I read on with growing concern. . . .

Friday, March 23rd – While in Verona yesterday, my carriage lost a wheel whilst being driven out to my friend Dami's estate. No real damage, but the driver suffered bruises and I was thrown clear. Upon examination, we discovered that the linchpin had been removed – and almost certainly in malice!

Throughout the months of April and May my father continued to receive these vague anonymous communications and meet with near-accidents. Eventually it became clear that he was considering the extreme of employing an armed bodyguard not only to protect himself, but also members of his family and household.

I came, at last, to the final entry of all – the fateful one that Father actually penned in my presence. It began with the news about the Cardinal Archbishop being able, after all, to officiate at my betrothal, and ended with these words – probably the last that my father ever penned in his life, and which were almost certainly written after I had left him alone in the library:

. . . trust I am doing the right thing. Now that the threats are being directed to that young couple, I was tempted to send them away for a while till this matter is settled and the scoundrel brought to book. Am afraid, however, that I shall have to confide in Bruno, at least.

I read that, the last entry, and sat back in the chair, blinded by sudden tears. The following page was blank, as was the remainder of the journal. That was my father's last testament, for the following morning, he was found at the foot of the Whispering Stair with a broken neck.

I remained seated for a long while, re-reading that last entry. It was some time before my mind began to accept – without any surprise – that I was not alone in the room. Oddly, the sensation, when it became clear to me, held not the slightest suggestion of fear or unease.

Instinctively I felt myself to be in the presence of a great warmth of affection, a groundswell of love which, like the tide of the great lagoon, cleanses and purifies all that it touches.

Presently, when I felt the strength to move, I turned to see who was with me in that room – and found myself looking into the eyes of my beloved sister whom I had counted for lost.

But – was she alive, or in the spirit?

I had barely risen to my feet and taken a pace towards the apparition when Julietta moved forward, arms outstretched, and embraced me. And I knew then that she was real, whole and vibrantly alive.

We sat together, hand in hand, my sister and I, in our dear mother's old sitting room, throughout that long night, till the dawn crept over the pantiled roofs of our native city, till the dawn chorus of birds gave way to the early cries of Venice born anew on the new day. In between long silences which were no burden – for where is there strain in silence where love is? – Julietta told me of her adventures, beginning with the day she fled from the villa on the Brenta, taking in all her experiences of the years between, and ending with her return home – incognito – to the very room in the very palazzo where, in fact, she had first seen the light of day.

The details of her tale I have cobbled together in later times, adding them to the disjointed narrative as she told it to me piecemeal that memorable night. It is as complete as I shall ever make it, and though rendered in my own words, after my own fashion, I have put it down as if it came from her lips, since it is, in every way, Julietta's story.

Fourteen

JULIETTA'S STORY

I was back in Venice by noon, and had not allowed myself to think all the way along the dusty road from the Brenta, but shut my mind to what had happened, fearful that I might go mad if I let the truth of it all take over and become part of me.

I let myself into the palazzo with my own key and went straight to my old room, where I busied myself with collecting together the things I simply could not leave behind. There was the fob watch that Father had given me on my twelfth birthday, the daguerreotype of my dearest mother taken on the beach at Torcello, my First Communion prayer book, the silk gloves I wore at my first ball, a palm leaf crucifix that had hung above my bed for as long as I can remember. These were the souvenirs of a life.

Next, for practical things, I selected three suitable costumes to fit into the medium-sized travelling valise light and small enough for me to carry unaided. I then made myself a cup of coffee and thought things out – in practical terms. By then, it was six o'clock.

Upon paying off the carriage that brought me from the Brenta, I had instructed the driver to arrange for a gondolier to pick me up at the water gate in good time to catch the night express for Paris, which leaves Venice at nine every evening. This arrangment just gave me time to go up to my mother's apartment for one last look, a hurried prayer for her darling soul – and then away.

The sleeping-carriage they provided me with was most comfortable, with a let-down bunk, wash-basin, luggage rack, etcetera. Upon our departure, I removed my outer garments, said my prayers, and laid me down to sleep.

What chance of sleep? When I had done all I had to do to get away, when there was nothing left but to lie and think, the pain of that dreadful day closed in on me – as I had known it must, sooner or later. But at least I was alone. No one had seen me collapse. That I did all alone, as the express train steamed on through the night, northwards, towards the towering Alps and all the world that lay beyond.

From my earliest recollection, Isolda had been my idol. My mother aside (and she was a different case entirely, a goddess incarnate, while Isolda was more like an angel), I looked up to her as to no other living being. When they sent her away to school in Switzerland, I pined and went off my food, and only regained the roses in my cheeks when she ran away and had to be brought home.

Alas, poor me! I reckoned myself to be so plain. People said I was plain. I once overheard one of the ladies at mother's soirée saying to her companion, 'What a very ordinary child dear Angelina's youngest has turned out to be.' I cried my heart out that night. Isolda, hearing me, crept into my bed and comforted me. When I told her what had been said, she only laughed and recounted the wonderful Hans Andersen story about the ugly duckling. From then on I was the Ugly Duckling to both of us. And then, years later – it was on that same twelfth birthday when father gave me the fob watch – and I had my friends to a tea-party in the *piano nobile*, with a three-piece orchestra playing quadrilles and waltzes, Isolda met me on the stair as I was on the way down to greet my guests in my party dress, and she said, 'Our Ugly Duckling has turned into a swan.'

Bruno came into our lives at the Feast of the Redemption. I was very small at the time, but I remember this dark-haired boy who seemed terribly old, almost grown-up. I suppose I fell in love with him even then – in the same sort of way that I loved Isolda. Afterwards, when I discovered that Isolda was seeing Bruno against Father's orders, I never let on to her that I knew about their meetings, or about the boat that Bruno kept near the Fondamente Nuova. By this time I was old enough to ask questions and listen to servants' gossip. They knew all about Isolda and Bruno, long before it became public knowledge, but I never told Isolda that the servants were talking about them, for fear that it would spoil the magic for her.

It was about this time that my feelings for the things about me began to change. It seemed to me that the whole world and the people in it had taken on a new and exciting significance. For instance, when Father consented to the engagement, and Bruno began visiting the palazzo, I saw quite a lot of him. He was very kind and helpful to me. One day, when Isolda was out, I entertained him to tea in the old schoolroom and we played backgammon, which he was not very good at, so we changed to forfeits. I put three questions to him and demanded a forfeit if he was unable to answer all three correctly. He failed the first time and I made him stand on a chair and sing his Regimental slow march. After that, he deliberately made his questions particularly hard. After having to pay all sorts of silly forfeits, I rebelled and said, 'No, I simply will *not* hold my breath and count up to twenty.'

'Very well, Julietta,' he said. 'Then kiss me.'

'Kiss you?' I repeated, amazed.

'Kiss me,' he said.

So I did. And my whole life opened up like a flower under the spring sunshine, as he took me in his arms and taught me – a girl of fourteen – that the verb 'to kiss' may be conjugated in many more ways than the one which I had always been taught, that's to say the way one kisses one's parents, one's sister, friends and relations. I can say that, by the time we had finished our game of forfeits, I had taken an astonishing leap ahead in my education.

The servants had always said that Bruno was a flirt. 'No real harm in the lad,' they said when they thought I was not listening, but merely eating up my cake at the other end of the staff table, and pretending their chatter was of no interest to me. 'No harm in him, but a real heart-breaker.' I won't say that he broke my heart, not that day of the forfeits for certain. Whatever I felt for him was soon overlaid by my grief at Father's terrible death. I have not spoken about the passing of my mother, nor can I bring myself to do so, but Father and I were never so close as he and Isolda – despite the tyrannical way he forbade her to see Bruno – till it became useful to him for the pair of them to marry.

I grieved for Father very deeply, but his passing never left the same emptiness in my life as my mother's. Despite his death, plans for the betrothal ceremony went ahead. The Cardinal Archbishop blessed them in San Marco with great ceremony, and for a reason that I could not comprehend at the time, I wept my heart out – all alone and unnoticed – in the family pew.

I now have to bring myself to touch upon the sin I committed against the Holy vows that Isolda and Bruno had plighted to each other. It happened this way. Despite the betrothal, stories of Bruno's flirtations continued to reach my ears – not from the servants, I hasten to add, they knew better than to gossip in front of me any longer, but from such as Carlotta Salvatorelli, Zöe Bonomi and their set, who never troubled to keep their voices down when I was around. It seemed that Bruno never made the slightest attempt to resist Carlotta's advances, which were of a very obvious sort, and I heard tell that he and Isolda had had a most terrible row at a ball over just this issue, when she had slapped his face and come home alone.

I think I both resented and envied Carlotta for her shamelessness in provoking the attentions of a man bound by Holy vows. In any event, I spent long and sleepless nights imagining myself in a position when I might flirt outrageously with my brother-in-law elect; to entice him, lead him on, bring about a situation where he would again take me in his arms and kiss me – once more and for the last time, for all time – like he had kissed me before.

251

The thought having been planted in my mind, it became an obsession. Standing back from myself and judging myself with the harshness I deserve, it is quite obvious that, though I could not possibly have admitted it to myself at the time, my intention went far beyond mere kissing. What I really yearned for was a love affair with Bruno.

I nursed this secret yearning, this hunger for kisses, for several months, working and re-working the scenes over and over in my mind, day and night. And then – a heaven-sent opportunity arose.

Isolda had to go to Verona on some business connected with Father's will, and it was necessary for her to stay over-night with some distant relations of ours in the city. I knew at once that this was a chance that would seldom occur again, and I decided to make the most of it.

Bruno had moved from the Giolittis' – which he found unbearably stuffy – to a rather bohemian little apartment which suited him very well. Like most men living on their own, he was incredibly untidy and claimed that he couldn't find a woman to 'do' for him. Actually, as I very soon guessed, he simply couldn't be bothered to look for anyone. This provided me with an opportunity, an excuse to visit him alone in his apartment. Well – scarcely alone, that was quite out of the question, and Bruno, flirt or no, would never have permitted me inside his door if I had simply arrived on my own.

There was a daily woman – a useless creature, pathetic beyond belief – who had several times presented herself at the kitchen door at the palazzo and begged for work, only to be sent on her way by the housekeeper. She was a familiar sight in the neighbourhood, and I sought her out and arranged for her to accompany me to the apartment of 'a friend of mine' where, so I told her, she might find regular employment if she suited.

Oh, by what devices do we serve the desires of our hearts!

I had contrived to meet the woman at six in the evening of the night that Isolda was away in Verona. She was there on time, and together we went to Bruno's.

'Julietta, what a lovely surprise. How very nice.'

If he was dismayed at the impropriety of my visit, the sight of my companion must have been an added puzzlement.

'This is Signora So-and-so,' I told him. (I have forgotten the woman's name.) 'You're always saying that you can't find anyone to "do" for you – well, I've found someone. Can I come in?'

I marvelled at my coolness, my worldly sense of intrigue, worthy of Carlotta at her shameless best. One could see that he was slightly put out, but his own coolness and suavity soon took over.

He showed us the apartment, and I took charge of things by telling him to settle himself in the sitting room with his pipe and his newspaper and leave it to me to give Signora So-and-so her instructions. This I did, and told her to start by preparing him some supper – tagliatelli, I think it was – and then clean out the kitchen and hallway while the meal was cooking. Having put her to work, I then proceeded about the business of bewitching Bruno.

My hands trembled as I fixed my hair just-so in the mirror outside his sitting room. Was it in such a disordered state of mind, I asked myself, that Carlotta set about her seductions of half the eligible young men in the city? Seductresses, surely, should be able to prevent their knees from knocking.

My entrance, however, was splendid. He looked up from his newspaper and there was no missing the flash of admiration in his eye. He offered me a glass of wine, which I naturally accepted, and sipped it – very much the woman of the world – while we indulged in light small talk. Presently I brought matters to a head in the manner I had practised over and over again in countless sleepless, passionate and lonely nights in my bedroom at the palazzo, till I had it word perfect.

I brought him to the point where he had to answer me a direct question of fact – something concerning a date on which we had all attended some party or other. . . .

'Wrong,' I declared. 'It was on the following Friday. And that will cost you a forfeit.'

He smiled – that broad, hearty smile which made his whole face light up.

'If you think, my dear Julietta,' he said, 'that I'm going to get up on that chair and sing all seven verses of my old Regimental slow march, you're very much mistaken.'

This was just as I had pictured it in my mind times without number. He was even saying the words I had planned for him!

I drew a deep breath. . . .

'Then you must kiss me, Bruno,' I said.

Still smiling, he replied quietly, 'Are you sure that's what you want, Julietta?'

I nodded, my throat too choked with emotion to utter the word, closed my eyes, held my face to him and waited.

The kiss, when it came, was everything I had dreamed in the uncounted and uncountable nights and days of yearning. It was like the first kiss that I had known from his lips, yet enriched by my own maturity of comprehension. It was – very heaven.

'Bruno – oh, Bruno!' I remember whispering against his mouth. 'I love you so much – so very, very much.'

He gently disengaged my arms and kissed me on the brow.

'And now, little sister, we must talk,' he said. 'We must talk about the love we have for each other, which is of a very special sort, and then of the love that binds me to Isolda, and she to me. . . .'

And then, gently and with the natural delicacy of a true gentleman, so that neither was my heart broken nor my pride hurt, he led me by the hand through the pitfalls of my unrequited passion, pointing out that he, himself, was not above temptation – but that a secret affair between us would only mean the ruin of three lives and the spoiling of the chaste love that was really the bond between us. And – closing the door to any protest – he told me, simply and sincerely, that he loved Isolda and would love her all his life.

I scarcely spoke during all that time, but listened, learned, and understood. At the end of it he again kissed me on the brow and then on the lips. But it was quite, quite different for me.

In the aftermath of this exchange I made some attempt to lower the emotional temperature by the pretext of serving up the pasta which Signora So-and-so had cooked for Bruno's supper. He was eating this very unappetizing dish when there was a knock, and Isolda came in.

Blessedly, Signora So-and-so provided the excuse for which she had been introduced into my pathetic little charade in the first place. Isolda took one look at the tagliatelli and another at the standard of the poor woman's housework – and she was sent happily on her way with a handsome payment. We laughed about the tagliatelli and the housework, the three of us.

But I thought I saw my sister giving me a thoughtful sidelong glance, and to my guilty mind it seemed to me that – *she knew.* . . .

Whether Isolda ever took Bruno to task about my being there I never knew, because I made an excuse and took my leave of them shortly after. I walked the streets for a long time, and up and down the shore, thinking over my idiotic little attempt to play the Carlotta Salvatorelli and being full of love and admiration for the way that Bruno had made everything all right between us.

My only worry was Isolda, and I realized then how incredibly foolish and thoughtless I had really been.

Supposing, I asked myself, that Isolda had not come in when she did, and we had parted company, Bruno and I, after our 'sensible' talk together. Would we then, either of us, ever have told Isolda about my visit? Perhaps so – but perhaps not. Perhaps, to spare her even an anxious moment of suspicion (knowing, as she did, Bruno's greatly overexaggerated reputation for flirting), we might have decided to keep quiet about the whole thing.

In which case, we would have introduced a lie into the love that the three of us shared mutually, and another lie into the special bond there was between the betrothed couple.

It was all very difficult, I told myself. And an object lesson for me that the world of the 'grown-ups' in which I had tentatively and inexpertly dabbled that evening was far more complex and fraught with pitfalls for the unwary than I had supposed.

Having thought that through, I went home to supper and bed.

But it was a long time before I was able to meet Isolda's eye without looking away.

Before he died Father had made arrangements for me to round off the education that I had received in the old schoolroom at the hands of various governesses by going to a highly-regarded convent school in Ireland. Though it was not a prospect that I greeted with any enthusiasm, I nevertheless accepted that I should start after Easter in 1878.

However, the uneasiness, real or imagined on my part, between Isolda and me after the Bruno incident left me quite looking forward to Ireland. This break, I told myself, was a golden opportunity to get away from both her and Bruno, turn myself around, get my thinking straight, and come home in the holidays for a new start.

But, oh! . . .

I shall never forget the morning that I was rushed off to stay with our relations in Verona at a moment's notice; almost literally pulled from my bed, bundled into a carriage, and sent away.

Bruno's name was mentioned, but everyone was pale-faced and tight-lipped. Isolda was simply not to be seen. In the days that followed, the story gradually unfolded, and it took the course of – Bruno had the fever – he was gravely ill – there were fears for his life. . . .

And then, my Great-Uncle Pietro, head of the household in Verona, broke the news to me. Bruno was dead. Isolda was inconsolable. The palazzo was no place for me. Arrangements had been made with the convent in Ireland to receive me immediately in the mid-term.

So it was that I departed from Venice, nor did I return till – ironically – the selfsame fever which was supposed to have struck down Bruno caused a swathe of death in Castlebar, and I came home to Venice.

And to the villa on the Brenta.

Two things stand out in my mind when I look back to my return. It struck me as very odd that the bustling palazzo – which had always teemed with servants and, even after Mother's passing, had thrummed with life, with visitors coming and going, parties being arranged, excursions being organized – that this beloved old home of ours had turned into a kind of morgue, where two lonely women lived like hermits.

The other thing was that my sister persisted in wearing the grey of semi-mourning, even though her betrothed had been dead for over a year. Furthermore, when I mentioned it to her, she showed no interest in putting it aside.

Despite all that, the days at the villa on the Brenta were an unspoilt delight – right up until the day I met the English officer, whose name now evades me. Isolda was her sweet, charming, amusing old self. The image of resentment that I had supposed she harboured against me – of that there was not the slightest sign. As the days passed, I felt inclined to open my heart to her about Bruno – to tell her frankly that I had gone through a phase of experiencing a carnal desire for the man she had been betrothed to marry, but that, with the help of his wisdom and understanding, I had come through it unscathed. And still loving him and revering his memory, as she did.

The cruel charade that blind fate played with the old scrap of newspaper – a thing that changed my life out of all belief – still remains clouded in my mind in matters of detail.

The part that I still find difficult to accept is that of my immediate reaction. Upon first reading that appalling report, I said to myself: You were right. She *did* suspect you and Bruno! Her love meant no more than that after all – Bruno's finer qualities were brushed aside in her insane jealousy. He was judged in the light of worthless creatures like Carlotta. And she put *me* in the same category as Carlotta. . . .

(Even then, I was overwhelmed with self-deception, for I had deliberately put myself in the same category as Carlotta in order to seduce my sister's fiancé.)

I recalled again how he had reasoned with me that evening, how he had brought me down from the clouds of fumbling misunderstanding and made me realize that there was more to loving a person than stealing kisses like apples from someone else's orchard.

And that she should kill him out of jealousy.

And confess to it! Without – as it said in the paper – without coercion! Of her own free will!

Unashamedly. Regretting nothing. Explaining nothing.

Shedding not a single tear of remorse.

And – the final appalling act of wilful defiance of all that was good and Holy on his side of the betrothal – to have slaughtered him in sacrilege!

I lived through all this during the long night's train journey through Italy, Switzerland and France. When the grey dawn found me, grey-faced and haggard-eyed, I had been through an examination of my own soul and found it to be defiled by hatred and remorse in equal parts. Hatred for the woman who had forced me into the role of her lover's seductress, remorse at having put myself in hazard of being chosen to play that role.

(How much easier to hate another when one's own wounded pride is involved in the transaction!)

It is true to say that I boarded that train a frightened, confused girl – and alighted from it a bitter, cynical woman.

But my life had to go on, and – calculating in all things – I had already decided what I must do.

The Mazzini-Forscas had distant relations and powerful friends in Paris, but I naturally avoided them at all costs, reckoning that Isolda would decide to come, or send someone after me to fetch me back, and that these people would naturally be the first she would contact. Instead, I found myself a cheap room across the river in the Latin Quarter, an attic under the eaves, where for over a year I lived quite comfortably by doing some modelling work for various artists of the *quartier*, using a false name.

To say that – in the popular phrase – I 'went to the bad' would be an exaggeration. For a woman of my upbringing and natural fastidiousness, it would have been out of the question. On the other hand, living where I did, choosing the occupation I chose, making the sort of friends and acquaintances who came my way, it was not to be wondered at that I soon stepped outside the narrow compass of formal behaviour that the strict upbringing of a Venetian aristocrat and convent-school girl imposes upon a person.

I did not take lovers, but was loved, and loved in return. When times were hard, I went short, but retained my independence. In all things, I was my own woman. Only once did I allow another person to bend my way of life away from the pattern I had imposed upon myself.

He was a Spaniard, a dedicated painter named Luis — brilliant and just beginning to make his name. In a series of portraits that he did of me, he broke out of the jostling ranks of the hopeful young artists of the *quartier* and won himself the beginnings of a reputation, a rich patron, a one-man exhibition and the promise of a dazzling future.

Luis was desperately in love with me. He was a fulfilment of something I had been seeking for as long as I could remember, certainly since I had lost the three people in my life — my mother, Isolda and Bruno — who had been my sheet anchors against fate. Alas, what I had to give Luis fell far short of his need, and in this I proved that my immaturity was as great as his. I was seeking a replacement mother, sister and knight in shining armour; Luis wanted me, the whole of me — to be submerged into himself. This I was not willing, or able, to give.

The day they brought me news that he had been run over and killed in the busy street, I shut myself in my one-room attic apartment and did nothing, saw no one, for weeks. During that time, I found that I was carrying Luis's child.

He was born on New Year's Day, baptized, and died soon after. A very great deal of me died with him. I was ill. Somehow, I managed to survive an appallingly hard winter when in truth I would have much preferred to go under. With the spring, I took stock of myself and decided that merely being one's own woman was not enough. After a lot of heart-searching, I presented myself at the door of a convent belonging to a strict order of contemplative nuns, and asked no more than to be allowed to stay as a layworker in the kitchens. Six months later I felt strong enough, convinced enough, to request acceptance as a novice nun.

The Reverend Mother, herself Italian, having heard the story from my own lips, took me on probation — for there are many who turn to the religious life out of despair, and despair is not enough.

259

My novitiate passed quickly and, for me, with no doubts or difficulties, though it was clear, even to myself, that I was closing my mind to an unresolved problem of my life that centred in Venice, in my family, in Isolda.

The time came for me to take my vows – not the final vows which would bind me to silence, prayer and contemplation for the rest of my life, a condition for which I yearned with everything in my heart and soul – but intermediate vows, strict and binding nevertheless.

The Reverend Mother sent for me. She told me that she had given my case much thought and a lot of prayer, and she was reluctant to allow me to progress further in my vocation – for which, she hastened to add, she was convinced I had a unique calling – until I had made my peace with my sister. Accordingly, she granted me leave of absence, a retreat back into the world, to go where I wished, do what I would, to put myself to rights with the world before taking on the life of the spirit.

And so, I came back to Venice.

I had money – the little that I had earned in the convent kitchens – enough to travel by the cheapest possible means, and to feed myself on the way. Upon arrival in Venice I got work in the kitchen of a trattoria. There only remained the question of where to stay. The answer to this was simplicity itself, and in view of the task that I had set myself, particularly suitable.

Years before, I had heard from Assunta about my English grandmother who had complained that her apartment was haunted. No one had believed her tale, of course, but the story so intrigued me that I spent a very great deal of time, when no one was about, exploring the interior of what was then my mother's personal suite. One afternoon, idly fingering the finely-carved panelling surrounding the fireplace, I pressed against a certain spot, and a whole section of the woodwork turned smoothly on a counter-balance to reveal a flight of stone steps leading down beside the chimney stack.

I can offer no explanation for the footsteps, bangings and mutterings that my English grandmother complained about, but throughout my childhood — I discovered the hidden staircase at the age of eight — I never revealed its secret to a soul, not even to my mother, and I never encountered anything in there more alarming than mice and spiders. The bottom of the stairs ended in the courtyard, and there was a similarly-operated secret door in a piece of exterior stone-work by the side of the chimney stack. Many was the time that I used my secret way in and out of the Palazzo Mazzini-Forsca, but in my childhood games I never guessed that I should one day find a real, pressing need for secret admission to my old home.

Quite simply, I moved into my mother's apartment. This posed no problems because no one ever entered its dust-sheeted solitude — at least, until Giuseppe burst in on me one morning!

I had just risen from a night's sleep on the sofa and was pinning my coif at a pier-glass when this giant of a fellow came in through the open door and met my gaze in reflection. He demanded to know who I was, and I told him. It was fortunate that I was wearing my novice's habit (which I had brought with me as protection in emergencies, the Reverend Mother having granted me permission to wear ordinary clothes at my discretion during my leave of absence), and he was a religious man, so I had little difficulty in convincing him that my only intent was for my sister's good. This much he accepted without demur. It took me a little longer to enlist his aid in keeping my presence a secret, but he agreed in the end — and said that he would tell his mistress that the noise she heard in the night — caused inadvertently by me — had been the rattling of a loose window frame.

Giuseppe became a loyal ally to me in my comings and goings. I initiated him into the secret of the staircase and he performed many useful errands for me during the double life that I carried on in my native city in those unforgettable months. My great fear was that we might disturb Isolda with our whispering and our coming and going at all hours. . . .

My intention was this: to investigate the murder of Bruno Ferrara in the light of the transcript of my sister's trial which I had sent for and studied before even setting off from my convent. This travesty of justice had certainly suggested that Isolda might be innocent, but I kept an open mind about that, for my only concern was to arrive at the truth. If I managed to clear her name, well and good. If my inquiries revealed that, trial or no, she was guilty of the dreadful crime, then I should have to find it in my heart to forgive her without any reservations. The issue was both a test of her innocence and of my love.

Working in the evenings at the trattoria, where I was known simply as Julietta and wore a cotton dress and apron, making my inquiries by day and in the late hours after work – sometimes in my novice's habit, sometimes in my persona of Julietta the kitchen hand – I began to assemble several lines of inquiry. Through listening to gossip and casual conversation everywhere I went – in the trattoria kitchen, in public places, and a thousand and one haunts around the city – I learned all about my sister and the wounded American colonel who lay between life and death in the hospital. I also heard tell of Isolda's dramatic public statement in Florian's, and it was this that convinced me – if by that time I needed to be convinced – of her certain innocence.

Casting a wide net, I soon found myself treading over ground that Isolda and Delamere had covered before the inquiry. I learned, for instance, about Carlotta's tragic death. From this it was only a step to discovering that she had had a baby by some unknown man. There was never any doubt in my mind but that Bruno was certainly not the father of that child, and that the man's identity might well be the key to the entire mystery.

At about that time Isolda began to take what seemed to be a renewed interest in clearing her name, though I was not sure if this happened before or after the fiendish attempt upon her life on San Michele, an outline of which I had from Giuseppe, but not the full details.

The trail of deaths that marked the tragedy of Isolda Mazzini-Forsca inevitably led me to think that our father, also, could have been the victim of this tangled web of plot and counter-plot, so I searched for, and found, his last journal and examined it very carefully, as well as the one for the previous year. What I learned there about the enigmatic person who had been threatening him convinced me that I was on the right track. Father had been murdered – I was sure of it!

It was then I stumbled over the trail that led to Signora Gucci of Burano. Wearing my habit, I had gone to see old Signora di Ventris, who did not recognize me (no one ever looks into a nun's face, and her habit allows her to walk about unnoticed, particularly in Italy), and in answer to my questions concerning the tragic Carlotta, she directed me to the professional foster mother of Burano.

I never actually found Signora Gucci, but left a message for her with neighbours, asking her to contact Giuseppe the odd-job man at the Palazzo Mazzini-Forsca. I said that she might learn something to her advantage, and mentioned the one word 'Carlotta'. By this I hoped that her poverty and her peasant's acquisitiveness might overcome her caution and persuade her to seek me out. Imagine my surprise when, returning to the palazzo in the afternoon, I was met by Giuseppe, who informed me that a woman from Burano had arrived that morning asking for Isolda – who had interviewed her, after which Gucci had gone on her way. And Isolda had left the palazzo only a few minutes previously – as if to keep an appointment.

What was I to think? Was it possible that Isolda – and perhaps Delamere – had already had dealings with Gucci? And had I in some way only helped to confuse matters?

I spent a most anxious hour or so in my mother's sitting-room, and occupied my mind by re-reading my father's journals by the light of a candle. My alarm may be imagined when I heard Isolda's footsteps approaching the apartment, and I managed to escape into the secret staircase only in the nick of time.

There is a spy-hole in the panelling, and I was able to witness Isolda's discovery of the two journals, and her long and careful perusal of the same. I waited till she had finished reading the last, sad entry that Father had made on the night before his cruel murder. I saw the tears pouring down her dear cheeks, and there was no other course for me but to emerge from my hiding place and reveal myself.

To offer her my love, my comfort. . . .

Fifteen

Julietta and I had much to talk about that night, but it was the question of Signora Gucci whom – as she explained – she had enticed from Burano with a hint of a reward that most concerned my sister. I who had just returned from witnessing the tragic remains of that unfortunate woman, recoiled from the idea of telling her the worst.

'She asked for you when she arrived here this morning,' said Julietta. 'Does that mean you had already been in contact with her?'

I replied that this was so.

'Had she previously told you the name of the baby's father, Isolda?'

'She gave me – us – the name "Bruno",' I replied, 'but that was obviously false.'

'Of course it was false!' cried Julietta with some heat. 'A deliberate attempt by either the true father – or perhaps Gucci herself, do you think? – to mask his real identity.'

'It may have been Signora Gucci's intention to deceive us at the time,' I replied, 'but she had certainly changed her tune since then. This morning she made arrangements to meet me at six o'clock to give me the real name – at a price.'

'You met her this evening?' cried Julietta excitedly. 'She gave you the name? You know now who has been behind all this?'

I shook my head.

'She played you false? Took the money and ran away?'

'No, Julietta,' I said. 'It wasn't like that at all. She was willing to tell, right enough. And she wanted the money to

264

enable her to go to America and join her son and his family. But she'll never see them, or America,' I added. 'Not – not now . . .'

Julietta stared at me, her fine eyes wide with dawning horror as she took in the import of my words. 'Isolda,' she breathed, 'you don't mean? . . .'

'They killed her,' I said flatly. 'Or *he* killed her – the enigmatic person from Father's diary. Just as Father was killed, and Bruno, and perhaps Carlotta. Certainly Zöe Bonomi.'

She gasped. 'Not Zöe as well!'

'And there could have been – and may yet still be – Jamie Delamere to add to the death-roll,' I said. 'And they've tried to kill me at least twice. You see, Julietta darling, there is more to this than a simple crime of passion – of the kind that the court tried to lay at my doorstep. This whole affair is more like one of those appalling Sicilian *vendettas*, when murder follows upon murder the way night follows day, and with as little chance of halting the process.'

We stared at each other in silence for a very long time.

Presently she took my hands, and I marvelled at the change that had been wrought in my impulsive little sister. Here was a mature woman who had stared unflinchingly into the dark side of the world and grown in stature during the process.

'We'll face this thing together, Isolda,' she said quietly. 'You and I – just like in the old days, when I used to creep into your bed and we'd plan what we were going to do the next day. Before – before all this horror began to happen.'

It wanted only a few brief hours till dawn, but my sister and I quit my mother's apartment and went down, hand in hand, to my room, where we lay down upon the bed, pulled the coverlet over us, and slept together till we were woken by the sunlight streaming in from the east. We then rose, bathed and changed, ate a simple breakfast of coffee, bread and fruit, and planned our day.

'I've been neglecting Jamie,' I told her. 'Yesterday was such a turmoil. I must go to the hospital first thing.'

'I'll come with you,' replied Julietta, 'and see this wonderful man who, with God's will, I shall have one day as my brother-in-law.'

I had told her all about the second and mature love of my life, and how my whole existence rested upon his return to the world to people and things.

Julietta had understood perfectly.

The instant I entered the hospital I had a sense of disaster. One or two of the sisters passed me by and averted their eyes, or greeted me only with a shy smile, and a swift glance to the woman by my side in the novice's habit. As soon as we came to Sister Mary Joseph's ward, I found the reason for the disturbing atmosphere.

'Steel yourself, my child,' said Sister Mary Joseph. 'The colonel is very poorly.'

'Oh, no!' I whispered.

'It's pneumonia,' she explained, 'always a danger and a threat with long-term bed cases.'

It was serious, she told me, and his life was feared for. I went in to him. He looked quite different from when I had last seen him, with an unhealthy flush to the cheeks, a wasted look to his whole countenance. Little Sister Agatha was seated beside him, dabbing his brow and lips with a cloth from time to time. She was crying, and did not look up from her task.

'I should have come to see him yesterday, no matter what,' I breathed. 'If I had been here – no, that's unfair to the good sisters. What's happened is no one's fault.'

Julietta squeezed my hand. 'We'll stay with him today and on through tonight, if needs be,' she murmured in reply. And to Sister Agatha she said gently, 'Rest a while, Sister, you look worn out. Leave him to us.'

The child thanked us and went about her other tasks with a tearful backward glance towards the figure in the bed. 'Oh, Signorina Isolda,' she said, 'I shall pray for him. We shall all pray for him, for both your sakes.'

My sister and I took turn and turn about to sit beside Jamie, attending to his few needs throughout the day, pausing only for a bowl of soup each around noon. The physician came in the afternoon and examined the patient, giving his opinion that the crisis of the malady might come within the next twelve hours and it would be make or break.

He offered the consolation that Jamie's excellent constitution would serve him in good stead in his fight for life, but added that the protracted coma had done little to sustain his defences against illness.

'He is truly in the hands of God,' was his verdict.

The long afternoon brought no change. Neither Julietta nor I could bring ourselves to rest, but stayed with the other, who sat close by the bed, watching for any sign of deterioration or improvement, wiping the feverish brow, alternately drying and moistening the burning lips.

It must have been about five o'clock, it was certainly growing dark, when Sister Agatha tiptoed into the room and, tapping me on the shoulder, whispered into my ear.

'There's Inspector Lippi come to see you, Signorina Isolda,' she whispered. 'Says it's important and will you please spare him a few moments? He's waiting in Sister Mary Joseph's room.'

I glanced at Julietta, who was with the patient. She met my questioning eye and nodded.

With reluctance I quit the sickroom and hurried along the corridor, where Lippi was waiting for me in the ward sister's little cubbyhole. He was about to rise upon my appearance, but I waved to him to remain seated, crippled as he was, and no longer a potential enemy.

'I can't be away long, Inspector,' I said.

The sensitive, pain-lined face was a mask of sympathy. 'They told me about the colonel's condition,' he said. 'You have my commiserations, Signorina, and my sincere wishes for his recovery.'

'We shall know how things are before dawn,' I replied. 'And now, Inspector. What have you to tell me?'

'As regards the matter we spoke of last,' said Lippi, 'we have made inquiries concerning the possible whereabouts of the man who attacked you at San Michele, but to no avail. There have been no reports, since then, of any male person seeking treatment in Venice city for such facial wounds as might have been caused by a thrust from the ferrule of an umbrella. However, since the scoundrel has carried on his activities as far away as Rome, he may already have quit Venice and sought help – if needed – elsewhere.'

'And the gondolier?' I prompted him.

The bland eyes swam away from me and made a play of examining his well-kept fingernails. 'We found the gondolier without much difficulty,' he replied. 'Obviously well rewarded for his part in the assault, he spent it in a tavern and boasted of what he had done. We had no trouble in locating him.'

'Did he – was he able to identify the persons who employed him to abandon me?' I asked.

'He was not,' replied Lippi shortly. 'When we found him, his throat had been cut from ear to ear.'

'Another murder!' I cried. 'Will there never be an end to them?'

'He may, or may not, have been killed for what was left of his money by anyone who heard him boasting in the tavern,' said Lippi. 'On the other hand, as you say, our opponents are likely to have silenced him.

'As to whether we shall see an end to it all, Signorina,' he added, 'I have every hope that the business will be finished within twenty-four hours. And that brings me to my real reason for coming to disturb you amidst all your troubles.'

'I am listening, Signor,' I replied.

He let a few moments pass, as was his habit when he had something particularly striking to impart – a habit with which I had grown disturbingly familiar during his interrogations. I waited in patience, but with growing apprehension, for I thought I knew what was coming. I was correct. . . .

'You are – or were – familiar with a woman named Gucci,' he said at length.

'Yes,' I breathed.

'When did you last see her, Signorina?'

'Yesterday,' I said.

'*Alive?*' The word was strongly inflected.

'Dead.' What else to say?

'I see,' he said. 'But you did not see fit to inform the authorities. Why not?'

I thought for a moment, then tried to explain that I had had to run for my life from Signora Gucci's killers, and had arrived back at the palazzo to find that my long-lost sister, whom I had thought to be dead, had been living under our

roof in conditions of secrecy – but I gave up explaining half
way through, and decided that simple candour would cut
more ice with this strange man.

'But, in any event, I doubt if I would have reported it to
you,' I admitted, 'for fear of being accused of her murder.'

He smiled his austere, smooth smile. 'Thank you for your
frank speaking, Signorina,' he said. 'I might, indeed, have
had grave doubts about you, for after all, you have shown
a marked tendency to be discovered in the proximity of dead
bodies.

'However, there is mute testimony here, to corroborate
your story of having run from the scene in panic. . . .'

So saying, he produced from his cloak the money bag in
which I had carried the money to pay the unfortunate woman
– and he shook it to make the coins jingle.

'This, you dropped in your headlong flight,' he continued.
'It was a bribe for Signora Gucci – yes?'

I nodded.

'In return for information that you sought?'

'Yes.'

'Which information you arrived too late to obtain – for
the woman was already dead?'

'Yes.'

'This information' – he stroked his cheek and looked at
me sidelong, down his very straight patrician nose – 'this
information concerned the paternity of a child, perhaps?'

I nodded. And must have betrayed my surprise, for he
smiled.

'We of the Judicial Police are also well capable of pursuing
a simple trail of cause and effect, Signorina,' he purred. 'Be
assured that we, also, are well aware that the father of that
child may well provide us with the answer to the questions
we are posing.'

'I hope so, Inspector!' I replied fervently. 'Oh, indeed I
hope so!'

'Amen to that,' he said. 'And I have to repeat, Signorina,
that I have every hope of being able to reveal that name –
and much else – before many more hours are past. And when
I do' – he looked keenly into my eyes – 'I shall send you
word, and you will be among the first to know. After what

you have been through, dear lady, you well deserve the courtesy.'

I thanked him. He then laid the bag of money on the table in front of me. 'You may take it now,' he said. 'It has been entered in evidence in anticipation of some future trial, and you may be required to produce it in court, but you may retain it for the present. Are you not going to count the money? Do you trust the Judicial Police so implicitly?'

'I think, Inspector,' I said, 'that I am going to have to learn to trust you.'

We both smiled.

When he had taken his leave I chanced to see him again through the window of the corridor, as he crossed the square beyond: a tall, limping, stooping figure with the cloak billowing out behind him like the wings of some giant bat. As he disappeared into the gloom beyond the street lights, another figure detached itself from a pillar opposite and followed after him. I recognized the second man from the distinctive slouch hat he wore. It was my feared and hated enemy, the man I called the First Interrogator.

'But there's one officer of the Judicial Police I don't trust,' I whispered to myself.

The long watches of that interminable night were spent by Julietta and me alone with our patient, with instructions from Sister Mary Joseph that on no account were we to fail to summon her if there was any change in his condition.

The hours drifted slowly past. We took turn and turn about as we had done that whole livelong day: watching closely over our charge and making him as comfortable as possible. They had brought in a reclining chair from the nuns' parlour for one or the other of us to take turns for a rest and a nap, but neither of us could bring herself to close her eyes. Not that the temptation of the weak flesh was ever very far away, and one fought to keep one's eyelids from treacherously drooping and being borne off into the sleep of the utterly fatigued. It is to be remembered that the pair of us had spent most of the previous night, also, in a wakeful and highly emotional state.

'Talk to me and keep me from nodding off' – that had

been Julietta's heart-cry, so I recounted almost everything that had happened since we had parted on the Brenta – with particular attention to my meeting with Jamie, our early association as a latter-day damsel in distress and a knight-errant, culminating in the earth-shattering realization that I was in love with this remarkable man, closely followed by the knowledge that my love was returned. When I had done, and silence fell between us again, I could not help noticing that my sister was crying.

'We seem doomed to suffer in our loves, Isolda,' she said at length. 'For you it has been Bruno – and now poor Jamie, here. What have we done, we two, to have been punished so harshly? I say this, though I have the consolation of my faith to bear me up, and the certain knowledge that every-thing in our lives is part of the pattern of a Divine Will.'

'I wish I could share your faith,' I told her. 'As far as I'm concerned, it seems a very odd sort of divinity to me, which decides that a young man should be murdered in the full splendour of his manhood, and that another has to eke out his days' – I gestured towards the figure in the bed – 'like this!'

She shook her head, and there was a serenity in her expression that silenced my bitter tongue.

'We're not to know why these things should be so, Isolda,' she said quietly. 'But occasionally one is granted an insight into the way that misfortune – tragedy, even – has a certain pattern that turns out to be for the good – in the long run.

'Take my own case. . . .'

'Oh, Julietta,' I interposed. 'You're surely not going to tell me that the tragedies of your life were for the good? Great heavens, you lost the man you loved, your baby was taken from you, and now you have – you have. . . .'

'Nothing?' She smiled, a sad smile. 'Were you going to say that I have nothing, Isolda? Well, you may be right by the harsher standards of the world, but that would be a very narrow view. I could have ended up so very much worse.

'And so could – Luis. . . .'

She had told me about Luis, though only briefly. How he had been run over in the street by a speeding carriage and pair, and she carrying his child. What could be added to that

271

tragic tale, I asked myself, that could possibly lessen its poignancy.

I was soon to learn. . . .

'On the face of it,' said Julietta, 'as the world views success and the promise of success, Luis had everything to look forward to. In his early twenties, he was already poised on the brink of fame, with a rich patron to support him through the lean days that every young artist must go through, plenty of ambition, an effortless talent. Add to that, he possessed charm, looks, sparkling good health. And he also had me – who adored him.

'And yet I tell you, Isolda, that poor young man was doomed to destruction.'

I stared at her. 'But why, Julietta – why?'

'The charm, the sparkle,' she said, 'were all on the surface. At heart, Luis was a self-doubter. Life, to him, was a constant struggle from the moment he woke up till the instant he put his head on the pillow. The times when he was not aware of this struggle – and these times were pitifully few and far between – he scintillated like a rocket, bursting into the sky and showering sparks, totally irresistible, catching everyone alight with his colour, his dazzling gaiety.

'But I saw the other side of Luis, and I was afraid for him. Earlier on, before success began to beckon, the painting that he then regarded as his masterpiece, his passport to fame, upon which he banked his all, his everything, was rejected by the Salon. The night he received this news, I found him in the bathroom in a pool of blood, both wrists slashed with a razor. And that was neither the first time, nor the last, that he had either attempted, or threatened, suicide.'

'Yes, but he was an artist, with the artist's temperament,' I protested. 'It isn't for the likes of us, Julietta, to measure such people's feelings against our own. Compared with such people, you and I – who've been known to do some wild things in our lives – have both feet firmly on the ground.'

She nodded. 'You're quite right, Isolda,' she said, 'and the difference is greater than you think. But in Luis's case, the difference was fatal.

'I didn't tell you about his patron – or, rather, his patroness. She was a brilliant woman of Paris Society. No longer in the prime of her youth, but still beautiful, a great hostess, rich beyond belief, the friend of princes and presidents, confidante of politicians and millionaire businessmen. She would take up an aspiring poet or painter, musician, actor, rising young politician, and advance his career – for so long as he amused her, paid court to her, was sufficiently successful to allow some of his glory to reflect upon her. And then – successful or not – when she grew tired of him, whenever a new face, a fresh talent, swam into her orbit, she would drop the old one with no more thought than she gave to changing her gloves.

'The night that Luis died, he was on his way to a reception that Madame X – I won't divulge her name because she is still in Society, still advancing the careers of young men and dropping them on a whim – that his patroness was giving for him in the Petit Palais. All Paris was there. I had not been invited, of course, but I doubt if I would have gone if I had been.

'Luis departed in his new evening dress suit, on the lapel of his coat the insignia of a minor grade of the Légion d'Honneur that Madame X had obtained for him. Joy in his heart, and the world at his feet – so the world would have thought.

'When they brought me the news, Isolda, I wanted to die with him. Like him, you see, I had caught a feel of the fame and splendour just within his reach, blinding me to the truth about Luis the man. I followed the cortège to his grave, grieving for a lost splendour, with his child under my heart.'

'And then, after your illness, the death of your baby, you despaired,' I prompted her. 'And you turned to your religion for consolation.'

She shook her head. 'It wasn't quite like that, Isolda,' she said. 'There was much that came before that. First came realization, a facing up to what might have been – if a Divine Will had not ordained that Luis had been killed that night of all nights when it could truly be said that he was at the height of his fame. As high as he could ever have hoped to get.'

'Surely, Julietta,' I said, 'that's a very pessimistic view, isn't it? I mean, you yourself said that as an artist he was brilliant?'

273

'As an artist – yes,' she conceded. 'As a human being, he was like a child. Worse – most children are extremely capable. Luis was a butt of fate, one of nature's buffoons, doomed to destruction. And fated to destroy others with him.

'Isolda, if he had lived only a few more weeks, he would have learned about our child. Immediately, he would have been torn in two ways. On the one hand, the lure of domesticity which, as an essentially kind man, he would have embraced with joy. On the other, the siren call of fame, and Madame X constantly at hand to point him away from home and hearth towards fame's dazzling prizes.

'Ever weak, he would have tried to compromise by taking on both roles. It would have ended in disaster. Finding that he was not at her beck and call day in and day out, Madame X would have dropped him. The one-man shows that she sponsored would have come to nothing. No more receptions and soirées. The invitation to dine at the presidential palace would somehow not materialize. The Salon would regret that, after all. . . .

'And, meanwhile, Isolda, I would have had to sit and watch my man destroying himself from within, eating his soul away with the canker of bitterness. Hating me for holding him back. Shunning our child, who would have become like a fetter about his ankles, holding down his free spirit and preventing it from soaring up on high – you can imagine the images that a frustrated artist creates in his disordered mind when he's on the point of ending everything.'

'He would have killed himself,' I said, and it was not a question.

She nodded. 'Yes, he would have been driven to that mortal sin,' she said. 'There was an inevitability about it. As it was, he died at the height of all the fame he was ever going to get. He died happy, and I grieved for him without any bitterness.

'A man was taken on the high tide of happiness. An infant was gathered up to heaven, untouched by evil. A woman suffered and found her refuge and her vocation.

274

'Things could have turned out so very much worse. That is my consolation, Isolda.'

The remainder of that night we scarcely spoke, but my sister was seldom far from my thoughts, and I found my eyes moving towards the contemplation of that serene profile as it looked down in gentle compassion at the tormented face of the man I loved.

Did I have the strength, the courage, to rise above misfortune as she had? If Jamie were taken from me, if he remained locked inside his mind for the rest of his days, would I be able to snatch a few crumbs of consolation from the disaster and build a whole new and joyful life upon the wreckage? From where I stood, I doubted it very much. . . .

Julietta broke in upon my thoughts.

'Isolda, his breathing's becoming more violent. Fetch the sister!'

Sister Mary Joseph came. I had found her sitting upright in her cubbyhole, not asleep but only dozing. One look at the patient and she declared that the crisis was upon him. By this she meant, I knew, that he was now at the Bar of Judgement: he was either going to live, or he was going to die.

We grouped about him, we three women: an elderly nun, her long life a monument to devotion and the service of others; a novice, my sister – but, in the stature she had gained in the years between, a stranger to me; and myself – what of me? . . .

'The breathing is very painful,' murmured Sister Mary Joseph. 'But less so than it was, I think.'

It was true. The awful strain that suffused those beloved features seemed to have abated, and the rise and fall of the poor, tortured chest had grown less violent, the awful shuddering that tormented the limp frame was perceptibly lessened. I glanced towards Julietta, and saw my own hope reflected in her eyes.

With the coming of the dawn, when the soul most readily yields up its earthly tabernacle, my love was drawn back from the grave and re-entered the narrow world that lay somewhere behind those closed eyes. And I rejoiced.

275

For this was my consolation – while ever Jamie lived, there still remained my hope: a flag to nail to the mast of my life through all adversity. Dead, I should have had a dear memory that would see me through the dark days. Alive, I had both the memory and the eager anticipation of better things.

My sister had taught me to recognize consolation.

The doctor came later that morning and confirmed that the patient was out of danger and resting peacefully. At Sister Mary Joseph's insistence, Julietta and I went back home to rest. She would have us sent for, she promised, if there was any change. Meanwhile would we get out from under her feet and allow her to run her ward? This last injunction was delivered in a voice that quavered between laughter and tears, and was accompanied by a kiss on both cheeks.

It was a frosty morning, and we walked quickly through the windy, empty streets, arriving home to find that Giuseppe had lit roaring fires in every grate in anticipation of our return. And how was the colonel? he wanted to know. Oh, and it was a blessing that the worst was over.

I made some coffee, and the two of us sat huddled before the fire in my sitting room, till sleep overcame us, and our heads fell back against the sofa and we drifted away together. The last thing I remember was taking Julietta's hand in mine.

When I awoke it was late afternoon and already dark. Julietta stirred beside me.

'What was that?' she said. 'Something woke me.'

'It was a knock on the water gate,' I said, and went to the window that commanded a view of the canal below. There in the gloom by the water-gate steps, a small steam launch swayed gently in the ebb and swell of the tideway. And a dark figure had alighted from it and stood by the gate.

'Who is it?' I called out.

'Judicial Police,' came the reply. 'Message for Signorina Mazzini-Forsca.'

'I am coming down!' I replied.

Gathering up my shawl, I answered Julietta's unspoken inquiry with excitement. 'The police. From Inspector Lippi. Julietta, this may be it – this may be the end of our agony.

He told me he would send word when he had unmasked our enemy!'

She followed me down the steps to the garden and the water gate, which we unchained with fingers trembling in excited haste.

The messenger was a middle-aged man, bearded, softly-spoken like his chief.

'Signorina Mazzini-Forsca,' he said. 'Inspector Lippi's compliments and will you please accompany me back to the headquarters?'

'Oh, is there no other message?' I asked, disappointed. 'No – *news?*'

'The inspector was most particular that he gave you the news himself, Signorina,' was the reply. 'He said most definitely, "I must tell Signorina Mazzini-Forsca with my own lips." That's what he said.'

'Very well,' I replied. And, turning to my sister, 'Julietta, I probably won't be long. If you need anything, just call Giuseppe.'

She embraced me. 'I know how much this means to you, Isolda,' she said, 'and to me, also. Tonight, I shall join my prayers for Jamie's recovery with a special prayer for a happy outcome to tonight's events.'

'We must go, ladies,' interposed the bearded man. 'Inspector Lippi doesn't care to be kept waiting.' Obediently, I stepped into the boat.

They cast off and the launch moved out into mid-canal, turned, and went on up in the direction of the Rialto bridge.

'But your office isn't this way,' I remarked to the bearded man.

'It's to the new headquarters we're going, Signorina,' he responded.

'Ah.'

It was cold, but I had my good grey shawl with me, and I drew it more closely about my shoulders as the craft nosed under the bridge and shaped course round the hairpin bend which leads to the longest straight stretch of the Grand Canal. We had not progressed more than half of this stretch before the coxswain of the launch slackened speed and, turning to the left, headed for the narrow opening of a dark canal leading off into a shadowy maw of high walls and darkened windows.

For some reason I felt the first stirrings of a nameless unease, and turned to the bearded officer.

'Are we coming the right way? I've never been near this district, but I know it has rather a bad reputation.'

'Used to have,' replied the other carelessly, 'but times have changed now, Signorina. The police have cleared out most of the undesirables and shut down the gambling dens and such. You could bring your maiden aunt down here now.' He laughed shortly, and – I thought – rather unpleasantly. Moreover, standing close to him as he spoke to me, I distinctly caught the tang of spirits on his breath. This further increased my apprehension, and I instinctively shrank away from the man.

The boat followed the course of the narrow canal, under humpbacked bridges and past high-walled, silent squares lying like private enclaves of secret squalor, through a tunnel that pierced the side of a blank-walled, roofless building with top windows that revealed the night sky, and on again. A Venetian, born and bred, I would not have believed that there was so much I did not know about my native city which, let it be said, one can walk right round in half a morning. But here I was, lost in this labyrinth of twisting waterways and dark monoliths of silence.

Presently our speed slackened. Ahead lay a sharp bend in the canal, and right opposite, on the far side of the bend, facing us, the façade of a palazzo, a semi-ruin, with the green slime of long ages darkened on its lower storey that told of past immersions in times of flood, of uncaring neglect for decades past. Between the row of flaking columns that grandiloquently graced the ruined façade, rows of dark windows reflected the shifting moon from broken panes of glass. A single light burned in a top room.

To my considerable alarm the launch shaped course to bring us alongside this house of grim decay.

'Is this the new headquarters of the Judicial Police, then?' I demanded of the bearded man.

'It is, Signorina,' he replied, and the concept seemed to

278

give him much amusement. 'You'll find it altogether more opulent inside than out, though.' He laughed.

The moon illuminated our surroundings as the boat touched the foot of the steps below a battered water gate. Fearful of falling, I stepped carefully out on to the slippery stonework and made my way after the bearded man through the gate, which was held open by one of the crew. Two others followed after us. I had the clear impression that they came not as escorts, but guards – if not gaolers.

The interior of the building conformed to the traditional courtyard set about with the four interior walls of the palazzo and open to the sky. Its former role as a garden was indicated by a broken fountain bowl and a mass of tangled rankness that had once been a flower border. A dead palm tree drooped forlornly over a marble cherub with a broken face, and a rat leapt from out of the fountain bowl and scurried away into the shadows at our passing.

'This way, Signorina,' murmured the guide, and led me up the staircase into the dark recesses of the upper storeys.

The unease that had taken hold on me earlier in the journey now took on the form of a nagging suspicion that all was not as it should have been and that my guide was not what he claimed to be. I quickly dismissed this as pure fantasy on my part. But I decided to be on my guard.

Upon arriving at the first landing the bearded man tapped gently upon a deeply-recessed door and was answered by a loom of candlelight appearing from under its lower edge. There came the sound of a key turning in the lock and the door creaked open to disclose a pale-faced youth in a cassock of clerical cut, who stood aside to let us enter.

I exclaimed in surprise to see the interior of the room to which we had been admitted.

The bearded man smiled thinly. 'You see, Signorina,' he said. 'Did I not tell you that this palazzo was more impressive inside than out?'

Like the great chamber in the Doge's Palace in the days 'when Venice ruled the Adriatic and held half the eastern Mediterranean in fief!'

The phrase sprang to my mind as I gazed around at the chamber in which we stood.

Vast, indeed, it was – and the candelabrum carried by the pale youth revealed only a portion of the interior, for the far end was lost in darkness. The sheer size and scale of our surroundings could only be guessed at, but the candlelight picked out tantalizing details. . . .

The silk-covered walls were hung – as far as I was able to discern – with life-sized, mostly full-length portraits of Venetian dignitaries of the past: doges, senators, warriors and merchant princes. For anyone with an eye for the superlative, there were at least half a dozen magnificent Titians and Tintorettos, several Giorgionis, a pair of superb Tiepolos, and hints of many more receding into the darkness. Above our heads two massive, unlit chandeliers dominated the visible part of the ceiling void, their innumerable crystal droplets picking up the tiniest pinpoints of light from the only source in that vast room – the candelabrum carried by the pale youth in the cassock. All the rest was gloom, and bathed in sombre drama by our shifting shadows.

'Will the signorina be seated?' said the bearded man who, now that we had arrived at our surprising destination, had assumed a more solemn, formal air. He indicated a gilt and brocaded chair that stood in the richly tiled centre of the floor beneath a glittering chandelier.

Full of puzzlement and mounting unease, I did as I was bidden. The pale youth set his candelabrum on a small table beside the chair. This done, he walked away on silent, slippered tread. Somewhere behind me he quietly closed a door.

I was alone in the vast chamber with the bearded man, my guide.

'What now?' I demanded. 'Where is Inspector Lippi?'

'Have patience,' he responded from out of the shadows behind me.

My feelings of total mystification and growing disquiet gave way to a sense of outrage that I can only compare to the way I felt during the early stages of my interrogations, before the two tormentors had bruised my spirit almost to breaking point. Whatever the meaning of this mummery, I thought to myself, why should I be subjected to it? If *this* was the manner in which business was conducted in the new headquarters of the Judicial Police (supposing that this was indeed where I had been brought!) I thought little of it.

'How much longer do I have to wait?' I asked, turning to address the bearded man standing back there in the shadows. 'You told me that I should see Inspector Lippi. Would you please inform him that Signorina Mazzini-Forsca is here – and make an end to this charade?'

He did not reply.

There followed a pause of total silence and stillness, during which time the conviction took root in my mind and hardened to a certainty. I had been inveigled to this sinister place for reasons other than had been represented.

In short, I had been tricked. And trapped!

The certainty fired me to action. I leapt to my feet.

'I am leaving!' I announced.

The voice answered me mockingly from the shadows. 'So, you are frightened, Signorina. That is good. You are now prepared for what is to follow.

'Sit down!

'Be still – and watch!'

I obeyed. The menace in that harsh command brooked only unquestioning and immediate submission. I suppose that, given time, my innate courage would have reasserted itself. The time was not granted me. . . .

The atmosphere in that dimly-lit chamber was now of a sort that one could have reached out and touched. Scarcely daring to breathe for fear of the sound snapping the unbearable tension, I simply sat, watched and waited.

And then, by some mysterious agency, the three pinpoints of light on the candelabrum beside me flickered out and died. I waited through an eternity of suspense, till at length there came a spurt of flame from the darkness far ahead. It was borne upon a scarlet-gloved hand. The hand carried the tiny tongue of fire to the dead heads of a candelabrum – one – two – three – and the candles were lit.

By the rosy glow one could see a robed and hooded figure seated behind a table, upon a throne-like chair.

Robed and hooded like a monk. But no order of monks were ever dressed from head to foot in shimmering scarlet.

281

Distant from the seated figure as I was, I distinctly heard the rustle of silks as the gloved hands were raised to the hood that entirely concealed the head.

A moment's pause – and the hood was drawn back, revealing the face and gleaming blonde hair of the most strikingly beautiful woman I have ever had the disturbing experience to behold.

The bone structure of the face, refined by experience that was hinted at by the smouldering eyes, was so marginally near to that of a skull – showing, as it did, the cheekbones, the deep-set eye sockets, the angle of the jaw – that it commended both admiration and unease. Such faces I have seen in the carvings of tormented martyrs. But there was something else added – some other factor that had shaped that face, those eyes that bored into mine across the distance that separated us.

'Do you know me, Isolda?' Her voice was deep, resonant, sepulchral.

'I do not,' I replied.

A hint of a smile played upon her lips – lips that were a trifle too thin, too cruel.

'Then I will cast your mind back,' she said. 'I will ask you to recall a ball at the Casa Crispi many years ago – so long ago that it seems like a lifetime –' So saying, she raised a gloved hand to her temple and closed her eyes as if in pain of recollection.

'I remember it well,' I heard myself say. 'But. . . .'

'Four girls,' she continued. 'Four tremulous virgins in the forbidding charge of Signora di Ventris.

'Yourself – Isolda – and three others.'

'Three others,' I breathed, suddenly full of a great fear.

Silence – and then. . . .

'*Carlotta Salvatorelli!*' she intoned.

I shrank back in the chair and felt the hairs at the nape of my neck stiffen and stand out.

'NO!' I cried out. 'Not you! You were drowned in the Grand Canal long ago. You had a babe that died. After that, they found you in the canal. . . .'

My voice tailed away. She was about to speak again.

'*Zöe Bonomi!*'

'Not Zöe!' I responded in a voice which, slipping beyond my control, had taken on the edge of hysteria. 'They said that Zöe died in a riding accident – but it wasn't true. But die she did. And she died by another's hand. You can't be her – come back from that grave off the Appian Way!'

The cruel lips smiled.

'I am neither of those,' she said. 'I am the third girl who accompanied you to the ball at the Casa Crispi all those years ago.'

'Not? . . . .' I stared at her, uncomprehending.

'*Edda di Rienzi.*'

'Edda?' I echoed.

Was it true? Could it be true? I thought back to the Edda I had known – and scarcely known. Very quiet in manner. Pretty as a picture in a blonde, peaches-and-cream manner. Rather plump. . . .

'The very same,' she said. 'But somewhat changed by circumstance. Nevertheless, the veritable Edda – as you can see. . . .'

She picked up the candelabrum in her scarlet-gloved hand and brought it nearer to her face, so that the flattering, rosy light softened the hardness of its bone structure. So that, with the eye of faith, I could reassemble that face as it had once been – softly rounded with puppy fat. The face of Edda di Rienzi who had never found very much to say for herself.

'Yes,' I whispered. 'It's you.'

The smile touched those cruel lips again. A shifting of the light, as she moved her hand, dramatically quenched the vision of the long-gone Edda di Rienzi I had known. In its place was the face that had been refined by experience, that had – in her own words – been changed by circumstance.

'It is I,' said the cruel lips.

'And I am your secret enemy!'

It was then I recognized the other factor that had re-shaped that face.

Its owner was insane!

Sixteen

'You are surprised?'

Surprised! There was no answering her question, which was put to me with a touch of gentle, almost playful, mockery. That the bizarre creature before me was a reincarnation of tongue-tied little Edda di Rienzi was something I was only just beginning to accept. That she should also be my enemy – the agent of all my misfortunes, and worse, much worse – was a fact that my mind was simply unable to encompass.

But, yes, it could be said that I was 'surprised'. . . .

'I wished very much for you to be found guilty of murder,' she said. 'There would have been a certain poetic justice in it, an elegant paradox, a sombre irony. Pity. The evidence was well presented, the actors richly rewarded for delivering their set lines. I fancy that only the absurd susceptibility of the old fool of a judge and the shrinking delicacy of the burghers of Verona saved your neck.'

'You killed Bruno,' I said. It was not a question.

'I did.'

'Why?'

She sat back in the throne-like chair and regarded me for a few moments before she replied.

'So now begin the lies,' she said. 'Now you are going to tell me that you never noticed me on that night of the ball, and my behaviour. When it *must* have shown, even to the most insensitive, that I was madly, hopelessly in love with Bruno Ferrara. That he was my all, my life, my only hope of happiness.'

284

I shook my head. My lips framed a denial. But she continued her remorseless tirade:

'And a marriage had already been arranged between us – perhaps you will now tell me that you were unaware of it. My father and his guardian drew up the draft of the betrothal contract on the very week of the ball. And then' – she paused – 'and then it all fell apart. I was told that Bruno had changed his mind. My father said it was all for the best, because he, after all, could not bring himself to ally our family with the Ferraras for political reasons.

'Political reasons!

'I hated my father!' She spat out the words. 'Do you know that he used to have me beaten by his valet? Beaten by a valet! And he used to have me shut up in a darkened room whenever I was upset and used to have my little tantrums.

'He drove my mother to her grave. You *must* know that, all Venice knew. He accused her of killing her own baby – my brother – in his cot. If she did, he must have driven her to it.'

A tense silence followed these dreadful revelations. I waited for it to end, fearful that anything I might say would worsen everything.

Presently she spoke again, and now her voice had taken on a curiously matter-of-fact tone – which, considering the content of her narrative, was grotesque to the extreme.

'However, my father wanted rid of me – I reminded him too much of my mother. So he arranged an alternative marriage. Ha! – as if there was any alternative to one's only hope of happiness in life.

'My intended was a Milanese merchant. Rich beyond belief – rich enough to buy and sell the di Rienzis and the Mazzini-Forscas, both. He had palazzos and castles, villas and country mansions throughout Europe, from Scotland to Spain and Greece. He wanted me dearly, for my bright golden hair, my baby-blue eyes, my plump little body.

'And he was twelve years older than my own father who arranged the match in a hurry, and afterwards walked me up the aisle of the Duomo at Milan, to meet my aged groom.'

With little or no effort I could have felt pity for her at

that moment; I withheld pity in anticipation of what I might hear next. How right I was!

'I will not bore you with a litany of the vile indignities I endured at the hands of that old goat. Suffice to say that it did not last long. Barely a week after the wedding, my husband suffered a fall from the balcony of our bedchamber. I became a widow, and wore black to good effect. I took lovers – a succession of lovers, because an attractive widow who is rich beyond belief has no difficulties in this regard.

'But I never found the happiness I sought. That had been taken from me.

'Later – much later – I learned that Bruno was to become affianced to you. And then I knew the name of she who had schemed and plotted to steal Bruno from me and deny me my lifelong happiness.

'*And so – I set out to destroy you and yours!*'

'First – you killed my father!'

I threw the accusation in her face. She did not flinch.

'You tormented him with threats – letters and messages, mysterious attacks upon his person. I read it all in his diaries. Right up to the last entry, which he penned the night before he was found at the foot of the staircase with a broken neck!

'And then – when you realized that nothing else would stop us – you killed Bruno!'

There was no sign of remorse, no consciousness of guilt, in her. She simply shrugged her scarlet, silk-clad shoulders.

'As in the case of your parent, I ordered the manner of his going,' she said with devastating calm. 'Apart from the assistance I rendered to my late husband in falling from the balcony, I have never soiled my hands with such work.'

Details of what must have been an incredibly complex and hellishly contrived conspiracy came back to me – and I had to know all the answers. 'And the woman whom Poeta Longhi saw leaving the chapel – what of her?' I demanded.

'That was evidence which the young man recited to order – for the mere price of a steamer ticket to New York.'

'And the rest of the – *actors* – at my trial?'

'Mostly all bribed – as your excellent Colonel Delamere supposed. By the way – how is he today?'

'He will live.'

The beautiful mask – so like a death mask – sketched an approximation to a sneer. 'Not a life that most of us would greatly covet.

'But, leaving aside your new love for the moment – we will return to him later – is there any detail of my activities on which you would care for enlightenment? You and Delamere have spent a lot of time in trying to unmask me. In view of your present wretched position, it seems only right that your natural curiosity should be satisfied.'

She sat back in her richly carved chair. The creature was thoroughly enjoying herself. She wore her madness like a proud decoration.

'Did Carlotta Salvatorelli drown herself?' I asked. I had a compulsion to know this.

She smiled. 'With a little assistance. A broken heart and the loss of her child quite turned her mind. It was a merciful release.'

'Who fathered the child?'

'Not Bruno,' she replied, and to my great relief, 'but one of my assistants – indeed, my principal assistant, whose acquaintance you made in Rome, and also on San Michele. He is a man of many parts. Ruthless and personable beyond belief. Little Carlotta chanced to find his attentions irresistible. Nor did she resist.'

'You contrived to put the blame for her death on Bruno.'

'Yes,' she said. 'There was a poetic justice in it. I loved that man, I love him still, beyond the grave. But with his absurd flirtation with Carlotta he virtually brought the blame upon himself. And, in turn, this also helped to involve *you*, Isolda.'

'And you killed Signora Gucci.'

'Again I repeat – not with my own hand. Gucci knew too much. She could have identified Lorenzo – he is my principal assistant, whose acquaintance you will renew again in a short space of time – and she was ready to tell all, as you will have divined.'

'And Zöe. . . .'

'Zöe simply could not still her chattering tongue about the affair that Carlotta had with Lorenzo. Happily Lorenzo disposed of her adequately well before she was able to do any real harm – even though he botched his attempt upon you in Rome.'

'And again at San Michele,' I added, with a shudder of recollection.

It was then I summoned up my resolve to make the denunciation that cost me more than I could tell – for to throw it at that grotesquely beautiful face without having the means at hand to destroy her on the instant was totally insupportable.

But I uttered the words: 'And you condemned the man I love to a living death!'

Edda di Rienzi exhaled a long, slow breath.

'Ah, I thought we would eventually come to that,' she said. 'Now, what is it, I wonder, that you find so devastatingly attractive in that rather ponderous American? Is it his fine line in psychological small talk, or his tales of derring-do on the battlefields of the old and new worlds? You see, I have taken the trouble to study him, even to converse with him, and he unknowing. Or is it that you have some girlish fancy to marry him and live in a log cabin on the American prairie?'

She laughed. I could have killed her there and then. Instead, I drew breath and shouted my defiance, my bitter wrath, loathing and resentment of this creature who had wrought such havoc in my life.

'A she-devil lives and walks the streets of Venice!' I cried. 'She tortures mind and body, and kills without mercy. And all in the name of her jealousy – her insane jealousy!'

My words stung her. I saw them strike home. It may have been my allusion to her madness, but it brought her to her feet. She came round the table and in a dozen swift strides was standing before me and, before I was truly aware of her intent and could back away, had closed with me, seized hold of my wrist and was staring closely into my eyes, white teeth bared, her perfumed breath fanning my face.

'Listen to me, Isolda Mazzini-Forsca,' she said, and her voice had taken on a note of terrible calmness that was more unnerving than any fury. 'I have instructed my paid executioners. One of them awaits my word to take a fast

288

conveyance to Treviso – to a certain clinic run by a certain German doctor. . . .'

'Assunta!' I breathed. 'You wouldn't – not even you could bring yourself to – that innocent old woman. . . .'

'Upon a word from me,' she said remorselessly, 'my man will go to Treviso. The woman Assunta will suffer a sudden demise which will be put down to a massive failure of the heart.'

From her crazed eyes I knew that she meant every word. Furthermore, she was relishing every word, as a wicked child delights in pulling the wings from flies.

'I have also instructed another of my executioners to present himself at the Palazzo Mazzini-Forsca when I say the word,' she continued. 'Ah! – did you say something, Isolda? Did I hear you exclaim?'

She smiled wildly and resumed, staring-eyed: 'Posing as an officer of the Judicial Police with a message from you, he will gain admission to your sister. There will be a covered gondola lying alongside the water gate, and her remains – you cried out, Isolda? – her *remains* will be transported to the middle of the lagoon, where, well-weighted, they will stay till Doomsday. It will be put about that she was recalled to her convent. Very neat, *n'est-ce pas?*'

'You she-devil!' I shouted into her face.

Again that hateful smile. 'And, finally, at the hospital. . . .'

'*NO!*'

'The man assigned for this task is – or was, till he had the misfortune to have himself struck off – a physician of some standing,' said this monstrous creature. 'On the pretext of having been summoned by you to give a second opinion of the patient, he will examine the unfortunate and prescribe a formula of his own devising, which he will then inject into the patient's vein. Unfortunately, however. . . .'

'What do you want?' I cried. 'Name your price to let them be. Do what you like with me – but spare them!'

She looked at me with searing contempt, her finely-boned profile turned to its best advantage, eyes slanting in my direction, searching me from head to foot.

'What do *you* have to offer?' she mocked. 'Riches, perhaps? Are you tempting me with the family fortune? I tell

289

you that I have gladly spent as much in the pursuit of my vengeance – and will spend as much again before I have settled for you all, and bought the silence of all those concerned in my great work.

'Will you, perhaps, give me back the love of Bruno? Will you raise him from his marble tomb and give him back to me – whole, young, vibrant, adoring – as I knew him before you cast your spell on that disastrously flawed Adonis?'

Mention of her supposed relationship with my dead fiancé prompted me to another fatal – fatal for me – indiscretion.

'He never gave you a second glance!' I said. 'Bruno would never have spared a thought for the speechless pudding of a creature you were in those days.' Disregarding the frightening fury that I saw mounting in her countenance, I went on. 'Oh, I grant that your dreadful father and Bruno's guardian may have hatched up some kind of half-baked nonsense between them – but they most certainly never told Bruno about any marriage plans with you, or he would have told me.

'*And we would have laughed about it!*'

Too late, I saw that my hasty, bitter tongue had run away with me and sealed not only the fate of my remaining loved ones, but also my own. Edda di Rienzi was now staring at me with a coldness that was beyond hatred, beyond reason, beyond humanity.

'You will be taken from here and locked up,' she said. 'At tomorrow's dawn – at the hour when criminals are led forth to execution – my principal assistant Lorenzo will call upon you. You will know him, for he carries the marks of your fingernails on his cheek, still, and the stab of a ferrule on his brow.

'He greatly resents those blemishes upon his masculine beauty.

'So he will enjoy his – *work!*'

After the silence following her pronouncement, which had been delivered with the dry calculation of the truly insane, she clapped her hands, in answer to which the bearded man who had brought me to that place stepped out of the shadows.

'Arturo,' said Edda di Rienzi, 'convey Signorina Mazzini-

290

Forsca to her quarters and see to it that she is made comfortable till dawn.'

Without another word, or a glance in my direction, she
turned her back and walked away into the shadows.

'This way, Signorina,' said the man Arturo.

Like the rest of that grim palazzo, save for the chamber we
had just left, the staircases and corridors were festering places
of damp and decay, with formerly priceless tapestries and
silk wall-coverings peeling like snake skins from the
mildewed folds of dissolution.

My guide – now gaoler – led me to the uppermost floor
and into a suite of rooms of a sumptuousness that almost
beggars description: a bedroom, sitting room and bathroom,
furnished in the seventeenth-century Venetian style and
embellished with superb murals depicting the rise of the old
Republic from the sea. And there the man Arturo left me,
and by the sound of a key turning in a heavy lock, I knew
that there could be no escape.

With no idea of the time – though I guessed it must be
late – I resolved to husband my faculties in preparation for
the coming dawn. Already I had decided that, far from being
a lamb led to slaughter, I would fight for my life when the
Lorenzo creature came to do his 'work'.

I reasoned this way: if Edda, in her madness, was not to
be swayed by bribery, the same could not possibly apply in
the case of a paid hireling killer. Well might the she-wolf
reward this Lorenzo person; I was willing – happy, even –
to lure him with every last coin I possessed, to set me free
and enable me to save my loved ones.

I have always had the facility to sleep in whatever stressful
situation. Without undressing, I laid myself down upon the
canopied bed, closed my eyes, thought firmly of the freedom
that I should gain for myself on the morrow – and fell fast
asleep.

Dawn. . . .

There were no windows in my luxurious apartment, but
even thick walls cannot shut out the sound of Venice's church
bells, and there is nowhere in the city – even in that labyrinth

of decay where they had brought me – where one is beyond the sound of a church bell.

I washed myself, smoothed my hair, and firmly bringing my nerves under control as best I was able, sat down to await my fate.

I was not kept waiting for long.

There came the sound of footsteps outside, then the grating of a key in the door lock. I steeled myself for the coming encounter, and rose to my feet. The door swung open – and he was there.

He was much as I remembered him from a fleeting glance on the station in Florence, but better looking than I had pictured. There was a soft, almost feminine beauty about him: a self-conscious handsomeness of which he must have been very proud – if not conceited. As I stared at him, one hand flew impulsively to his cheek, to cover up the perfection that had been hideously – and permanently – marred by the rake of my fingernails. And his brow – that smooth and noble brow – was scored and pierced by the thrust of the ferrule. I knew then with what agonized fury he must have pursued me that night in the graveyard of San Michele.

'You at last,' he said. 'I've waited a long time. But now I have you.'

I drew a deep breath to summon up my spirits, for I had an uneasy feeling that my deep-laid plan was just about to go very badly awry. . . .

'I don't know how much Signorina di Rienzi has paid, or is about to pay you for killing me,' I said with a calmness that astonished even myself, 'but I will double that sum. And I am willing to negotiate even further.'

He did not respond. A sly grin spread over those well-shaped, almost girlish lips.

'Did you hear what I said?' I demanded.

'Yes, I heard you, Signorina,' he replied, but did not move, and continued to regard me, still with that feline grin.

'Then you no doubt agree to my terms?' I said, knowing in my heart that he did no such thing.

He shook his head. 'Oh, no, my fine signorina,' he said. 'You don't escape so easily. You marked me, you did' – he touched his disfigured cheek again, delicately, with his fingertips – 'and I'm never going to lose these scars. You'll pay for what you did, for haven't I promised it to myself?'

He advanced towards me, but I stood my ground, convinced that I had the means to command him.

'I am rich,' I said. 'Not so rich as your mistress, perhaps, but I am willing to give my all to save my life, whilst she will only pay you whatever is the going rate for murder.'

Again that leering smile.

'I might accommodate you on those terms, Signorina,' he said. 'But not just now. Before we start discussing money, there is much to be done – as between the two of us. That's to say, as between a man and a woman. And after that, there's the matter of what you did to me. . . .'

Again, the hand went to the cheek, and then to the ravished brow.

A knife flashed in his hand – a dagger, of the kind that had plucked the life from Bruno.

The knife point came close to me. His beautiful, defiled features were a mask of gloating triumph. I backed away till I reached the far wall and there was no more retreat.

'She told me – the signorina told me – that I could take as long as I liked,' he said, leering. 'So it will be that way.'

The knife point moved to within an inch of my throat. The back of my head was pressed hard against the unyielding wall.

'To put last things first,' he continued, 'I think that, when all's done, we'll talk, you and I, about money. You're willing to give everything you have to save your life. Well – I might be tempted. Me having expensive tastes – in clothes, for instance, food and drink. Women. . . .'

The knife came closer; its point briefly scraped my cheek.

'But before then,' he went on, 'there's the matter of settling accounts for what you did to my face. And that will take quite a while. . . .'

Again, the knife point touched my cheek, and described the shape of a phantom slash from the corner of my right eye to the angle of my jaw.

'But first,' he said, 'before I spoil the fruit, I must taste it. So it's first things first, my fine signorina. . . .'

The knife point descended. I drew a sharp intake of

shocked breath – as the blade slashed down and rent my bodice from neckline to waist.

I closed my eyes and steeled myself against his next assault.

There was a shattering detonation. Opening my eyes again, I saw Lorenzo crumple up and fall, his face twisted in an agonized rictus.

Raising my eyes towards the open door, I saw a stocky figure replace a smoking pistol in his pocket.

'A close thing, I think you will agree, Signorina,' said my rescuer, whom I knew well from former acquaintance as my Number One Interrogator!

He introduced himself as Sub-Inspector Minghetti – quite formally. One would never have believed that he had probably saved my life, let alone that he had once subjected me to a most cruel and gruelling series of interrogations that had left me like putty, to be shaped and fashioned to his own requirement.

'It's all over, Signorina,' said Minghetti. 'We have them all in custody, the killers. Apart from this one' – and he looked down at the assassin, now stretched lifeless at his feet.

'I – I don't understand, Signor,' I faltered. 'That you of all people should be here to rescue me. I know that Inspector Lippi had a change of heart about my guilt or innocence. But you. . . .'

'I have always had a sneaking belief in your innocence, Signorina,' he said. 'Only – I had nothing to go on but my intuition. A word in the wrong place, and I should have been out of the service without a pension. And I am a family man, Signorina.'

I nodded, trying very hard to assemble the idea of my former tormentor as a family man, pension and all.

'Anyhow,' said Minghetti, 'I have kept a close watch on you and your doings all these years. Particularly after Colonel Delamere took up your case. I have a great respect for the colonel's methods of deduction.'

'I am most deeply grateful to you, Signor Minghetti,' I said, and had the inestimable pleasure of seeing his uncomely countenance colour up like that of a shy young girl.

'Well, it is all over,' he said. 'Acting on the information of your servant Giuseppe. . . .'

'Giuseppe!' I exclaimed. 'So it was he who alerted you.'

He nodded. 'Giuseppe saw you being taken away in the launch,' said my companion. 'Upon questioning the signorina your sister, and learning that you were being taken to the headquarters of the Judicial Police, he was puzzled to observe that the launch was proceeding in the wrong direction, whereupon he hailed a passing gondola, gave chase at a safe distance and saw the launch arrive at this place. He then came to the office, where I was just about to shut my desk and go home for the night. I immediately realized that here, at last, was the opportunity I had been waiting for – the culmination of the patient inquiries I had carried out at my own initiative, and at considerable risk to my career.'

I thought of the time that he had watched Jamie and me at luncheon in the Grand Hôtel des Bains on the Lido, and elsewhere – and blessed his name.

'But, Signor Minghetti,' I asked, 'what of the other assassins?'

'All apprehended, Signorina,' he replied, with a touch of justifiable smugness. 'No sooner had I arrested one of them than he gave me the names of the rest. They all talked. Your friends are all safe, Signorina.'

'And Edda di Rienzi?' I asked.

I saw his answer in his suddenly crestfallen face.

'Regrettably, she slipped through our net,' he said. But, more animatedly: 'We shall have her before nightfall, have no fear of that.'

Sub-Inspector Minghetti had two launches and a score of officers at the crumbling palazzo. As I left the building with him I saw a dozen crestfallen prisoners, the bearded Arturo among them. Many bore signs of having resisted arrest. As I watched them being shepherded into one of the launches I remarked to myself how similar they were, each to each. Killers all. And I shuddered.

'What will happen to them?' I whispered to Sub-Inspector Minghetti.

'They are all wanted by half the police forces of Italy,'

came the reply. 'But it is Venice that will have the pleasure of ending their careers. They will be tried together, along with di Rienzi. And will hang, every one.'

He took me back home in his launch. Julietta and faithful Giuseppe were there to greet me. My sister embraced me in tears of relief.

'I never thought to see you again, Isolda,' she said. 'After Giuseppe summoned the Judicial Police and we heard from Signor Minghetti of what might be afoot. . . .'

I drew her close, blessedly thankful to have and to hold her. Nor did I speak a word of how near she had come – along with Assunta and Jamie – to the assassin's attack.

'I must go and see Jamie,' I told her. 'Now – immediately. I shall never rest till I know that he's alive and well amidst all the turmoil I've been through. No, dearest, don't trouble to come with me. I shall be all right, and, in any event, I'd be happier to see him on my own.'

She understood perfectly. We kissed, and I went down to the water gate to rejoin Sub-Inspector Minghetti, who had agreed to escort me on to the hospital.

He left me there, at the door. His unaccommodating countenance was twisted into an expression of grave concern.

'Bring word when you're ready to leave here,' he said. 'I have two men on watch in the vicinity of here and San Marco. One of them will escort you back home on foot.

'Remember – the devil is still at large, and neither you, nor anyone concerned in this case, will be safe till we have her either dead or behind bars. Promise me, Signorina, that you'll do as I say.'

I promised this ugly man whose professional manner had so conspired to destroy me, but who had displayed to perfection the old adage that many a true heart beats within an unprepossessing breast – and went on inside.

Jamie had almost quite recovered from the pneumonia, save for a severe loss of weight, but his cheeks were pallid, his hands wasted and fine-boned like those of a bird. Sister Agatha was delighted with him and said that his eyelids had flickered again that morning and she was sure that, by prayer and hope, we might yet bring him back to wholeness again. I thanked the child, attributing the issue of the flickering eyelashes to her ready imagination, but grateful for her ever-ready concern.

I stayed with Jamie for a few hours, till dusk began to fall, helping with giving him his supper. When he had been settled for the night, I took my leave of the good sisters and went out.

It was only a stone's throw to the office of the Judicial Police. I could see the figure of a man strolling with seeming unconcern in the arcade at the far side of the piazza, and another one was wandering aimlessly down at the end of the piazzetta, by the foreshore. Either or both of these could be Minghetti's men.

I craved to go into San Marco and light a candle for Jamie, and decided to do this first and then go along to his office and ask for an escort home, as I had promised Minghetti.

Slipping my shawl over my head, I entered the sacred gloom of the great cathedral, that multitude of pillars and white domes, clustered in a long, low pyramid of coloured light, with its sculptures of alabaster, clear as amber, delicate as ivory. A thousand indifferent paintings and a million garish representations have failed to vulgarize its splendour. I have loved it all my life, this glorification of religion and the city of my birth.

Somewhere in the sombre, coloured shadows, an organ was playing an extempore as I went to the altar of Our Lady and lit a candle for the safety and health of the man I loved, sealing the offering with a short prayer.

There was no one else in the great edifice when I rose to my feet – no one, that is, but the ever-present figure of an old nun kneeling close by. She did not look up when I passed on my way towards the stair that leads up to the balcony which commands a superb view of the piazza – one of the favourite views of my childhood, to where, in the old days, my father would take me on his broad shoulders.

The sharp night air met me as I emerged from the balcony and stood there, flanked by the four great bronze horses, two each side of me, relics of Imperial Rome and brought from Constantinople as prizes of war. And I looked out over my native city and gave thanks for my deliverance from the evil that had worked to destroy me and mine. I gazed towards the north, to the isle of the dead, where Bruno slept in peace, to the south and the Guidecca, where he and I met all those years ago at the Feast of the Redemption, and to the Lido beyond, with its memories of both Bruno and Jamie. I looked along the line of the Grand Canal, picked out by the lights of moving gondolas, and could almost identify the roofs of my dear old home.

Venice at peace.

Or – nearly . . . for the heart of the evil still remained, lurking in some dark alleyway, or some gilded palazzo, perhaps. Waiting for her moment to emerge again and resume her vendetta against me and mine. I shuddered at the thought.

Something stirred in the corner of my eye. The dark-habited figure of the old nun came out on to the balcony. She walked with the aid of a crutch.

'Good evening, Sister,' I murmured.

She nodded and sketched the sign of the cross towards me.

I returned to the breathtaking view, the more dramatic now that lights were going on throughout the city, along the canals, in the squares, and, further off, on the far-flung islands of the great lagoon.

There was a footfall close at hand. Turning, I saw that the old nun was moving behind me. She stopped, leaning heavily on her crutch, and seemed undecided about whether to address me or not.

'Are you all right, Sister?' I asked.

The black-habited figure did not answer, but lifted her head, so that I could see the grinning countenance framed in the starched white coif.

And the well-known tag came back to me – '*No one ever notices the face of a nun.*'

'There is no escape for you, Isolda Mazzini-Forsca,' said Edda di Rienzi. 'If you ran to the end of the earth you would find me waiting there.'

With these words she launched herself upon me, throwing aside the crutch as she did so. Two lean but powerful hands took me by the throat and bore me back against the balustrade of the balcony, close under the upthrust bronze hoof of one of the heroic-sized horses, so that I was staring up into the wide-open mouth of the prancing charger, and I had the wayward thought that this would be the last thing I should see before my eyes were closed for ever.

'Goodbye, Isolda Mazzini-Forsca,' breathed a wild voice close by my ear. 'Given other circumstances, we could have been friends, for you, also, have fire in your veins. But – alas. . . .'

My senses were slipping from me. There was a great ringing in my ears. From afar I seemed to hear the sound of many voices calling to me, calling my name, bidding me to hold on to life.

Then all at once the choking pressure was released. I clawed my way upright, to see the she-wolf in nun's habit turning in alarm as a pair of caped figures appeared on the balcony behind her.

There came a shout: 'Watch yourself, Signorina!'

Edda's wild eyes were upon me.

'I would take you with me now,' she mouthed, 'but I think there would be no place for you where I am going, Isolda Mazzini-Forsca!'

With these words and with one bound, she was standing on the broad parapet of the balcony and looking down onto the ornamental pavement of the piazza.

She raised her arms on high, above her head, and called out to the night sky, her voice echoing and re-echoing across the great square.

'I come, Infernal Master!' she shrieked. 'I have served you on Earth, make safe a place for me in Hell!'

She leapt, and fell with a fluttering of black habit, turning over and over. I covered my eyes before she struck.

Seventeen

Spring came to Venice like a blessing. The long winter passed, the streets miraculously came alive with flowers. In every window box, peering over the tops of ancient walls, in public parks, quiet corners, from out of the cracks in the pavements, sported in the buttonholes of the men-about-town and in the hatbands of smiling priests – spring flowers were everywhere.

But even spring has its overtones of sadness, though I know there was no sadness in Julietta's heart when Assunta and I accompanied her to the railway station and saw her off. No sadness – only a bright-eyed joy for the future that lay ahead for her now that she – now that we both – had settled the score that had lain between us like a bad debt.

'Shall I never see you again?' I asked her as we sat, hand in hand, while the express train stood steaming in the yard and the passengers trailed their luggage on to the long line of waiting carriages.

'You will be able to visit me sometimes in person,' she said, 'but you will be with me always in spirit, Isolda. After what we have been through together there can be no end to the bond between us.' Her eyes danced with the special joy that she had always expressed in that particular way, ever since she was a little girl. 'I'll tell you what . . .' she began.

'Yes – do tell.'

'If all our prayers are answered, and Jamie comes back into the world, write to me straight away, and I will ask Reverend Mother for a special dispensation, so that you can both come and visit me. Will you promise to do that?'

Would I promise? With all my heart. The very thought

that my darling would ever come back to me was the great consolation of my life, and living and believing in it was something I had learned to do from Julietta.

'And you have no regrets?' I asked her, though I knew the answer, and I also knew that she rejoiced in repeating to me, over and over again, that she felt like a young bride on her wedding morning, waiting – as she was now – for the carriage to carry her to where her loved one was standing at the altar with love and welcome in his eyes.

'No regrets,' she smiled. 'Be happy for me also, Isolda. For it will give me great joy to think that some of my own delight has touched your heart also.'

The guards' whistles shrilled. The huge locomotive gusted a gush of steam skywards. Assunta came hurrying. She had a posy of spring flowers that she had just bought from a flower-seller.

'For my spring bride,' she said, putting the posy into Julietta's hand and kissing her on both cheeks. 'With every wish for happiness.'

'All aboard for Milan and Paris!' cried the guards. 'The train is about to leave!'

Now that the time had come there was more to say than could possibly be expressed in words. It was only in looks, in the touching of hands, in silent promises and protestations of love, and in kisses, that the dreadful gulf of parting could be bridged. And all too soon there was no longer even that consolation. We were standing together, Assunta and I, and the train was slowly creeping away, gathering speed as it went, carrying Julietta from us. She, leaning out of the carriage window, was waving back, and continued to do so till she was taken from our sight, borne to her chosen vocation, and the embracing of her eternal vows.

Leaving us alone and diminished.

Freed of the dark cloud that had hung over my existence since that far-off day of the funeral on San Michele, I resolved to emulate Julietta and give some meaning to my life. Accordingly, I sat down and worked out the practicalities of opening up the palazzo as a home for orphaned children.

It was by no means an easy proposition. Loving kindness

301

and good will were one thing, determining how many children could be suitably accommodated in a great house designed for aristocratic living, the entertainment of politicians, prelates and international celebrities, was another. And a kitchen designed to provide haute cuisine for a score of discriminating palates may come badly awry when the call is for half a hundred bottles of warm milk four times a day and night, and as many servings of simple pasta. In the matter of knives, forks, spoons and plates, moreover, great changes had to be made. Apart from the servants' tableware, the palazzo stocked only the finest bone china for daily use, and solid silver plate for banquets. All this would need to be replaced by robust ware that would withstand rough treatment by small hands. I mention this detail merely by way of illustrating one of the minor problems.

As for the larger question of how the project was to be financed, the Mazzini-Forsca fortune consisted of land owned throughout Europe, and investments in various commercial and industrial concerns worldwide. The entire capital was held in entail for succeeding heirs to perpetuity and could not be touched by any of them, then or in the future. The incumbent heir, or heirs – that is to say Julietta and myself – simply lived on the interest accrued, which was considerable. After taking only a relatively small sum as her 'dowry' to the convent, Julietta had signed away her interests to me. In the event of my not marrying and producing heirs, the fortune would pass, upon my death, to the next in line – a distant cousin living in Naples. It was therefore necessary to obtain a promise from this cousin, that he would continue to maintain the proposed orphan home when I had gone. Happily, he agreed to this.

The orphan home was in business!

Staffing the home with both lay and medical staff presented no great problems, for I was able to offer good wages, there was a ready pool of unemployed peasant girls in the city and the isles of the lagoon. I took newly-qualified young doctors and nurses from the hospitals and training schools of northern Italy and gave them the opportunities which might not have come their way for years.

Three months after Julietta's departure we opened the

302

doors of the palazzo to the first twenty small guests – merely the first of the many, and with only a skeleton staff and a whole load of dreams and hopes to buoy us through the early days.

Of course, in all this I never forgot Jamie for more than a few minutes on end. As ever, I went to see him every morning early, helped to feed and prepare him for each new day, sat with him for an hour or so, and again in the evening. After the pneumonia, his general health sadly declined, so gravely had the illness undermined his constitution. The doctors, when I pressed them for the truth, gave it as their verdict that he could not possibly have a life expectation of more than another year or two, possibly less. And that, barring miracles, even the smallest infection could make an end of him. So it was that I lived my life, with him and for him, in tiny portions, measuring out the days with teaspoons, enjoying every day when it came and letting the tomorrows look after themselves. In this way I managed to be very happy after my fashion, got through my work at the palazzo, and made the time I spent with Jamie the reward of my existence.

On the afternoon of a day I shall remember till I die – and I was supervising the preparation of the older children's supper in the kitchen – old Anselmo, the porter from the hospital, arrived in a high state of distress.

'Signorina Mazzini-Forsca!' he panted, having clearly run all the way from the hospital, 'come quickly, come quickly!'

'The colonel!...' I stared at him in awful disquiet, wondering if this was the summons I had dreaded at the back of my mind, day and night, for so long.

So it seemed to be....

'The colonel's taken a bad turn, Signorina,' quavered the old man, 'and Sister Mary Joseph says you should come. But hurry – hurry, do!'

I needed no second bidding. Untying my apron and throwing it aside as I ran, I was out of the kitchen, across the yard, out of the gate and tearing down the street in the direction of the hospital with Anselmo trailing along far behind.

Little Sister Agatha was waiting for me at the main door. She had been crying already, and the tears started afresh in her red-rimmed eyes when she seized hold of my sleeve and urged me to follow her.

'What happened?' I asked.

'I only left him alone for a few moments,' she cried brokenly. 'And when I got back, he was lying on the floor beside the bed. They – they've taken him to the operating chamber. The doctor thinks that – thinks that. . . .' She broke off, still running with me, into heart-rending sobs.

The operating chamber was a high-ceilinged vault of a place which had been the convent refectory in medieval times. In the centre of the otherwise bare floor, a still form lay upon a wooden table. The principal medical officer to the institution, Doctor Guittone, stood beside the patient in the greasy old frock coat that he wore for operations. He turned as I came in.

'Doctor, what has happened?' I asked.

'Dear lady, I am afraid there is nothing to be done,' he replied. 'Clearly, while this young sister absented herself' – he glowered severely at the shrinking little nun by my side – 'clearly the patient suffered some kind of seizure and was precipitated from the bed by a violent muscular spasm, falling with considerable force and striking his temple – see? . . .'

He pointed to a contusion on Jamie's brow, which was already darkening angrily. 'There may be a fracture,' continued the doctor, 'but I am reluctant to probe too vigorously for fear of doing more harm than good.'

'And you say – you can do nothing for him?' I asked.

He shook his head. 'The fall, and the seizure that preceded it, have done their worst,' he replied. 'The blood pressure is falling rapidly. The breathing – as you can see – is perilously shallow and fading fast. There is scarcely any pulse. In these circumstances. . . .' He shrugged his shoulders tellingly.

'May I stay here with him, Doctor?' I begged.

He looked relieved to be able to turn his patient over into other hands. 'By all means, dear lady,' he said. 'Stay with him – an excellent idea. If you have any – ah – anxieties, if there are any developments, you have only to summon me. I shall be in the wards.'

I thanked him and he left. Little Sister Agatha would clearly have liked to remain and keep me company, but somewhat to my relief – for I did not want to share Jamie with anyone when this might be our last time together – she said she must get back to her work.

Alone with my love, I took hold of his limp hand and composed myself to wait for the end.

The end of a summer's day was marked by the shadow that moved across the stone-flagged floor of the operating chamber. Its limit began, when I first came in, at the far end beyond the direction in which Jamie's feet were pointing. Two hours later it had crept half way towards him.

In the way that one assembles trivial ideas to substitute for real emotion – the way, for instance, that children will tell themselves that they will escape the anger of their teacher for bad work if they don't tread on the cracks in the pavement – I composed a fantasy that Jamie would not die while ever he remained in the sunlight. I closed my mind firmly against any speculation about what would happen when the encroaching shadow overwhelmed him. That was a problem for the future to decide. All that mattered was the here and now.

Two hours. I held on tightly to the idea that Jamie was mine for two whole hours, and that we would have to make it last for all our lives. I began by telling him all the latest news from the palazzo. . . .

'We had three new admissions today. Two new-born babies from the mainland and a little girl of eight who has been gently ejected from every orphanage in the province. The trouble is, she was cruelly treated by a stepmother. It's the old story, darling, and we see so much of it. Happily, the treatment of patient kindness seems to work. . . .

'I worry about the children's diet. Why do young people always prefer the most unsuitable foods? Assunta, who's in general charge of the kitchens now, makes a horrible concoction of molasses, butter and cream as a special treat for Sundays and feast days. The children could eat the sticky stuff till it came out of their ears, and I'm sure it's bad for their teeth, let alone their digestions. . . .

'Assunta is so much better after her treatment at Treviso, She's taken on a new lease of life. . . .

'Oh, darling, you should see the garden now. I've taken out all the old bushes and planted cuttings of rhododendron and azaleas from the villa on the Brenta. Next spring they'll make such a wonderful show. . . .

'Next spring, my darling. . . .'

The shadow was creeping nearer, measuring out both our lives. I clung to his hand more tightly, willing for some of my lifetime to be granted to him.

'Jamie, everyone sends you love,' I went on, 'Julietta writes to say that she has taken her vows and is very happy. The Reverend Mother has ordained that some of the money from Julietta's dowry will be set aside for special Masses to be sung for you and me, Jamie. So, you see, everyone's on our side. God and all. . . .

'Oh, my darling, don't leave me. What shall I do? Where shall I go? How shall I hide?. . . .'

I bowed my head in agony over his still hand, his left hand, and closed my eyes, so as not to see the encroaching shadow which was already touching the far edge of the table upon which he lay, and must soon envelop his feet, and all of him.

And I prayed, as I have never prayed before in my life.

And all the time, I knew that the shadow was creeping nearer, ever nearer, and that my fantasy was played out and that I would soon have to pay for the brief hours in hard coin.

A light breeze ruffled my hair. Someone must have come in the door, I thought.

'Who's there?' I called, but without moving or opening my eyes. 'Is that you, Sister Agatha?'

There was no reply, and that was very odd. If no one had come in, from where else could the breeze possibly have come?

Again, it touched my hair, more noticeably this time.

Almost as if . . .

. . . as if someone was beginning to stroke my head!

306

When I opened my eyes, his hand – his right hand – was poised above my head. Looking beyond that hand, I saw, through my sudden tears of mingled joy and disbelief compounded with certainty, that his eyes were open and he was looking straight at me.

I saw in those deep blue eyes the light of perfect reason, touched by the warmth of his humour, the sweetness of his love.

'Isolda. . . .' he murmured.

'My love!'

'I feel as if I've been away from you so long.'

Epilogue

The Sunday midday promenade is the climax of the Venetians' week. Weather permitting, all Venice and his family walk from church to the main thoroughfares and piazzas, linger over the flower shops on the Rialto bridge and take coffee and aperitifs in the cafés along the way. A very fine orchestra plays outside Florian's, and frequently has to compete with another at the café across the square.

My story ends, as it began, with a walk.

This was on the first Sunday after my marriage, when I first went abroad in my native city and was generally addressed as 'Signora'. I wore my new blue organdie dress with the sprinkling of tiny white flowers at the ruffles and hem, and a broad-brimmed straw with an enormous blue rose at the crown. No longer The Woman in Grey, but the same person inside.

Too proud and happy to do other than gaze steadfastly ahead, waiting for the passing greetings and being quick to respond to them; wanting the experience to last for ever, but longing to be back at the palazzo where we could sit in the garden, by the flowering rhododendrons, with the fountain splashing and the sound of children singing upstairs in the old schoolroom, and Assunta's laughter coming from the kitchen as she jokes with giant Giuseppe.

'Good day, Signora Delamere. Good day, Colonel.' That was the new Marchese di Rollo, freshly succeeded to the title from his father. I shall never be cold-shouldered by the likes of the di Rollos again.

We progress out of the Piazza San Marco by way of the Merceria, the string of busy shopping streets leading to the

Rialto, and there the greetings come thick and fast. I see a short, thick-set man pushing a wickerwork bassinet overtopped by an enormous parasol, under which sits a baby who is the image of his father, poor little thing. But perhaps, when he grows up he will be as handsome as his mother who walks with one hand on her spouse's arm.

This time it is I who am happy to give the greeting, for I owe my life to this unprepossessing man who once nearly drove me to despair.

'Good morning, Signor Inspector Minghetti, Signora Minghetti.'

Inspector Lippi died in the spring, brought down at last by the wasting disease that had beset him since childhood. The assistant has taken over from that complex and devious man whom I had never really understood.

Minghetti raises his straw boater and beams at us – almost as proud of us as if we were his own creations – which, in a sense, we are. The baby is fine. His name is James, and we are his doting godparents.

We go on our way, and now we turn down the narrow, winding street that leads to the back of the Palazzo Mazzini-Forsca. It is a street of memories for me, for it was along here, years ago, that I took my first tentative walk after my trial and disgrace, and a disastrous occasion it was.

But all that is changed now. The old women in black no longer cross themselves or make the sign against the Evil Eye when they pass me by, but nod and smile, and I don't doubt but that they whisper to each other what a fine couple we make.

We are almost home. There is a woman sunning herself outside her door. With her are two children, both girls. On another occasion, the older girl ran to show me her doll, but has long forgotten that. The mother knows me as well as I know her. At the sight of me, she picks a flower – a pink – from the window box close by her door and stoops to give it to the younger child. I hear a whispered instruction: 'For the beautiful signora.'

The child runs over to me, smiling and unafraid, and gives me the flower. I thank her and look back at the mother, my eyes misting with happy tears. She waves a hand in shy greeting and mouths something like 'good luck'.

We go on our way, and I look towards the tall man who walks by my side, my arm in his. Our eyes meet and he smiles at me.

My husband, alive and whole and splendid after his long retreat into the secret world of the mind, where he stayed awhile, to allow Nature to perform the long task of making good his terrible hurts.

My own, my Jamie.